Praise for the Brittany Mysteries

"Bannalec's Breton adventures are some of the best French local color going, with a deft blend of puzzle, personality, and description of the indescribable."　　　　　　*—Kirkus Reviews* on *The Fleur de Sel Murders*

"Well-drawn, complex characters, the lovingly described countryside, and the area's culinary bounty make this a winner. Some fans will be inspired to take their next vacation in Brittany."
　　　　　　—Publishers Weekly on *The Fleur de Sel Murders*

"Jean-Luc Bannalec . . . has channeled his affection for the westernmost region of France into a charming first mystery."
　　　　　　—New York Times Book Review on *Death in Brittany*

"A setting to die for . . . The star of the mystery, though, is Brittany."
　　　　　　—Booklist (starred review) on *Death in Brittany*

Also by Jean-Luc Bannalec

Death in Brittany
Murder on Brittany Shores
The Fleur de Sel Murders
The Killing Tide

The Missing Corpse

—→ **A BRITTANY MYSTERY** ←—

Jean-Luc Bannalec

Translated by Sorcha McDonagh

Minotaur Books
New York

First published in the United States by Minotaur Books, an imprint of St. Martin's Publishing Group

THE MISSING CORPSE. Copyright © 2018 by Jean-Luc Bannalec. All rights reserved. Printed in the United States of America. For information, address St. Martin's Publishing Group, 120 Broadway, New York, NY 10271.

www.minotaurbooks.com

The Library of Congress Cataloging-in-Publication Data for the hardcover edition is available upon request.

ISBN 978-1-250-25295-1 (trade paperback)
ISBN 978-1-250-17337-9 (ebook)

Our books may be purchased in bulk for promotional, educational, or business use. Please contact your local bookseller or the Macmillan Corporate and Premium Sales Department at 1-800-221-7945, extension 5442, or by email at MacmillanSpecialMarkets@macmillan.com.

Originally published in Germany by Kiepenheuer & Witsch as *Bretonischer Stolz*

First Minotaur Books Paperback Edition: April 2020

D 10 9 8 7 6 5

for L.
for Dr. H. A.

There are people who make you happy
when they walk in,
and those who make you happy
when they leave.

—BRETON PROVERB

The Missing Corpse

The First Day

He was the biggest of the lot. He gave a loud cry. Brisk. Monosyllabic. His head craned arrogantly upward. The vigorous cry was to a buddy who peeped out from behind a rocky ledge and was now rushing over. It was cold, around zero degrees, and the air smelled of damp ice.

Commissaire Georges Dupin from the Commissariat de Police Concarneau was standing directly in front of him, not unimpressed. In spite of the fuss he was making, the figure opposite him really was imposing, and he was at least a meter tall.

A black head, piercing brown eyes, a black throat. Bright yellowish-orange patches on the back of his head. A long, elegant bill, dark on the top, a deep orange on the bottom. His chest a garish yellowish orange with radiant white below; his back shimmering from nape to tail, a silvery slate gray. Like the flippers. His feet and legs, on the other hand, were also jet black. The king penguin was an exquisite spectacle: royal.

By this point, his buddy, who was a little shorter than him, had joined him. Dupin knew that individual penguins could reliably recognize each other by their voices.

Suddenly they both began to cry out in a curt, clipped way. Threatening cries. Unmistakable. For a moment Dupin had thought the cries were meant for him. But he was mistaken. Three of his favorite penguins were standing on the other side of the ledge in the snow-covered Arctic pavilion: gentoo penguins who, along with a group of southern rockhopper penguins, made up the largest penguin colony in Europe here in the Océanopolis in Brest. It was why Dupin, the penguin lover, made a detour here every few months, whenever he was near Brest. Today he was with Henri, who had become his best friend in his "new hometown," a fellow ex-Parisian who had found his great love and happiness at the End of the World more than two decades before. "Everything begins at the End of the World," was what people said: *"Tout commence au Finistère."* One of the Breton sayings that got straight to the heart of things: this was what people thought and felt here.

Commissaire Dupin was on his way to a police training seminar in Brest, which unfortunately was part of his "promotion," and on top of everything else, he still didn't know what exactly the promotion meant. Officially speaking, he was no longer the chief commissaire but the "supervising commissaire," although as far back as anyone could remember, there had only been one commissaire in the Commissariat de Police Concarneau anyway. A very modest commissariat, yet it was the only one in France that, according to a never-checked claim, had a panoramic view of the sea. And also of the old town in the large harbor with its enormous fortress walls. A very modest commissariat, but one whose "regional jurisdiction" had expanded bit by bit in recent years—with every retirement of a commissaire in the neighboring districts and the serious financial difficulties in the public budget. Dupin's promotion had almost coincided with his fifth anniversary of working in Brittany. During the "ceremonial" phone call, the prefect had murmured something about "not bad" and that it was "a reasonably good job" that Dupin was "putting in." That one "could certainly talk about some respectable joint investigative successes, in fact." On the first of March five years earlier, Dupin had reported for his first day at work in Brittany following his unceremonious "transfer" from the metropolis—increasingly outlandish tales were developing around the reasons for this transfer.

The topic of the current training course—it had been assigned to him personally as a "bonus" by the prefecture—was "Conducting Systematic and Systemic Conversations in Investigative Situations." Based on the latest results from academic psychological research, of course. Dupin was downright notorious for his unconventional, undoubtedly highly unpsychological conversations during investigations. They were anything but "systematic," or at least not in the usual sense.

But taking part in the course was obligatory and the promotion came with a not very generous but still attractive pay raise. So it was blackmail. This was why Dupin wouldn't have had any problem skipping the introductory meeting today, if only it hadn't fit so nicely with Henri's plans. He had to go to a meeting of restaurateurs near Brest.

The two kings were now waddling toward the three gentoos, at which the gentoos appeared to give each other signals with their flippers. They started to move a moment later and dived into the pool in one daring leap. At breakneck speed, doing crazy turns, but most importantly in a provocatively good mood, they scattered, each of them going in their own direction, before abruptly turning around, darting boldly just past each other, and then disappearing into the waterways to other pools. The little show had lasted less than five seconds. As soon as the birds who looked so clumsy on land—and who had lost their ability to fly over the course of their evolution—were in their element, they turned into by far the most skillful and swift buoyant bodies in the aquatic world. They could get up to speeds of forty kilometers an hour, Dupin knew, streamlined to perfection. They could dive for up to twenty-two minutes on a single breath, reaching up to five hundred meters deep. Dupin read everything there was to read about penguins, and he had these facts and figures at his fingertips. He was particularly impressed by the penguins' sense of direction: they used keen eyes and unrivaled mnemonics to memorize the details of an area many kilometers square under the ice sheet and on the seabed. At any given moment, they knew the location of their nearest hole to the surface—vital to their survival. As it was for a commissaire too, in a way. Just like the ability to maintain a constant body temperature of 30 degrees Celsius at a perceived temperature of a hellish minus 180, during howling storms, weeks of darkness, and without food, a thought that horrified Dupin.

Henri and Dupin had been trying unsuccessfully to keep their eyes fixed on the three gentoo penguins. They were just about to turn away when the three of them shot out of the water behind the two king penguins in one almighty leap. A moment later they were standing sure-footed on the icy ledge—like an operation out of a film. So the gentoo penguins' scattering had been far from random—they had been planning an ingenious operation. Penguins were unrivaled for teamwork.

The two king penguins looked visibly annoyed. For a moment, it seemed as though they were contemplating some aggression: they drew themselves up to their full heights, their bodies ostentatiously tense. The larger one let out a few harsh cries as they did so. But then, just as suddenly, the kings slipped into the water without any fuss, in an almost lazy way, then looked up again and finally swam away.

The ledge where the feedings took place now belonged to the three gentoo penguins.

"They know how it's done!" Dupin said, and smiled to himself.

"In the end, cleverness is strength." Henri laughed.

The penguin colony in Brittany was the largest in Europe, but there was something else much more spectacular than that: these were *French* penguins. They came from official French territory, the Îles Crozet, sub-antarctic islands. And, even more crucially: these islands were, in fact, a Breton archipelago! Due to being discovered by the naval officer Julien-Marie Crozet in the eighteenth century. He came from Morbihan, near the famous gulf. A Breton! These penguins—they were Bretons. Which also meant there was an authentically antarctic Brittany! It might sound odd to Brittany-beginners—but Dupin had long since stopped being surprised. In recent years he had got to know the South Pacific Brittany, the Caribbean one, the Mediterranean one, and even the Australian Brittany. "There's no such thing as *La* Bretagne! There are many Brittanies!" was one of his assistant Nolwenn's basic philosophies.

"Did you know that penguins can catapult themselves up to two meters out of the water using explosive acceleration techniques? Weapons engineers have copied it for firing torpedoes and—" Dupin's raptures were interrupted by the high-pitched, monotonous beeping of his mobile. He fished it out reluctantly. Nolwenn.

"Yes?"

"This is completely unacceptable, Monsieur le Commissaire! This will not do!"

It was serious. That much was clear. Even though Dupin had rarely seen it in all these years: his assistant—all-around wonder woman and generally calm and composed in even the diciest of situations—was very agitated. She took a deep breath. "The last lighthouse keeper in France is going to leave his lighthouse in a few days! Then they'll all be controlled by computer. And they won't be called *phares* anymore, they'll be Dirm-NAMO!"

"Nolwenn, I—"

"An entire profession is disappearing. Over and done with. There will be no more lighthouse keepers! Jean-Paul Eymond and Serge Andron have lived in the lighthouse for thirty-five years, at a height of sixty-seven and a half meters, enduring the harshest storms with waves where the foam pounded over the dome so that all you could do was pray. How many times did they repair the lighthouse in storms like that and risk their lives to save others! Will the computer be repairing its own faulty cables in heavy storms soon? The smashed glass?" She took another breath and continued. "The lighthouse keepers—they are an important historical figure, Monsieur le Commissaire! As I say: this is completely unacceptable!"

As desperately sad as this news indeed seemed, Dupin wasn't sure what

Nolwenn actually expected him to do. That he intervene as a policeman? Arrest someone?

"A murder? Has something happened?" Henri spoke in a hushed voice, making an effort to be discreet, but still noticeably curious. Dupin's face had obviously reflected something of Nolwenn's emotional state or even just shown his bafflement. He played it down quickly with a soothing gesture.

"Are you already in the seminar center, Monsieur le Commissaire?" Nolwenn's voice had completely changed from one second to the next. Thoroughly unsentimental now, purely matter-of-fact. Dupin was used to this. The words "seminar center" conjured up images in his mind of flower-patterned plastic thermoses on brownish Formica tables, with dreadful, lukewarm water for coffee brewed hours before. He'd been under strict medical orders since last week to avoid coffee for a month anyway—and after that to "*drastically* reduce" his "excessive consumption of coffee," in the words of Docteur Garreg, his determined GP. Garreg had (once again) di-agnosed an acute inflammation of the gastric mucous membrane—painful gastritis, Type C. And that's how it felt too: painful. But Garreg had not only diagnosed Dupin with gastritis, he had diagnosed more fundamen-tally a "serious medical caffeine addiction with prototypical symptoms." Which was ridiculous. And the caffeine ban was a nightmarish command for Dupin. It was capable, if he took it completely seriously, of throwing him into a severe crisis psychologically, and that crisis would be a great deal more severe than any nonexistent addiction symptoms. So he had privately agreed on one *petit café* in the morning, and on the rule that a small coffee wasn't a coffee.

"I . . . no, I'm—"

"I can hear the penguins." Nolwenn wasn't saying this ironically. He sometimes had the creeping suspicion she had tagged him with a GPS transmitter. He wouldn't have put it past her.

"Monsieur le Commissaire, the seminar begins in exactly three min-utes."

"I know."

"Okay. Riwal still needs to speak to you. It's about the break-in at the bank last night."

"Is there any news?"

During the break-in at a bank branch in a tiny backwater, somebody had not only stolen the money from an ATM but the entire ATM. Which required heavy-duty equipment. And which, all things considered, did not sound like a good idea.

"He and Inspector Kadeg were at the bank earlier. They've just come back."

"Tell him I'll be in touch from the car straightaway."

"Have fun, Monsieur le Commissaire."

Nolwenn hung up. Henri was still looking inquiringly at him.

"Nothing important."

"I've got to go." Henri turned toward the exit.

"Yes, me too." Dupin followed his friend with considerable reluctance. But there was nothing for it. He would have to suffer through this seminar.

* * *

The water was coming from everywhere: from the side, from the right, from the left, from in front, from behind, obliquely from below—sometimes, and rather as if by chance, from above too. This rain was unique: you couldn't see droplets of rain, these were infinite numbers of infinitely thin threads, tentacles that worked their way into clothing, driven by fickle movements of the wind as it constantly changed direction. No clouds were even visible; the sky was a nebulous, dull gray material. A monotone block. And it hung very low. Which Dupin found depressing on principle and which practically never happened in Brittany—it would all go perfectly with the seminar center. On top of this, it smelled of rain, the whole world smelled of rain. Musty.

The thirty meters from the exit of the main building to the entrance kiosk where he and Henri were taking shelter had been enough to leave them literally soaked through to their underwear. In the past, in Paris, rain had simply been rain. It was here in Brittany that Dupin had first experienced what this was: *real* rain—the same was true of the clouds, sky, and light. And of all the elements. Of all the senses. He had learned to distinguish between all the types of rain, just like the Bretons did; like Eskimos with snow. Even worse than threads of rain was heavy, full-on drizzle—*le crachin*—which was even less visible and which you only really noticed once you were dripping wet within seconds. But the most important thing Dupin had learned was—an admittedly abstract realization on days like this—it rained far less than the persistent, mean preconception would have it. He had recently read in a Paris paper: "There are two seasons in Brittany—the short period of long rainfalls and the long period of short rainfalls"; all serious scientific statistics belied these kinds of defamatory claims. In southern Brittany, there was less annual precipitation than on the Côte d'Azur. But something else clinched it: Bretons didn't actually take any notice of rain—a sophisticated attitude, Dupin thought. Not because they were so used to rain, no, but for two significant reasons: it was, after all, *just* the weather, and some things were more important. Life, for example. People would never have dreamed of calling off one of the countless festivals here just because it was raining. What's more, Bretons were resistant to their very cores to having anything dictated to them from "outside." Whether it was centralized Parisian plans or simply the weather. That's how one of the Bretons' most beloved idioms had come about, with which they launched their attacks if other people complained about the rain: *"En Bretagne il ne pleut que sur les cons"*—"In Brittany it only rains on idiots." Going out the door during heavy rain without even noticing it had made it onto the legendary magazine *Bretons'* list of the ten unmistakable traits that mark out Bretons. Along with things like making a big fuss when butter is unsalted; within the first two minutes of meeting someone saying: "Shall we have a drink?"; or as soon as more than twenty people are together, getting Gwenn ha Du out of their pocket—the Breton flag—to make it into a Breton gathering.

Henri and Dupin had parked next to each other, in the first row at the front of the enormous parking lot. Right now, on an ordinary Tuesday at five in the evening in the week before Easter, it was practically deserted.

The loud, steady beeping sounded again.

"Brilliant."

Dupin took his phone out of his jeans pocket, the screen covered in streaks. Hopefully the device was waterproof; he went through at least two mobiles a year on average. This one was just a month old, the commissaire's first smartphone, a small revolution instigated by Nolwenn.

Dupin saw Riwal's number. Of course. But now wasn't a good time. They needed to get going.

"I don't want to be late, Georges," Henri said. He was getting ready for the second sprint of the day, about another twenty meters to the cars. "I have to put in my plea for Breton bacon. I'm absolutely dying to get it through. Nothing else has so much flavor! Especially the bacon from Terre et Paille in Bossulan."

It really didn't make any sense to wait and see if the squalls would die down.

Dupin let his phone ring. The call would be forwarded to Nolwenn. Henri's words had made his mouth water despite the circumstances. Henri's meeting was about the annual ceremonial vote on which foods or dishes would be the theme of this year's "Semaine du Goût," or "Week of Flavor." For a week, four or five foods were celebrated in schools, nurseries, cafeterias, and also restaurants. An homage to the sheer endless sensuous treasures of France.

"Everything starts with bacon!" Clearly Henri still had time to go into raptures. "Brown the bacon in salted butter in a large casserole dish and gently caramelize it with some wild honey: for a Friko Kaol, a Breton cassoulet, the bacon is the most important ingredient—along with smoked sausages, potatoes, onions, and kale from Lorient—hmmm, my instinct tells me I'll have several good ideas."

"I'll be interested in every single one."

The piercing, monotonous beeping again. Another call from Riwal. Dupin hesitated. Maybe he should answer after all.

"Stop by again soon," Henri said, and dashed out into the deluge. "*Salut*, Georges!"

"See you then, Henri!" called Dupin, his phone already at his ear. "This is not a good time, Riwal. We—"

"It's about the break-in at the bank. They've—"

"We'll talk later, Riwal."

"They've accidentally stolen the banking terminal, not the ATM!"

"What?"

"You know how the two machines look the same, you get money at one of them, and at the other you do your banking. There are still no clues to the whereabouts of the perpetrators."

"They've . . . stolen the printer that gives out account statements?"

"It's not just a printer, you—"

"Absurd."

"For example, you can make transfers or—"

"We'll talk about it tomorrow."

"Okay, I just wanted you to know, I—"

There was a loud thud audible on the other end of the line, like a door being flung open with some force, and Riwal abruptly broke off mid-sentence.

For a moment nothing happened, then Dupin could hear a voice, extremely clearly. A commanding tone. Kadeg, his other inspector.

"Hang up immediately. We've got to inform the commissaire straightaway. This instant. It's an emergency." Dupin could hear Kadeg perfectly: "We've got a corpse! Covered in blood. Not far from the Belon, in the grass next to a small parking lot. At the tip of the Pointe de Penquernéo. If you walk along the river from Port Belon to the estuary nearby, via the upper footpath that leads to Rosbras, there's a large field and from the right—" Kadeg's military style had given way to his equally typical long-winded, overly detailed style.

"What?" cried Dupin. "Riwal, what's going on?"

"Kadeg has just rushed in and reported that—"

"Hang up!" Kadeg seemed to be standing directly next to Riwal now and yelling into the handset at the top of his lungs.

"Kadeg, this *is* the boss!" Riwal desperately defended himself. "The boss is already on the line!"

"Riwal, give me Kadeg," Dupin ordered.

A moment later, the other inspector was on the phone.

"Monsieur le Commissaire? Is that you?"

"Who else, Kadeg? What's happened?"

"A man, he's currently—"

"Who is the man? What do we know?"

"Nothing. We don't know anything yet. The call has just come in from a colleague in Riec-sur-Bélon. An old woman was out walking her dog and saw a man lying there in an odd position, not moving. She says there was blood. She got to a restaurant as quickly as she could because it was closer than her house and she called from there. La Coquille, it's—"

"I know La Coquille."

Kadeg let an unnecessary pause develop.

"And?"

"Nothing. That's all we know. Two of our colleagues from Riec are already on their way; they ought to be there in a few minutes."

"I . . . fine. I want a report immediately. I'll leave right now and I'll be there in forty-five minutes. I'll see you both there—you and Riwal. Call me as soon as you know more."

"Will do, Monsieur le Commissaire."

"And tell Nolwenn to send me the exact details of this parking lot where the body is straightaway."

"As I say, up on the cliffs, if—"

Dupin hung up and stood there motionless for a moment.

"Shit."

Then he walked briskly to his car. At least he'd miss the seminar, and it wasn't even his fault.

* * *

Dupin had just taken the final *rond-point* before the four-lane road at a hundred kilometers an hour, which had pushed the old Citroën XM palpably and audibly to its physical limits. He would soon be on the Breton motorway, and wouldn't come off it again until Riec. Nolwenn had already been in touch, since the little roads on the Belon estuary headland—as usual—did not have names. His GPS wouldn't be any help. She had given him some preliminary rough guidance and he would call her again later. Forensics and the medical examiner were on their way. He and Nolwenn hadn't spoken for very long; Dupin hadn't wanted to tie up the line. The windscreen wipers swept frantically back and forth, struggling to do their job properly. He should really have been driving more slowly.

The low-pitched drone sounded again, the car phone, almost as old as the car. Dupin's fingers went to the tiny buttons.

"Boss, can you hear me?"

"Perfectly, Riwal."

"You can turn around again! No body after all. False alarm."

"Excuse me?"

"Apparently there's no body after all, boss."

Dupin sat bolt upright. "You're joking, aren't you?"

"Our two colleagues from Riec are at the parking lot. Where the body supposedly was. But there's nothing there. No body, no dead person, no injured person. Nobody. There is no visible evidence. And no blood either."

Dupin had taken his foot off the gas pedal slightly. Ever so slightly.

"What does that mean?"

"At the moment we can—"

"Have you spoken to the old woman who saw the dead body? Who is she? What do we know about her?"

This just couldn't be true.

"A former actress. Sophie Bandol. Very well known. She lives in Port Belon, on the outskirts of the village. Apparently she's somewhat eccentric. And gets confused sometimes. So our colleague says."

"Sophie Bandol? Sophie Bandol lives in Port Belon?"

This was unbelievable. Dupin adored her. All of her films. She was one of the greatest French actresses of the twentieth century, from the golden years, up there with Jeanne Moreau, Catherine Deneuve, Brigitte Bardot, and Isabelle Huppert. But he would have expected her to be on the Côte d'Azur or in Paris.

"Yes. Has done for a long time now. Although she's not from here. Parisian."

This was beside the point anyway.

"Is she with the police officers?"

"I don't think so."

"Maybe our colleagues aren't in the right spot."

"They know every nook and cranny of that place. And the description was extremely precise. Apparently Madame Bandol goes for a walk there every day."

"I want to speak to her, Riwal. She's to come to the parking lot. Immediately. I'll be right there."

"I . . . okay. I'll let our colleagues know. Kadeg and I are almost at Trégunc, so should we even—"

"Absolutely! I want to see everyone. On the scene."

"Maybe somebody hurt themselves. And just wanted to recover briefly. And then went home. It's possible, after all."

Dupin scoffed. It was possible.

"Or . . . Sophie Bandol is quite old, I'd say she must be eighty, and sometimes you can have a turn—"

"You mean that she's not fully with it anymore? That she imagined it?"

"It would be a possibility."

It would, in theory, be a possibility. Of course.

"How close was the actress to the body?"

"I don't know. As I say, there doesn't appear to be a body at all."

"Maybe the body disappeared?"

"Disappeared?" Riwal sounded baffled. And also a little as though he might be doubting the commissaire's sanity.

"Speak to you soon, Riwal."

A moment later, Dupin had hung up. He leaned back in his seat. Even if it really had been a false alarm, and there had been no body, and no incident of relevance to the police, this had to be established beyond doubt first, once a report had been made. Formal confirmation was called for. So he had no choice but to take a look at the would-be crime scene. Theoretically he could delegate this to his inspectors, of course. But then he would have to go back to the seminar. Plus there were some crazy stories out there.

Dupin put his foot right down to the floor.

* * *

Thirty-five minutes later, the Citroën's tires were screeching as he braked on the cracked asphalt of the small parking lot south of Goulet-Riec.

"Thanks, Nolwenn. I'm here now. I'll be in touch later."

Dupin hung up. Nolwenn had directed him perfectly, as always.

As he was drawing level with Quimper, it had brightened all of a sudden, the depressing gray getting increasingly sparse and translucent the closer he got to the sea. The rain had stopped. As he took the exit from the four-laner, the gray had dispersed and given way to a pale silvery magical sky, delicate, perfectly clear—crystalline, that was the word for it; a color, a shade, that only existed in springtime. Every single month, the various seasons had their own colors for the sky.

The change in weather could not have been more Breton. Dupin could have sworn that the dreary rain would set in for days; absolutely everything had looked and felt that way.

Three police cars were parked in the far right-hand corner of the parking lot. Both of his inspectors' Peugeots—Kadeg and Riwal were in the habit of generally driving their own cars—while the third must have belonged to their colleagues from Riec. Dupin had pulled up a little short of the parking lot, on the narrow grassy verge, half on the road.

There was nobody in sight.

The commissaire got out, stood still for a moment, and took a deep breath in.

Wonderful. There it all was again—the space, the sky, the light. And there was a particularly strong scent. The Atlantic was close by.

You could still taste the salt on the air here by the river; you could smell algae, seaweed, minerals. During his last big case, Dupin had had to get to grips with the exact makeup of the seawater, and he had been very impressed. It was no wonder life had emerged here. You could hear the waves crashing against the rocks. When the breeze was coming in off the sea, you could hear them from far away. Every single wave. If anything on earth would ever be capable of making Dupin deeply calm—which would not happen in this lifetime—then it would be wave meditation.

Dupin walked to the middle of the slightly sloping parking lot.

At the end of the parking lot was a path to a track that sloped upward between gnarled oak trees starting to form bright buds. Two narrow, stony paths led to the cliffs by the sea. Wind-blown hawthorn bushes and several stone pines were visible, but it was mostly bright yellow broom. It was in defiant bloom in these weeks, sprawling patches of scrubby bush all over the landscape. And beyond the broom: a wide, rich blue-green streak, the Atlantic, less than a hundred meters away. And the crystalline blue above it. An almost supernatural light.

Dupin looked around again. There was nobody visible from here either. Nothing was moving. The parking lot was definitely a secluded place, inland and covered with undergrowth meters high, with a little wood beyond it.

In the grass next to the parking lot, Kadeg had said. Intuitively, Dupin scanned the ground with his eyes, even though it was pointless.

He had no idea where exactly the brilliant actress claimed to have seen the body. It had been raining here too until not long before, and the wet asphalt was glistening in the sun.

Dupin dialed Riwal's number. Nothing. Kadeg's number. Nothing. His phone had two solid bars of reception. Why weren't they picking up? Maybe they had no reception. Dupin thought it over quickly and then headed for the dirt path between the oak trees that got closer and closer together.

The path went up the hill, unexpectedly steep. Dupin had almost reached the top. The landscape suddenly changed here. The native Celtic fairy-tale oak wood gave way to a gently undulating meadow complete with dozens of fresh mole hills that smelled of rich soil, and the odd apple tree. A gentle picture-book landscape. *Les terres* is what the Bretons called them: harmonious shapes, peaceful, tranquil, completely different from the rugged cliffs, the violence of the ocean. Such different landscapes so close together.

This hilly plateau lay between the estuaries of the Aven and the Belon, two mythical rivers—fjords, really—that flowed into the sea in the same rugged bay, one from the northwest, the other from the northeast. The broad incisions they made inland formed a symmetrical triangle. Three-quarters of an island, in a way. They created a distinct, sheltered territory that could only be accessed from the north, via tiny little roads between Pont-Aven and Riec-sur-Bélon.

No sign of anyone up here either. Dupin turned around.

And soon he was back at the parking lot. He would try one of the paths in the direction of the sea.

All of a sudden he heard voices, albeit faint ones. Moments later he could see them coming along the path: his two inspectors, along with a female and a male police officer, neither of whom Dupin knew.

"Where's the actress?" Dupin hadn't greeted them with a word or a gesture, and his tone had been grumpier than he had intended.

"She was desperate to get back to Port Belon, she was freezing," Kadeg gleefully shot back. "It's not like we could force the old lady to stay here until you'd come back from the penguins."

Riwal beat Dupin to a response, which would undoubtedly have escalated the situation. "She has shown us the place where—she thinks—she saw the body. Then we brought her to La Coquille." He remained pointedly matter-of-fact.

"And the dead body hasn't turned up again?"

"No, boss."

"Show me the spot where Sophie Bandol saw the man."

"Follow me," said the young policewoman, who had a blond ponytail and flashing green eyes, and she made a sharp turn to the left.

They walked back up to where the parking lot started—it was about twenty-five meters long, fifteen meters wide. The wall of undergrowth formed a kind of niche here. The wild, bushy grass was ankle-high.

"Here." The policewoman pointed to the spot, half a meter away from the asphalt, directly in front of the thick undergrowth.

"The man's head may have been bent in an odd way. And Madame Bandol says she saw blood. I've marked everything with string."

Only now did Dupin see the nylon cord parallel with the asphalt.

"This, em . . . this is our . . . new colleague. A policewoman. She is . . . still new. I think that should really have been the forensic team's job." The older policeman was stammering now. In his late fifties, Dupin guessed, and at first glance perfectly pleasant. "My name is . . . Erwann Braz. You know . . . it's extremely unclear whether there has been a, em . . . an incident worth following up. We've looked carefully at everything and couldn't find a thing. By the way, it's an honor to meet you, Monsieur le Commissaire."

He had said this last sentence in an embarrassingly submissive way. So that was the initial pleasant impression over with. Dupin couldn't stand people sucking up to him.

"I think that our colleague here . . ." Dupin said, and looked directly at the policewoman—who quickly supplied "Magalie Melen"—"our colleague Melen has done the exact right thing."

Magalie Melen didn't seem like she had needed the commissaire's support.

"Was Sophie Bandol able to see the man's face?"

"No, because of his contorted position and because she stopped some distance away," Melen answered.

"And where did she see the blood?"

"She couldn't say."

A car was audible and everyone turned around. A flashy off-road vehicle. Dupin recognized it straightaway: René Reglas. His favorite pathologist. The Mister Universe of forensics. Insufferable. Dupin's short streak of good luck in avoiding him had come to an end today.

"Well, bravo," he said.

"Madame Bandol was coming from the hill there." Melen continued undeterred, pointing to the path that Dupin had just taken. "She says she didn't see the body until the last minute; her dog suddenly barked fiercely. But she didn't get any closer than four or five meters away. She has shown us where she stopped. She says her dog lost its mind even at that distance. She was afraid it would go up to the body," Melen seemed hesitant, "and might catch something."

"Catch something?"

"Yes, that's what she said."

"She's an old lady," Riwal said. "It must all have been frightening for her."

"It's well known that she gets confused sometimes. Disoriented. Some form of senile dementia, no doubt. Not to mention her fundamentally rather eccentric, odd nature," Erwann Braz said impatiently.

"Who says that? How would you know that?" Dupin asked gruffly.

"It's widely known. She has come to the police several times in recent years about supposed burglaries. Trifling matters. And there was never anything concrete. A large boulder once went missing from her driveway. We know her at the gendarmerie."

Few phrases—in Dupin's entire life—made him more angry than "It's widely known . . ."

"The boulder really was gone," Magalie Melen said, undaunted.

"There you have it," added Dupin in delight.

Surprisingly, it was Kadeg who brought their conversation back to the point: "We've inspected the surrounding area, Commissaire. Nothing out of the ordinary."

"Well then, the forensic results are settled! Sensational! And we could have saved ourselves the trip," Reglas said as he came up to the little group from behind. "The police help carry out the work of the forensic team straightaway these days. Absolutely remarkable!"

Reglas was accompanied by his team: two young lads who were just as pompously and incredibly full of themselves as he was.

"I want to see every car removed from the potential crime scene immediately. And by that I mean the entire parking lot. Every single car parked here is in violation of official regulations. They may have contaminated crucial clues already."

Reglas and his team put down their imposing silver suitcases in synchrony and opened them. Neither the two police officers from Riec nor Dupin and his inspectors reacted to the forensic investigator's demand.

"It's possible," Riwal said, unfazed, "that there was *no body at all*."

"We don't have any reliable evidence at all," the older police officer said, showing his unsuitability for the job again.

"For the time being," Kadeg said, startlingly matter-of-fact, "we've got a yet-to-be-disproven statement that there was a corpse lying here. With blood visible on it. Despite it not being here anymore. There might be reasons for that—perhaps the murderer disposed of it."

"Show me where the corpse supposedly was," Reglas said. He was also a master of remaining unimpressed.

The older policeman shot Dupin an obsequious, inquiring look, and Dupin raised his eyebrows and shrugged.

"Here, that's what the old lady who made the statement claims." Braz showed Reglas the spot.

"This place has an aura about it," Riwal suddenly said in a low, mysterious voice. He was known for a tendency to do this, counterbalanced by a very practical side, and all heads abruptly swiveled around toward him. Dupin was glad nobody asked any questions, including their two colleagues from Riec. A moment later, Kadeg drew everyone's attention back to himself: "My informant suspects that sand has been removed from the Plage Kerfany-les-Pins and the Plage de Trenez in recent days. That's very near here."

Excellent. That was all they needed. For weeks now, Kadeg had been nagging Dupin and the entire commissariat about this topic like a maniac: *sand theft*. Dupin couldn't stand to listen to it anymore, although Nolwenn had urged him not to take the subject lightly. Cases of sand theft really did happen over and over again, and on a large scale on some coastlines. Contrary to popular perception, sand was an extremely valuable, almost universal raw material, and was used in large quantities for all kinds of purposes: for concrete, mortar, glass, paper, plastic; above all, the silicon in quartz sand was essential for microchips, computers, mobile phones, and so much more. Kadeg had the facts at his fingertips: two hundred tons of sand were needed to build a single house, thirty thousand tons for a kilometer of motorway. Seventy percent of all beaches in the world had already, at a conservative estimate, fallen victim to the industry. Most of them illegally. The sand was stolen in enormous quantities by criminal gangs and companies. A global phenomenon, Dupin had learned, that affected Brittany too, and caused catastrophic ecological consequences. A few years ago, a militant association had been founded to provide well-publicized opposition to protect the beaches: *le peuple des dunes,* the people of the dunes. Nolwenn had left a long article about it on Dupin's desk: "*La Guerre du Sable*"—"The War of the Sand."

No matter how urgent the subject might be, though, this was not the time or the place.

"We don't need that stuff about the sand now, Kadeg! We've got other things to worry about," Dupin said.

"You know that sand was being stolen from the wild beaches at Kerouini and Pendruc for more than two years until anyone even noticed. The culprit was only caught by chance."

Kadeg was fanatical. Although he was right: a skillfully executed sand theft was difficult to detect. The culprits drove trucks to isolated beaches on nights when the tide was low, and by the next morning the tide had removed all of their tracks. Nobody even noticed the absence of considerable quantities of sand, simply because the sea often carried tremendous amounts of sand away during higher tides and storms—and sometimes only brought it back days later and deposited it in entirely different places. Or only a proportion of it. And kept the rest. It happened many times a year. Dupin was always worried it could affect his favorite beach—that the sand might just not come back one day. It was crazy how the sea was constantly creating new landscapes. Sometimes a wide bay was full of the finest powdery sand and ran evenly for half a kilometer into the sea, and sometimes the same bay was stony, rocky, and was two or three meters lower, with no sand at all. In February, a storm on the Sables Blancs in Concarneau had taken away so much sand that the fossilized trunks of an oak wood thousands of years old had been visible for days. They had jutted half a meter out of the muddy ground like an enormous art installation.

"And you see a connection between the corpse that Madame Bandol thinks she saw, the disappearance of the corpse, and criminal sand theft activity here on the coast?" Melen asked.

Dupin was grateful to the young policewoman for this precise question. Although she couldn't stop Kadeg.

"I don't think the culprit in Kerouini was acting alone. Even though the building contractor is claiming that. There's a system behind it. Sophisticated organized crime. A mafia! One of these gangs has just been busted in Senegal!"

"This seems extremely vague right now," Magalie Melen said calmly.

"Everyone wants it: in Brittany we have the best sand in the world. The purest granite. They're particularly keen on that. It's not ideal for everything, for—"

"Enough, Kadeg. We know."

Erwann Braz showed some stubbornness. "I'd like to point out again that it's still highly questionable whether we actually have anything to deal with here."

"When exactly does the old lady claim to have seen someone lying here?" Reglas butted into the conversation. He was kneeling on the ground a few meters away from them.

"Shortly before five, she says," Melen answered.

"Excellent. It must still have been raining heavily here too then." It sounded as if Reglas took this as a personal insult. "In rain like that, all organic trace evidence dissolves within minutes. We'll have to take soil samples, and even then we probably won't have any luck."

Dupin felt a growing unease. "I'll speak to Madame Bandol myself."

As always, Kadeg had objections. "But what should we—"

"You wait here with Riwal and our two colleagues until Monsieur Reglas has a preliminary report for us." Dupin was already some distance away when he said this, making a beeline for his car.

"But we—" Kadeg couldn't be silenced.

"Speak to you later." Dupin opened the car door, got in, and stepped on the gas pedal as the engine started, the Citroën jolting forward.

It was an absurd situation. Not just Kadeg with his sand theft obsession. But also the great film star of the twentieth century playing a role; a corpse that had suddenly disappeared—and which, although it was impossible to tell, may never actually have existed. Although in principle Dupin didn't think the magnificent Sophie Bandol lacked credibility for now, just because she was old and apparently quite odd. It was true: older people really did get confused sometimes.

* * *

Dupin loved Port Belon, the enchanted little village that was somehow divorced from time and the real world. He loved its charm, its aura, its atmosphere. Like in one of those films from the seventies and eighties that celebrated life at long wooden tables in wild gardens by rivers, lakes, or the ocean.

Port Belon lay in the estuary of the Belon, which at this point, just a few hundred meters from the open Atlantic, was very wide. At high tide, the Atlantic thrust its water kilometers inland. From the other side, from the land, the Belon came, flowing as a stream through picture-book meadows and woods, over dark, nutrient-rich soil, always carrying a little of the soil along with it. At Le Guily, where there was another eight kilometers to go before the sea, it flowed as a small stream under a picturesque bridge, and on the other side it was suddenly a river, a sea river. Freshwater and saltwater mixed in ever-changing proportions. And something unique was formed.

A secret, a gift. Sea and river, that was the special thing about this place, something you noticed and tasted in the air, in the extraordinary smells: a unique mixture of land—with green meadows, grass, flowers, fields, the taste of rich soil and damp woods—river, and, depending on the direction and strength of the wind, the salt and iodine of the sea.

The village was tucked inside the middle of a thick Breton wood on a tapering flat headland. A wood like the one near the cliffs at the parking lot: ancient, full of ivy and mistletoe. All along the only street that led to Port Belon, the tall treetops grew together over the road so that they formed a dark green tunnel.

There were fewer than a dozen houses here, white or made of pale granite, and two centuries-old manor houses, proper châteaux, and anarchic gardens with several bushy palms towering up out of them. You could still see the old splendor in the properties, but you could also see the time that had passed, ubiquitous ivy and flaking paint. The charm of decay, of the transitory nature of things.

Dupin had left his car in the parking lot a little upstream and went to the village on foot the way he always did—down the narrow dead end that headed straight toward the water and ended abruptly at a small jetty.

Dupin loved standing here. On the dock, right by the water. A narrow staircase with a terribly rusty frame led down to the river, and at high tide it went directly into the water.

Opposite this, on the other side of the river, lay Belon, also just a few houses, white with Atlantic-blue shutters and dark slate roofs. They were also nestled in gently flourishing woods on slightly hilly banks, oak woods like on the Port Belon side, with several stone pines and fir trees towering into the air here and there in the gaps. A few local fishing boats were bobbing lazily to and fro on the flat, now dark turquoise water of the river, all of them in vibrant colors—orange, light green, yellow, sea green, and scarlet. They were called *Au Large, Horizont, Dauphin;* one was *L'Espoir II,* and every time he saw it, Dupin thought sadly about the tragic story of what the "first hope" might have been.

It was still low tide, very low tide; the Belon was truly a river now, you could see the current flowing toward the sea. Large stretches on either side lay exposed, sand and silt that reflected the dazzling sunlight. Extensive, glittering landscapes were formed. Dreamlike black-and-white scenery— the blinding light was so dazzling that it leached the colors from the landscape. Hundreds of artists had captured this unique nature. Like a bizarre, dark shadow, from here you could see what had made the enchanting village so famous ever since the nineteenth century—legendary, it had to be said—not just in Brittany and France, but throughout the world: the oyster beds. The extensive oyster beds that sank beneath the water at high tide.

Port Belon was—along with Cancale in the north—the mecca for oysters, or *huîtres,* and the art of growing and refining them, *ostréiculture.* Breton oyster farming was first developed here, and the Belon oysters were legendary throughout the world: they were swallowed in the best bars and restaurants in Tokyo, in New York, in Rome, in London, and of course in Paris. *This* was where they came from. And yet everything here was completely unpretentious, calm. It was like with the villages in Champagne: such exclusive delicacies made you expect incredibly fancy villages, and then they were totally down-to-earth.

Port Belon was not chic, but it was all the more beautiful for it. You got out of the car and you could feel it: a magic. Some places had it. The commissaire kept a private list of the places that cheered him up, brought him happiness, even though this was a big word—you had to seek them out in life. Just a few weeks ago he had come here with Claire, just like nearly every time she visited for the weekend (as a Normandy woman, she was crazy about oysters). They had generally met in Paris less often recently; Claire was coming to Concarneau more and more often, which Dupin had been pleased about, because this way they avoided the ceremonial visits to his mother. Claire had even come during the week, if she had worked another whole weekend at the hospital. "I want to get a feel for what normal life is like here. Your everyday life," she had said. They had walked along the bank of the Belon in glorious sunshine and fresh wind in the late afternoon. It was one of the most marvelous walks Dupin knew. With blissful fatigue and cheeks reddened by the wind and sun, they had stopped off. And had eaten until late. Sat, eaten, drunk, talked, and laughed.

Dupin shook himself. He could stand here and watch forever. Lose himself in it. But not now.

La Coquille was just a stone's throw away, on the edge of the village, in one of the fjord's last, sharp turns. The restaurant run by three elderly sisters was an institution, a paradise for seafood lovers. Only a few of the tables were occupied, but that would change soon. Dupin recognized Sophie Bandol immediately. She was sitting at one of the windows that looked out onto the wooden terrace. At a small table for two right by one of the wide windowsills crammed with carved seagulls, little brightly painted boats, a blue-and-white-striped lighthouse, a lamp with a protruding old-fashioned lampshade, and several picture frames with Atlantic paintings in them. Everything higgledy-piggledy. Over the decades, hundreds of objects had been collected in La Coquille, mostly maritime objects, and they had been hung on walls, put out however and wherever there was space, all over the place, bit by bit, in no particular order. Dupin really liked it. Sextants, life rings, shells and stones, little boxes with glass panels that had miniature models of beach landscapes behind them, ship's wheels, barometers, pieces of rope, and cabin lamps.

Dupin realized he was a little nervous. Which he found embarrassing and almost never happened; neither official authorities nor famous people ever affected him. Except when he admired them.

"*Bonsoir*, Madame Bandol, *enchanté*. Commissaire Georges Dupin, Commissariat de Police Concarneau."

In his bashfulness he had become formal, which felt awkward. Sophie Bandol sized him up with a mixture of skepticism and curiosity.

Dupin started again. "You . . . you notified the police, Madame Bandol, because you saw a man lying in a parking lot near the Pointe de Penquernéo. You assumed the man was—"

"I know when someone is dead. And I *did* see a dead body. A corpse. Dead as a doornail. A tragic incident."

She looked marvelous. Tousled, shoulder-length hair, elaborately dyed a dark blond with a messy center parting, sparkling pitch-black warm eyes—which had fascinated Dupin ever since the first film he had seen them in—a wide mouth with curved lips, elegant bright red lipstick, and a sumptuous smile without a trace of aloofness. Unaffected, generous.

The smile he knew from the films, the smile that was just as famous as her coquettish, sullen pout.

"I . . . Madame Bandol, it's a great pleasure. I mean, I'm so very glad to meet you, I can hardly believe it."

The words had just come tumbling out. But Dupin didn't mind. He was sitting here with Sophie Bandol!

"What do you intend to do, Monsieur le Commissaire? Now that the dead body has disappeared. How are you going to find it again? You can't just put up with a body going missing on you. I think the situation is looking rather tricky."

"What can I get you?" Jacqueline, one of the three sisters at La Coquille, was standing next to them.

"Jacqueline has already taken my order. I'm starving, you know." Madame Bandol suddenly spoke in a very intimate tone, as if she were sitting across the table from a good friend. "What will you have to eat, Monsieur le Commissaire?"

"I . . . no, thanks. I'll have . . ." Dupin was considering how many more *petits cafés* would fall under "no coffee"—you had to look at it in proportion to his usual amount of coffee. "I'll just have . . . a tea." Dupin knew it had sounded pitiful. Besides, tea didn't do anything for him; he kept trying it, it had no effect. In fact had no effect at all, no matter how black he drank it. "And," he hurried to say—Jacqueline had already turned round, but not before acknowledging his order with an extremely annoyed expression—"and a glass of Anjou." One of his favorite white wines.

"That's something anyway," Jacqueline said, somewhat placated.

"Something terrible has happened here," Madame Bandol whispered. There was real fear in her voice. Then, a moment later, a cheerful smile suddenly appeared on her face. "I'm on the champagne and I'll stick to it if you don't mind." She was holding an empty glass in her hand.

"What did you see, Madame Bandol? Please tell me everything again very carefully. In as much detail as you can, every little thing you can remember."

"Zizou was barking like mad all of a sudden," she said, and looked down at her legs—underneath the table, right next to her feet, lay a motionless, medium-sized, friendly looking brown-and-white dog. Dupin didn't know much about dogs, but he knew this breed: it was a fox terrier,

Tintin's dog. The dog lifted its head for a moment, then dropped it comfortably onto its front legs again.

"He was absolutely beside himself. We were still in the little wood at that point. On the path. Not at the parking lot yet at all. I immediately knew something was wrong. Zizou doesn't just go crazy out of the blue, you know, he has a very even temperament. It was obvious this wasn't just a wild boar, hare, or fox. He sometimes barks when Kiki is nearby too, but that wasn't it either. Luckily, I had him on the lead," she said.

"And then?" Dupin rummaged for his red notebook in the back pocket of his pants. And one of the Bic pens that he bought in considerable quantities at the Tabac Presse next to the Amiral, only to then lose them again with impressive speed.

"I asked him what was wrong. Then he dragged me right to the parking lot. Getting more and more agitated. Then I saw him. The man, I mean. He was lying in the grass. Right next to the asphalt. I showed your inspector the spot. I didn't go any closer, I didn't want Zizou to get even more agitated. Or to catch something."

Dupin ignored this final sentence. "Describe everything that you saw for me," he said.

"It was raining cats and dogs, the visibility was not particularly good. What can I say? It was a man. The head was oddly bent, it wasn't normal, and one of the legs too, I don't remember which one now, was sticking out strangely. I couldn't see his face. Or maybe a little. As I say, I wisely didn't go one step closer."

"How did you know he was dead?"

"That was obvious."

An indisputable fact, that much was clear. Jacqueline had set down the tea, the wine, and another glass of champagne as she went past.

"And the blood?"

"It was there. There was blood on the body!"

"Where on the body?"

"I couldn't say."

"A lot of blood?"

"No, I don't think so. But not a small amount either."

"How old was the man, would you say?"

"It was impossible to tell. But he definitely had hair. Short hair, I think." She paused and suddenly looked astonished. "His hair was dark brown." She screwed up her eyes. "Yes, dark brown. There, you've got a real clue after all."

"Are you absolutely certain about this detail, the dark brown hair?"

"Absolutely, I think."

"But not about the short hair?"

"No."

"And you hadn't told my colleague that earlier?"

"I didn't remember it then. I assume I was still in some shock. Otherwise," she raised her voice, "I would obviously have said so in my statement."

"Can you remember his face? Or anything unusual?"

"Well, I really only saw the man from the side."

"And you didn't notice anything out of the ordinary?" Dupin sighed quietly. "A particularly large nose, whatever it be?"

Madame Bandol looked surprised. "No."

"Do you think that . . ." Dupin broke off.

"You ought to be concentrating with all your might on the details that are certain, Monsieur le Commissaire!"

"Do you remember what the man was wearing?"

A definite sulkiness had crept into her voice. "No. It wasn't a situation that allowed for looking very carefully."

"What else were you able to see? Anything next to the man, on the grass? In the parking lot?"

"What do you mean?"

"Did anything in the parking lot strike you as unusual?"

"No."

"Did you see a car there?"

"No."

"Another person on their way to or from the parking lot?"

"Oh, yes."

Dupin pricked up his ears. "When did you see someone? Where?"

"No, I mean a car. There was a car there. A big car, I think."

"What does that mean?"

"Not one of those newfangled little cars."

"Do you remember the color?"

"No. Dark, maybe."

"Black?"

"No. Possibly red. I don't remember. It wasn't visible."

"It wasn't visible?"

"The visibility wasn't good. And Zizou and I were so preoccupied by the dead man, after all."

"Where was the car?"

"If you're coming from the road, on the left. Before the parking lot."

"Far away from the corpse?"

"Some way away. But not far. No."

"And that also slipped your mind just now, when you spoke to my colleagues?"

"Yes," she answered nonchalantly.

"And it was just one car—there was only one car there? Can you say that with some certainty—there was no other car?"

"I suppose so."

"Excuse me." Jacqueline came to their table with a remarkably large *plateau de fruits de mer,* one of the legendary platters with huge mounds of seafood served on them.

"Do have some . . . Jacqueline, please lay a place for the commissaire."

The kitchen had been generous to Madame Bandol; it was an impressive array. Various kinds of bivalves—*praires,* cockles, *amandes, palourdes grises,* and *palourdes roses*—large and small sea snails, large and small langoustines, pink prawns, half a large crab, a whole spider crab, and of course: Belon oysters. A few hours before, everything had still been splashing about in the sea, and in the intervening time they had been in one of the sea-water tanks on the restaurant's terrace. You could also buy everything very fresh from the tanks, to go, in the small shop next to the restaurant. Claire and Dupin loved to buy their seafood with lemons, a special vinaigrette, homemade mayonnaise, and brown bread.

Dupin's mouth was watering, whether he liked it or not. And the platter was certainly big enough for two.

"Am I one of the suspects?" Madame Bandol's voice was trembling now. "I've been a suspect before. Oh yes! In 1960, on the Côte d'Azur, there was a murder in my hotel, in the room right next door, a real murder, with a real gun, four shots at close range, the torso was riddled with bullets." Madame Bandol cracked a pink prawn. "A very good-looking young chap I'd flirted with at the pool bar the evening before and whom nobody else knew, very mysterious." She waited a moment and then said calmly, "*Voilà*—those were the days!"

"I don't think that you . . . that you're one of the suspects, Madame Bandol. But at the moment you're playing the lead role nonetheless: you're the only witness."

Her face grew serious. She was silent for a little while.

"I know what people say about me. That I'm a senile old woman who makes things up sometimes. Telling tall tales, imagining things. But I don't do that!" Madame Bandol was getting really angry. "A doctor has said I'm suffering from 'early-stage dementia.' Ridiculous, that is just nonsense. I'm old. That's all. And that's no joke! It makes you forgetful sometimes, so what? But the dead man, I saw him. Just like I see you here now!"

Madame Bandol was using one of the sharp, toothpick-sized skewers to pull the sea snails precisely and skillfully out of their shells.

"I believe you, Madame Bandol. I believe you." This was true; Dupin did believe her. The details seemed unreliable, but her having imagined the whole thing—or made it up—seemed unlikely, in his opinion.

Madame Bandol's features relaxed; the smile was back in a flash. She gave him a conspiratorial wink. "Then let's eat together!"

Jacqueline had already brought the second place setting. It would be silly not to use it, Dupin thought. And Madame Bandol's words made it clear that she had said enough about the whole "incident" for now. Dupin picked up a large langoustine.

"Langoustines from Loctudy. They're the best." Madame Bandol set about the crab with some pliers, the claw shattering noisily on her first attempt.

Dupin took some of the homemade mayonnaise. Along with half a lemon. And the fresh, white, nutty meat of the langoustines: yes, it didn't get better than this.

* * *

They had eaten—Dupin dropping his guard further with every bite. Madame Bandol had begun to ask him personal questions, bluntly, without beating about the bush—about his profession, his background, his career with the police, and about why he had become a policeman. About any women in his life. They had spent a longer time talking about Paris. About how if you had to decide, you would choose Paris out of all of Europe's most beautiful cities without hesitation—London, Barcelona, then Rome, classic—and about how there was that special sense of joy that you got in Paris. Only there. Dupin had drunk another glass of Anjou, and Madame Bandol another glass of champagne.

Dupin had—as bizarre as the situation was—enjoyed it. And what's more, he was doing his duty as a policeman. Strictly in the interests of the investigation. What Madame Bandol had said constituted all of the information they had. Dupin needed to keep checking whether anything else would occur to her after all. And most importantly of all: he could keep testing his sense that he believed the core of her statement. After all, everything depended on this. He had to build up as accurate a picture of her as possible. And he was doing a very thorough job of that over langoustines, clams, spider crabs, and the Anjou.

"So, what are you thinking of doing about the missing corpse,

Monsieur le Commissaire?" Madame Bandol had obviously decided it was time to get back to the "incident."

"We'll do everything we can to find it—or re-find it."

"And how will you do that?"

A good question.

"Perhaps some other detail occurs to you?"

Madame Bandol leaned back slightly. "You may be from the police"—her gaze swept carefully over Dupin's face as if she wanted to be certain before she continued speaking—"but I ought to tell you, I trust you." She took the last oyster, having eaten all twelve by herself because Dupin didn't eat oysters. She drizzled a spritz of lemon on it and swallowed it in an elegant way.

"I'm not Sophie Bandol." She smiled briefly and took a mouthful of champagne as if to wash down the oyster.

"Excuse me?" Dupin started.

"I'm Armandine Bandol."

"What do you mean?"

"Sophie's twin sister," she said, and smiled again. "Everyone mixes us up. They always have. Sophie lives in Paris. We bought the house here twenty-five years ago, right by the river. A gorgeous house. You simply must come and visit. But we didn't come here often. At first, Sophie came more than I did. Now she only comes occasionally. And I live here. Permanently. I've lived here for many years now."

She took another mouthful of champagne, slowly this time. She looked out the window, directly at the Belon.

"Why . . . I mean, how can this be?" Dupin rubbed the back of his head. He was confused.

"There's nothing complicated about it. There's not much to tell."

"Tell me what there is to tell."

"I'm a dressmaker. I worked with Yves Saint Laurent for thirty years. When I retired, I gradually relocated my entire life here. Some reporter thought I was Sophie Bandol and wrote a long story about the famous actress who was retiring to the End of the World. With photographs and that kind of thing. That was almost ten years ago. At first neither of us really understood it. Then we found it funny. It became more and more entrenched. People thought I was Sophie and Sophie was me. Sophie was glad the tabloid reporters in Paris suddenly left her alone. And here—nobody is interested in celebrity here, Bretons aren't impressed by that kind of thing. So the famous actress is left in peace."

It was unbelievable. Dupin had never heard a story like it. He had indeed known that Sophie Bandol had a twin sister who was her mirror image, that was common knowledge. But nothing else.

"I'm always a little hungry still," Madame Bandol said, and gestured discreetly to Jacqueline. "What about you?"

"I . . ." Dupin was still struggling with the elaborate story. "And here in Brittany you've never—for example you've never used your ID in an official context?"

"Yes?" Jacqueline was standing next to their table.

"A few more *palourdes roses* from the Glénan, please!" Madame Bandol said, and a moment later she turned back to Dupin. "In the supermarket, at the fishmonger, at the bakery, while buying a newspaper, nobody has asked me for ID yet. I live a somewhat reclusive life. I've got Zizou. I've got a good female friend and a male friend of many years. My walks. My workroom where I still tailor things for my friends and myself sometimes. Now and again I go to Paris. Or I have visitors. That's it."

She looked inquiringly at Dupin, perhaps a little reproachfully.

"I've never claimed to be Sophie Bandol. And nobody has ever asked me either."

Dupin smiled. The more you thought about it, the more believable and plausible it became, oddly enough. Of course it was possible. And Madame Bandol wasn't guilty of any crime. She hadn't deliberately misled anybody. Not even him. Interestingly, he wasn't disappointed, although he had to admit he would really have loved to meet Sophie Bandol.

"And your two friends know who you are?"

"Oh yes, of course. What do you think? That I'm putting on an act for them?" Her indignation was comical. But genuine.

"And what do they say about it?"

"They find it funny."

"Who are these two?"

"Oh, just Monsieur Kolenc, one of the oyster farmers. He mainly produces the *huîtres plates*—those are the best of all!" She looked contentedly at her plate. "In size two or three, so the smaller ones! My girlfriend is Maëlle Gilot. She makes marmalade and jams. She lives on the outskirts of Riec."

"And your doctor, for example?"

"His practice is in Paris. I've been there twice in the last twenty years. A quack, just like all doctors. I have a room in Sophie's Paris house."

"I think—" Dupin was interrupted by the beeping of his mobile. Riwal.

"Excuse me a moment, Madame Bandol." Dupin stood up and walked toward the door to the terrace.

"Yes, Riwal?"

"Reglas. He just left. He has given us a preliminary report. Nothing. He has found absolutely nothing so far. He has also taken various soil samples from the spot where the corpse is supposed to have been lying. To test them for blood, scraps of material, and so on."

"It was raining cats and dogs," said Dupin.

"What is Madame Bandol saying? Have you been able to find out anything else?"

"She . . ." Dupin paused. If he told the story about the sisters being mistaken for each other, it was bound to cast more doubt on Madame Bandol's credibility in the eyes of his colleagues. "Madame Bandol saw a car parked a little way outside the parking lot. Our colleagues from Riec didn't see a car when they arrived, did they?"

"No. What did it look like?"

"Dark."

"Black?"

"Dark." Dupin hesitated. "Or red, she says."

"Or red? Has anything else come to her?"

"The man potentially had short hair, definitely dark brown."

"That's new too."

"Yes. Otherwise she confirmed all of her statements in detail. You've always got to bear in mind: Madame Bandol was standing maybe five meters away—with not much light and heavy rain, so visibility was poor, and with a panicked Zizou into the bargain."

"The dog?"

"The dog."

"All right, boss. Our Riec colleagues will make inquiries in the area. About whether anyone noticed anything unusual in the late afternoon. Or happened to be near the parking lot. Kadeg and I are thinking of driving back to Concarneau now."

"No problem." A rare sentence for him, Dupin knew. He put his mobile back in his trouser pocket.

Although all of Port Belon was enchantingly beautiful, the terrace at La Coquille, built directly on the river, was perhaps the most enchanting place. You sat on barstools along a counter made of wooden planks, with a real ship's mast soaring into the air at one end with the Breton flag flying proudly from it; the two seawater tanks had been installed in the roofed section of the terrace. You had a view of the Belon, the very last stretch of it before the open Atlantic. No painter could have dreamed up a more picturesque view: on either side, densely wooded hills fell gently away to the river, regular, practically symmetrical. Every single treetop stood out clearly against the sky. A perfect display of nature. And beyond that, the vast sea began. Dupin looked toward the west. The sun was still quite far above the horizon, but it had already started to change the color of the sky around it. The orange hour had begun.

The commissaire sighed. He wished this was a different evening. And that he was here with Claire. He turned around and went back into the restaurant. To Armandine Bandol.

* * *

Madame Bandol was holding a fork in one hand, a piece of *tarte tatin* on it. She smiled frankly.

"I've ordered you a slice too," she said, and gestured with her head toward his place, where there was a particularly large slice of the apple cake on a prettily decorated porcelain plate. "Yes, Jacqueline definitely likes you!"

Dupin had just remembered what else he'd wanted to ask. He had circled it in his notebook when he was making notes. "Kiki. Who's Kiki?"

Armandine Bandol looked amused at first and then, when she realized he'd meant this question seriously, aghast.

"Impossible, Monsieur le Commissaire! You must know Kiki. How long have you been here, did you say? In Concarneau, in Brittany?"

"Five years."

"Don't you read any papers?"

"*Ouest-France, Le Télégramme,* every morning, every article."

"The ten-meter-long shark that comes to our coastline every April. He likes this bay, the Aven, the Belon. Sometimes he even swims into the Belon at high tide."

Of course. Dupin had read about it. A few times, in fact. With very mixed feelings.

"The name had just slipped my mind." It sounded absurd.

"Have you never seen him then?"

Dupin had indeed never seen him. And he was in fact rather pleased about this.

"A basking shark! After the whale shark, the second largest fish on earth, you see. It belongs to the same family as the great white shark," Madame Bandol said triumphantly.

"But it only eats plankton," Dupin hastened to add, having once looked it up himself on a specialist zoological website as a precaution, even though Nolwenn had assured him of it many times before. "It is, even if it wanted to, anatomically incapable of consuming other food. Meat, for example."

The basking shark was indeed from the same family as the great white shark. And Dupin had admittedly found it an alarming idea, to be swimming and then suddenly see the fin of a ten- or twelve-meter-long shark next to you; the animals liked to come close to the coast, and Dupin personally loved swimming far out into the large bays. As much as he hated being on the sea—in boats, for example—he loved being *in* the sea; he went swimming before work in the summer. He loved it and didn't want to have to think about sharks while doing it. And yet he knew that they were not that rare; quite a few basking shark videos had been collected on the *Ouest-France* website.

"We call him Kiki, like the preserved specimen on display in the Concarneau aquarium. An extraordinarily loyal creature. Zizou and I saw him just last week, in the estuary. The Belon carries so much delicious plankton. The oysters are crazy about it too. But let's stop talking about Kiki. There are more pressing matters. How shall we proceed with the case, Commissaire? Count me in. *The only witness!*" She paused and then intoned pensively, "A difficult witness who can't say much because she didn't see much. And whose memory plays strange tricks on her now and again."

Dupin would have liked to say more about the shark, for instance that Kiki was more of a name for a budgie. But he let it go. He had shaken off his astonishment at the—in the eyes of a city man—highly unusual animals of Brittany. They were a part of everyday life: extravagant sea and land creatures, porpoises, bottlenose dolphins, small penguins. Most recently he had encountered Skippy, the giant kangaroo. One day he would probably come across the Great Mammoth, the rhinoceros, the bison, and the giant panther who had lived in Brittany in ancient times, up until recently in effect, if you were judging by the Breton sense of time.

"I suggest we make plans to meet here again tomorrow. And keep talking." Madame Bandol signaled to Jacqueline as she spoke.

"We've conducted soil tests at the spot where you saw the corpse."

"Very unlikely that they'll find something. With that rain. And I only saw the blood on the upper body."

Dupin gave a start. "You said you weren't sure where it was."

"Well, apparently I do know. It was on the upper body, I'm telling you now. It has just come back to me," she said with conviction. "It helps when we talk about it. The lower section of the coat was clean, for example."

"A coat, you remember a coat now too?"

"Yes, dark green. Or a long jacket."

"Dark green? You could see that?"

"I could see reasonably well at that distance."

Confused, Dupin noted it all down. Blood on the upper body. Coat or longish jacket, dark green. Then he crossed out a few other things.

"I've got to go now, Monsieur le Commissaire."

Jacqueline had brought the bill on a plastic saucer.

"I'll take the liberty of settling this," Madame Bandol said. She had taken out her purse and was placing a few notes on the saucer without even looking at Dupin.

"Thank you very much, Madame."

"This has been fun. We're a team now." She looked at Dupin, and it was clear she was waiting for a reply, even though it couldn't have been a question.

"I guess so, Madame Bandol."

She stood up and Jacqueline appeared with the bright yellow oilskin jacket that had become one of the many emblems of Brittany. When their "inventor," Guy Cotten, died some years before, public mourning had taken place here for several days. He had designed the iconic yellow jacket for the professional deep-sea fishermen in 1966, and they were now well known around the world. The jacket also answered one of the questions that Dupin had still had: how Madame Bandol could have taken her daily walk in the heavy rain. She was also wearing sturdy shoes, he now noticed. Proper hiking boots, dark brown. Dupin was seeing Madame Bandol in full for the first time now. She was wearing a long, black, elegant yet comfortable-looking skirt and a kind of casual blazer with a matte silk top underneath, also in black. She looked fantastic. The bright yellow of the coat reaching almost to her shoes was a dramatic contrast to the black underneath. Zizou stood next to her, fully awake now. He obviously knew the procedure, the evenings spent here, the sequence of events.

Dupin had stood up too.

"See you tomorrow then, Monsieur le Commissaire. Jacqueline can tell you how to reach me."

"Yes, see you tomorrow then. It was a pleasure to meet you, Madame Bandol. A great pleasure!"

"Oh, Monsieur Dupin." Madame smiled mischievously and left.

Dupin sat down again. He was not in any hurry. The whole business was too crazy.

He looked out the window. At the river. The ships on the buoys were bobbing harder now, the tide was coming in. He reflected on the corpse that had disappeared, the extraordinary and baffling Madame Bandol, and on what he should do about this whole case.

And he had no answer.

*   *   *

The sea at the horizon, at the end of the Belon, was shimmering a violet and orange color now, the sun having sunk quietly into the Atlantic. And the sky too had only changed color in one narrow stripe this evening—sometimes the colors clung to the horizon—otherwise it was nothing but that lucid, crystalline blue, as if the sky were trying to defend it to the last. It was only in the east that it was enveloped by the oncoming blackness.

Dupin was standing on the small jetty, very close to the water, as always. He got out his phone.

"Monsieur le Commissaire?"

"That's all for today, Nolwenn."

"Riwal has already told me." This was how it always worked—Nolwenn was perfectly up to speed at all times. "No new findings. So nothing else useful has occurred to Madame Bandol."

"No, there are a few details," Dupin said, and passed on the new information.

"So did she seem confused to you?"

"No. Now and again, maybe. She told some eccentric stories, and I've seen how impressively oddly her memory functions. She—" Dupin broke off. Of course it couldn't be ruled out that she really was confused.

"I mean, is she genuinely not with it? Suffering from dementia? Could she have imagined the whole thing?"

"No."

"So you believe her then. Good! Follow your instinct, Monsieur le Commissaire!" As Nolwenn saw it, instinct was the most reliable thing a person could have.

Dupin's forehead creased. "I really do believe her. I think she saw someone lying there. I think there are too many details and they're too precise."

Dupin knew that these random, precise details were not surefire proof. They could equally be a hint at the opposite assumption. But his instinct still told him—including after the more in-depth conversation—that what Madame Bandol was saying was essentially true. That there had been an injured or dead man there in the parking lot.

"All right. Then we *have* got a case," Nolwenn declared matter-of-factly but full of energy. "So, here we go. First of all we should check if anyone was reported missing yesterday or today, somewhere in Finistère or in Morbihan. Throughout Brittany. If there was a corpse, then someone is missing somewhere now! Male; dark brown hair, possibly short; dark green jacket or coat; injury to the torso; drives a dark car. Or a red one. That's something anyway."

A pitiful set of facts, thought Dupin. Still, they had to start somewhere. Sometimes routine helped.

"Have someone call the hospitals and doctors in private practice in Riec and the surrounding districts. As far as Lorient and Quimper. Ask whether a man was brought in early in the evening. Or made his own way there injured," he said.

"Noted. Inspector Kadeg will deal with that. Inspector Riwal will have to do some cramming tonight." Nolwenn left an artful pause and then switched into a solemn tone: "For tomorrow, for the diploma."

The diploma. Of course.

For weeks, Riwal had kept the whole commissariat on its toes with it. The final exam for the seminar "Breton Languages and Cultures" at the Centre de Recherche Bretonne et Celtique at the University of Brest. A three-hour class every Tuesday evening for two semesters. Dupin had to admit he had found it ludicrous to see Riwal of all people—the particularly proud Breton—taking part. But on the other hand that was the very reason it made sense. Nolwenn suspected it had something to do with Riwal's impending fatherhood; that he wanted to prepare in a suitably "well-grounded" way for the birth of his son. A suspicion that Riwal, and they were eight months in now, had not contradicted. The seminar comprehensively covered the various Breton languages, the culture, art, literature, but especially the history. Which essentially meant—judging by what Riwal talked about with great enthusiasm every week in the commissariat—one thing: looking at all of human history and working out what Bretons had invented, discovered, and completed first. It was a quintessentially Breton discipline—Dupin had long since internalized it—that was practiced everywhere, in magazines, books, on the radio; a popular sport. In recent weeks Riwal had been questioning his colleagues in the style of a quiz show, so in the afternoons the whole commissariat sat together. The first monumental construction of humanity? No, not the Egyptian pyramids, as everyone would assume, but the seventy-five-meter-long Breton stone tombs, the Cairn de Barnenez. Built when? 4500 BC. The pyramids weren't built till two thousand years later!

"I've already signed Riwal's application for those two days off on your behalf. Tomorrow it's the written exams, next week it's the orals," Nolwenn said.

"Then Kadeg will have to take it on. Of course. He's to call me straight-away."

"He will. And tomorrow morning the two of us will speak about your party. Whether you like it or not. There are only a few days left."

Dupin did not want to. He absolutely did not want to. He hadn't wanted to from the beginning, he hadn't wanted the party at all. At first he had been able to delay the ridiculous idea of throwing a party for his five-year work anniversary. Once the "promotion" that Nolwenn consistently referred to as an "honor for the entire commissariat" had also come along, he no longer stood a chance. It had become an obsession. Besides, Nolwenn had threatened a "surprise party" in the event that he continued to refuse to cooperate, the ultimate threat for Dupin.

"Let's do that." He sighed.

"I'm not in tomorrow afternoon, if you remember?"

Dupin had forgotten. "Of course."

The funeral. Somewhere inland. Aunt Elwen, one of the many aunts in Nolwenn's clan, with all of its branches. Nolwenn didn't seem to have been all that close to her. Last week when she announced she had to go to the funeral, she had immediately added a joke, some typical Breton humor, which was in no way inferior to the dry humor of British Celts. An elderly Breton meets someone of their own age at a guild meeting. "Harryston, old chap, I wanted to express my condolences. I heard you buried your wife last week." "I had to, mate, she was dead, you know."

"Well, I'll make the calls now and then I'll go home. *Bonne soirée*, Monsieur le Commissaire."

"*Bonne soirée*, Nolwenn."

She had hung up.

Dupin looked at the waters flowing inland. They were surging with such incredible force and speed. It was impressive every time: the enormous quantities of water that flowed toward the source, conquering the land. He walked slowly up the road to the parking lot. To the right and left were the two old manor houses of the oyster dynasties. He would drive to Concarneau and drink a Lambig at the Amiral. Paul, the owner, had got some of the new vintage from his brother-in-law.

The parking lot was deserted—Dupin's Citroën was the only car there. It was almost dark; the tall, densely packed trees didn't let much light through.

Suddenly, when Dupin was just a few paces away from his car, there was a strange sound. He started. A kind of croaking. Eerie. Hard to identify. But close by. It seemed to be coming from the other side of the car. Dupin remained motionless. His muscles tensed. His right hand had moved automatically to his weapon. For a moment nothing at all happened.

Then suddenly a misshapen brown head appeared from behind the bumper. Dark eyes focused on the commissaire. And then the misshapen body followed.

A goose. A large, majestic goose.

The strange croaking had turned into unmistakable aggressive sounds. Dupin knew a lot about geese. In the little one-horse town in the Jura that his father came from and where Dupin had spent nearly all of his holidays as a child, he had had enough unpleasant, distressing encounters with geese to give him enough respect for bad-tempered specimens to last him the rest of his life. They could turn into monsters. And this one was not just any old goose, it was the most capricious, temperamental breed of all: a Toulouse goose.

It was coming toward him in a fierce, gaggling rage, with a grim look in its eye. Dupin shrank backward as quick as a flash. The goose suddenly stopped, scurrying slightly to the left and then back to the right as if it was drawing an invisible line that was supposed to mean: you will not cross this.

Dupin knew how fast geese could be. His chances of outsmarting it with a special running maneuver were extremely poor. And betting on wearing it down, waiting until it gave up and moved, was a bad tactic with geese—they were even more obstinate than he was. Things looked bad. There was just one option left. Dupin turned round and walked briskly back into La Coquille. He stopped at the counter. One of the sisters was busy polishing the glasses. She cast him a curious glance.

"I need some vegetable scraps," Dupin said very firmly, quickly adding a "please."

"You're well informed for a Parisian." There was genuine respect in the old lady's friendly voice. She turned around, disappearing into the kitchen and returning with a plastic bag a few minutes later.

"Carrot peelings, salad scraps, cucumber peelings—our special mixture for Charlie, he loves it. He's not having a good time of it at the moment. Lovesick. Good luck."

Dupin just nodded. It would no doubt have turned into a funny conversation, but he wanted to get going. The commissaire knew there was only one thing more powerful than the mysterious wrath of geese: their love of eating. And vegetable scraps had been his grandmother's tried and tested home remedy. They worked every time.

The goose, Charlie, was standing—just as Dupin had expected—exactly where he had left him earlier. The angry gaggling started up again immediately. Dupin took aim, throwing the bag to the left, in the direction of the hedge, not so far away that Charlie could have remained uninterested, but far enough to ensure he could walk past safely on the right.

It worked. Although only just. Dupin sprinted to his car, wrenching the car door open on his last stride and jumping inside. Just in time to escape a beating from Charlie, as he had in fact decided to go on the attack after a quick snack. The commissaire started up the engine, put the car in reverse, and drove out of the parking lot in a sweeping arc. Charlie followed the car for a few meters, then returned to his special mixture, gaggling.

Dupin had a smile on his face. He actually liked geese.

The call from Kadeg didn't come till he was almost in Concarneau. An extremely short call.

Kadeg didn't have any news to report. Not even anything minor. Neither his nor Nolwenn's calls had turned up anything. No recently missing man in all of Brittany.

That would have been too simple anyway.

Dupin was looking forward to the Lambig.

The Second Day

Yes, no doubt about it—we've got a dead body, Monsieur le Commissaire. A corpse. It's definitely there, why do you ask?"

"Is someone near it?" Dupin was standing there thunderstruck, the phone pressed hard to his ear.

"Me. I mean, I'm near it."

"Are you keeping an eye on it the whole time?"

"I'm standing here a few meters away from the corpse, I can see it the whole time." The policeman sounded stressed. Stressed and bewildered.

"I don't want the corpse to be unsupervised for a second. And where, tell me—*where* is the body?"

"In the Monts d'Arrée. Almost underneath the Roc'h Trévézel. I'm sure you know the D785, the mountain road that runs along the mountain ridges of the Monts d'Arrée—on the other side, where—"

"Unbelievable!"

He knew the mountain road over the "mountains," but it was a hundred kilometers away from Port Belon, a little way north of Quimper and far inland. A secluded area in the middle of absolutely nowhere.

"Is he wearing a dark green jacket? Or a dark green coat?"

"A dark green jacket?" The policeman—a gendarme from Sizun—was increasingly despairing. "No, he's wearing a beige jacket and it's covered in blood. And torn. Jeans. Brown leather shoes or sneakers."

"Short, dark brown hair? Injuries to the upper body?"

"He has injuries everywhere, Monsieur le Commissaire. The body is horribly contorted. He's lying directly beneath one of the steep peaks. He must have fallen from it. But there's something else," the policeman said.

"What?"

"There are terrible hematomas on his neck. The doctor thinks he could have been strangled. Before the fall. He is positive the hematomas didn't happen during the fall, anyway. It doesn't look like an accident."

"Strangled?"

This was all difficult to believe. Dupin didn't wait for an answer.

"What kind of doctor are you talking about?"

"Our GP from Sizun. He came straight with us. As a precaution. The man could still have been alive, of course. He's a very good doctor, eighty, but very fit."

"And he's certain about the hematomas? Already?"

Medical examiners always said they wouldn't give any opinions until the final results of the autopsy.

"Yes, absolutely. Do you want to speak to him directly?"

"No, no. And the short, dark brown hair?"

"It's not long, I'd say. What do you mean by short? Buzzed?"

"Averagely short."

"Could be. And the hair definitely isn't blond or red, anyway. It's hard to tell because it's covered in blood and anyway the head is hard to—"

"And there's nothing to identify him?"

"There's nothing in the pockets of his pants or jacket. It looks as though someone made sure there was nothing left to find."

"What age would you say he is?"

"Oh—that's hard to say too. Mid-sixties perhaps. As I say: the corpse is in a bad state."

"And the official medical examiner? Where's he coming from?"

"*She* is coming from Brest. She ought to be here soon."

Dupin had almost reached his Citroën. The call had come in as he was on his way from his apartment to the Amiral. He had walked straight to his car, which as always was parked in the big square right by the harbor—in contravention of all official regulations that provided obligatory parking for the police in the exclusive spaces at the commissariat.

"I need to know the time of death as soon as possible. Whether he died yesterday around four or five in the evening. And if there's anything on his clothes or hair that doesn't come from the place where he's lying. Soil, grass, whatever."

Could this in fact be a case with two corpses all of a sudden? And two—in all likelihood—murdered men? If Madame Bandol's statement was correct, and Dupin still assumed it was this morning—although of course it couldn't be completely certain—but in any case, if it was true, then it would be absurd: two capital crimes, two murders within just twelve hours in southern Finistère? A male body was missing here, while one was suddenly found there, albeit a hundred kilometers away. Of course the obvious thought was that the corpse in the Monts d'Arrée was the missing corpse from Port Belon.

The Monts d'Arrée were an extremely remote area, hence a good spot to dispose of a dead body. On the other hand, there were also extremely remote places around Port Belon, closer places—and above all, the much safer place: the Atlantic. But maybe there were reasons for this place that they simply didn't know about. Or this really was a question of a second corpse.

"I'll inform the medical examiner of everything as soon as she is here."

"Shit," Dupin said, still absorbed in his thoughts.

The policeman seemed—understandably—not to know how to respond. Dupin picked up again where they had left off. "Who found the man? And why so early?"

It was just quarter past eight.

"A group of hikers. An organized tour with a guide. Twelve people. They set off from Sizun at seven o'clock. They wanted to get to the summit. And then on to Lac Saint-Michel. The hiking season is just beginning here."

Dupin knew how high the Roc'h Trévézel was: 384 meters, the highest elevation in Brittany. He could never help smirking when people talked about a "summit," even if the hill fell steeply away facing the west, toward the Atlantic. Especially because Dupin knew *real* summits. Real mountains. His father's home village was at 700 meters' altitude, on the edge of the Alps. In less than half an hour you could be at 2,000 meters' altitude; a little further and you were at 3,000 meters and above.

"And he was lying in the middle of a hiking trail?"

"No. On a rock slightly off the trail. And it's just a narrow path that's not used much anyway. One of the group wanted to take a photograph and left the path—he discovered the corpse. As I said earlier, it was directly below a steep rock face. It's a good hundred-and-fifty-meter drop. He probably fell or was thrown. In any case he was probably already dead."

"And a local would have known that a path runs along there?"

"Yes."

"Is there a car anywhere in the vicinity?"

"No."

"No dark car? Or a red one?"

"No."

"How did the man get there?"

"We can't tell at this stage. My colleague is up on the mountain ridge. He's looking for footprints. Perhaps that will tell us more. He's very good at looking for footprints."

Dupin had reached his Citroën.

"I'll be there," he checked his watch, "by just after nine, I think. As soon as the medical examiner has anything to say, she's to call me. And take a photo of the corpse on your mobile, from above at an angle, and send it to my assistant. Immediately."

They would show it to Madame Bandol. Her memory sometimes behaved in an extremely arbitrary way, suddenly and selectively, but that meant it could be full of surprises anytime. Even if the chances were slim, they needed to try everything.

Without waiting for an answer, Dupin hung up.

It was baffling. A string of baffling incidents that had started yesterday at the penguin exhibit in the Océanopolis. And hadn't stopped. Dupin firmly believed in the principle of accumulation. He always had. If extraordinary incidents occurred, no matter if they were good, bad, funny, or even baffling, then several happened in a row. They didn't like to be alone.

There had also been something baffling about the equal parts surprising and mysterious message Claire had given him this morning on the phone when she had woken him at seven o'clock. Dupin was to meet her early that evening in Quimper. "At about six o'clock." She would be in touch again to tell him where. At first he had thought she was joking. It was also mysterious because no train came in from Paris "about six o'clock." The TGV came in at four forty-five or six forty-five. Dupin hoped he would be able to make it. Now that there was definitely a corpse.

* * *

The landscape was surreal, rugged, bizarre, wild, like in a sinister fairy tale. The perfect place for whimsical fantasies, stories, and legends—and in fact there were huge numbers of them here. The ideal dwelling place for druids, sorcerers, fairies, dwarves, and other magical creatures. It was creepy and utterly inhospitable to poor human beings. A setting for stunning fantasy films, where scenes about Frodo, Gandalf, and their companions could have been filmed.

The Monts d'Arrée, the "Breton mountains," formed the border between southern and northern Finistère. Dupin remembered how overwhelmed—and above all, deeply shocked—he had been when he had driven through them for the first time, up the D785 to Morlaix, because of some little bureaucratic issue. He would never have suspected Brittany had landscape like this. The road ran through forests of black fir until a new world suddenly opened up: gentle mountain ridges of granite and sandstone, rounded by the weather—the *menez*—alternated with rough, rugged mountain crests, jagged quartz, oddly contorted rock formations: the *rocs*. There were a few spacious plateaus too. It looked as though the ground had cracked violently open. The *rocs* towered high into the air, jutting out of a barren landscape of heather, gorse, ferns, mosses, and springs, streams, and bogs steeped in legend. There were several secluded chapels here and there, themselves the topic of various stories. And a smattering of mysterious menhirs.

"Supernatural" was the best word for this area, Dupin thought. The everyday world, the world on "this side," ended here in the heart of Finistère. Deserted realms where thick fog fought for the upper hand against bitter winds and raging storms. With no trees at all, which looked even more odd; they simply didn't grow here, like at dizzying heights above the tree border. Winds and storms carried the infinitely fine salty spray of the raging Atlantic as far as here; it fell straight down onto the chain of mountains and the salt prevented any more luxurious vegetation growing. That was the scientific explanation. There were legends about it too—probably the most ridiculous legend that Dupin had ever heard: when Jesus was born, the heavens had sent the trees on the Monts d'Arrée to Bethlehem to welcome the Messiah. When they stubbornly refused (simply Bretons) they were condemned to wither and never be able to grow again.

During his trip to Morlaix back then, Riwal had drummed it into Dupin—emphatically and using many vivid stories—only to venture across the chain of mountains in broad daylight. Dupin couldn't tell how serious Riwal was being. But as always, Riwal had managed to provoke a slight sense of unease in Dupin, as crazy as this was. Impure souls wandered around here before and after sundown, in desperate hope of salvation, apparently; dwarfs danced with wild movements in the darkness on the heath; eerie stone depictions of Ankou, Death, came alive at night. The devil himself had hidden his treasure here, and whoever tried to dig it up would be grabbed by the legs and dragged down into the depths. It was even rumored that the entrance to hell, Youdig, was located here, in the Yeun-Elez, the ancient bog surrounded by rugged *rocs*.

At some point Dupin had interrupted Riwal as he reeled off stories. It was probably a good thing he was not around today.

The commissaire was almost there. The Roc'h Trévézel towered up imposingly to the left of the road.

A moment later he spotted a small police Peugeot in the unpaved parking lot next to the road.

Dupin had intended to take a look at the corpse and to meet Kadeg, the policeman, and, most importantly, the medical examiner there. But if the perpetrator had left footprints, then they would probably be up there and not where the corpse had hit the ground.

Dupin drove up on the right and parked directly behind the police car.

The weather was doing its best to heighten the dramatic effects of the landscape further. Vast jet-black banks of cloud drifted menacingly across the sky with misshapen holes in them, light falling hauntingly through them in dazzling streaks. Roving spotlights illuminating several sharply outlined sections of the landscape: a peak, a section of heath, a lake. Like with religious or paranormal phenomena.

Dupin couldn't resist a smile: a weather-beaten signpost pointed the way to the "highest mountain in Brittany." It was perhaps three hundred meters high, and a narrow, stony footpath ran up it. It must have rained heavily during the night, because the path had turned into a stream. To the right and left of Roc'h Trévézel were more rugged peaks.

He would have a good view from above. Dupin broke into a run, which quickly turned into a wearying trudge over the rich soil. Within a few meters, his shoes were soaked through. Even the faded grass had been, like everything up here, blown askew by the wind. There wasn't much here: low, gnarled undergrowth that looked like overgrown bonsai trees, bright splashes of green and purple here and there, large fragments of rock in between.

Dupin had to scramble the last few meters up to the summit. He was pretty out of breath when he got up there.

The views were spectacular in every direction. And it was as he had suspected: down below, on the other side from the one where he had parked his car, he could see a little group of people. He noticed Kadeg's new dark red jacket; the others must have been the policeman who had called him and their colleagues from forensics. He could only just make out the hiking trail. They were standing a few meters to the side of it.

Dupin could also see the large rocky ledge with a misshapen silhouette lying on it. The dead body. Someone was standing next to him, presumably the medical examiner. There were two more figures in front of the rocks.

Dupin had another hundred or hundred and fifty meters of the ridge to climb before he would get to the place from where—according to the plausible hypothesis—the victim had been thrown. Already dead. If what that doctor from Sizun said was true. The rocks were slightly lower there.

Dupin was almost there when his mobile started to beep loudly. He almost didn't hear it in the strong wind up here.

"Monsieur le Commissaire?"

"Yes, who else would it be, Kadeg?"

"Where are you, boss? We're waiting for you."

"Look up."

"What do you . . ."

Dupin could see Kadeg moving. Raising his head. It still took a while.

"Is that you up there?"

"What do you think?"

For some ridiculous reason, Kadeg now began to wave.

"What are you doing there?"

"What is it, Kadeg, fire away!"

"The medical examiner has given some preliminary details on the possible time of death. In light of the rigor mortis and livor mortis, of course the weather has made the corpse's core temperature—"

"Kadeg!"

"The man died yesterday between nine o'clock and twelve. Probably, as I sa—"

"Yesterday morning?"

"Between nine and twelve, yes."

This was unbelievable. It had a significant impact on everything.

Madame Bandol had—if this was true—seen the corpse around five o'clock in the evening, before the perpetrator could get rid of it, in the parking lot near Port Belon. So the murder would in all likelihood have happened during a timeframe before five o'clock. It would make absolutely no sense to strangle someone yesterday morning—seven to ten hours beforehand—and then place them in the parking lot in Port Belon at five o'clock, or rather leave them there until five o'clock, and then drive the corpse into the Monts d'Arrée that evening or that night and throw them off one of the rocky ridges. It would be utterly ludicrous.

But then—then they were in all likelihood dealing with *two* corpses! With *two* murders.

"Hello? Are you still there, Monsieur le Commissaire?"

"What about the strangulation, what does the medical examiner say about that?"

"She agrees with the GP from Sizun. There's a strong probability that death occurred due to mechanical asphyxiation. He was probably strangled, in any case. We will only know for certain whether he was already dead during the fall, or simply unconscious, after the autopsy. But she thinks strangulation is the most plausible cause of death."

"I presume nothing has been found yet that could identify the man?"

"We would have informed you," Kadeg grumbled. "Are you going to come down to where we are? The medical examiner wants to have the body picked up as soon as possible."

Dupin's thoughts were elsewhere. "Yes. I'm coming."

He hung up and remained motionless for a few moments. He ran a hand roughly through his hair. Then he looked around. During the phone call, he had continued to climb slowly.

It could have happened somewhere here, in the next few meters. The victim was thrown down the slope here. They, the perpetrator and victim, had probably come by car. The path from the road to here didn't look quite as arduous as the one he had taken.

There were several possible scenarios. The murder, the strangulation, had taken place up here, or it had happened earlier and the victim had been brought up here, either dragged or carried up. It wouldn't have been a stroll anyway: the perpetrator must have been fairly strong. Or they weren't alone.

A deep bass voice cut into Dupin's thoughts. "Are you the Frenchman?"

The commissaire turned around. A few meters away, a head appeared from behind a rock, then the uniformed body. A very old policeman, by the looks of it anyway. Snow-white hair, a face weathered by the sun, weather, and life. This had to be the colleague who was looking for footprints. He stood still and scrutinized Dupin from head to toe.

"Nothing good has ever come out of France. Don't take it personally," he said.

"And with whom do I have the pleasure of speaking?" Dupin made a point of being pleasant in his response. He generally ignored it when he was spoken to like this. And the sentence "Nothing good has ever come out of France" had long since become an everyday Breton phrase to him.

"Brioc L'Helgoualc'h."

"Pleased to meet you, Monsieur . . ." This was the exact kind of Breton name that Dupin couldn't remember for the life of him, let alone pronounce. "Have you found anything up here?"

"Are you in charge of this now?"

Dupin remained calm. "If you mean the murder investigation: that's right, monsieur."

"This just gets better and better!" The old policeman's intonation was far less unpleasant than his words. "Is this your first time here in our neck of the woods? In the Monts d'Arrée?"

"Do you think it could be relevant to solving the case, the question of whether I've been here before?" Dupin said, remaining even-tempered. There was nothing hostile about the grumpy chap.

"Oh yes."

"You were going to tell me whether you'd found anything interesting."

Brioc L'Helgoualc'h grunted something Dupin couldn't make out, turned around, and disappeared behind the rock again without any further explanation. A hint of movement with his head could be interpreted, with some generosity, as a request to follow him. Dupin sighed—and followed.

This was going to be a wonderful investigation.

* * *

When Dupin rounded the rock, Brioc L'Helgoualc'h was already some distance away. As old as he might be, he walked fast.

He was kneeling in the heather a little below Dupin.

"Here," he called.

Dupin approached. Only now did he spot the small path. He crouched down too and saw what the policeman had meant: two faded but still clearly visible footprints on a patch of ground between some stones and moss. A right foot and a left foot, almost parallel at this spot. Deep imprints. Someone stood here for quite a long time. One single person.

Dupin looked along the path. It ran directly from the road and led to the rough, rocky ridge with the slope where the dead body lay.

"There's another print down there. And further up there too. But the path is mostly stony or mossy."

Dupin's mobile rang. Kadeg again. He answered anyway.

"So where are you, Monsieur le Commissaire? You're the only person we're waiting for. The medical examiner wants to leave with the corpse."

"I'm investigating," Dupin replied drily. "I hope there was another reason you called me. A good reason."

"The medical examiner says that she sees indications of a struggle. Apart from the strangulation marks, she means."

"Yes?" This was relevant.

"Hematomas on the right side of the face, on the chin, on the stomach, that very likely were not sustained in the fall; a twisted, broken right wrist that doesn't look like an injury from the impact either. But she wants—"

"A broken wrist?"

It must have been a brutal struggle. The victim had grappled ferociously with his murderer. "Has she said anything else?"

"No, but that is quite a lot—before the autopsy."

"I'm coming—until then, everyone stays where they are." Dupin hung up.

He turned back to L'Helgoualc'h. "I—"

"Broken wrist?" L'Helgoualc'h's voice had changed. He sounded insistent.

"A broken wrist, yes."

"When night falls, the Kannerezed Noz, the washerwomen of the night—bony, pale women—begin to wash the shrouds of the dead in the bog. If you encounter them, you've got to copy them. But if you don't wring out the washing in the same direction as them, they break your wrist and you bleed to death." He looked Dupin in the eye imploringly.

"He didn't bleed to death," Dupin said, "much less from a broken wrist."

But he had to admit that the eerie imagery had thrown him slightly. Although he never really reacted to these kinds of stories anymore. They cropped up in every case: myths, legends—they weren't in Brittany for nothing. They were essential. And what's more, he found them somewhat comforting in the absence of Riwal—who would otherwise no doubt have told these stories long before. Riwal would have really embellished them, however, and delighted in telling them with style. L'Helgoualc'h had told them downright prosaically by comparison. And appeared to intend to leave it at this interjection—a moment later he was back to the footprints.

"As I say, I've found the same footprints down there. Shoe size eleven or twelve. I suspect an especially heavy man, or a man who was carrying something heavy. Another man, for instance. The footprints are deep." L'Helgoualc'h stood right next to the footprints and stayed there for a moment. Then he stepped aside.

"Have a look."

Dupin crouched down again. The policeman's footprint was practically invisible. And looked tiny compared to the others. "I'm a size seven and a half."

Dupin was impressed. The estimate of 11 or 12 was precise.

"I think he brought the man up here once he was already dead, although I don't see any drag marks. They won't have been deep enough. With the rain. The man stopped a number of times to catch his breath where the ground was even and he could get a solid foothold. If there was a struggle, then it wasn't on the rocks here, it was down there, earlier."

Dupin nodded.

"He was wearing sneakers. Nikes. He—"

"Nikes?"

"Easy to identify by the tread marks."

Dupin took another look. He would not have been able, no matter how sharp the edges of the footprint, to identify any tread marks. L'Helgoualc'h seemed to Dupin like some Native American tracker. No doubt there was also an ancient connection between the Celts and Native Americans that Dupin just didn't know about yet.

"Bigger structures like honeycombs, wavy lines in between . . . A common design," L'Helgoualc'h said.

"I see."

If this was correct, they had their first clue to the perpetrator. Apart from the fact that he must have been reasonably strong. Nike sneakers in

11 or 12. This was potentially a crucial lead. Dupin was intrigued about what the forensic team would say, but he had no doubts about his colleague's expertise.

"It wasn't a hiker. No sensible hiker wears sneakers like that."

"Are there footprints belonging to anyone else?"

"No."

"And you haven't found any other trace evidence up there on the ridge?"

"No. It's all rocky. Not a chance."

"I want to go up anyway."

Dupin turned away and followed the path up the ridge. It was in fact a much easier walk than the earlier path. Soon he had reached the last rocks. The slope that now came into view was brutal. Steep, a long way down, and dotted with sharp, rocky outcrops. Dupin averted his gaze. He turned around slowly. Amongst the ominous banks of cloud, bigger and bigger sections were being broken up by clear blue sky, opening up views far into the distance of the breathtaking peninsula of Crozon and of the bay of Brest where you could see the Atlantic—Ar Mor Braz: the large sea. The bog with the washerwomen of the night in the east, surrounded by the three *rocs*. The reservoir Saint-Michel, and beyond it, one of the largest unspoiled Breton forests, the Chaos of Huelgoat. Also a place of wild stories.

"This—this is the balcony of the west."

Dupin practically jumped. He hadn't heard L'Helgoualc'h coming. Suddenly he was standing next to him and speaking huskily, but with unexpected melancholy. "The balcony of the western world, they say. The Monts d'Arrée might look to you like strange hills—in reality they're *mountains*. Majestic mountains; the Massif Armoricain is a vast mountain chain that stretches hundreds of kilometers, from Normandy to here. And for a long time its peaks were higher than Mount Everest is today. They were over nine thousand meters. The Himalayas, and also the Alps, the Pyrenees, the Caucasus, they're all young mountains in comparison to this one; not even fifty million years old. The Monts d'Arrée are ten times as old. That, monsieur, that is the truth of these mountains."

Dupin had to concede that even he was moved. For Bretons, the commissaire had learned, the past was as real as the present, and a point in time three hundred million years ago, for example, was just as valid as one in the present, so that it was deeply unfair and presumptuous to arbitrarily pick today as the only valid point from the continuum of time. Just because you were someone who happened to live right now, it was pure arrogance, modern pretension. If you looked at the world in a Breton way, the Monts d'Arrée were real mountains, even today.

"This is Bretagne *bretonnante*—the heart of Brittany beats here like nowhere else." L'Helgoualc'h put it as a quintessential truth. In the last few years, Dupin had received many hours of Nolwenn-lessons about Bretagne *bretonnante*, or Breton Brittany. What this meant was the westernmost tip of the Breton peninsula, Basse-Bretagne, which in the old language meant "far from the capital," far from Rennes and Paris. Which was the greatest compliment for Bretons, who were rebellious on principle.

They spoke the "genuine" Breton here, Celtic, not the Gallo of eastern Haute-Bretagne that, like French, had developed independently from Vulgar Latin and was therefore a young language. Celtic was at least a millennium and a half older than French, a very important fact for Bretons. Thus had Bretagne *bretonnante* taken on the aura of the "real" Brittany over the centuries. If Finistère was the center of everything—the beginning of the world: Penn Ar Bed—then Breton Brittany was the center of the center.

"I'm going to take a look at the corpse," Dupin said. He really did need to make a move. "Excellent work, monsieur."

L'Helgoualc'h did not respond to the compliment in any way, of course. His expression darkened instead.

"The perpetrator isn't from round here."

"Why do you think that?"

"To a stranger, the steep slope must have looked like a place where it was possible to dispose of a body forever. But everyone even slightly acquainted with this area knows that there's a path not too far away down there. A local would have disposed of the victim in the bog. The Yeun-Elez is just a few kilometers away." He gestured vaguely westward with his head. "The body would never have reappeared."

There was something to that.

"There's a path that leads directly into the bog at Kernévez. There are peat banks meters deep there. It contains water, mud. It would be easy. This was someone who doesn't know their way round here. A stranger. They were just passing through. It has nothing to do with *us locals.*"

It was as though L'Helgoualc'h was speaking about his tribe.

"So many people have disappeared in the bog. At night, but also during the day, in the most beautiful sunshine." As he had done earlier, he explained sinister things with no warning. "Suddenly you see mist, a kind of bubbling on the surface as if the water underneath is boiling—if you stop and stare, you're done for. Your curiosity will cost you your life. The ground you're standing on gives way. The howls of a dog ring out. And you disappear forever in the Youdig. The portal to hell. To a cold hell. We had our last missing person's report just several years ago: three men went missing in the bog during perfectly clear weather."

"And they were never found?" Dupin blurted out, and instantly felt awkward.

"They were never found. The bog was combed systematically for days."

That must have been before his time. Dupin couldn't remember news along those lines. He was glad.

"That's the way it is here. Every night you hear howling somewhere. Demons, the souls of the dead who were able to escape for a few hours. Now and then figures appear in the villages that are not what they look like, and that are not what or who they claim to be. Up until a few years ago, Catholic priests performed exorcisms here: they cast the demons out and into the bodies of black dogs and threw them in the water of the

Youdig." L'Helgoualc'h looked at the sky. "These mountains are a special place. To this day, the druids hold their most important ceremonies here, mainly at the bog. Just recently there was the Celtic end-of-year festival. A large group, three hundred druids were there."

Dupin had heard of it. From the modern druidic associations. Riwal had explained it to him. Riwal may not have been a member of these societies himself—surprisingly—but he knew several members and of course couldn't see anything odd about it.

The druids had apparently been the finale of the fantastical stories. L'Helgoualc'h looked inquiringly at Dupin.

"Yes, that sounds plausible. That it was a stranger."

Dupin tried to shake off the images of devious demons.

"They're waiting for me down there."

He instinctively looked in the direction of the bog before setting about his descent.

Back to the car.

Back into the normal world.

He had to concentrate on what was concrete: a strong person, according to the current scenario, had brought the victim from the road to the rocks and thrown him down from there. At that point, the victim was probably already dead, strangled. There had been a fierce struggle. The perpetrator wasn't from round here. And he wore sneakers. Nikes.

Now that was something.

* * *

The corpse looked truly horrific. Dupin had grown used to quite a lot. But this was amongst the worst that he'd ever seen. "Severely contorted" would have been an appropriate description. The dead man must have hit rock numerous times during the fall. His body had literally burst open in many places. The entire ledge he was lying on was covered in blood. Blood and other sticky fluids.

"Do you want to spend longer looking at him? I'd like to take him to Brest immediately and get started on the autopsy," the medical examiner said. She was a surprisingly pleasant-seeming representative of her profession—just forty perhaps, curly brown hair, a focused look on her face—and was standing on the rock next to the corpse. Dupin was at the edge. The landscape down here was different again; the bushes grew tall and there were small copses. A single vast oak tree stood a few paces away and cast long shadows.

Dupin had had to walk quite a distance—by car you could only get within a few hundred meters of the site via a grassy path.

The man, as far as it was possible to say, looked rather slight; he wasn't tall, perhaps one meter seventy-five. Dupin guessed at dark blond hair, an inconspicuous color. He saw exactly what had been described to him earlier.

"Take him away. Are there any more findings yet?"

"I've already shared everything I'm able to say right now with your inspector. Just one more thing: above the broken wrist, you can see the edge of a tattoo. That could help with identification. I'm going to have to remove the clothing with a scalpel and hope that there's still enough skin there to be able to make it out fully." She sounded unfazed, professional. "I'll be in touch as soon as I have news."

"Right, okay. Thank you."

The medical examiner gave a signal to two young men who were waiting next to the rocky ledge with a stretcher.

Dupin turned away and walked toward the small group standing in the heather a few meters away. Kadeg was on the phone. It looked important, of course.

A young policeman was coming toward him. Dupin greeted him with a vague gesture. "We spoke on the phone?"

"Exactly. Gendarmerie de Sizun. You've already met my colleague up on the rocks there."

"So do we have a better picture of what might have happened here yet?"

"No."

"Anything relevant? A missing person's report? Reports from people in the area who've noticed something unusual?"

The policeman's expression verged on alarm. "No. I mean, not yet."

It would have been too perfect anyway.

"Our colleagues from forensics want to know whether you'd like them to do anything specific down here at the rocks. Otherwise they'll go up to the summit and carry on with their work there."

It was hard to believe that even the forensics team seemed to be easy to work with here.

"That's fine." Dupin bit his tongue, not remarking that they probably wouldn't find anything up there other than the Breton Native American. The word "summit," he realized, didn't make him smirk anymore. He would look at these mountains differently from now on.

"So we know nothing, then? Nothing at all?"

"Yes. I mean, no." The policeman practically stood to attention as he answered.

"Good work," Dupin said in an upbeat way, although he noticed his mood was worsening. The policeman looked a little relieved anyway.

There was nothing more for him to do here. And the same was true of the summit.

In fact he could have done with a coffee now. To prevent his mood getting even worse for one thing, certainly, but mainly because he needed ideas and a razor-sharp mind. He had—by the looks of it—two cases on his hands all of a sudden. And both appeared utterly mysterious. This case, and of course the one in Port Belon too.

"Is Sizun far from here?"

"Just a few minutes by car."

"Is that the nearest village?"

"Yes."

"I'll take a look around there."

It was obvious the policeman would have liked to ask why. And also that his instinct told him he'd better not.

"Here I am, Monsieur le Commissaire." Kadeg, Dupin's overzealous inspector, had come over to them. "The phone call is over, everything is okay."

Kadeg's facial expression told a different story. He looked worked up and jittery, but he was trying to hide it.

"What's wrong, Kadeg?"

The inspector hesitated.

"No. Nothing. Everything is absolutely fine."

"All right then."

Dupin wouldn't try to drag it out of him, whatever it was. Without another word, he turned around and walked back to his car.

* * *

Sizun was tiny; a pretty village. And indeed just a few minutes' journey from the mountains.

Dupin was sitting in the most glorious sunshine outside the bar at the Hôtel des Voyageurs. He could feel the warmth of the sun's rays on his skin; it was as though the sun wanted to demonstrate with all its might what it was capable of as early as the beginning of April.

A few plain wooden tables and chairs. One of the simple, authentic bars—brasseries, restaurants—that every French village had, no matter where they were, even in the sleepiest backwater, and Dupin loved them on principle. And also because without fail, you could rely on getting a decent *entrecôte frites* and a respectable red wine—one of the foundations of the Grande Nation. The Hôtel des Voyageurs was, like all of the buildings on the village's small central square, an old stone building; a long building, whitewashed, with window frames, awnings, and other details in a flamboyant green. People gathered here every day, in the mornings, afternoons, and especially in the evenings—this was where it happened: the daily life that made up people's existence. Dupin could sit at places like this for hours and watch people, watch them simply going about their lives. This was where everyday things were celebrated and special things too: births, baptisms, engagements, weddings, big birthdays—and funerals.

Dupin had in fact only ordered one coffee, and that didn't count. And he had already drunk it. Which had caused a recurrence of the stabbing pain. As a precaution he had ordered a *jambon-fromage* sandwich to give his stomach something different—and because he didn't know when he would next get something to eat; during a case, food was always tricky for him. The baguette was an impressive size: it was lying on a large plate in front of him and it was still jutting out over the edge.

Dupin had spoken to Nolwenn briefly. Brioc L'Helgoualc'h, the tracker, was obviously a police institution in Finistère, although Dupin had never heard of him. The deep respect in Nolwenn's voice had been unmistakable.

Nolwenn had not heard anything about Riwal and his exam yet; she had commented on it three or four times. The written portion of the exam was today and it had begun at nine o'clock. However—and it was already overdue, in fact—the prefect had been in touch. Lug Locmariaquer, as unpronounceable as he was unbearable—he was sadly unavoidable too. Dupin was to call him. "Urgently. Immediately." Which didn't surprise Dupin one bit—the prefect immediately became self-important if there was a crime that promised some attention. The only odd thing was that although the prefect, according to Nolwenn, did want to talk about the dead body in the Monts d'Arrée, he *primarily* wanted to talk about something else entirely. "Something extremely delicate."

Dupin didn't have the slightest idea what this was about. And no desire whatsoever to find out. But he had had to promise Nolwenn, and she seemed to take the request seriously, so Dupin knew it would be sensible to take it seriously too. That was ten minutes ago now.

The commissaire sighed, took another bite of his sandwich, and reached for his phone.

It was already in his hand when the monotonous beeping started. A withheld number. Dupin hesitated for a moment before picking up.

"Commissaire! Madame Bandol here! I need to speak with you urgently. It's important." She was speaking extremely fast.

"What's this about?"

"The incident. I've remembered some more things after all."

Dupin pricked up his ears. This was unexpected. She sounded very firm and clear.

"Go ahead."

"It all depends on what I remember, doesn't it? We haven't got anything else yet," she said.

"Exactly, Madame Bandol."

"The man was wearing jeans. Definitely. He did have very short hair, dark brown or even black, very dark!" She was still speaking with urgent speed. "And shoes with birds on them. Or a bird, it might only have been one. It was a jacket, not a coat! Not as long as a coat. And it was dark green. As I said! Dark green! I saw it clearly last night."

"You saw . . . it clearly at night?"

"Everything. I saw everything. In my dream."

"In your dream?"

"Oh yes, I saw it crystal clear!"

Dupin was hesitant. "You dreamed it?"

"I see everything in my dreams. And everything that was gone earlier."

"You mean that in your dreams, you remember things that you've forgotten?"

"Heaven knows I do! So, note everything down exactly as I said in your little red notebook. I only use Clairefontaine notebooks too, by the way."

"I . . . anything else, Madame Bandol? Did you dream anything else?"

"That was rather a lot." Her intonation was stern, but Dupin was already used to it. "Taken together, a pretty decent picture is emerging. You can work with that. It should be enough for identification. And then we'll know more!"

"I think—"

"You ought to pass the information on quickly, Commissaire."

Dupin still didn't know what to say. He pulled himself together.

"I'm going to do that, Madame Bandol. Soon."

"Fine, keep me up to speed, then. And the man in the photo, there's no way that was him, it's out of the question. Your young colleague, she's standing next to me here. I've already told her. That photo doesn't get us anywhere. It might also be a fresh corpse—but it's not mine, anyway! Speak to you soon, Monsieur le Commissaire."

She hung up, leaving Dupin bewildered. He rubbed his temple.

The waiter brought over a small bottle of water that Dupin had only ordered out of sheer desperation that he wasn't allowed another coffee. Even the waiter had looked at him oddly—and initially forgotten to bring it, not all that surprisingly; drinking water didn't have a good reputation in Brittany, for health reasons. Bretons said it caused rust—*"l'eau ça fait rouiller, l'alcool ça conserve!"* Dupin poured himself some anyway and got out his notebook. He had immediately started again this morning, from the back and upside down. For the Monts d'Arrée. The commissaire added a few things.

He was just finished when his phone beeped again. The prefect. He really was serious.

"Yes?"

"As always, you cannot be reached when you're needed, Commissaire."

Dupin had learned how to have phone calls with the prefect in recent years without them inevitably ending disastrously. First of all, in the irritable phase, it was best to say nothing. Then Locmariaquer carried straight on, you just had to let him speak.

"Always the same. But there are more important things right now. It's about Kadeg. Your inspector. We have a problem."

Suddenly Dupin was paying attention. "What kind of problem?"

"We have reasonable suspicion of criminal activity. He is accused of being involved in conspiracy to commit sand theft on the Plage de Trenez. The commissariat in Lorient let me know. They have initiated disciplinary proceedings against him; the most senior authorities are involved. The commissariat has been on the trail of a criminal ring for months, undercover, and they have the preliminary evidence. With support from Paris. They—"

"What's Kadeg meant to have done?"

"They steal sand, in large quantities, simply transporting it away during the night, he—"

"This is utterly absurd. Nonsense, absolute rubbish," Dupin interrupted the prefect. "About Kadeg, I mean."

"There's evidence. Photos of Kadeg systematically reconnoitering the beach at night. On nights when he wasn't on duty, mind you. Wearing dark clothes. With a female accomplice."

"An accomplice?"

This was getting more and more ridiculous.

"He conspired to establish contact with some building firms under a false name, in order to offer consignments of sand. The evidence is comprehensive and has come from the last three months. It's serious."

Unbelievable. It sounded like their colleagues from Lorient had set up an elaborate undercover operation.

"Of course he did. He . . ." Dupin was stupidly getting into difficulties. How was he meant to explain to the prefect what he had spontaneously suspected: that in his sand theft obsession, Kadeg had been investigating single-handedly and outside of his work hours?

"He's in serious trouble, Commissaire, and he's your guy, we've got to—"

"Of course Inspector Kadeg is investigating entirely on my orders, Monsieur le Préfet. Undercover."

Dupin surprised himself with these words. He hadn't thought it through, he had just felt himself getting angry. Kadeg was definitely many things, including insufferable, but he was absolutely not a criminal. The accusations were ridiculous. And the inspector was part of his team; Dupin took that very seriously. If circumstances got tough, it didn't matter how great any personal differences and antipathies were.

"You . . . he . . . you mean to say, he . . ." The prefect struggled to compose himself. Dupin's words had thrown him. "What are you talking about?"

"We've been working on the subject of sand theft in Concarneau for some time now too. We were obviously alarmed by this business on the beaches in Kerouini and Pendruc. Kadeg was doing some specific investigation, especially on the Plage de Trenez." Dupin had to risk a few shots in the dark to sound credible and cover as much as possible of whatever else Kadeg might have done. "He inspected suspicious sites and activities for us incognito outside of his official work hours. I ordered it."

"And who is this female companion?" Unfortunately this question put Dupin in an extremely difficult position. "He came to the beach in the middle of the night on numerous occasions, with a woman, half covered up, you can only see her hair."

Dupin kept improvising. "A disguise. He took a woman with him so that it looked as if they were a couple in love."

Dupin suspected that she was, speaking of romance, Kadeg's wife, the police martial arts teacher from Rennes—but he preferred not to say anything.

"You don't believe that yourself. Why was I not in on it?"

"We still only had a vague level of reasonable suspicion."

Dupin was partly taken aback, because he had always assumed that the prefect had a soft spot for the overeager inspector, who was always obsequious to him, and because he enjoyed using Kadeg as an extension of himself. Now he was dropping him like a hot potato. It spoke volumes, it was a question of character.

"I ordered everything, every single thing," Dupin insisted—there was nothing for it but to forge right ahead. He just hoped that Kadeg hadn't done anything too idiotic in his sand theft mania—in all honesty, he feared the worst.

"You've just made that all up!" The prefect remained strangely calm as he said this.

"As you can see, Monsieur le Préfet, we were right all along. There was obviously something to our suspicion."

Although it didn't really matter right now: Dupin was stunned that Kadeg's obsession had apparently had a kernel of truth to it.

"We will of course listen to what Inspector Kadeg has to say in his defense. He is being picked up by a squad car right now, in the Monts d'Arrée. They're taking him to a hearing."

"They're having him picked up?"

"The accusations need to be clarified. It's out of my hands now. The sooner, the better. And if the situation is as you say, then he has nothing to be afraid of anyway."

Kadeg, picked up by a squad car, on the way to a hearing in serious disciplinary proceedings—Dupin could not believe it.

"We have more pressing matters right now anyway, Commissaire! What's all this with the corpse in the Monts d'Arrée? And the one in Port Belon yesterday? That then disappeared again?"

Dupin would have to call Kadeg immediately. He wouldn't get anywhere talking to the prefect right now.

"We've only just begun the investigations in the Monts d'Arrée. Two hours ago."

"And you don't know anything yet, I hear."

"No. But everything's been set up. We'll have preliminary findings soon."

"Good. That's what I want to hear. The press is already making an enormous fuss. It says 'The Body in the Hell-Bog' on the internet."

"It wasn't in the bog. It was underneath the Roc'h Trévézel."

Luckily Dupin wasn't aware of anything in the press. But they would obviously have a field day over this. And when he thought of the hiking group alone, there were plenty of people who would happily tell their stories.

"On the topic of Port Belon, the headline says: 'A Corpse—or No Corpse?' And it says that even the police themselves aren't sure whether there was a serious crime there yesterday or not. I don't need to tell you these are not the headlines I'd like. I'll have to make a statement, you know, I have a responsibility."

Dupin had to force himself to remain calm.

"We're assuming there was a crime. Yes. In Port Belon too."

The prefect remained silent for a while. Dupin let him.

"Good. Then I expect you to solve it quickly! And the business in the mountains too. And, Commissaire: this Kadeg thing—don't get carried away! Be careful!"

Dupin didn't intend to respond.

"And stay in touch! Do you understand? You're going to get in touch regularly. That is an order. Now, I have a more important meeting to get to."

A moment later, the prefect had hung up.

Dupin was dumbfounded. The craziness continued unabated. One crazy thing merrily followed another. And they were getting increasingly serious.

What on earth had Kadeg been thinking? The trouble was, Dupin could answer that question himself. Kadeg would have become increasingly worked up over this sand theft theory. Sunk his teeth right into it like a terrier. That's what happened.

What was equally incomprehensible was this: Dupin may never have been able to stand that commissaire from Lorient, but they had never had any serious run-ins. A squabble here or there, but nothing more. Why hadn't he simply called Dupin? Then they would have been able to work it out at the beginning. And been able to speak to Kadeg.

The commissaire gave himself a shake. Now was not the time for questions like this; there were more pressing matters. His inspector was capable of doing serious damage to himself.

Dupin dialed Kadeg's number. It took a while for the inspector to answer.

"Mons—"

"Kadeg, keep your phone to your ear and listen to me. I know you're in a squad car. No doubt someone is sitting next to you. You are going to answer with a yes or no only, in a casual tone of voice." Dupin paused briefly, as a test. It took Kadeg a moment before he uttered a relatively neutral "Yes."

"Good. Now make a mental note of the following: not only did I know everything that you did, I ordered it all. Me, personally. In its entirety. That means all of the idiotic activities you undertook in connection with your sand theft investigations. Do you hear me?"

This time it took even longer before the confirmation came: "Yes."

"Was that your wife, Kadeg?"

"Yes." He sounded miserable, though he was trying to pull himself together.

"Did you . . . do anything seriously illegal during the course of your . . . investigations?"

"No."

"Is that a definite no?"

"Yes. I mean, no."

"Good."

Silence.

"And you're . . . you're not actually mixed up in anything? Anything illegal?"

Just as a precaution.

"No."

"Then nothing can happen. I'll take care of everything. You'll be back on duty soon."

"Yes." There was an audible hesitation, then a relieved "Thanks" and also a childish, sulky "You see, I was right. They're stealing sand."

Dupin hung up.

The whole thing was a farce. He absolutely had to keep a cool head. There were—probably—two murders, and he was dealing with his inspector's ludicrous antics!

* * *

Dupin had summoned the two policemen from Sizun—the tracker L'Helgoualc'h and the young man from earlier—to the Hôtel des Voyageurs for a brief meeting. He would have no support for the next few hours. One of his inspectors was completing an exam on Breton history, the other was at a police station on suspicion of criminal activity. Brilliant.

He had spoken to Nolwenn again while he was waiting. Mainly about Kadeg. She had heard about it already, of course, but had still been beside herself. She intended to call the prefect personally. She hadn't come up with anything else on the dead body in the Monts d'Arrée.

The two policemen had sat down with Dupin at the outdoor table and given brief reports. The corpse was in Brest and the autopsy had begun, while the forensic team had completed its work with no new findings. As expected, they hadn't found anything at the summit that L'Helgoualc'h hadn't found, and they had confirmed everything he had said without exception. They had checked the footprint tread in the databank: the specific tread of the footprints they had detected came from Nike. The company used it for three different models. Another important thing was this: nobody had found footprints belonging to anyone else. In all likelihood there had been just one perpetrator at the Roc'h Trévézel.

"The man must be missed somewhere. Since yesterday lunchtime or yesterday afternoon." Dupin really didn't understand it. "There's been no report anywhere?"

L'Helgoualc'h had not said much so far; his young colleague had taken on the reporting.

"No, Monsieur le Commissaire. No report anywhere. The medical examiner cleaned up the dead man's face and emailed a photo to us. I think he's recognizable in it despite the significant injuries."

"Send it out. And to the media too." Dupin was fed up. They needed to do something. They couldn't just wait and see if someone would get in touch. "To all Breton *départements*—and nationally too."

"We're planning to show it around in the bars and restaurants in the area," the young man said. "An effective method round here."

The commissaire nodded.

"When was the last time there was a murder in this area?" Dupin had been thinking about it. It was bound to be a long time ago.

"In 1962. A farmer killed her drunken husband after he ran over their pet horse when he tore into their yard in the car while wasted one night."

Dupin didn't inquire any further. He knew the status horses had in the Breton countryside. Nolwenn knew dozens of astonishing horse stories through her clan. For centuries, a horse had been the most valuable item for a family. Wealth and status were determined by the number of horses you had. Sometimes they even lived in the houses with the family and, like the housewives, were called Charlotte, Marianne, or Ma Chérie. The violent loss of a horse, therefore, was a genuine motive for murder.

"That's it, nothing else?"

"Nothing major. Lots of alcohol offenses, but they're harmless," L'Helgoualc'h said, and shrugged. "Hardly ever a theft. And if there is one, then it's because of a feud, for revenge."

"The dead man's clothes? What about those?" Dupin asked.

The young policeman took over again: "The medical examiner will let us know. Brands, sizes. Any potential unusual features that would allow them to be traced. We ought to get those shortly."

Dupin felt uneasy. Something had occurred to him.

"Anything else on the tattoo?"

"Not yet."

"I—" Dupin paused. He was absorbed by a thought. It had come to him when they had been talking about the clothes. An odd thought, perhaps— but then again maybe not. It was about something Madame Bandol had said. About one of her memories from her dream last night.

Dupin stood up without explanation. He needed a computer. He had to take a look at something. His smartphone! He was always forgetting all the things it was capable of doing.

"One moment." He had spoken more to himself than the others.

He bent over the small screen, found the browser, and opened it. Typed in what he was looking for, making a few typos as he did so. After a couple of seconds the first images appeared. There was a quizzical astonishment on the young policeman's face, profound skepticism on L'Helgoualc'h's.

"That could be it." Dupin kept scrolling. "Yes." He looked at the two policemen. "I've got to go. It's important."

It was important, and he had to look into this issue himself. Speak to Madame Bandol himself.

"Get in touch straightaway if there's any news."

"Understood," the young officer gasped out, still visibly confused about the commissaire's sudden departure.

"Thanks. And again: good work!"

Dupin placed some cash down on the little plastic plate and walked briskly away.

He was in a hurry.

* * *

"It's done! He's out." Nolwenn was worked up.

That had happened quickly. Not that Dupin would have been surprised, but the prefect was—precisely because of his slow-wittedness—often a tough nut to crack. Besides, the issue wasn't in his hands alone—disciplinary proceedings were highly official affairs.

"How did you manage that? Kadeg has . . ."

"Not Kadeg—Inspector Riwal! The exam, the diploma! He says he knew everything." Her worked-up state was tempered now with pride. "I didn't expect anything less, of course."

Dupin had parked his car in the parking lot in Port Belon and walked down the small road toward the quay—this was where Nolwenn had got through to him—and he would be there any minute. He had given the young policewoman from Riec a task to do during his journey and she had responded not with questions but with a "No problem, I have some at home." Magalie Melen had also organized the meeting with Madame Bandol in a few minutes' time.

"What do you think, Monsieur le Commissaire?" Nolwenn cut across his thoughts.

"I . . . I'm glad."

"Do you know what one of the topics was?" With her enthusiasm, Nolwenn could hardly be stopped. "America!"

"Very good. I'm sure Riwal gave a thorough account."

A pitiful attempt on Dupin's part.

"America exists thanks to Bretons! Who discovered America? Breton fishermen from the Île de Bréhat! And centuries before Columbus. They landed on Newfoundland. Everything is documented. American independence?" Dupin could practically see Nolwenn's shining eyes. "Won by a Breton! The Marquis de la Rouërie and the corps he was leading dealt the English the decisive blows. And Halloween. But you know that, don't you?"

Dupin hoped it had been a rhetorical question.

"All Breton! When it's getting cold at the beginning of November, the Celts celebrate the Feast of Samhain. That night the hidden portals to the dark world open up and creepy creatures dash through our realms! In the eighteenth and nineteenth centuries, Celtic emigrants brought these legends and customs to North America and *voilà*: Halloween!"

That was genuinely interesting, but not right now.

"Don't worry about Kadeg." Nolwenn had seamlessly returned to harsh reality. "The prefect and I have thoroughly . . . let's say *spoken*. And I've also made my opinion plain to the commissaire from Lorient." It was on the tip of Dupin's tongue to ask for details, but he refrained. "I think you'll get him back soon."

"Excellent." Dupin would never have dreamed he would ever say that in reference to Kadeg. But this really was good news, and in truth it took a load off his mind.

"And Riwal is already on his way to you. Where exactly are you?"

"I'm standing in front of La Coquille. I want to speak to Madame Bandol. And then take another look at the parking lot. Where the corpse was."

"So you're still assuming that Madame Bandol saw a corpse?"

"That's right, and I have a little theory that I want to test."

"Has Madame Bandol trawled through her memory again? Has anything else occurred to her?"

"She saw the corpse during the night in a dream." Dupin was aware that it sounded odd. "More clearly than in her memory. So she was able to see a few extra details."

"Just like with Aunt Marguerite! When she's dreaming, lots of things come back to her that have completely slipped her mind while she's awake. Sometimes you ask her something and she says you're to ask her again tomorrow morning. And that's how it goes: she knows it again then. That, Monsieur le Commissaire, is nothing unusual."

Any worries that Nolwenn might doubt his sanity had been completely unfounded; he might have known. For a Breton, the truthfulness of dreams was self-evident.

"Who knows, maybe even more things will come to her this way—it's astonishing sometimes. In any case: don't let yourself be put off, Monsieur le Commissaire, even if you don't have anything concrete yet. You know the Breton motto: nothing is more real than what you cannot see! The world is an enchanted forest. There's hidden meaning everywhere. And dreams are a tried and tested signpost. I"—again the switch to practical things was seamless—"will tell Riwal he's to meet you at the parking lot."

Dupin was already pacing up and down outside the entrance of the restaurant with the dozens of colorful signs. *Huîtres de la Bretagne. Le plaisir à l'état pur,* promised the largest of the signs: "Pleasure in its purest form." He was impatient; he wanted to know what truth there was to his idea. Perhaps it was just too far-fetched.

"Thanks, Nolwenn. I—"

"Your party the day after tomorrow," she said, sternly now, and Dupin jumped, but luckily she didn't say what he was afraid she would. "You won't be dealing with that today, you've got things to do, the murders come first. I've confirmed the menu with Alain Trifin. Almost everyone has accepted. Even Commissaire Rose let me know today she's coming. As long as a crazy shoot-out in the salt marshes doesn't get in the way, of course, I'm to tell you, and: 'wind and sun permitting.' That's it. Any comments?"

"No."

"Then I'll call Inspector Riwal now." She hung up on the last word.

Dupin was standing in front of the door to the restaurant. He took a few deep breaths and then went inside.

Jacqueline nodded to him from the bar. She seemed to have been expecting him.

"It's over here."

She gestured to the end of the bar with her head, where a package lay.

"Brilliant." With a satisfied expression, Dupin picked up the package as he walked past. Magalie Melen had completed the small task immediately.

Madame Bandol was sitting at the same table as yesterday, which was absolutely fine by Dupin—it was in keeping with his way of quickly developing habits everywhere. Her dog was standing at the terrace door today, his nose on the windowpane. He seemed excited.

"Come on, Commissaire, come on! What is it? It seems extraordinarily urgent."

Madame Bandol practically pulled Dupin toward the table. She was dressed in shades of pale blue from head to toe, another long skirt and a simple blouse with a wide, round neck. She looked almost girlish, her hair even wilder than yesterday, expertly wild.

"I've got to show you something, Madame Bandol." Dupin had remained standing. "You spoke about shoes with birds on them. On the phone earlier. Is that right?"

"Oh yes."

"Shoes with birds on them. Which was what came back to you in a dream. One of the new details."

Dupin had pulled a pair of sneakers out of the package. Covered in mud, they had clearly been heavily used in all kinds of weather. But the thing he was interested in was still clearly visible. In a garish neon green on dark blue. A kind of elongated check mark—or even: a stylized bird.

The trademark.

"I'd like to know—"

"You really know a thing or two, Commissaire! You'd never think it to look at you! They were different colors—I've just remembered, the shoes were black and the birds were red—but yes: that's them! The shoes that the dead man was wearing. Just like those! We've got the man."

Somewhere in the recesses of his mind the thought had been sparked when Madame Bandol had talked about the "shoes with birds on them." That's often how it was for Dupin: the associations, the deductions began and he only really realized later. One of the reasons why he really disliked talking about his "method."

"Are you one hundred percent certain, Madame Bandol? Absolutely certain?"

This was a crucial point.

"I swear it! I did tell you, I could see the birds down to the last detail in the dream."

"And now you even recall the colors?"

"As if I were seeing them in front of me."

Dupin sat down.

"Nikes. The victim was wearing Nikes," he murmured almost inaudibly.

"What's that supposed to mean, Commissaire?"

Instead of answering, Dupin got out his phone. There was something else he could still check. This could be another lead. A further validation.

"A black shoe, you say." Dupin was on the manufacturer's website again. He put in the color and a few moments later he saw the range. "With a red symbol," he said, going through the list model by model. "Completely black—apart from the red symbol, I mean. No other colors on the soles or anything?"

"Completely black!" Madame Bandol looked put out by the query.

"Here!" He had found what he was looking for. "Like this?" Dupin held the phone out to Madame Bandol.

"Exactly! The colors. The model. These exact ones! Bravo!"

Now for the most important thing. Dupin clicked on one of the extra pictures with a view of the tread. A moment later he saw it blown up: honeycomblike patterns and wavy lines. It was obvious. This model existed. This exact model: plain black Nikes with red symbols—and most importantly, they had the special soles that left footprints like the ones from the Monts d'Arrée.

Dupin ran a hand roughly through his hair. He needed to concentrate.

"Tell me what you're thinking, Monsieur le Commissaire! How else can I help you?"

Dupin's brow creased. "We've found exactly these footprints from this type of shoe," he said, and pointed at the mobile screen, "by the place at the Roc'h Trévézel where the murderer threw off his victim. The perpetrator there was wearing shoes like this."

Madame Bandol's eyes widened, there was profound fear on her face. Then she steadily shook her head in a theatrical gesture.

"Then it was my dead body!" She was quite agitated now. "My missing body from the Belon—and he was the murderer from the Roc'h Trévézel! It's got to be!"

The implication was spectacular. The exact same thing had struck Dupin. Assuming Madame Bandol was remembering the shoes (and anything else) correctly, they were dealing with a turn of events that was just as confusing as it was dramatic. He tried to express it as a potential sequence:

"The man with the Nike sneakers killed the man *yesterday* morning, whom we then found at the Roc'h Trévézel *this* morning. Only to be murdered *himself* a few hours later, a hundred kilometers away in Port Belon."

The two cases—they would be one case.

"Maybe they were both just wearing the same shoes. The murderer yesterday and the dead man yesterday," Madame Bandol said.

"I don't think so." His instinct told him this was no coincidence.

"I don't either." Madame Bandol gave him a conspiratorial smile. "And it's much more exciting this way too."

Dupin didn't delude himself. It sounded far-fetched, highly speculative. Radical. But if the assumption was correct, there was a strict logic to the consequences.

"I'd like to have a facial composite of this man done—of your dead body. And send it round with the other photo. We might get lucky. Perhaps the pair of them have been seen together somewhere."

They didn't have enough details to produce a face, of course, but they did have some details of what the dead man—the perpetrator—had been wearing. They were clutching at straws to some extent. But they only had straws right now.

Madame Bandol shook her head again.

"The chances are definitely slim. But all right. Have a composite done! Maybe something else will occur to me then. We'll see. Memory is a grab bag."

"I'll arrange for one of the sketch artists to visit you."

If the story that was just emerging was true, the case would be on a large scale. There would be at least a third person involved in the matter. And still out there somewhere. The murderer of the murderer. Yet they didn't have the slightest clue as to what it was about, what dramatic intrigues were going on. They were groping about in the dark.

Dupin felt an urgent sense of unease. He was used to feeling this way; it was a state he always got into if cases became complicated.

"Thank you, Madame Bandol." Dupin stood up. "If anything else comes to mind, get in touch immediately."

There was considerable disapproval in Madame Bandol's expression.

"You're not going to leave me here by myself with these extraordinary developments, are you? Besides, it's lunchtime, you ought to have something to eat. And we can keep investigating together as we eat."

Dupin reached for the sneakers and put them back in the crumpled package.

"I've got to go, Madame Bandol, I'm sorry."

After a brief reflection, her generous, open smile reappeared.

"Well then, what are you waiting for, my dear?"

* * *

"I would narrow down the time of death to between eleven o'clock and twelve noon yesterday. And finally, I can confirm what the village doctor suspected: the man was strangled. He was already dead during the fall down the steep rock face. The broken wrist probably came from a struggle, along with a series of hematomas that occurred antemortem. Unfortunately, we didn't find any tissue or skin from the perpetrator underneath the fingernails."

"Anything else?"

The old Citroën groaned; Dupin had taken a sharp turn at too high a speed. The medical examiner had called him just after he got into the car. He had delegated some new tasks to Magalie Melen beforehand.

"At the moment, I'm assuming that the injuries sustained in the struggle, strangulation, and subsequent fall occurred within the space of an hour at most. When he was thrown off, he had not been dead for long."

This wasn't much, but it did to an extent make it easier to sort through the scenarios about the sequence of events.

"That means it could all have taken place there at the Roc'h Trévézel."

"That's possible. But another possibility is that the victim was murdered somewhere nearby and then brought there."

Dupin liked the medical examiner's precise, unflappable, and unassuming manner.

"Are there any clues to the identity of the dead man?" he asked.

"Nothing conclusive. Mid-sixties, one meter seventy-six, central European. Very bad teeth, conventionally treated, the dentistry could have been done anywhere. Heavy smoker. Not a balanced diet. But surprisingly healthy overall, on first impressions. Limited personal hygiene. Non-branded clothing and shoes. Nothing striking."

"The tattoo?"

"We've taken a careful look at it. Unfortunately the right arm suffered severe injuries during the fall, and part of the tattoo was torn to shreds with the skin. We couldn't fully reconstruct it. But what you can still make out looks maritime. A stylized sail, a kind of building, I guess, a letter, an *S*. One or more letters could be missing. An old sailor perhaps. He has had the tattoo for a long time."

"A sailor?"

"Perhaps he went to sea in his youth. Or maybe not; maritime motifs have always been amongst the most popular ones. So perhaps it doesn't even mean anything."

"Can you send my assistant a photo of it?"

"Of course. There are the remains of a second tattoo on the left upper arm. He has had that one for a long time too. Unfortunately you can make out even less there due to the considerable injuries. Just a line, three centimeters long, that tapers at the top. I presume the rest is missing."

"Just a line?"

"A kind of shallow wedge. Or beam. I don't have a clue what it could be. I'll take a photo of it too. That's it for the moment."

"Thanks. Call if you have anything else."

As the call ended, Dupin turned onto the narrow road to the parking lot.

He ran a hand roughly through his hair again. It was maddening. What was all this about? On top of the statistical considerations, his instinct said something else pointed to a connection between the two cases: the utter mysteriousness. Two dead men suddenly lying somewhere and nobody knew who they were or where they came from. And nobody seemed to have reported them missing yet.

Dupin parked his car just outside the red-and-yellow tape that had been used to cordon off the parking lot. Magalie Melen had spent the morning making more inquiries round Port Belon and also Riec. Not one person had noticed anything unusual anywhere or had had anything to say about the—purely officially speaking—"potential" corpse.

The spot where Madame Bandol had seen the body was still cordoned off separately. The four neon yellow mobile pillars and the tape around an empty section of grass looked absurd. Especially in the middle of this desolate landscape.

Dupin stooped and slipped underneath the tape. He was now standing exactly where the corpse had been lying. Cautiously, ever so cautiously, he turned in a circle, not looking for anything in particular. Why this place? He had been wondering this all along. And the same went for the Monts d'Arrée. Why the Monts d'Arrée, why Port Belon?

The murderer of the dead man at the Roc'h Trévézel had—according to the hypothesis—come here in the afternoon—why? Or had he been murdered somewhere else and brought to Port Belon already dead? The fact that the corpse had apparently only been lying here for a short time before it disappeared pointed more to a spontaneous crime and not to a plan, let alone a clever plan. Which was equally true of the murder in the Monts d'Arrée and the disposal of the body there. How had the corpse been taken away from the parking lot—in a car? Taken away forever; perhaps it would never turn up again.

Dupin's thoughts were interrupted by an approaching car.

A police car. But not Riwal. The car stopped directly behind his. A moment later the unpleasant policeman from yesterday was clambering out and heading straight for Dupin. Erwann Braz.

"What are you doing here?" Dupin grumbled irritably, having been glad to be alone briefly.

"I'm checking Madame Bandol's statements. They are not consistent."

"Excuse me?"

"She said she took the same route yesterday that she always takes. That is not true." Braz spoke quickly and eagerly, but Dupin felt he also spoke with a brazen personal antipathy toward Madame Bandol. "I have two witness statements saying that she stays on the lower path along the Belon every single time she takes her daily walk, and walks as far as the cliffs, where you have a view of Port Manech. Then she turns around and walks back the same way. But not yesterday!" He was trying to inject some pathetic suspense into his long-winded sentences. "Yesterday she didn't come via this path by the Belon, she came via the little path that leads to the parking lot! From that direction." He pointed to where their cars were parked. "Beyond the first branch in the little road, where the left fork goes to the *gîte* and the right to Port Belon, there's a footpath up from the river. That must have been where she walked. She left the path by the Belon *before* the estuary and came around here."

"Yes, and?"

"So the statement that she came down the path from the hill is false." Braz was acting as though he had solved the case with this extraordinary discovery. "She gave a de facto false statement. Possibly even deliberately."

This did need to be cleared up, but the policeman was making Dupin's blood boil. First wanting to declare Madame Bandol of unsound mind and now even suspecting her—it made him extremely annoyed.

"Whether Madame Bandol came from here or there doesn't affect her statement on the corpse in any way."

"It drastically reduces the overall credibility of her statements even further—and certainly raises more questions."

"I think—"

The monotonous beeping of Dupin's mobile sounded. Nolwenn. He took a few steps to one side without saying anything.

"It's instantly recognizable, Monsieur le Commissaire! *Shelter House!*"

Dupin was slow on the uptake.

"We went through it, do you remember? It's similar to the Abris du Marin."

Nolwenn's longer explanation didn't help.

"The hostels and homes that Jacques de Thézac established in various Breton ports at the beginning of the twentieth century, to provide stranded sailors with a home, food, accommodation, and work. To rescue them from the clutches of alcohol."

Dupin knew what the Abris du Marin were. One of the old hostels was right next to Henri's Café du Port in Sainte-Marine, a beautiful building. *Dieu—Honneur—Patrie* was written in large letters above it and Dupin was deeply moved every time he saw it.

"And?"

"The tattoo! It's the symbol of the Shelter Houses. The north Scottish counterparts of the Abris du Marin. Very well known, as is the symbol! There's just an *H* missing on the tattoo—the arm looks badly injured. Good thing the man was already dead before the fall."

"Tell me more, Nolwenn."

This was so difficult to take in. Nolwenn could only just have received the photo. She had recognized it straightaway. And now—now they suddenly had their first real lead. And it possibly pointed to Scotland.

"It's a Celtic sister association—there are close links between the Shelter Houses and the Abris du Marin." That had been one of the big topics in Nolwenn's Brittany lessons recently: "Intercelticism," the connection between the regions of Europe where the millions of remaining Celts lived nowadays and who were *finally* bonding again. Scotland, Ireland, Wales, Cornwall, the Isle of Man, and Brittany, they were known as the "six Celtic nations." Millions of representatives of a three-thousand-year-old, enormous, proud, ancient civilization! Which, at its largest in the third century B.C., had taken up almost all of Europe (Brittany had been Celtic even in 800 B.C.). It stretched from the British Isles via Gaul, down the entire Atlantic coast as far as Spain and Portugal, and in the east, to the modern-day countries of the Czech Republic, Slovakia, Serbia, Croatia, and Poland.

"We ought to contact them immediately, Nolwenn."

"I was just on the phone to the headquarters in Thurso. They have hostels in Portree on Skye, in Oban, Drumbeg, Hope, and Armadale. Lots of sailors who live in the Shelter Houses have a tattoo like that."

Nolwenn was fantastic.

"Are they all registered?"

"Yes. The current residents and the former ones too. Most of them come back every once in a while. Things are very personal, that's the principle of it. I asked them to make inquiries everywhere as to whether someone is missing. I've also sent the photo of the dead man over to them already. The employee in Thurso didn't know him, but that doesn't mean anything."

"Brilliant."

Perhaps they'd be in luck. It was a real opportunity.

"I've got to go, Monsieur le Commissaire. The funeral. Poor Aunt Elwen. Otherwise she'll be in the ground before I get there. I'll be in touch as soon as I hear anything. The woman in Thurso has my mobile number."

Dupin could see it now: Nolwenn at the grave, the shovel with soil in her right hand, the mobile in her left, that's how it would be.

She hung up a moment later. Dupin stood there for some time, lost in thought. Then he turned with a start. Another car was approaching the parking lot. This time it really was Riwal. The inspector brought the car to a stop with a violent jolt. Dupin walked over to it. He was glad that Riwal was back.

Erwann Braz was clearly unsure whether to follow Dupin. At first, he walked a few paces in Riwal's direction, but then for some reason he stopped and tried to catch Dupin's eye. Unsuccessfully.

Riwal's pride was clear to see—he seemed to have grown a little.

"The remedy for scurvy?"

"I . . . sorry?"

"It says in all the history books that James Lind discovered it at the beginning of the nineteenth century. In reality it was François Martin, a Breton pharmacist from Vitré, and it was in 1601! He was on an expedition to East India when a dreadful storm sprang up, the boats were drifting about, unable to maneuver. All of the sailors got scurvy, apart from the ones on his boat. He had given the seamen oranges and lemons to eat."

"Congratulations, Riwal!" Dupin had phrased this too openly—a mistake, the story was not over yet.

"They were rescued by Dutchmen and the Dutch king asked the pharmacist if he could keep the secret for the Dutch navy. Out of gratitude for his rescue, he agreed."

Dupin was getting impatient. "Riwal, a number of the first important clues have just emerged."

Riwal's facial expression changed instantly.

"Clues that could lead us to the identity of the dead man at the Monts d'Arrée," Dupin said, and told him about Nolwenn's discoveries.

"We need—" His mobile rang again. Nolwenn once more. Dupin imagined she was already in the car.

She launched right into it:

"Seamus Smith!" She had uttered the name like it was a sensation.

"A regular guest at the Shelter House for decades. In Oban. Sixty-two. Scottish. They recognized him in the photo straightaway. He—"

"We've got the identity of the dead man? We know who he is?"

Things were happening thick and fast now, and this was Nolwenn's favorite speed.

"He moved back into the hostel last November. He set out very early yesterday, but didn't tell anyone what his plans were. Much less that he wanted to take a trip. Apparently he didn't take any luggage either. They noticed he hadn't come back this morning. Which never really happens. He doesn't have any family left. They were already considering reporting him missing. Nobody can understand how he got his hands on a plane ticket; he didn't have a cent."

"How . . . did this happen so quickly?"

"There was no witchcraft, Monsieur le Commissaire. My Scottish friend is very good." Dupin could hear genuine respect in her voice. "She's on the phone to Oban again right now. They're trying to track down the director of the hostel, she wasn't in just now. My friend has only spoken to the assistant so far."

Their dead man was a Scotsman. Dupin had only been in Scotland twice, and that was a long time ago. In Edinburgh. He had really liked the city. He didn't know Oban; only the wonderful whisky.

"What else do we know? Was he a fisherman?"

"Yes. But he hadn't been at sea for many years now. Too much alcohol. Probably a screwed-up kind of existence on the whole. No luck. Casual jobs in fish markets, mainly at mussel and oyster farms. Only ever temporary jobs. We don't know any more at the moment."

"Oyster farms?"

"They have them on the west coast of Scotland too. Right up into the north! But now I really must go. My friend is going to call Riwal, I've given her his number. I might not have any reception at the cemetery. Has Riwal arrived?"

"Yes."

"Have you congratulated him?"

"Yes."

"Good." Nolwenn hung up.

* * *

Dupin put the phone in his pocket and placed both of his hands on the back of his head.

They had their dead man. One of their dead men. They knew his identity.

Although, it made everything even more mysterious for now. Why on earth did an aging day laborer from a Scottish backwater, who lived in a hostel for stranded sailors, leave Oban out of the blue one morning, only to then be murdered a few hours later fifteen hundred kilometers away in the Breton wilderness?

Dupin had—as he usually did while on the phone—been walking around without noticing. With no purpose in mind, no destination; it was almost like sleepwalking. When he hung up, he occasionally didn't know where he was.

He had walked from the parking lot as far as the cliffs. Way out. Large, pale granite blocks rounded into whales' backs over millennia, in the midst of thick, scraggly heather, a deep purple. The rocks were covered in lichen—neon yellow, bright orange, and bilious green areas in endless shapes—oval, oblong, round. Like ominous, enigmatic signs, ancient symbols.

Dupin took off his jacket. He was wearing one of his navy-blue polo shirts. It was really warm today, the sun hinting effortlessly at summer. A gentle, velvety breeze was blowing. One of those great Atlantic days, as Dupin called them, when the radiant, clear blue of the sky was everywhere. The sea seemed to want to show off its endless palette of blue shades too. Directly below him lay the turquoise bay. Far out there on the horizon there was a deep, rich blue to admire, while the horizon itself was a delicate, pale blue line. To the left was the Belon estuary; the Aven's estuary to the right. You could see the bay, and on a small headland beyond it was Port Manech with its cozy harbor, the lagoon-like beach, the two tall palm trees at the front, and the small red-and-white-striped lighthouse.

The view was extraordinary. It was one of those days when a baffling optical phenomenon occurred. The air above the ocean acted as binoculars. Riwal had explained it to him once. At great length. But it was true. Faraway islands that you could usually only see the contours of suddenly seemed very close. You could make out several trees, sandy beaches, houses. So close you could almost just casually swim over.

Two large sailing boats were coming out of the Aven one after the other, and a green fishing boat was coming out of the Belon. Dupin's gaze roamed farther out over the sea. Suddenly it snagged on something. Something dark was moving in the water. Not a boat. He briefly closed his eyes. Then stared at the spot again . . . gone! It was gone. He opened his eyes wide, standing there motionless. Was that Kiki? The direct relative of the great white shark? Perhaps it was just a rock that had been briefly exposed by the swell. In any case, there was nothing visible there now.

Dupin shook himself.

The new updates were significant. They had a lot to do. There were tasks to be delegated. Specific measures to implement, investigative steps. They needed to learn as much as possible about Smith as quickly as possible. But for a moment the commissaire was overcome by a strange feeling. Not the usual unease, tenseness, his typical restlessness. He was oddly relieved. Relieved that he could finally do something.

He was keeping an eye out for Riwal. Braz and his inspector seemed to have stayed in the parking lot.

Dupin walked back along the bumpy path he had taken earlier.

"Hello, boss."

Dupin almost jumped. Riwal. But not from the direction Dupin was expecting. He was not far away and had called out unnecessarily loudly.

"Here, boss."

Dupin turned and saw Riwal, Erwann Braz, and also Magalie Melen heading for the cliffs along a different path from the one he had just been standing on. Dupin turned round.

"We saw you'd walked to the cliffs." Riwal knew that Dupin couldn't stand being followed when he was on the phone. "I thought you—"

"There have been important developments," Dupin announced firmly.

They had no time to lose.

They would have a discussion here on the cliffs.

Erwann Braz stopped in the middle of the path, unfazed. Riwal and Magalie Melen looked for a place to stand in the heather.

Dupin explained the extraordinary news in just a few words. And also his theory that the missing body from Port Belon was presumably the murderer from the Monts d'Arrée. That it would therefore all be one case.

It was clear all three were astonished.

Dupin had pulled out his little Clairefontaine notebook. "Smith must have flown. To Brest or Quimper, maybe. We need all the information on that, especially whether he traveled by himself."

"I'll take that on." Riwal seemed to be full of energy, the triumph of passing the exam. "I'll deal with Smith."

"I want to know everything about him. Someone needs to speak to every resident of this hostel in Oban. To everyone he knew."

Riwal nodded. He knew about the commissaire's obsessions; he would want to know every little detail straightaway, no matter how insignificant it seemed.

"The police in Oban will be investigating now too. We need to make sure that they know our questions and ask them. You're to establish contact with someone there as soon as possible, Riwal."

"I'll do that right away, boss."

"And then I want us to make his identity public. And for the police to request the assistance—"

"I'll take care of that," Magalie Melen said quickly.

"Braz—you put in a call to the Monts d'Arrée. To the gendarmerie in Sizun. And inform both of our colleagues. Ask them whether they know anything about a Scotsman in the area."

"Will do," the policeman confirmed.

"Melen, send a sketch artist to Madame Bandol. They're to produce a photofit image of the man she saw for us. There are a few new details. As soon as you have it, send it out too."

Dupin had kept an eye on Braz as he was speaking.

"Who actually told us that Madame Bandol didn't walk down by the Belon yesterday?"

Braz looked at the commissaire in astonishment.

"Matthieu Tordeux. One of the oyster farmers. He owns Super de Belon. A very successful business."

"What was the man doing there when he supposedly saw her?" You could always turn the tables, thought Dupin. "He was obviously not far from the crime scene at the relevant time. What was he doing there?"

"I—I," Braz stammered. "I don't know. I'll ask him."

"You ought to. How did you come to hear about it?"

"Well, we did speak to everyone in the area about whether they noticed anything unusual yesterday."

"And you didn't think it was unusual that he was there himself?"

This was really a question that arose straightaway.

Braz squirmed. "I will speak to him immediately."

Dupin turned pointedly to Magalie Melen. "Tell me about oyster farming in Port Belon. Who does what with oysters here?"

"Oysters?"

"Oysters."

"There are four companies. The old Château de Belon, Madame Laroche and her family, she's a descendant of the Breton founder of oyster farming. Then there's Baptiste Kolenc, the owner of the second manor house, another old hand, he has been running the business Armoricaine de Belon for decades and he's a friend of Madame Bandol." The one who knew her secret, as Dupin was aware. "Then there's Matthieu Tordeux's farm. If you go down the ramp at the quay and then left along the high stone wall: the small white building there. And there's a trader, Madame Premel, who also does refinement, *affinage*. Her farm is on the other side, toward the estuary."

"That's the entire oyster scene here?"

Dupin had been making notes.

It was relatively easy to get an overview of the oyster industry here in the world-famous oyster village.

"Only part of the oyster industry takes place in Port Belon, of course. In total there are around thirty companies on the Belon, most of them have their headquarters in Riec or right next to the production line at the river, they—"

Dupin's phone beeped.

Magalie Melen broke off and looked inquiringly at the commissaire. He glanced at the screen and picked up.

"Where are you, Kadeg?"

"I . . . there is . . . there is still an issue after all, Monsieur le Commissaire." Kadeg seemed even more subdued than this morning. Even more pitiful. This didn't sound good.

"One moment," Dupin said, and turned around. "Everyone is to get in touch as soon as they have anything."

Then he set off. Back toward the cliffs. "Go ahead, Kadeg."

"I've . . . there's sand on an undeveloped piece of land belonging to my wife near Lorient. From various beaches. Including from Kerfany-les-Pins and Trenez beaches."

"What do you mean?"

"We had to offer the building firms samples. We needed to convince them."

Dupin could see why Kadeg was feeling pure fear. What he was saying amounted to no less than the fact that he *really had stolen sand*. Irrefutable in the legal sense too. It was enough to make Dupin tear his hair out.

"You assured me earlier that you hadn't done anything illegal. You—" Dupin broke off. This was absurd, he had been naive, he ought to have known better.

"How much, Kadeg, how much sand?"

"A reasonable amount. I—"

"You've lost your mind!"

Kadeg couldn't control himself any longer. "They are unscrupulous crooks. They are destroying the beaches, entire biotopes that Brittany . . ."

Dupin had never seen Kadeg as a committed ecologist or patron saint of Brittany before. This must have been his wife's influence. But right as Kadeg might have been about the issue—that wasn't what mattered.

"Kadeg! Do you realize what you've done?"

Getting him out of there would be really complicated now. But they had more important things to do! After Nolwenn's intervention, Dupin had hoped it would be over.

"I'll say you knew nothing about the . . . sand samples, of course."

"Nonsense. Then you'll be in a real mess."

"I can't drag you into it any further."

Dupin was almost impressed. This was not Kadeg's usual style.

"You're an idiot, Kadeg. Is that clear? A complete idiot."

Kadeg was really just the terrier he always was. He had sunk his teeth right in.

"Do internal affairs know about the sand yet?"

"No. But I'm going to tell them. I should have done it already."

"I ordered you to do *that too*. To procure sand samples and to offer them—do you hear me, Kadeg? It happened on my orders!"

Dupin had no choice, he had to keep going down the road he'd chosen. Not knowing whether it led straight to disaster. For Kadeg—and for him.

"All right." It had taken Kadeg a while to answer. He was audibly relieved.

"Any other illegal activity I should know about?"

"No. That . . . that's all."

"If you keep anything else secret from me, then it's over."

"Do you know what, boss?" Kadeg's voice was suddenly firm again. "Do you know where one of the managing directors of Construction Traittot owns a house? In Port Belon! That's really something, isn't it?"

"What do you mean?" Dupin rolled his eyes.

"Construction Traittot! A large construction company angling to get a foothold in Brittany with knock-down prices. I've been keeping tabs on them for some time. We've made more progress than our colleagues in Lorient."

"If you have any serious evidence, Kadeg—then out with it! Tell our colleagues! Tell them everything!"

"They receive deliveries of sand in Lorient on trucks that aren't registered to any company."

"You've seen this?" Dupin couldn't believe he had got mixed up in this.

"Absolutely. Gracianne did too. And took photographs."

Kadeg's wife, the stout martial arts teacher, was in fact called Gracianne; Dupin always forgot.

"That's not reliable at all."

"We need to tackle their books, all their business records."

"We have no chance of getting a look at their books without reliable suspicion. You know what a search warrant requires. Pass on everything to our colleagues from Lorient, Kadeg! And let them do it. We're staying out of it—do you understand? We are staying out of it!"

"They're just poking around so far, my instinct—"

"Kadeg, stop. What matters now is preventing a charge being brought against you, a suspension. And we're in the middle of a double murder here!"

"I—"

Dupin was furious. "I'll have to speak to the prefect again and somehow explain the sand on your land. Before he hears about it from the other side."

"I—"

Dupin hung up.

Kadeg was driving him up the wall. This whole issue. Utterly pointless. This had to end.

* * *

It had—like all phone calls with the prefect—turned into a nerve-shredding conversation, ten infinitely long, wasted minutes of his life; but somewhat successful in the end. However, Dupin had foolishly put his neck on the line again.

At first he had given emphatic but undetailed updates on the first breakthroughs in the murder investigation—"A start at least, keep up the good work, mon Commissaire" was the prefect's response—and then he had come to the sand theft issue. And he quickly appealed to the prefect's boundless narcissism this time. This matter presented "potentially, a genuine coup for the prefecture," Dupin had claimed. Especially, of course, if a criminal French firm was engaged in destroying Brittany for profit, in the macabre form of the theft of original Breton resources to boot. If this was all true, there would be extraordinary media interest and Locmariaquer would become—Dupin had described this in glowing terms—the celebrated green hero. The fact that Dupin thought the chances of this vanishingly small was an entirely separate matter. Eventually the prefect had said that the issue, in spite of the "completely unacceptable methods" of the commissariat in Concarneau, could probably be resolved amicably. "In the interests of Brittany!" which really meant "in my own interests." It was disgusting, but it didn't even matter.

This time Dupin hadn't stopped at the cliffs, walking farther down the path instead and into the bay, as far as the water. When he hung up, he was standing on fine, dazzlingly white sand. A gorgeous little beach that he knew well. Tiny waves lapped on the bank, like at a lake. From here, so close to the water, everything seemed even bluer today. When he and Claire did the wonderful walk along the Belon, they often ended here, and always did in the summer. With a little dip. Then they had a picnic: baguette, *brie de Meaux,* boar sausage. Dupin was reminded of the mysterious plan to meet "around six o'clock"; he had no idea how he was going to manage to get away now that they found themselves on a real case. In any case, he would have to be there.

"Monsieur le Commissaire? Hello?" Riwal was standing above Dupin on the cliffs and was frantically scouring the surrounding area. If someone were watching from a distance, it would be an amusing sight— the way they had run around this landscape in the last half an hour, met, parted, met again.

"Down here."

Riwal lowered his gaze to the sea. A moment later he took off running.

Out of breath, he soon came to a stop just in front of the commissaire, his cheeks reddened.

"What is it?" Dupin had walked toward him.

"A second man, there's a second Scotsman—on the plane, the two of them came together, he . . . his name is Ryan Mackenzie . . . They flew from Glasgow to Brest. They left yesterday morning at seven forty-five, Glasgow, I mean"—Riwal took a deep breath—"they rented a car in Mackenzie's name, a silver Citroën C4. Everything via a travel agent in Glasgow— booked and paid for by Mackenzie."

Dupin was standing bolt upright, as if thunderstruck. A bull's-eye. Two men. Smith had not been alone. The two of them had come together. That strengthened their hypotheses.

Erwann Braz had joined them by now too. Riwal must have had him in tow.

"What did he have on?" This was the all-important question now.

Riwal didn't understand at first. Dupin repeated: "I mean this second Scotsman, what did he have on yesterday? What did he look like?"

"They weren't able to tell me that. I've asked the airline to get in touch with the aircraft crew immediately and ask whether anyone remembers the two men from 15A and B. Our colleague Braz has—"

"I have," Braz interrupted Riwal, his voice thin, barely audible, "just spoken to the car rental company on the phone." He hemmed and hawed. "He was wearing a jacket. Dark green."

"Dark green—a dark green jacket?"

That was it! Unbelievable.

There was no way that was a coincidence.

"And he had sneakers on, yes, dark sneakers, that's what the man who gave them the car remembers." Braz's embarrassment was clear, and with good reason. "Jeans. Short hair. I . . . It appears as though Madame Bandol did in fact see this man."

It was all true.

Madame Bandol had seen a man lying in the parking lot above them. And it was this very man. The second man. Ryan Mackenzie. Who had flown from Scotland to Brest with Smith. Dupin almost made a fist and shouted "Yes!"

Gentle, mystical chords rang out. Riwal's mobile. Dupin had asked him to change this psychedelic ringtone countless times but to no avail.

"A Scottish number. I'd better answer it." Riwal picked up. "Hello? Inspector Riwal, Commissariat de Concarneau."

Riwal held the phone slightly away from his ear, but Dupin couldn't make out anything anyway.

Away from the phone, Riwal whispered:

"A Scottish policeman. From Tobermory. Isle of Mull. I had requested information on the second man."

"Yes," Riwal said in English, speaking to his Scottish colleague again. And listened carefully for quite a while.

"Yes." The Scottish policeman was obviously telling him an awful lot. "Yes, thank you."

Riwal hung up. Dupin knew he spoke very good English, although that hadn't been clear from this conversation.

"So." Riwal was trying to get his excitement under control, which he was only partially successful in doing. "A sixty-two-year-old small business owner from the Isle of Mull, married .. he . . . he has been missing since yesterday evening."

"Well, that's pretty obvious now," Braz interrupted sulkily, but Riwal carried on unfazed:

"His business is in a secluded bay on the island, around fifteen kilometers from Tobermory, that's where they live too." Riwal's intonation made it clear the climax of his report was coming. "It's called Oyster Culture—they're oyster farmers!" He paused briefly and then carried on in measured tones. "They also fish other species of bivalves, but they mainly farm and sell oysters."

Maybe this was their link.

"The policeman is going to get in touch with more information soon."

"We've got to speak to the wife immediately; after all, she ought to know what her husband was up to in Brittany. Why he made this trip— and why he came with Smith."

Dupin noted down the most important points.

"We need to find out what Smith and Mackenzie's relationship was like and how they knew each other. When exactly did they intend to fly back, Riwal? Do we have the return flight?"

"Yes. On the same day, yesterday evening at seven forty-five."

This was odd too.

"They wanted to go straight back? On the same day? They flew to Brittany for just a few hours?"

"That's right. The flight only takes an hour and a half. Whatever they were planning, judging by their itinerary, it would have been possible to get it done in a matter of hours."

That explained why Smith hadn't had to officially sign out of his hostel. He would have been back again that night. Nobody would ever have known anything about his trip. This sensational news raised a string of questions.

"Are there any leads on the location of the Citroën C4?" Dupin asked.

"No. We'll put out a search for it immediately. It will probably have been somewhere near here yesterday afternoon." Riwal craned his neck vaguely in the direction of the parking lot. "Mackenzie probably came to Port Belon from the Monts d'Arrée by car."

"Mackenzie could also have been brought here by someone else—by his murderer, for instance. Perhaps he met his murderer in the Monts d'Arrée," interjected Braz, who was trying to make up for lost ground.

"In any case, after renting the car, the two of them drove directly to the Monts d'Arrée—why? Why there?" Dupin was aware that neither Riwal nor Braz knew. "Braz, have you spoken to one of the gendarmes from Sizun?"

"Yes. They don't know Smith and had no idea what a Scotsman might have been doing in the area either. They don't know any Scottish people at all."

"Call again and bring them up to speed. Perhaps something else will occur to them about it."

It was unlikely, but still.

"There might at least be a completely banal explanation for why they drove through the Monts d'Arrée." Braz wanted to score more points. "That's the shortest route from Brest, although it's actually quicker via the four-laner. Older GPS devices often just go by the distance in kilometers."

It was a plausible idea.

"But why do the two of them fly here together, which suggests that they know each other—only for one of them to kill the other right after they land?" Riwal had articulated one of the key questions. "It would have been easier to do it in Scotland. It can't have been planned, there must have been a spur-of-the-moment argument."

"How far is it from Glasgow to Oban and to this island?" Dupin was still thinking about how they had wanted to travel there and back on the same day.

"I think it's two hours to Oban by car, and another hour to the Isle of Mull." Riwal was good at geography. Especially the geography of the sister nations. "That will have been the oyster farmer's car; Smith won't have owned one, I'd say."

The speculation was pointless—they needed more solid information; they had to be patient. It was awful.

"Have a search put out for Mackenzie too. Find out whether someone saw him yesterday evening. I want to see his photograph in every newspaper, along with this Smith's photo. Online, on the Breton television channels, everywhere."

"Most importantly, we need his corpse," interjected Riwal thoughtfully.

"Where's Magalie Melen?"

"Creating the composite with Madame Bandol is proving, how should I put it, rather complicated," Braz gloated. "She had to go and help the artist."

"Well, it's pointless now. Call your colleague, let her know! Tell her to arrange for the search for Mackenzie. She'll work directly with Inspector Riwal." Dupin paused. "The oyster farmer who's friends with Madame Bandol," he glanced at his notebook, "Monsieur Kolenc. His business is based in that manor house?"

"Yes."

"All right. Then I'm going to find out whether anything occurs to an oyster farmer in Port Belon about a Scottish colleague's trip to Brittany. Perhaps the Scotsmen knew someone here." Dupin's expression became grim. "And, I'll pay a visit to this Monsieur"—he took another look at his list of people's names—"Monsieur Tordeux, Matthieu Tordeux. And ask him what he was up to yesterday in the general vicinity of the presumed crime scene. I'm assuming you haven't got round to it yet."

Braz looked utterly shamefaced.

"Back to the Scotsmen: we obviously need, as quickly as possible, the call records from their phones. Landlines. Mobiles. And access to the email accounts."

"Of course, boss." Riwal's nodding indicated that it had long since been on his radar.

"Right. Off you go then. We have no time to lose. Get in touch as soon as there is anything."

Dupin turned away.

"And another thing. Melen is to bring Madame Bandol up to speed on the latest."

They both stared at Dupin, Riwal even more astounded than Braz. The commissaire was notorious for preferring not to let anyone in, not even his inspectors, let alone "outsiders."

"She is to share everything we know with her."

Dupin couldn't resist a grin.

* * *

"My father is in the oyster beds. Down in the river. You'll find him there."

Dupin guessed Kolenc's daughter—she had introduced herself as Louann Kolenc—was in her mid-thirties, a short, slender woman with delicate, soft facial features, but undoubtedly a bundle of energy. You could see it in her sparkling blue eyes. Thick, shoulder-length black hair. Very friendly. A small smile.

"I'm happy to come with you."

She was wearing dark blue jeans and a plain V-neck sweater in the same color, and mid-length rubber boots.

"I'll find my way there, thanks."

Dupin was standing in the inner courtyard of the old manor house. Everything around them was made of stone; centuries of atmosphere. A few camellia bushes in full bloom, deep pink with an intense smell. A tank about five meters wide and three meters deep containing green-and-blue boxes full of oysters. A half-open wooden sliding door that revealed a glimpse of the workroom.

The young woman was standing at a kind of wooden counter—clearly a workspace—with a few boxes on it. Next to them were round raffia baskets in various sizes. And two towering piles of brown algae. The stuff with the little round lumps that went "plop" if you stood on them. They were hollow, only containing water—Dupin had found them interesting even as a child, during holidays by the sea; they exploded like snowberries used to do on the way to school back home.

"If you go down this road, then left and past the garden of the château with the high stone wall. That's where the oyster tables start. Lots of rows of them. The ones slightly farther back in the river, those are ours. That's where he should be."

"Do you work in the family business too?"

Louann Kolenc gave Dupin a piercing look. But she was still friendly. Then she pointedly took one of the raffia baskets and put it directly in front of her.

"My father and I think Madame Bandol really did see a dead body. We don't think she's crazy."

"She did. We're sure of it now."

Dupin wondered whether Monsieur Kolenc had confided in his daughter about the truth of the Bandol sisters.

"Madame Bandol is passionate about oysters. She is tireless in doing her bit for the prosperity of Port Belon," she said, and laughed.

Dupin understood. "I had that impression already."

The young woman took a couple of oysters out of the blue box and tapped them against each other. She saw Dupin's astonished face.

"Listening to the oysters, we call it: *écouter l'huître*. You can hear if they're alive. If they're good or not. These ones are alive." She placed them in a raffia basket.

"I'm glad to hear it," replied a perplexed Dupin.

"I've helped out since I was six years old. I've done it on a regular basis since the death of my mother. My whole life. This is a wonderful job, you—"

"Monsieur le Commissaire!" Riwal was standing at a narrow wooden gate that separated the inner courtyard from the street, breathing hard. He must have sprinted again. "New information. There's news!"

"I'm coming." Dupin was already moving. "Thank you, Mademoiselle Kolenc."

"Good luck!" It sounded genuinely encouraging.

A few moments later, he and Riwal were through the gate.

"The wife. They've spoken to Mackenzie's wife. Only on the phone for now. She's probably quite far away from them. The wife says she doesn't know anything."

"What did they tell her about her husband?"

It was extremely difficult to convey. Both pieces of information. That he was dead was, strictly speaking, still an assumption (even though it was certain for Dupin). But on the other hand, it was very probable that he was a murderer—that he had taken a secret trip to Brittany during which he had committed a murder.

"For the time being they've just said what has been established beyond doubt. That her husband has gone missing in Brittany. That he was here and has now disappeared. They haven't mentioned probable cause yet. Mackenzie's wife is of course beside herself with worry."

"And she didn't know anything about this trip?"

"No, she claims her husband told her he needed to go to Glasgow urgently. He has a share in an oyster bar, if I've understood correctly. He goes away for a day or two now and again. She presumed he went alone; he didn't mention Smith anyway."

Riwal seemed strangely weary in comparison with earlier, and also a little as if there was something on his mind.

"And she knows Smith?"

"Yes, she knows him by sight. She met him at the oyster farm a few times. He was one of the people who helped out during the season or on other occasions. She didn't know anything more about him. And she says her husband can't have known him very well either."

"He didn't know him very well, but spontaneously takes a secret trip to Brittany with him." This had not been a question. "And the wife can't make any sense of what her husband might have been doing in Brittany either?"

"No. She says she was only peripherally involved in her husband's business dealings."

"Well, then probably nobody will be able to tell us. Or want to." Dupin rubbed his temple.

"He traveled to Cancale every two or three years, she says. To one of the numerous oyster fairs. He got to know an oyster farmer from Cancale there. The two of them had formed a loose friendship, she says, and were considering launching something together businesswise. But that hadn't been fleshed out as yet. After staying in Cancale, Mackenzie then always traveled to Holland and Belgium for a few days."

At least there was a known connection to Brittany. And again: oysters.

"The last trip was just under three years ago. In theory it would have been time for another one—but she didn't know anything about a planned trip."

"Do we have the oyster farmer's name and details?"

"It's all there."

"Anything else? Does she have no idea at all what might have been going on?"

"Not the foggiest, according to the policeman who spoke to her on the phone. He's on his way to see her right now to speak to her in depth. A colleague is also making inquiries."

"Does the policeman find the woman credible?"

Dupin wasn't pleased about the situation. They were completely dependent on other people, on the police in Oban and Tobermory; Dupin would have jumped at the chance to speak to Mackenzie's wife in person. It all went against his instinct: a significant portion of the investigation would be out of their hands, a situation that the commissaire couldn't stand on principle.

"He didn't say it in so many words, but I suspect so."

This wasn't a particularly helpful statement. But what could they do? Riwal couldn't change anything about the situation either.

"Get in touch with the man in Cancale immediately," Dupin said. "No, I'll call him myself. I'll need the name and number."

"I'll send both to your phone. You'll have them right away."

"Any news on Smith?"

"Not yet. They haven't managed to track down the director of the Shelter House yet. She was probably the only one he spoke to now and again."

"Don't tell me she's missing too?" said Dupin.

"They're assuming that she drove to Fort William to do a few errands. She does this once or twice a month."

"No mobile?" Dupin felt uneasy.

"No mobile reception. Northern Scotland!" Riwal said with emphasis, clear reproach in his voice.

It took a Breton of all people to say that.

"Do we have access to their communications yet?"

"Smith didn't own a computer, but he did have a prepaid mobile, although he probably didn't have it on him very often. They're working on Mackenzie's documents. It's taking a little while. Mobile, landline, computer. I . . ." Riwal's eyebrows knitted; he didn't go on talking.

"What is it, Riwal?"

"The medical examiner was trying to get through to you. Then she called Nolwenn at the funeral." Suddenly Riwal's voice almost seemed to crack. "Next to the first line of the tattoo, she has found the beginnings of a second one, she—" Riwal broke off again, as if he wanted to check something in his head, then he got out his phone. "Here, take a look."

He held the little screen out to Dupin. "The second tattoo. Smith's left upper arm."

There wasn't much that could be made out. A line, tapering at the top, grazed skin, hematomas. He had almost forgotten this second tattoo.

"I know this symbol. A mythical symbol. It's the *tribann*." Riwal was pale; his lips had almost disappeared.

Dupin looked at him: "Yes?"

"Three beams, sunbeams, coming from a central point."

"What does it symbolize?"

"It goes back to Edward Williams, the founder of the Welsh Gorsedd of Bards. Early nineteenth century. The three beams symbolize the virtues of love, justice, and honesty. It's called"—Riwal's forehead was becoming more and more furrowed—"*the magic mark*."

Dupin remained focused. Using the first tattoo, they had found out the man's identity, and hence the second man's identity too. Perhaps the second tattoo would lead them to the "story of the case." Or at least put them on the right track.

"Who uses it?"

"Apart from the Welsh bard society, there's also the society from Cornwall, it's called Awen there, and the Scottish one—and the Breton society as well. The Goursez Breizh."

"A bard society?"

"A druidic society."

This answer did not help.

Dupin had of course heard of the modern—"contemporary"—druidic societies. He had had to unpick many of his prejudices in recent years—most of the existing societies followed a strictly humanistic religion and were a little like freemasons' lodges. The druids were—from a historical point of view—the sages and philosophers of Celtic culture, but also the scientists, doctors, and above all the guardians of history and tradition. Systematic druid training took twenty years. Riwal had explained it in detail during one of his quiz rounds at headquarters; even Caesar had written about these druids with great appreciation. In accordance with strict philosophical beliefs, you had to make a mental note of everything, all knowledge was preserved only orally and passed on; written knowledge was regarded as inferior because it let things become fixed and static and thus killed the essence of them. Storytelling became the highest form of science. Being a druid thus meant one thing above all: telling stories to pass on knowledge. Only if you grasped that, Dupin had learned, could you understand Riwal. Or Nolwenn. The love of storytelling was something fundamentally different to just talking. "Real" storytelling that deliberately blended history and mythology reached the status of a fine art—it was no coincidence that Celtic culture had produced some of the most powerful literary stories in the Western world and in all of European literature: King Arthur and the Knights of the Round Table, Tristan and Isolde, The Holy Grail, Perceval.

"You're saying Smith belonged to a druidic society? He was a druid?"

"Lots of the members have the symbol as a tattoo. I think so. It's possible. The druidic societies have been very popular again in the Celtic nations since the seventies."

Dupin needed to be careful or the conversation would drift into obscurities. Although Riwal was not a member of any of these societies—thank god—he knew all about them.

"And what does this Goursez Breizh do?"

"The aim is to promote and preserve Celtic culture and the Breton language. *Goursez* means throne. It's a Celtic neopaganist movement."

"Do you think Smith could have come to Brittany in his capacity as a druid, on some kind of druidic matter?"

"The societies work together very closely, you know: Intercelticism. There are joint activities. Not just the big gatherings."

Riwal had not embellished these topics much by his standards; in fact he hadn't embellished them at all. They had been dictionary entries instead. But he was known for his passions for the supernatural, fantastical, and also the occult. He still seemed strangely reticent. He usually loved these kinds of stories, but he appeared to find the idea that something druid-related could actually become part of a case extremely distasteful.

"So are there druidic societies around here?"

"Of course." Riwal sounded outraged now. "Throughout Brittany! There are local, regional, and national societies, all-Brittany ones. As early as 1850, the famous linguist and classical scholar Hersart de La Villemarqué founded the Breuriez ar Varzed association, Bards of Brittany. He was so famous, the Brothers Grimm proposed him as a corresponding member for the Berlin Academy of Arts! In 1899, a delegation set off to the Eisteddfod in Wales; at this big Celtic festival, under the symbol of Excalibur, King Arthur's sword, a Breton Gorsedd was founded. Today it's called Breuderiezh Drouized, Barzhed hag Ovizion Breizh, the Brotherhood of the Druids, Bards, and Ovates of Brittany. Most of the local and regional associations are part of this association. But not all of them, of course, there are significant differences. *Philosophical* differences."

That was enough for now, Dupin felt.

Riwal's expression darkened again. "The mythical symbol is increasingly being sported by the druids. Based on the order of the freemasons, there are three ranks: the ovates who wear green robes, the bards in blue, and the druids in white. Perhaps he really was a druid."

"What could be going on here? If this is to do with druids, I mean?"

"I couldn't say."

Dupin left it at that. Everything was so speculative anyway. For now at least.

"Tell our colleagues in Scotland to look into whether Smith really did belong to a druidic association."

"Maybe it was just a decorative tattoo. It's a very popular symbol."

This was a topsy-turvy world. Riwal was making an unusually strenuous effort to play down the significance of the druidic symbols and all things fantastical. Something about it truly seemed to frighten him.

"We'll see. I'll go and speak to Monsieur Kolenc now, down in the oyster beds."

Riwal looked very relieved.

"We've made one of the wooden tables outside the château into the command center; La Coquille is too busy. It's where you eat the oysters outside and look at the Belon, you—"

"I know the tables, Riwal, even though I don't eat oysters."

It was a good place for a provisional command center. Dupin was notoriously inclined to use unusual places to work—outdoors, in cafés, restaurants, or bars—the main thing was not working in the commissariat.

"Even better. We'll be sitting there if you need us. Magalie Melen is there too."

"See you soon, Riwal."

Dupin walked down the dead end toward the quay and the oyster banks in the Belon, while Riwal turned right. To the command center.

Dupin had never tried the "Queen of Seafood." He thought the outside of the shellfish was very pretty—the dark, creviced, sharp-edged shell in distinct gray shades that made the oysters look like bizarre stones. On the inside the shells were even prettier: iridescent mother-of-pearl. Dupin had particularly liked collecting them as a child, along with the *ormeaux*, and piling them up by the dozen. He was definitely fond of the oyster as a creature. Dupin had read that they led a simple, but admirably peaceful life in their protective shells: either they were resting (or sleeping)—or they were eating. Doing just these two activities—some reproduction also happened once a year—they eked out their modest, contemplative existence. An exceedingly comfortable existence to Dupin's mind. They didn't even need to move to eat; the food came to them. Plankton delicacies were washed directly into their shells without any effort on their part. Dupin also thought highly of oysters because Aphrodite had come out of an oyster, the most beautiful of all women and the goddess of love. And because they called for such excellent wines. And frankly he even believed the stuff about the health benefits, on the whole at least. And also that they tasted exquisite, in theory. Like the sea refined—a truly lovely thought, Dupin had to admit.

But the commissaire had never brought himself to eat a single one—although he had been firmly planning to several times. But it wasn't the idea of eating a living organism that bothered him, not at all; he managed it with other bivalves with no trouble. What had stopped him at the very last moment was the sight of it: the sliminess and the gooeyness of the whitish-green jelly. And it didn't help that absolutely everyone said that once you'd eaten a single oyster, you couldn't help but be addicted to them for life.

* * *

The air tasted like a salty sea floor; it smelled most intensely at times like this when there was low tide, sunshine, and gentle wind. Dupin liked this. You could smell everything the sea was made up of. Sunshine and warmth made it evaporate and hover, creating a fleeting ocean of almost infinite numbers of water vapor particles.

The current was visible as the Belon flowed through the bizarre landscape of white, dazzling silvery expanses toward the sea in a twisting, not very wide channel. Even at low tide it was impossible to tell how much water really belonged to the river; even at the lowest point of low tide, huge quantities of seawater were flowing away from the riverbeds and banks. To the right and left of the channel, the oyster tables jutted out of the silver expanses everywhere in long rows, the *tables à claire-voie*. Slender structures made of dark brown rusty metal rods, thin, grooved, and perhaps half a meter high, fitted with more supporting rods at the top, each ten or fifteen meters long. Steel centipedes. And there they lay on the tables: the large, coarse-meshed, flat bags called *poches* with the oysters growing inside them. Masses of brown algae had become tangled in the tables at high tide.

Dupin had followed Kolenc's daughter's instructions and had

turned left at the little quay and walked down the gently sloping ramp—which was currently dry—into the riverbed. A handful of people were visible in the vast landscape. Dupin headed for two men working at the tables near the water channel. He walked across the muddy seabed and the stones, crushed shells, and small sandbanks. After just a few meters, his shoes were dirty up to his ankles and completely soaked through.

"Monsieur Kolenc?"

Dupin called vaguely in the direction of the two men. The taller of the two turned round to him.

Dupin walked toward him. "Monsieur Kolenc?"

The man nodded.

"I'd like to speak to you. Commissaire Georges Dupin."

Baptiste Kolenc did not betray any surprise. He looked perfectly cheerful. "Because of the dead body from the parking lot?" he asked.

Dupin would have put Kolenc in his early sixties. A tall but well-built man, broad shoulders, large jet-black eyebrows, dark eyes, thick short gray hair, and a distinctly receding hairline. He had extremely friendly features and an open smile like his daughter's that took over his whole face. He was wearing some of the yellow workman's oilskin pants, held up by wide blue suspenders and a light gray sweatshirt covered in splashes of sludge.

"The dead body from the parking lot. Yes. A Scottish oyster farmer from the Isle of Mull, we now know, he probably farmed other bivalves too, but mainly oysters, but we don't yet have any idea what he was doing here. Why he came to Port Belon. He made a . . . stop-off in the Monts d'Arrée and then came here."

"An oyster farmer?" Kolenc asked in astonishment.

"Apparently they farm oysters in northern Scotland too," Dupin said carefully. He didn't know if this sounded like sacrilege to a Breton oyster fisherman.

"I know there are a few farmers up there." It didn't sound scornful. Kolenc carried on removing algae from the rods on the oyster bank. Then he picked up one of the large bags, shook it hard, set it down on the right, on the left, gave it another vigorous shake as if he wanted to make sure that the oysters were really tumbling over each other, and then put it back in its place the other way up with a deft movement. The oysters already looked big, and there must have been quite a few kilos of them.

"They love nestling up to each other. You've got to shake them regularly so that they don't grow together or form shapes that are too crooked," Kolenc murmured when he saw Dupin's gaze.

"Ryan Mackenzie is his name. Does his name mean anything to you?"

Kolenc was holding the next sack, his eyes fixed firmly on the task. "Never heard of him. Should I have?"

"I had hoped he might be known here. Or that you'd have some idea why a Scottish mussel and oyster farmer might come to Port Belon?"

"Business? Maybe he has his oysters refined here. That wouldn't be unusual, lots of people do that, including some overseas farms. It wouldn't have been about the sale of seed oysters."

Dupin had already heard this term in connection with oysters, *refinement*. Magalie Melen had talked about it earlier too—but he didn't really know what it meant.

"What do you mean by that, Monsieur Kolenc?"

Dupin fished out his Clairefontaine and the Bic.

"He could bring his fully grown oysters here to the Belon for a few weeks, for refinement in the nutrient-rich fresh and salt waters. Then they can be called Belons. And sold as such. That's common."

Dupin's brow furrowed.

"Belons are amongst the most famous oysters in the world. You can imagine how coveted a label it is. With oysters, the provenance determines the price."

"They just lie around in the water here for a while, once they're ready, and are then traded as Belons?" It sounded dishonest to Dupin.

"It's . . . all right." Kolenc shrugged.

"What do you mean by 'all right'?"

"In the space of a few weeks an oyster renews itself physiologically from the ground up. It's entirely replaced. So it takes on the classic Belon character in terms of taste and color here."

For a Breton, Kolenc was astonishingly talkative, practically chatty.

"Do all oyster farms do that here, including you?" Dupin still found the idea dubious somehow.

"You don't know much about oyster farming, do you?" The question had not been phrased in a malicious way, but Kolenc did now sigh audibly.

Dupin didn't have the slightest clue about oyster farming; of course, quite a few people had told him about it on quite a few occasions over the last five years, but, of course, he had often not listened; generally that was one of his greatest talents: pretty elegant "not-listening" when something didn't interest him.

"You need to know the differences between reproduction, farming, and refinement."

"Really?"

Dupin particularly wanted to understand refinement.

"Reproduction only takes place in a few areas. In Brittany, for example, it takes place in Cancale or in the parks between the Couesnon and the Loire. Then farther downstream by the Atlantic, in the Arcachon Bay. The *creuses* come to us at eighteen months for farming, including refinement. That takes another eighteen months. We get the *plates* once they're fully grown—just for refinement. For proper refinement."

"And how long does that take?"

"Different lengths of time. Everyone decides for themselves. We say six months."

"Is there a minimum?"

"It's strictly regulated. Fifteen days. What you really have to know the differences between are farms who cultivate the oysters in their own parks and refine them properly and then finally sell them as their own oysters from here, and the farms," Kolenc sounded scornful now for the first time, "who do nothing more than refine other people's oysters for the minimum time—and then send them back. They do nothing more than rent out their parks, the spaces in the water here. Including to foreign companies."

"Do you know of farms round here that refine oysters from Scotland? In the proper way or in the minimal way?"

This was the point Dupin was essentially interested in. Possible connections to Scotland. Direct, indirect, it didn't matter. Refinement would be, if he understood correctly, a plausible reason why a Scotsman, a Scottish oyster farmer, would actually come to Port Belon.

"No. But it's possible. *We* only refine our own oysters."

He sounded proud. Kolenc turned aside and got out a steel brush. He began to brush the bags down vigorously, dirt, shells, and scraps of seaweed falling away.

"Is it big business? Refinement in general?"

"It is indeed. The oysters come from many European countries. I've heard they even come from Japan and China. But most of them are from France, from the less famous oyster regions."

"Who does that kind of business here?"

"In Port Belon, you mean?"

"Yes."

"The trader, Madame Premel. And Matthieu Tordeux, one of the three farmers. You'll need to ask them about business ties to Scotland. Just like us, the Château de Belon doesn't do it."

Dupin had heard of those two before, too.

"You'll just have to watch out, there's no love lost between Tordeux and Premel. Apart from them, some of the big farms in Riec do it. They have much bigger nurseries all the way along the stretch of the river between here and Riec. It's four or five kilometers; they have factories everywhere there."

Pretty little Riec-sur-Belon was the oyster capital on the river. Just a few minutes away from Port Belon by car. Dupin was fond of it. There was a wonderful bakery there, a well-stocked newsagent, and a lovely market.

"You said something about . . ." The commissaire searched for a term he had just noted down. He generally made a lot of notes—although usually just single terms. You never knew when it might come in handy. "Seed oysters. About seed oysters, you said this couldn't be about them. What does that mean?"

"Seed oysters are the oyster babies. As I mentioned, reproduction only happens in a few areas. From there, they are in turn sold to other areas for farming and refinement. In Scotland, for example, the oysters don't spawn. The water is too cold. There's no reproduction there."

"Where do the seed oysters here in the Belon come from?"

"Some are supplied from other countries, mostly from Holland, the largest seed oyster producer in Europe. Lots come from the Arcachon Bay too. We only get our seed oysters from Brittany. And the *plates* that come here already fully grown, ours are from Brittany too. They love the Belon."

"And this is big business too—the seed oyster business?"

"Oh yes."

"And the *plates,* what kind of oysters are they?"

Kolenc's eyebrows went up. This was quite clearly the question of a rank amateur.

"You don't even eat them?"

"No."

It took a moment for Kolenc to respond. He seemed torn between bafflement and disgust.

"The *huîtres plates* are the indigenous ones, the original European oysters. Almost extinct. They are flatter, rounder, smoother, smaller on average." Kolenc sighed again. "And the *creuses*—they are, as their name implies, deeper, longer, more dome-like. Originally a Pacific oyster. The *creuses* make up the lion's share of the market, throughout Europe and around the world. Like the château, our farm specializes in European oysters, but we also cultivate *creuses*—most other businesses only cultivate *creuses*."

"And in Scotland?"

"Both kinds. Like in England. But the European oysters only make up a very small proportion of production everywhere. Of the forty-five thousand tons of oysters that Brittany puts on the market every year, only a thousand tons are *huîtres plates*." Kolenc seemed pensive now. "Perhaps this Scotsman just wanted to buy oysters."

"What do you mean?"

"It's quite simple. That he buys finished oysters from the Belon, imports them to Scotland, and sells them on there. Some farmers are also traders. Or he puts them directly on the market himself. Perhaps he has specialized in the *plates*, they love them in Britain. And he gets them from the Belon. They're the best."

This was of course conceivable. It would be completely plausible, just like the refinement theory. A plausible reason for Mackenzie's connections to Brittany—and for business trips to Brittany.

"And the *plates*—those are the better ones?"

Kolenc looked amused.

"It's a question of taste. We think so." Kolenc smiled. "But not all *creuses* are the same. With oysters, everything depends on the local composition of the water they live in. It depends on the plankton, for instance, the various species of plankton available—we call them the 'green flavors'—or on the makeup of the minerals, principally the salt content, of course. Oysters do nothing more than concentrate the taste of the water they live in. They are pure sea." Kolenc's voice took on a poetic tinge, which was an amusing contrast to his down-to-earth nature. "Just as the climate and soil of a cultivating area determine a wine and make it unique, so it is with the water and the taste of the oysters. It's *terroir* for wine, *merroir* for us. So the *creuses* from the Belon are of course wonderful too."

Dupin had never looked at oysters this way before. It was a lovely idea: that oysters allowed you to taste a very specific sea, a very specific place, very specific water. Yes, like wines. Dupin realized he was digressing.

"So you don't know this Scotsman—Ryan Mackenzie?"

As he had earlier, Kolenc looked confused. It was an abrupt change of topic.

"No. But do ask the others. And in Riec."

"Does anything at all occur to you about what might have happened here? I mean why in the oyster world such"—Madame Bandol's word came to him—"incidents might come about? And serious conflicts too—going as far as murder?"

Kolenc's expression became very serious. "No, no idea, but this much is for sure: there's a lot of money at stake. Along with image, ambition, greed. Oysters may be the most contented, amicable creatures, but people are not."

Dupin knew what Kolenc meant. That's how it was. Everywhere.

There was one thing that still interested him: "What do you mean when you say there's no love lost between them: Monsieur Tordeux and this trader?"

"They were married once, for half a year."

A succinct explanation.

"And it didn't turn out well."

"Not at all well. It looked like true love at first. She wasn't running the business at the time, it still belonged to her father. She's more than twenty years younger than Tordeux and has long since remarried and had two daughters. Tordeux has become a dyed-in-the-wool bachelor."

"I see. And now they're fighting?"

"They've just gone up against each other. There was an oyster farm for sale near La Forêt-Fouesnant and both of them wanted it. Tordeux got it. They"—he seemed to think it over—"always clash at every opportunity actually, even at our association meetings—they never seem to happen without a fight."

Both the Amiral and Henri with his Café du Port sourced their mussels and oysters from a farm near La Forêt-Fouesnant. But the business in question must have been a different one; Dupin would have heard about a sale. He would ask Henri or Paul.

"Otherwise, since we're already on the subject—any other rifts here in the area? With or without Scottish involvement?"

"Not that I know of. We all get on well with each other. Not that they're friendships. But we respect one another."

"Do you think—"

"Monsieur le Commissaire!" Riwal was running toward them and shouting at the top of his lungs from far away. It was starting to resemble a slapstick comedy.

"I'm coming." Dupin turned to Kolenc. "Thank you, you've been so helpful."

"Armandine Bandol said you two were a team." Kolenc laughed; he seemed to like this idea. "Maybe I'll be your consultant," he said, and then added: "Armandine likes you. She trusts you."

Dupin understood what he meant. He was pleased that Kolenc was protecting Madame Bandol's secret.

"An extraordinary woman!"

"So come by if you'd like to know more about oysters."

"I will—see you soon, Monsieur Kolenc."

Kolenc turned his attention back to the oyster tables and with a vigorous movement he tore a thick cluster of brown algae off the supporting rods.

While Dupin was saying good-bye, Inspector Riwal had set off back to the bank. Dupin caught up to him before the ramp up to the quay.

Suddenly the commissaire stopped walking.

Without any explanation, he turned around and walked briskly back to Kolenc, who was watching him curiously.

"Just one more question. Perhaps it's slightly off topic. A building contractor has a house here in Port Belon."

"Pierre Delsard. Yes. A pompous show-off."

"What do you mean by that?"

"Delsard isn't here often. He comes with friends or 'business partners' and throws huge parties. On the days when these parties are happening, there are Porsches, Jaguars, and Range Rovers parked here. From all over

Brittany. And from Paris, of course. There's a steady stream from the best *traiteurs* in the region. Oysters, rare mussels, lobster, champagne, foie gras."

Dupin's mouth automatically watered. He hadn't eaten for far too long.

"Where's his main home?"

"In Lorient. His company is there too. They say he has invested in an oyster farm or two. For fun. Because he doesn't know what to do with his money."

"Here in Port Belon?"

"I couldn't say. Nothing is official knowledge. Ask Tordeux. He's a good friend of his."

"Do you think he got into business with Monsieur Tordeux?"

Those would be confusing entanglements—the building trade and oyster industry. Which Dupin had not considered before.

"I don't know, Tordeux acts aggressive; he's constantly expanding his business. Besides the farm near La Forêt-Fouesnant, he bought a business in Cancale recently," Kolenc said.

"Cancale?"

"Yes."

Kolenc added, "It's not that unusual. Cancale is by far the largest Breton oyster location for everything, including seed oysters. Lots of larger oyster farms have a site there."

"I see. Where does the building contractor source his oysters from—for all those parties?"

"I assume his mate supplies him."

"Thanks again, Monsieur Kolenc."

Kolenc's open smile was back. "That's what consultants are for."

Dupin turned round once and for all. Riwal was waiting for him on the quay.

"News on Smith and Mackenzie. Most importantly: the director of the Shelter House has turned up again; she was shopping in Fort William as suspected."

Dupin was relieved to hear this.

"The director of the hostel knew that Smith was in fact an active member of a druidic society in the past, but"—there was noticeable relief on Riwal's face—"definitely not for the past several years. The group is called Seashore Grove and is a direct member of the Scottish Gorsedd. At most, Smith still went to special celebrations, but even then, not on a regular basis. So it's unlikely that this is about a druidic matter." He had uttered this sentence with emphatic certainty. "And nobody knows anything about Mackenzie having any interest in druidic matters."

Dupin was torn, but he let the subject drop for now.

"Go on."

Riwal looked downright grateful. They walked along the quay, turning right and going up the road.

"Smith has been a guest in the Shelter House for twenty-seven years. He's actually from the Isle of Skye. A complete loner, according to the director. No family ties or other strong social bonds—he never spoke about them anyway, and in the hostel they never heard of any. A reserved man, he generally spent his evenings alone, a lot of alcohol, but no medical problems as yet. And a good eater." Riwal's description was thorough. "There's a man around his age in the house whom he chatted to now and again, but he doesn't know anything relevant either, our colleagues have already spoken to him. The two of them told each other tales of the high seas. Talked about old times, fishing, rugby, Celtic sports, bagpipe competitions. That kind of thing. Smith often went fishing and every now and then he brought the cafeteria a big fish. All in all, a guy who wanted to be left alone. On occasion, when he had had too much to drink, he lost it. Over small things. But that didn't happen often. He was very amenable, really."

"Physical violence, bodily harm?"

"No. It descended into a brawl once, but nobody was hurt. It happens more often with other residents. The other thing the director had to report was this: he had been involved in a bank robbery that went wrong."

That was a major crime, at any rate. Riwal mentioned it last and almost in passing.

"When was that?"

"In 1970. He was nineteen."

"That's almost half a century ago." Dupin's interest was waning. "Has he come to the attention of the police again since then?"

"No."

Dupin was noting everything down; the notebook was filling up.

"And his casual jobs?"

"Only very seasonal, never anything permanent. As we already knew: as a young man he had been a deep-sea fisherman, on the big boats far out in the North Atlantic, the truly wild sea." Riwal's respect was palpable. "But the director didn't know any more details about that."

"And his links to Mackenzie?" Dupin asked impatiently.

"I was just coming to that. It seems he has always worked for Mackenzie, a few weeks here, a few months there. Seven years ago he worked for him for nearly twelve months straight, then suddenly it was less; it was only weeks at a time in recent years. The Shelter House residents have to document their working circumstances precisely, that's one of the requirements for being admitted. It's all there."

"What happened? Why did he work there so much less often as time went on?"

"We don't know. Perhaps because of the devastating events in oyster farming at the time. In 2008, the *huîtres plates* across Europe caught a brutal bacteria that almost wiped them out. Widespread oyster death. Or because of the major economic crisis—businesses collapsed all over the place."

"Here in the Belon too? I mean, did the oyster death happen here too?"

"Everywhere. There's another wave now. At this very moment."

Dupin gave an involuntary start. "Right now? Here in Port Belon?"

He looked around, an absurd reflex. Nobody had told him about this yet. They had all seemed so relaxed.

JEAN-LUC BANNALEC

He and Riwal had arrived at the tables outside the château some time ago. At their "command center." They had chosen the last table, away from the others. There was nobody there apart from them. Braz and Melen seemed to be out on duty.

"It's not in Port Belon yet. It started in the Arcachon Bay and is just arriving in the Île d'Oléron now. The border of Brittany. Catastrophic. And a complete mystery. An unknown bacteria. It's been killing off oysters wholesale for a while now. Mainly the *plates*. It strikes with terrible force and it strikes the fully grown animals. Up to two-thirds of the oysters are affected."

Riwal had sat down, but Dupin stayed on his feet. He knew that Riwal knew what he was talking about when it came to oysters. Apart from the obligatory langoustines, he usually brought a dozen oysters to the commissariat for lunch and complained vociferously about the price every day—in Paris, Dupin knew, it was four or five times as much!—and then he and Nolwenn set about them with relish. Riwal naturally put his never being sick down to this daily oyster consumption. And of course, oysters were a symbol of Brittany and that meant it had to be defended.

"And it could strike here too?" Dupin's question sounded unintentionally melodramatic.

"Any time. At any second." Riwal's answer was equally melodramatic.

Dupin didn't have a clue how this could be connected—but perhaps it was no coincidence that the Scottish oyster farmer and his seasonal worker had set off for their trip to Brittany right at this moment. At a moment when—possibly—a fresh disaster was happening in the oyster world.

A single high-pitched note was audible, but only just. A text message. Dupin got his mobile out of the pocket of his jeans and looked at the screen. Claire. The promised details for their meet-up. *The corner of Rue de Kergariou and Rue du Sallé, 6:30.* That was it. Riwal blinked curiously at him.

"Back to Smith. What else is there on him?"

"That's all for the moment. Our local colleagues are trying to find out whether there might still in fact be family members whom they have to inform."

"When did Smith last have a job with Mackenzie?"

"Over the last Christmas and New Year's holidays. That's the high season in oyster farming. For three weeks."

"And not again after that?"

That was almost four months ago.

"And Mackenzie. What news is there on him?"

"The policeman is with Mackenzie's wife right now. We'll hear about that soon. I had given him a quick call because of the druidic issue. Riwal pulled a face. "Our colleagues have looked up what they can find on his company. He has tried to expand a few times. He set up the company thirty-five years ago, he had a branch in Kirn, but he sold it again two years later. Then he bought a smaller oyster farm in Lochgilphead ten years ago. And after that he opened an oyster bar in Tobermory where he offered his own oysters and mussels to eat or buy. Six years ago he deregistered these two businesses again."

"Why?"

"It wasn't clear from the official documents. The recession, I suspect. Tourism must have severely declined in northern Scotland too. Or the impact of the oyster death at the time; even if Scotland was spared, he definitely wouldn't have got any more seed oysters. Or both of those reasons."

"So in the end he only had one business left?"

"Mackenzie did in fact invest in a bar in Glasgow last year called Oyster Heaven—he's a co-owner. His oyster farm on the Isle of Mull and this bar, those were his two current businesses."

Mackenzie was someone who had obviously always kept trying. Had tried to build himself something bigger. And kept failing. Due to adverse circumstances perhaps, Dupin thought.

"We need to know as soon as possible whether Mackenzie imported oysters from the Belon. Or whether he had any refined here. Whether he specialized in European oysters. Tell our Scottish colleague to grill his co-workers."

"We'll do that, boss."

"Are our colleagues working on Mackenzie's business records yet? They ought to be logged . . ."

"If they even existed—and were legal. If not, they definitely won't be on the books. And also not if he was only just setting it up. Perhaps that's why he came."

Dupin was walking up and down in front of the tables. The panorama was enchanting. In front of the magnificent manor house, straight across the Belon, stood a handful of extremely weathered long wooden tables with benches. Lined by old, wildly overgrown oak trees was a view of the Belon estuary, shimmering an emerald green in the afternoon sun.

"So does it happen often, such a large-scale oyster death?"

Dupin was still, he realized, preoccupied by the blight issue. The potential catastrophe.

"Not on the horrific scale of 2008, but on a smaller scale, it happens over and over again. In 1920, an infection wiped out ninety percent of the *huîtres plates* in Europe. Up until the end of the nineteenth century, it was the only species of oyster in Europe, from the Norwegian fjords to Gibraltar, apart from smaller cultures of the Portuguese oyster. Even in the years before the infection, it had been badly affected by the excessive rise in consumption, after the Sun King really made it into a delicacy again, which it had previously been amongst the Greeks and Romans." Riwal's eyes gleamed. "In the Middle Ages, oysters were just for poor people, they were out of favor. But Louis XIV later had every guest at his sumptuous parties served exactly one hundred oysters. His chef could never source enough of them." Riwal suddenly sounded glum. "And the chef threw himself into the Seine because of a delayed oyster delivery. He—"

"Riwal—the oyster death!"

This was not the time for historical digressions. It had also sounded a little macabre; Riwal seemed fully capable of understanding the motive for this desperate act.

"The millennia of European oysters were followed by the great half century of the Portuguese oyster." Dupin almost burst out laughing at Riwal's words. "The year 1868 is the crucial date. A Breton ship loaded with six hundred thousand Portuguese oysters sought shelter in the Gironde estuary from a terrible storm that wasn't letting up. At some point, the captain figured the oysters were spoilt. He had them thrown into the water—and some were still alive." Riwal had begun to speak very quickly—he was aware that Dupin would interrupt again otherwise. "They quickly spread out all the way along the Atlantic coast. When the disease almost obliterated the European oysters, people were glad to have them. The Portuguese oysters were more delicate and could be sold all year round because of their spawning habits!"

"Kolenc talked about a Pacific oyster," Dupin said.

"In around 1970, the Portuguese oyster caught two deadly viruses one after the other and was almost wiped out itself. Luckily an oyster farmer had brought a small culture of the Pacific oyster from British Columbia and Japan a few years before, which was immune to the viruses. The 'giants.' More were soon sourced and people began to farm them. They are the most robust kind of oyster. Tragically, there was another terrible virus lurking in some imported specimens, which almost completely eradicated the by then slightly regenerated cultures of European oysters." Riwal took a deep breath for his finale: "The Pacific oyster makes up over ninety percent of the world market today; the European oyster makes up point two percent."

Dupin was—whether he liked it or not—impressed. Clearly the history of oysters was an extremely violent one—a history of mass death and disaster. And, like everything else in the world, a history of coincidences.

"At some point, the European oyster will die out completely," Riwal said wistfully. "It has just received the award for Mollusk of the Year, an important award!"

Dupin almost laughed, but Riwal was serious.

"The award is for mollusks whose survival is under threat and who have an important ecological function. The Desmoulin's whorl snail, the great gray slug, the mouse-eared snail, the thick-shelled river mussel, the door snail. In this way, they inform the public about select species and try to bring more attention to mollusk-related issues, they—"

"Riwal! We are not at the university!" There were some moments when you had to step in. Although Dupin could easily see why mollusks with names like these needed someone to champion them.

"Kolenc didn't mention anything about a potential epidemic. Or that they could possibly be on the brink of a catastrophe here in Port Belon." The commissaire was pensive. "But it could actually mean the end for the farms. Including his."

"There are many reasons the bacterium might stop before the river. Just a few currents would need to change. And it would all be irrelevant to the Belon."

"Riwal, do you think that the *plates* taste superior to the *creuses*?"

For a moment there was astonishment on Riwal's face, then joy. Unalloyed joy at Dupin's unexpected interest in oysters. For years they had all—Riwal, Nolwenn, but also Paul Girard from the Amiral, and Henri—tried in vain to give Dupin an understanding of oysters.

"There is something uniquely nutty about the *plates,* something delicate, something subtle, and there's an undercurrent of saltiness. Here in the Belon anyway. They taste of the extraordinary water they live in. A mixture of river flavors and sea flavors." Riwal's face was rapt now, transformed like a wine critic's at a tasting. "The river flavors are reminiscent of cucumbers, melons, or fresh soybeans—on the other hand, they have that very specific metallic clarity of the iodine flavor. Which the oysters from the refining pools in Marennes-Oléron, for example, have almost none of, although they are of course fantastic. With the oysters from the large sea bays or the open sea, the iodine component is even more pronounced. It all just depends on . . ."

". . . *merroir*," Dupin finished his sentence.

Riwal nodded appreciatively.

"You have to close your eyes if you're eating oysters. Smell, taste, feel. The sea, the place! Only philistines wash oysters down." These words were resonant with anxious disgust. "You've got to chew them slowly and pay attention to the flavor with all of your senses. And anyone who really wants to do that will avoid any added flavors like lemon, pepper, or vinaigrette. The water is as exquisite as they themselves are. Another bad habit is eating oysters ice cold, that damages the flavor!" Dupin would need to intervene again; Riwal was digressing. "They taste best at a temperature of between eight and twelve degrees, like the young, lightly sparkling Muscadet with its mineral taste and the flavors of apples and citrus fruits that you drink on the side!"

"You can't beat a Muscadet," Dupin blurted out. His mouth was watering, but not because of the oysters.

"A wine that can stand up to oysters is important and it depends on flavor, region, and species of oyster. But not all white wines are appropriate by a long shot. For Belon oysters, the Muscadet is the absolute perfect wine! But what also goes well is a Chablis. A Pouilly-Fuissé. A Puligny-Montrachet. Why not? Excellent!"

"All right, Riwal. All right!"

Suddenly a pleased, delighted expression appeared on Riwal's face.

"Do we have an oyster case, Monsieur le Commissaire—what do you think?"

Dupin furrowed his brow. At some point Riwal, Nolwenn, Kadeg, the whole commissariat, and last but not least the Breton press had started to refer to the cases from the last few years like this. The "art case," the "island case," the "salt case." Absolutely ridiculous. When he heard this, he feared the worst for the party the day after tomorrow; it occurred to him again that he needed to elicit a promise from Nolwenn that there would be no speeches. Or any kind of funny retrospectives. Or amusing anecdotes.

"Riwal!" Dupin was desperate to get back to the investigation now. They needed to concentrate.

"We need to know whether any of the other oyster farmers knew Mackenzie. All along the Belon. Whether anyone has done business with him."

"Absolutely, boss."

"We should build up a picture of who on the Belon maintains business ties with Scotland. No matter what kind. There won't be that many. Call in our two colleagues from Riec. Make inquiries at every farm."

The staffing situation was still poor. Riwal might have been back but Dupin could have done with Kadeg and Nolwenn.

"I'll take on the farms here in Port Belon." Dupin looked at his watch. He still had about an hour, then he needed to leave to get to Quimper more or less on time—for his mysterious plans with Claire. His instinct told him that he should under no circumstances risk being late. During their first relationship, he had been far too late far too often. Or hadn't turned up at all.

"Did you get through to the man in Cancale, Monsieur le Commissaire?"

This was important. Dupin hadn't tried again yet.

"I'll do it immediately. On my way to see Monsieur Tordeux." Dupin leafed through his notebook. "Ah yes—at Super de Belon."

"Okay. I sent the name and number of the man in Cancale to your phone. You ought to have everything."

"See you later, Riwal."

"Another thing, boss." Riwal seemed embarrassed all of a sudden. "This business with Kadeg. Just briefly, so that you're aware: internal affairs is having him painstakingly show them everything on the site right now. The sand samples. To get a complete picture of *our* undercover operation. Nolwenn just let me know."

"From the funeral?" Dupin stopped moving.

"Yes. Aunt Elwen was already in the ground, don't worry."

"And when will we see Kadeg?"

"This evening, I think. Or else tomorrow morning."

"Thanks, Riwal."

Dupin left the tables at a brisk pace. He had just turned the corner when Magalie Melen suddenly appeared in front of him. This was inconvenient.

"Commissaire—Madame Bandol is asking when you're seeing each other again today. She has been trying to call you."

"Has she recalled new details? Did something else spring to mind?"

That could happen at any moment.

"I don't think so. It was about her next 'meeting' with you, she said. And how you propose to progress with the investigation in general?" Magalie Melen had no doubt repeated Madame Bandol word for word.

"Tell her that unfortunately I won't make it today anymore. *Unfortunately.* That I'll be in touch tomorrow."

Dupin really was sorry.

Something else had occurred to him during his conversation with Kolenc. He had even made a note of it:

"What exactly has happened to this madame who owns the château?"

"Morocco, Agadir. She's away until the end of the week. With her whole family. Her husband and two children. They've been gone since Sunday of last week. They take two weeks' holiday a year. Traditionally always in the weeks before Easter."

"And who's staffing the tastings there now? If you want to eat oysters at those tables?"

"Her niece. Late twenties. She's actually a baker. She comes here every year for these two weeks. But only does the tastings here on-site. And reads a lot. Things aren't very busy round here yet, as you can see. And then there's also the three employees who look after the oyster beds. They come from Riec."

"You know the owner?"

"Quite well."

It sounded more like "very well."

"Suspicious in any way?"

The young policewoman remained unfazed. "I don't think so. No."

"Call her in Morocco—and inquire about Mackenzie and Smith. And Scotland in general—about any possible connections to it."

"Will do."

"I've got to get going." Dupin hurried on.

A call and a visit were still doable—he would no longer manage the conversation with the trader before Quimper. He actually really needed a coffee. The commissaire emitted a loud, deep sigh. It could be heard far and wide.

* * *

"Hello?"

The phone had rung for a long time—Dupin almost hung up again.

"It's Commissaire Dupin here. Commissariat de Police Concarneau. Am I speaking to Monsieur Cueff?"

"Speaking." An irritated tone of voice.

"We're investigating a murder case, monsieur. A man you know disappeared last night."

"You're pulling my leg, right?"

"No, Monsieur Cueff. It's about Ryan Mackenzie."

"Ryan Mackenzie?" There was concern in his voice.

"Yes. It's highly likely he was murdered in Port Belon."

"Highly likely?" A legitimate question, expressed with undisguised condescension. "Do you mean it's highly likely he was murdered—or do you mean it's highly likely he was murdered specifically in Port Belon?"

"Both."

This was correct. And it ought to have been enough. There was quite a long silence and Dupin didn't intend to break it.

"That's crazy. He called me just last week. Wednesday afternoon."

"He did what?"

"I hadn't heard from him for a good year, I've known him for almost twenty years, we—"

"What did he want?"

"He told me that business was good and that he might want to come by in the near future to discuss the idea of taking a share in the company. His last visit was two or three years ago."

"He wanted to come to Brittany?"

This was getting more and more interesting.

"To see me in Cancale. Yes. So?"

"What were these plans about a share? How far did they progress?"

"It was still just an idea. Nothing more. He wanted to buy in to my oyster farm. Potentially twenty percent of it or so. He'd had the idea a long time ago, I was very interested." What Cueff was saying was very informative, in contrast to the undisguised reluctance audible in his voice. "But the considerations never progressed very far."

"Why was he interested in it in the first place, do you think?"

"Breton Oysters is an attractive business in Britain. Plus he would have had a reliable supply of seed oysters."

It was a good thing Dupin had spoken to Kolenc in some detail; he was up to speed.

"And how long have you known him exactly?"

"Since 1997, I think. We met at a fair for European oyster producers here in Cancale. He was sitting at our table, next to my wife and me. He has visited us every few years since then, whenever he made a trip to the Continent."

"Did he mention anything about an imminent trip to Brittany he was planning? Soon, this week?"

"No. He . . ." Cueff hesitated, an uncertain hesitation. "Nothing. He only said he wanted to come soon, without mentioning a date. He was going to get in touch again."

"Nothing else?"

"No."

"No hint, nothing indirect or implied?"

"No."

"Did anything seem unusual during the phone call?"

"He was in a very good mood. The call lasted maybe three minutes. No. You now know pretty much every word we said to each other."

Dupin had reached the quay. On the left-hand side, the little white building directly beside the high, overgrown stone wall of the château was easy to see from the ramp. A neat white sign that read *Super de Belon* in enormous blue lettering pointed the way.

"A share in a business like this, what kind of figures are we talking about?"

"We didn't get as far as figures in our considerations at all."

"How much is your farm in Cancale worth?"

It took Cueff a while to answer. He seemed to be considering whether he should answer at all.

"Right now you'd pay a million for a business like mine."

"Do you own other businesses? Or shares in businesses? In Port Belon, for example?"

"No."

"And the name 'Seamus Smith' probably doesn't mean anything to you either?"

"No."

"That's it for the moment, Monsieur Cueff. Just one more thing: where were you when Ryan Mackenzie's call came through?"

"At home."

"A landline call?"

"I barely use the landline. A mobile call."

"Were you home alone?"

"I was working in the office. Yes."

"Nobody saw you?"

"Not till that evening." The displeasure in Cueff's voice grew again and he didn't try to hide it. "When my wife and son came in around half past eight."

"Thanks very much. We'll be in touch again soon."

No response from Cueff. Dupin didn't wait long. He hung up.

It was just a few more meters to Tordeux's farm.

The same outsized sign as at the quay hung resplendent over the entrance to the building: *Super de Belon*.

Dupin dialed Riwal's number and he answered on the first ring.

"Boss?"

Dupin launched in with no preamble. "This man from Cancale, Nicolas Cueff. Speak to the police in Cancale. We need information about him and his business activities. Anything we can get access to. And I want someone to go over right now and talk to him in detail. They should have him tell them everything in meticulous detail, every aspect of the conversation with Mackenzie. Go over his alibi with him again. And most importantly: the policeman who is with Mackenzie's wife is to ask her specifically whether she knew about her husband's plans to invest in Cueff's oyster farm. And in particular, about how he had apparently just taken up this idea again and called Cueff because of it last week—it would certainly have meant quite a large financial investment."

"All right, boss."

"Riwal, is Nolwenn back?" It made Dupin nervous when Nolwenn wasn't in the office during a case. Her presence didn't just mean great help and support, but also moral and psychological stability, and also a kind of superstition that everything would turn out well.

"The funeral meal ought to be over soon."

"Thank god," Dupin blurted out. "See you soon."

* * *

The river had risen again slightly, the channel widening. Right next to Tordeux's building was a long oyster pool. Next to that was a bright red tractor, the shovel facing upward, just above the ground. Two men in the apparently obligatory yellow oilskin pants were busy loading large red sacks full of oysters onto the shovel. Dupin strode up to them, wading through deep mud again. His shoes would not dry out again today.

"Monsieur Tordeux?"

They clearly hadn't heard Dupin coming, both men turning round with a start at the same time.

"Inside," said one of the two men with a vague gesture. A moment later they were fully focused on the sacks again.

Dupin turned on his heel without saying a word. The door—which was more like a gate—was standing wide open.

"Monsieur Tordeux?"

Not waiting for an answer, Dupin went inside. A sparse room stretched out in front of him. The walls had been roughly plastered and whitewashed in days gone by, becoming brown and gray. The room was crammed with junk and mountains of oyster sacks in untidy piles. In the far right-hand corner, which you could only get to by walking in a zigzag, he spotted a crude set of wooden steps that looked like the result of DIY carpentry. There was a single small window, the light was mainly coming through the open door.

"Up here."

Monsieur Tordeux had taken his time with his response.

Dupin worked his way over to the stairs. The steps were twice as high as normal steps, so it was practically mountain-climbing.

Everything was different upstairs. The contrast was enormous. You were suddenly standing in an exquisite designer room. Luxuriously furnished. Windows on three sides—the largest looking out onto the river—and most importantly, an enormous skylight made of aluminum that showed off a considerable amount of sky. Next to the large window with the river view, a snow-white table stood in the middle of the room. It looked expensive, with an equally expensive stainless steel lamp on it, a large flat screen, and an elegant white chair behind it. There were two chairs in front of the table. Perfectly fitted steel shelves on the walls, white paneling. In the other corner of the room was a black leather sofa with a low, matching coffee table.

"Monsieur Vannec?"

Tordeux didn't stand up till the last second and was now walking purposefully toward Dupin, holding out a friendly hand to him. Medium height, slim, lightly tanned, short black hair discreetly gelled back, a silvery shimmer on the sides, an elegantly narrow face—perfectly shaved—dark gray slacks, light gray shirt, gray tones that went too well with his hair to be a coincidence, three shirt buttons open, studiously casual. Perhaps late fifties or even early sixties; it was hard to say—he had stayed young without appearing to be making a desperate effort to do so.

For now Dupin didn't intend to clear up the obvious misunderstanding, letting Tordeux talk.

"You're absolutely right to come to me. Belon oysters! There's nothing better! It's great that you found us okay. We'll make you an excellent offer. Do sit down!" He pointed to one of the two chairs.

The expert approach of a shrewd salesman. Dupin stayed standing.

"Commissaire Georges Dupin—Commissariat de Police Concarneau."

Tordeux looked surprised for just a moment and then smiled in amusement. Self-assured.

"I was expecting a new customer. A restaurateur. He was meant to be here at five," he replied, "but of course it's a pleasure to welcome the police too."

Dupin was not in the mood for joking.

"Do you maintain business links to Scotland, Monsieur Tordeux? To Scottish companies?"

"To our sister nation?"

Dupin did not answer.

"Yes, with a trader in Edinburgh. And a farmer in Dundee." Tordeux spoke in a pointedly casual way.

"Edinburgh and Dundee?"

A hit on the first try. Scotland, two links. Albeit eastern Scotland.

"Yes."

"One of your business partners is called Ryan Mackenzie, I take it."

It couldn't hurt to give it a try.

"Ian Smollet. That's the name of the trader in Edinburgh. I sell our delicious *plates* to him. And James MacPhilly is the farmer in Dundee—I refine his oysters into superb Belons. I see them both, I'd say, every two years. The business is worth it. Edinburgh is a fantastic city, they cultivate an exquisite flavor there!"

Dupin had fished his notebook out of his pocket. "You don't know a Ryan Mackenzie, Monsieur Tordeux—I'm asking you straight out. You've never met him? Never heard of him?"

"Definitely not."

"He was the victim of a murder yesterday, very near here."

"So it's true then. There's been some unsettling news going round since last night. And you mislaid the corpse. That must be seriously annoying for you."

"Seamus Smith? Do you know him?"

"Same thing. Never met him, never heard the name."

"And your trader and your farmer—are they in contact with one of them?"

"You're kidding me! Do you think I know all of their business partners? Who are these two gentlemen you're asking about, are they oyster farmers too?"

"One of them is, yes. Ryan Mackenzie."

"My partners aren't accountable to me. And just for context: I maintain business relationships with sixteen European countries."

"And how long have you had ties to Scotland?"

"Twenty years, I think. At least twenty years."

"Was either of the two—your Mr.," Dupin checked the names, "Mr. Smollet and Mr. MacPhilly—here in Brittany recently?"

"Most recently, I saw them both at the beginning of last year. In January and March maybe. They were here briefly. There's nothing more to tell."

His answers came very casually.

"But you're in touch regularly? By phone, email."

"You don't give up—what are you actually trying to get at?"

A smug smile suddenly flitted across Tordeux's lips. For a split second.

"I'm investigating. So?"

"Of course we stay in touch. There are regular deliveries. The trader gets a shipment of *plates* every two weeks. The farmer sends me quite large quantities of his oysters twice a year. And I send them back to him."

Again, it was like water off a duck's back with Tordeux.

"Do you fear the outbreak of an oyster infection here in the Belon, monsieur? That the catastrophe from Arcachon will spread as far as here?"

"We'll see."

He didn't seem surprised by the question. He didn't seem worried by the topic at all. Or he was hiding it very well.

"Is there talk of that round here yet?"

"Ask the others. I'm certainly not talking about it." Tordeux's eyes flashed suddenly. "Who supplies the commissariat in Concarneau with oysters? I'll make you an unbeatable offer."

Dupin wasn't sure if this was meant to be a joke.

"I hear you've just bought and expanded a farm near La Forêt-Fouesnant?"

"That's right. And two years ago in Cancale. Yes, you've got to position yourself well strategically! And business is good. If you work hard for it."

"And why so extraordinarily good? We're talking about significant investments here."

Tordeux looked Dupin right in the eye. "We've increased turnover here by a factor of twelve in ten years. Increasing year on year. And we've saved capital." He spoke in a pointedly calm voice.

"Pierre Delsard. The building contractor. A good friend of yours, apparently. You supply him with oysters and mussels."

"A very good friend. And a very good customer. Yes."

Dupin felt it was almost provocative, how willingly Tordeux gave information.

"Monsieur Delsard didn't go into business with you, by any chance? As the financier? A silent partner?"

The answer came promptly; Tordeux didn't betray any emotion: "No. I do my own thing."

"Are you sure?"

"Absolutely," he said, and burst out into loud laughter.

"Financially, is your business based more on farming or refinement on the whole?"

"Refinement."

Dupin glanced at his watch. He would need to get going soon.

"And now for the most important question, Monsieur Tordeux." Dupin paused for a few moments, as if he was waiting for something. "What were you doing yesterday at the scene of the crime at the time that it was happening?"

The question caught Tordeux by surprise—there was a flicker of shock on his face.

He made a big effort to make his tone breezy and sarcastic. "So that's how it is. I'm your suspect. I would never have thought you capable of so much humor—Parisians are normally more on the grumpy side."

"That's right, Monsieur Tordeux," Dupin said sharply. He was fed up with the rhetorical dancing around. "I alone decide who is under suspicion. You're absolutely right to worry. So?"

"Oh, so you can be a bit more aggressive. I'm glad. That's important in your profession. So, my official statement for the record: I own a *gite rural*, a kind of guesthouse, inherited from my aunt, around a kilometer from the parking lot, and there's only one way to get to it: via the road with the little dead end to the parking lot off it. I came via that street. A completely legal action, as far as I know. Around four forty. Because I had something to do at the *gîte*. And I saw old Madame Bandol with her dog. She was coming up the path from the Belon. And that was it. As befits an upstanding citizen, I accurately reported this to the police when a colleague of yours asked me whether I had by any chance been in the area in question at the time in question and whether I happened to notice anything."

"To summarize: at the time of the crime you were at least in the vicinity of the crime scene. What did you need to do in your *gîte*, monsieur?"

"I was expecting guests."

"And you do all of that yourself?"

"Of course I've got someone who looks after the building." Tordeux was acting almost indignant. "Making the beds, cleaning, and so on. But there are things I need to do there too."

"Do you have many guests?"

"There could be more, if I wanted. I just do it on the side. I mainly rent to friends and acquaintances."

"And what were these things that you had to do?"

"I had the key."

Dupin had been thinking more of the heating or something along those lines. "The key?"

Before Tordeux could respond, the commissaire carried on: "We'll get in touch again very soon, Monsieur Tordeux. Then you'll tell us the rest. A colleague will speak to your guests too."

Dupin turned around and headed for the stairs.

"I'll be here." Tordeux seemed completely calm, not a trace of irritation. "And have another think about the supply to your commissariat. Your festive occasions, receptions. There must have been plenty of them since you've been there." This didn't sound sarcastic in the slightest. "I make the best offers. Real Belons!"

Concentrating hard, but moving quickly, Dupin climbed down the neck-breaking steps.

It was 5:45.

Outside the exit, he could see a short, dumpy man approaching the stone building, keeping close to the wall and wearing an ugly pale yellow suit. Making an effort not to get too close to the mud. It looked ridiculous. Presumably the restaurateur whom Tordeux was expecting.

Dupin hurried on.

He could see Riwal at the turnoff for their command center. The inspector noticed him too, although Dupin had been trying hard to scurry past.

Riwal immediately rushed over to him.

He got started before Dupin could even say that he really didn't have the time right now.

"Boss, the policeman who drove over to Mackenzie's wife has just called, we spoke in depth. Our colleagues—"

"And?"

"Jane Mackenzie has confirmed she didn't know what her husband was doing in Brittany. She—"

"I'll call you from the car soon, Riwal, I mean, straightaway, in a minute."

He wanted to hear the details of what the Scottish policeman had to report from this conversation.

"From the car?"

Dupin hadn't told anyone about his "field trip" to Quimper.

"In a minute."

"There's more important information, the phone records belonging to—"

"In a minute, Riwal. I promise! Tordeux has two Scottish business partners, by the way. In Edinburgh and Dundee. An oyster farmer and a trader. Have them checked out by the Scottish police, Tordeux is to give you their contact details. Find out whether they were in touch with our two Scotsmen."

Dupin was already walking on, but he turned round again briefly. "And work out where I can find this trader. Tonight."

* * *

It was 6:37. Dupin was almost on time. And nervous. Why was Claire acting so mysterious?

He was already at the Place Laënnec that he liked so much, at the imposing cathedral. He would be there any moment now, at the corner of Rue de Kergariou and Rue du Sallé, a little cobblestoned street with quite a steep rise to it—hilly, medieval Quimper had a good number of them—with old houses in shades of pale beige, ochre, and gray that made the light glow in an atmospheric way.

Riwal had been reporting to him in great detail for almost the entire journey.

The conversation between the policeman from Tobermory and Mackenzie's wife had ended up taking a long time; the policeman had had to stop a few times. Jane Mackenzie had been in a miserable, nervous state.

She definitely didn't know of her husband having any business ties to Brittany. Her husband had apparently spoken to her about the idea of getting into business with Cueff, but her impression was that this had remained vague. Most importantly, she had had no idea that her husband got in touch with Cueff last week or that he was considering this issue again at all. Mrs. Mackenzie didn't have much of an overview of the business or finances. She outlined the history of the farm for the policeman in broad brushstrokes, including various attempts and plans for expansion, along with the setbacks. Apparently it was indeed the great oyster death in 2008 that led to the sale of the other companies, combined with the poor economic situation. The Mackenzies' company had experienced many highs and lows. Her husband dreamed of building something big, and despite all of the adversity, never gave up. Ryan Mackenzie had told his wife he was going to drive to Glasgow and possibly stay overnight—and he really did have a meeting with his business partner that he had arranged three weeks ago. They had found an email in Mackenzie's outbox canceling it with no explanation. It must have happened in the days leading up to that: something in Ryan Mackenzie's life that made him—along with Smith—plan the fateful Brittany trip. Something that possibly began with the call from Smith.

According to Jane Mackenzie, Mr. Mackenzie was a "good man through and through." Riwal had noted several phrases and read them out: "introverted, honest, and had no enemies." She couldn't—it was always the same old story, Dupin had heard it often enough—for the life of her imagine that he would have been caught up in something bad. He had had trouble with alcohol when he was young, but not for a long time now. She had got to know him when he was thirty and she was twenty-two. Jane Mackenzie had confirmed again that Smith and her husband, as far as she knew, hadn't known each other well. That her husband had felt "somehow sorry" for him and gave him work now and again.

Dupin had wanted clarifications and more details, even asking questions as if Riwal were Jane Mackenzie. It had quickly descended into the ridiculous.

While one policeman spoke to Jane Mackenzie, two of his colleagues had paid a visit to the farm. The employees were completely in the dark about Mackenzie's trip to Brittany, and also had no idea what their boss might have wanted in Port Belon; they didn't even know about Cueff. What was also significant was that they were sure the farm had never done business with the Belon, or with any farm in Brittany, for that matter.

A different topic had been more productive. The Scots were quick: they already had all of Mackenzie's phone records from the last six months. From his landline and mobile. Almost entirely local calls and some to Glasgow too, to Oyster Heaven. No calls to France or Brittany, apart from the one to Cueff the previous Wednesday at four thirty (matching up with Cueff's statement). Almost four minutes long. What was interesting was this: nine records of calls between Mackenzie and Smith, whose prepaid mobile they had also examined already. A call from Mackenzie three weeks before Christmas, then not again till the Tuesday of the week before last: half an hour, in the morning, an outgoing call from Smith followed by two more in the early evening of the same day, eight and fifteen minutes long, this time outgoing from Mackenzie. Then a call every few days, always around three o'clock in the afternoon, and two calls on the day before their trip, on Monday of this week. As if something had begun two weeks ago, that's what it looked like—but what?

Dupin had reached the corner of Rue de Kergariou and Rue du Sallé some time before.

But Claire was not there yet.

He looked around. Maybe she was in one of the shops. Some of Claire's favorite shops were here in the narrow streets on the slope. The one with the kitchen towels, tablecloths, and pottery in every color under the sun; the bustling shop with the wonderfully silly knickknacks, objects that were made from other second-hand objects. A little bit farther up you came to the venerable *lycée,* the medieval city walls, enchanted gardens laid out in an interlocking pattern and labyrinthine paths. You could see it here: Quimper in its atmospheric, majestic beauty, its old charm.

Just before Quimper, right after the long phone call with Riwal, Nolwenn had called. They hadn't been able to talk for long. Dupin was deeply relieved: she was on her way back to the commissariat.

She had given a brief update on Kadeg. Internal affairs had finished the inspection of the sites and also the sand deposits misappropriated by Kadeg. There were endless statements to write now. But then it would all be over. Nolwenn had learned in a call from the prefect that two men from Lorient's "sand theft" special task force had been present for the inspection. And had apparently found everything "highly interesting." The prefect had been in a very good mood. And had ordered that all information about these "unspeakable goings-on" be systematically pooled and that they now officially include Kadeg in the operation in order to deal a "devastating blow" to "these sorts of environmental villains" as soon as possible. It was ridiculous. But it made Dupin smile—the special unit would have some fun with Kadeg.

There was still no sign of Claire. The commissaire—whose agitation was worsening by the minute—was walking restlessly to and fro.

He was now standing in front of the display window of the knife shop he liked so much. The one with hundreds of hand-crafted pocketknives from the Cévennes villages that he had visited as a child with his father. Laguiole, Thiers, Perceval. Mythical names. Knives that you owned for a lifetime, that you inherited, from generation to generation. The way he had inherited his father's little collection, fourteen completely different knives that his father had selected over the decades: with handles made of walnut, juniper, olive, cherry wood, ironwood, ash, oak, and beech. They had seemed magical to him as a child. They had decorations, symbols, and names like magic wands: Gwarlan, North Wind; or Aile de Pigeon, Pigeon Wing. Dupin had started to expand the little collection one day. He did so here too occasionally, in this shop, but mainly in the excellent fishing shop next to the Amiral, which carried an impressive collection and whose owner he liked very much.

* * *

"Georges! Over here!" a familiar voice suddenly cried out behind him.

Claire sounded absolutely euphoric.

She took his arm in greeting and pulled him with her.

"You're not going to believe it." She headed up the road with him, toward the shop with the strange objects.

Shortly before the shop, she turned left—into the small shop with the pottery.

"Choose one. The one you like the best."

They were standing in front of an impressive shelf of bowls, little dishes in all kinds of shapes, sizes, and Atlantic colors.

Dupin was dying to know what was going on. What was Claire doing here? On a normal Wednesday, a working day, in Quimper. She clearly hadn't just got here, she didn't have any luggage with her, nothing. What was wrong?

"When did you arrive, Claire? Have you taken a little time off?"

"Choose a bowl, Georges, go on."

She was being serious. He knew Claire. He wouldn't find out anything until he had chosen a bowl. And until she felt the moment had come to tell him.

His eyes roved along the shelf and came to rest on a classic, quite small bowl: opal blue with a beigey white on the inside.

Claire picked a warm orange one.

"They go perfectly together," she declared.

She took his bowl out of his hand, went to the cash register, and paid. Soon, they were back outside.

"A little bit farther." She pulled him on up the street, as impatient as before. "Any minute now, Georges, you'll see."

Suddenly, Claire stopped in front of one of the old houses. A particularly beautiful one in a light yellow with pale granite stones on the sides and around the windows. She rummaged in her handbag. Then she walked toward the door. Dupin saw that she was holding a key in her hand. She opened the door and quickly went inside. She knew her way around. Dupin followed her.

They went up to the second floor. Then Claire fiddled about with the door to an apartment, pushed it open wide, and gestured to him to go in.

It was still not the time to ask questions yet—she would be the one to let him know what was going on here.

A little hallway, a room to the left with a view of the garden. An empty apartment. Pale, old oak parquet. A second room facing the front, flooded with powerful sunlight shining right inside.

Claire had gone into the second room. She opened the balcony door. On the narrow balcony there was a small, round marble table and two blue folding chairs with peeling varnish.

Claire took the two bowls out of the paper bag and one of those stylish silver thermos flasks out of her handbag. She opened it and poured something into the little dishes that Dupin instantly recognized by its aroma, *café au lait*. Then she sat down in the chair on the right and looked at him, completely relaxed now.

Still she didn't say anything.

Dupin sat down next to her, becoming more and more nervous by the minute. He looked around. The view was magnificent. Gorgeous old houses exuding tradition, soft colors, you could look up and down the Rue de Kergariou, see the bustle of people outside all the little shops; directly opposite, a rather wide alleyway revealed a view of the sky. Everything was wonderfully tranquil.

Claire took a mouthful of coffee, then carefully put the bowl down. A smile flitted across her lips.

"Welcome to my apartment."

She had said it perfectly matter-of-factly. With that typical smile that Dupin instantly fell for every time.

"I . . . Claire—What?" He was struggling with what her words meant. "You've . . . That's . . ." Dupin rarely stammered, but he did so now. "Claire, this is your apartment? *Your* apartment?"

"Since five o'clock today. It's more practical this way."

Claire always stayed with him when she came to Brittany; his apartment was big enough for both of them, even if Claire was staying for a few days. Weeks, if she wanted.

It was clear that this was—in Claire's opinion—a wonderful piece of news that she was revealing to him—although this wasn't yet evident from Dupin's reaction.

"You've rented this apartment? For yourself?"

They had already been over that much.

"As I say, it's much more practical!"

This sentence didn't help to clear up Dupin's confusion.

He took a big mouthful of the milky coffee—to hell with Garreg's ban.

"From here, I can get to the clinic in a few minutes. So I'll be on time in the mornings. As is appropriate for the head of cardiology."

Dupin stood up abruptly.

"You applied for a job here in Quimper, you looked for an apartment—you . . ." He waited a moment before he dared to say: "You're moving here, you're moving to Brittany!"

Claire had also stood up. "Well deduced, Monsieur le Commissaire."

This was absolutely crazy. Dupin could scarcely believe his luck.

Claire, the Normandy woman, the Parisian cardiologist, would become a Breton woman.

"I thought I'd just give it a try," she said firmly and clearly.

Dupin pulled her toward him and kissed her.

Claire loved to surprise him. She often did it. Although this time it was on a different scale. She hadn't even vaguely hinted that she was considering this kind of step. Never. But this was what she was like, he knew she was like this. And he loved her like this. She was never afraid of a big decision if it was about creating the life she imagined for herself. *We only have this one chance,* Claire always said, *it could always all go wrong. It's so easy to be afraid of that and leave things as they are. It's simple.*

This moment with Claire, on the balcony in the sun, a few meters above the hustle and bustle that seemed infinitely far away—this, Dupin realized, was definitely one of the happiest moments of his life.

"I saw the clinic's job listing two months ago, at the beginning of February." Claire's eyes sparkled. "I called the head of the clinic and then came for the first time a few days later. We agreed on everything three weeks ago. Then I signed. It all worked out perfectly, Georges. And I had a little bit of help."

This certainly explained Claire's recent behavior. That she had come in the middle of the week, citing altered shifts and rhythms in the Paris clinic. And also sentences like "I just want to see what everyday life is like here in Brittany" ought to have given him pause.

"I looked at the apartment last weekend," she said, and smiled.

Dupin's mobile rang, interrupting Claire in the middle of her story. With a reflexive movement, he took it out of his trouser pocket. This reminded him that Claire didn't know anything about the case—she didn't even know there was a case. He had almost forgotten it himself over the last few minutes.

Riwal.

Now was absolutely not a good time, of course. This moment with Claire was too important. And no doubt she had made plans for the evening.

Dupin answered.

"Yes?"

"We've got the car, boss. The rented C4 from Brest. It—"

Dupin was immediately focused. "Mackenzie? Is his body in the car?"

Claire's eyes widened.

"No. But we have the car anyway."

"Where?"

"On the secluded headland below Kerfany-les-Pins and Kerdoualen there's an old road that goes into the sea. Not far from the Plage de Trenez. Somebody let the car roll into the Atlantic there."

One of the countless coastal roads that went right into the sea so that boats could be launched.

"And no trace of a corpse?"

"No."

"Shit."

It was going to be crucial to get their hands on the corpse eventually.

"Other traces?"

Dupin gave Claire an apologetic glance and went inside.

"The windows are wound down, the doors are open. Somebody wanted to make sure that everything would be washed out of the car. It's very effective."

"How was the car found?"

Dupin walked on through the apartment. It really was beautiful.

"Two divers. On the hunt for crabs and spider crabs. The season has started." There was unalloyed joy in Riwal's voice, but then he switched back into his professional tone: "A skillful perpetrator."

"What do you mean?"

"That we're dealing with a competent perpetrator." No doubt all terms from that infuriating psychological training course on the "Perpetrator Profile" last year, thought Dupin. In the months that followed, Riwal had rather tested Dupin's patience with his "expert comments." "The perpetrator knows the area. And not only that. They knew how to sink a car and hence remove trace evidence. Perhaps they also dumped the body there at the same time; we're experiencing extreme tides at the moment, so the currents are brutal. If he did throw the corpse into the sea there, it will never come to the surface again."

Riwal's reasoning was plausible. If somebody in Port Belon wanted to dispose of a car and a corpse in the sea and knew their way around, they wouldn't start by driving around the Aven, through Pont-Aven, and back down again on the other side of the river. And they also would not drive farther along the coast toward Lorient, where it was difficult to get to the water. They would choose this exact headland. And another reason was that it was very secluded.

"But how did the perpetrator get away again?" Dupin wondered aloud. The perpetrator must have needed to get back to the parking lot where—possibly—his own car was parked. A dark or red one perhaps. "A lone perpetrator would have had to walk back. Or at least to a bus stop."

"Kerfany-les-Pins would be the nearest stop."

"Tell our colleague from Riec he is to see whether there was a bus that stopped in Kerfany at around five thirty in the evening—and if so, ask the bus driver if he remembers the passengers who got on there. There and wherever else the bus stops nearby."

"If there were two perpetrators, one of them could have driven in Mackenzie's rental car, the other in their own car. They could both have come back that way. And, someone who knows their way round that well probably wouldn't have taken the risk of a journey on a public bus."

"Have it looked into anyway!"

Any scenario or conclusion was possible; it was enough to make your head spin.

"Trenez, Kerfany—you know those are the beaches where Kadeg suspects sand theft," Riwal remarked in a deliberately offhand way.

This had completely slipped Dupin's mind.

"And?"

"That's all. It's an interesting coincidence."

Now and then Riwal could drive Dupin mad too. He just hoped that Riwal wasn't falling victim to this obsession too. The commissaire ignored this.

"Where exactly are you, boss?"

Dupin had rather gracefully avoided this question from his inspector during the phone call earlier on the journey to Quimper.

"I'm coming to Kerfany, Riwal. Wait for me there."

Dupin hung up.

And went back out onto the balcony. Claire hadn't moved. She was leaning back, her legs crossed, looking along the little alleyway. Relaxed.

"You've got to go, Georges. Nab the perpetrator," she said, and turned to him.

It hadn't sounded at all sarcastic, or angry either, Dupin realized with relief. Not even disappointed. She meant it exactly as she said it, he could see it in her eyes.

She stood up, gave him a kiss, and left the terrace. "I'm going to take a bit of a look around my new town. I definitely need some new furniture,

Georges. And I still need to drop into the clinic and discuss a few official things with the director."

Dupin suspected her working hours would no doubt be roughly as long as in Paris.

"And then I'll go and sit in the Amiral, okay? That's how it works here, isn't it?" Claire looked at him with her warm smile.

"Exactly. That's how it works." Dupin returned her smile.

"Just come when you're done. Then we'll have a drink together. And raise our glasses! I'll cancel the reservation here in Quimper."

"I won't be too late," Dupin said quickly.

His phone rang again.

"Has the car disappeared, Riwal? Or what's wrong?"

"See you in the Amiral later, Georges," Claire whispered to him, and vanished into the kitchen.

"Tordeux's house is on fire—his home, boss." Riwal was almost shouting. "The house is ablaze, nobody knows if Tordeux was inside or not. Kolenc's daughter called the fire brigade. She—"

"What?" Dupin was standing there thunderstruck.

"The fire brigade is on its way. Melen and I are already on the road too. Braz is staying at the site where they're salvaging the Citroën."

"Is there a police officer at the scene yet?"

"No. The call came in two minutes ago."

"Was it arson?"

"We don't know yet, boss."

"We need forensic fire experts. Immediately."

"I'm on it, boss."

"Where is Tordeux's house?"

"In the middle of the village. You can't miss it. It's on fire."

"I'm on my way, Riwal." Dupin had already left the apartment and was running down the stairs. "See you shortly."

* * *

His mind was racing.

The probability that at this point in time and in this place, this was an accident, a coincidental fire—that Tordeux had maybe just forgotten to turn off the oven—was low. But still. It urgently needed to be investigated. If it were arson, that would change everything. Up till now he had intuitively assumed it was a "finished" crime. A brutal crime with two people dead, yes, but one that was over with and now needed to be solved. Arson would mean that events—whatever they were—were still taking their course, and right under their noses too. And on top of that, the matter would be much more complex than assumed and would probably involve more participants.

* * *

There were four fire engines in the garden. Two squad cars were parked on the road down to the quay, which was completely cordoned off. Dupin had stopped directly behind them. Even from a distance he had been able to see smoke, grayish-white smoke shaped into a strangely slanting column by the wind that had picked up again.

It looked crazy—the front of the house appeared completely intact, there was no trace of a fire from the street.

"Boss, I'm here!"

Dupin followed Riwal's voice into the garden. There must have been a dozen firemen going about their work in expert order, no sign of a hectic rush or nerves.

Riwal was standing behind the big ladder truck. At the end of the extended ladder was a basket with two firefighters inside. They were each holding a hose. Magalie Melen was standing next to Riwal.

Although the wind was carrying the smoke away, the stench near the site of the fire was so acrid that Dupin's eyes immediately watered and hurt.

"It's the annex that's on fire. A wooden structure. Tordeux has his office there. The fire is under control now, they'll have it put out soon.

They were able to stop it spreading to the main house, also thanks to the strong—"

"What about Tordeux?" Dupin interrupted Riwal.

"We don't know yet. We're trying to reach him on all his numbers. He wasn't in the main house, that's already been searched. His car is not in the driveway and it's not down at the oyster beds either. Which probably means he wasn't here. It will be a while before the fire brigade can get into the burnt-out rooms."

"Has everyone been informed that we're searching for him?"

"Everyone here in Port Belon is aware. We've passed it on to the radio station—and that he is to contact the gendarmerie in Riec immediately."

"What are the firefighters saying? Where did the fire start?"

"The fire chief has seen indications that it might have started at the outer wall onto the garden," Magalie Melen reported calmly and coolly. "But he can't say any more yet."

Dupin walked around the annex in a large arc, Melen and Riwal following him.

"First of all, we need to know if Tordeux was inside. Arson attacks with murderous intent generally take place late at night while people are sleeping, and not in the early evening, but there could obviously have been an argument and Tordeux was lying injured or unconscious in his office." Dupin had tried to go through all the scenarios on his journey. He was feeling uneasy.

"Where are the specialists?"

"On their way. It will be a while before they can get to work anyway."

Dupin went closer to the annex. Everything was charred. At the corner where they were standing, the annex's pointed Breton slate roof had caved in and there was a gaping hole two or three meters wide.

"They've already tried to look inside from the ladder." Riwal had guessed what Dupin was thinking. "They couldn't make out anything."

The commissaire turned to Magalie Melen. "Do we know of any friends? Family?"

"He has an ex-wife . . ."

"So I've heard, the trader."

"He has a steady stream of girlfriends, a woman from Saint-Malo at the moment, apparently. His best friend is . . ."

"Pierre Delsard, the building contractor."

"That's right. Although Delsard is much younger than him. Delsard is also uncontactable."

Dupin pricked up his ears. "Is that not odd?" he asked.

"Not really," Melen said drily. "He could be at a dinner and have his phone off. Or he has no reception. There are lots of places in Brittany with no reception."

Who was she telling.

"No wife, family?"

"A bachelor like Tordeux."

Dupin took a few steps to one side, stopped, and ran a hand through his hair. "This was his office? And the first floor of the little white building by the oyster beds, what did he do there?"

"Met his business partners, did presentations, and so on," Melen reported. "The ground floor is used by the oyster bed workers. But this is where he has his business computer, data, and papers for all of his companies. His business headquarters, in a way. He gets administrative help on Mondays and Fridays."

"If Tordeux doesn't turn up soon, we'll get a search warrant."

"Good idea, Riwal. You take care of that."

Dupin reflected. "We need to find out as much as possible about Tordeux, so use every source of information you can."

"If Tordeux is mixed up in Mackenzie's murder"—Riwal was speaking a little like he was in a trance—"or is mixed up in any criminal activities at all, he could even have set the fire himself in order to destroy evidence." This was a plausible assumption too; it was definitely one of the possible scenarios. "I would—"

"Tordeux! He's on the phone." A young policeman whom Dupin didn't know came running up to them, stopping just in front of the commissaire. "Commissaire, I mean, Tordeux is on the line. From Saint-Brieuc. He's having dinner there. He—"

"Give him to me!"

Dupin took the phone. "Monsieur Tordeux?"

"In person and speaking. I'm not lying charred in my office at all!"

Dupin was furious that his quick-wittedness deserted him at this exact moment.

"What—"

"Your colleague informed me that my house's annex is on fire," Tordeux said in the same seamless switch from odd humor to distinct businesslike coldness as this afternoon.

"That's right. A major fire."

"Your colleague said the fire was under control, almost extinguished already. I really owe the fire brigade my deepest thanks." The incident didn't seem to have made too much of an impression on him: no horror, no fear; he seemed relatively calm. "I will—"

"Monsieur Tordeux, your office is completely burnt out, are you aware of that?" Dupin interrupted him gruffly.

"The main thing is that nobody was hurt. This kind of thing happens. I hear everything is all right at the main building, *that* would have been truly unpleasant. It's just my office in the annex. The computers can be replaced, and almost all of the data is in the cloud anyway. It would have been much more difficult for my businesses if the fire had got my little building at the oyster beds."

Either it really didn't bother him or he was pretending. And if so, he was pretending perfectly. Or, even more devious than that, he knew that the commissaire wouldn't fall for his calmness—and he was pointedly putting it on. Perhaps it was even a self-confident declaration of superiority. "I've been considering renovating the office from the ground up for several years so that I can have guests there too; it was all very old."

"How might the fire have started, Monsieur Tordeux?" Dupin was equally pointed in switching into a detached tone.

"Maybe the kettle in my office short-circuited. Or it was the computer, one of the many cables, the WLAN router has been faulty for months. It's ancient."

"Did you go directly to your house after the visit from the restaurateur, and then set out for dinner from there?"

"That's exactly what I did!"

"When exactly did you leave?"

"Around five thirty."

Dupin didn't respond.

"I'll be on my way soon, Commissaire. And we can talk more at the scene later."

"You're to leave straightaway, Monsieur Tordeux."

"Is it normal to haul the unfortunate victim over the coals in Paris? The person who has been affected?"

"I'll be expecting you immediately. What exactly are you doing in Saint-Brieuc?"

"A big meeting for restaurateurs, I was invited."

"Have you met a Monsieur Cueff from Cancale there?" Saint-Brieuc was in the north, not too far from Cancale.

"Never heard of him."

"As I say: I'll be expecting you." With these words, Dupin hung up.

Tordeux's behavior was sheer mockery. It doubled or tripled Dupin's suspicion that he'd set the fire himself. Which he must have known, he was so shrewd. But then that prompted the question: what was he trying to achieve by it?

If there had been any data or potential evidence linking him to something, whatever it was, it could be permanently destroyed now. Or did he just want to confuse Dupin with his behavior? Unusual behavior might be the best protection. Dupin's instinct told him Tordeux was capable of anything.

"What did Tordeux say, boss?"

Riwal and Melen had joined him.

Dupin repeated it succinctly.

"I want you to investigate this man thoroughly. And I want to know what everyone in this village was doing between, let's say, six thirty and seven thirty this evening, where they were, who they were with, and so on. No exceptions. And I want to know who Tordeux has feuds with. And what his relationship with this building contractor is really like."

"Will do, boss! Are you aware that the restaurant above the Plage de Trenez, where they're salvaging the car right now, was burnt out two months ago? Down to its foundation walls. Under mysterious circumstances."

Dupin recalled the reports in the *Ouest-France* and *Le Télégramme*.

"Mysterious how?" he asked.

"It happened at night, around three o'clock in the morning. The way the fire spread, it actually looked like a fire accelerant. So, an arson attack. But strangely, no traces of a fire accelerant were found. Nothing."

"One of those attempted insurance scams, no doubt," Dupin replied.

"The owners are drastically underinsured. They wouldn't have wanted a fire."

"Do you see a connection to this incident, Riwal?"

Riwal's bad habit of suggesting sinister, vague connections, usually in delicate situations, but not openly saying them or drawing conclusions from them really drove Dupin mad. The ridiculous thing was that you could never dismiss them wholesale. Sometimes Riwal was actually right in his almost "prophetic" moments, although unfortunately you never knew when they were happening.

"I don't know." Riwal hesitated, then said: "What you should perhaps also bear in mind is this: the plot of land directly next door belongs to Pierre Delsard, the building contractor. Who, it seems, might in fact be mixed up in sand theft intrigues."

"And?"

This was all he needed.

"We should bear everything in mind," Riwal added calmly.

Which was of course correct in principle, although Dupin couldn't for the life of him see a connection between the two dead Scotsmen from the oyster world and the sand-thieving building contractor. Not even remotely . . .

Melen brought the conversation back to earth. "By the way, the forensic team has just arrived. It will be a little while until they can start their real work, but they're here!"

"Is there news from the salvaging? Should we go over there?" Dupin asked.

"Not long before you arrived, I spoke to Reglas on the phone."

"I want to hear everything. But not here."

* * *

"So, any new findings on the car? Clues on Mackenzie's corpse?"

Dupin, Riwal, and Melen had left Tordeux's land and were walking down the idyllic, ivy-lined path to the quay.

"Reglas was cursing like a fishwife when Melen and I had to leave 'just because of a fire.'"

"Findings?" Dupin ignored everything else.

"No. As I said, the doors of the Citroën were open. Sea, tides, and currents did a good job—everything was washed away. The forensics team still haven't found anything. No blood in the trunk, none on the front or back seats, no DNA."

"Has the car been secured?"

"A fire engine pulled it out of the sea using a rope winch with help from two coast guard divers. A spectacular operation. They'll take it away now."

While it was frustrating that they did not yet have the second corpse, the discovery of the rental car added something solid and conclusive to the current scenarios—or hypotheses, strictly speaking. The probability that Mackenzie had not been lying dead in the parking lot had been low before, but it was now dwindling to zero.

"Reglas is to keep us up to speed. Go on, what else is there?"

"Yesterday evening," Riwal got out his notebook, "a bus did in fact drive from Kerfany to Riec, via Moëlan-sur-Mer. At six twenty-five. That could fit timing-wise. Three people got on in Kerfany. Two young girls who probably wanted to go to Moëlan, and one woman."

Dupin stood up straight.

"What kind of woman? Did the bus driver know her?"

"No. He says he had never seen her before. She was also difficult to see. Quite a long blue jacket with a hood."

"Where did she get off the bus?"

"Riec."

It was approximately three kilometers from there to Port Belon. A stone's throw away.

"Did any of the other passengers know the woman?"

"We don't know yet."

"I want to know who this woman was. Find out."

"We will."

They had arrived at their command center, the tables outside the château.

"What about Tordeux's two business partners in Scotland?" Dupin got out his Clairefontaine and leafed through it. Riwal beat him to it:

"Smollet. A trader in Edinburgh. MacPhilly, a farmer in Dundee. The Scottish police have spoken to them both in depth. Both have stated they knew neither Mackenzie nor Smith. And that they have never had business ties with any other French firm. I also had the policeman from Tobermory speak to the staff in Mackenzie's farm specially. The upshot was the same: they were sure that Mackenzie didn't do business with Smollet or MacPhilly. Apart from Oyster Heaven in Glasgow, he only supplied local and regional caterers directly. Our colleagues have finished examining his books, by the way. In terms of imports, only the seed oysters are in fact recorded, and nothing on the export side."

They weren't making any progress this way.

"What about the oyster farmers in Riec?" Dupin said urgently. "The ones with potential business ties to Scotland? What do we know on that?"

Melen was responsible for this part: "Three connections to Scotland. That's it. Three farms in Riec—they refine oysters in the Belon for one Scottish farm each. The Scottish farms then sell them in their own country."

"Any links to Mackenzie? Or Smith?"

"We don't know of any right now, direct or indirect links, business links or personal ones. By the way, I've also got hold of the owner of the Château de Belon, who's in Agadir at the moment. Her farm has nothing to do with Scotland, and she doesn't know any Scottish people either."

Dupin's forehead was furrowed. "What if Jane Mackenzie is in fact part of this business herself, or is at least in the know or suspects something that she doesn't want to reveal? She could be lying to us through her teeth."

"That's right, boss. She could be feeding us a pack of lies. That's also why the Scottish police have had a few more conversations with people who knew Mackenzie. They've spoken to the mayor of Tobermory, two restaurateurs who bought oysters and seafood from him, a landlord, and an old school friend he occasionally went hiking with." Riwal cleared his throat. "It's the same story: nobody knew of any links to Brittany, not even the relationship with Cueff that has been proven to exist. None of them knew about a planned trip. Only the hiking friend and the landlord knew about the bar in Glasgow. Mackenzie didn't have many friends and acquaintances. And he clearly didn't reveal much about himself."

"Who owns the rest of the"—Dupin leafed through his notebook—"the Oyster Heaven bar? Has someone spoken to the other owner?"

"A man called Paul Phorb. They haven't been able to get hold of him yet. Forty-eight, from Glasgow, but lives in the Highlands."

"They haven't been able to get hold of him? Is the bar closed?"

"No. But he's not there. The two young people who work in the bar don't have a clue where he is."

"Has he disappeared?"

Dupin knew it probably didn't mean anything, but even so . . .

"They say he comes by every two or three days. That they generally don't know where he is."

"But they'll have his number and call him regularly."

"He's not answering. The police have only been trying for a few hours. I don't feel it's too suspicious yet."

Dupin thought about it. "Where are the three Scottish farms that have their oysters refined in the Belon?"

"One farm is on Loch Fyne." Melen had obviously expected this question, and replied straightaway. "It's on a very long fjord on the west coast, northwest of Glasgow, one of the few well-known oyster spots in Scotland. A large firm."

"Very similar conditions to the Belon," Riwal added. "The extreme tides are constantly bringing new plankton, as well as a mixture of saltwater and freshwater. Dolphins and basking sharks—"

"Riwal!"

"The second one is near Thurso, right up in the north, and one is in St. Andrews in the northwest," Melen concluded.

"Anything unusual about these three farms?"

"No. All reputable businesses."

"And that's it? No other business ties between the Belon and Scotland?"

"Just those. And of course sales via wholesalers and agents, but we definitely can't check all of those channels."

This wasn't much. And it made Tordeux's connections to Scotland even more relevant—theoretically—if they weren't dead ends like all the rest at the moment.

"There are plenty of links to England and Ireland," Riwal started again while Dupin steeled himself. "After France, Ireland is the second largest oyster producer in Europe. England is traditionally a great oyster nation too." Riwal's storytelling fever, there it was again. "Henry IV always ate four hundred oysters on feast days, before having other foods served. Even the ancient Celts enjoyed the ritual of oysters with their *uisge beatha*, the water of life. Or whisky, as we call it today."

Dupin had—unintentionally and carelessly—looked intrigued.

"These days they drink Black Velvet with the oysters"—Riwal's expression revealed undisguised disdain—"a mixture of Guinness and champagne. And they eat them wrapped in bacon and fried, they're called 'Angels on Horseback.'" He sighed. "But the British do produce wonderful oysters. Even the Romans sung their oysters' praises and transported them to Rome using glacial ice they fetched especially from the Alps for the purpose. Caesar loved oysters so much that he wanted to occupy the British Isle just because of them. He—"

Riwal broke off. He seemed to realize this was not the situation for such digressions.

Melen returned to the topic unfazed: "Incidentally, we have spoken to the trader, Madame Premel, on the phone to question her about potential contact with Mackenzie or Smith. You wanted to speak to her yourself too, we—"

"I will," Dupin said. He would in fact do that next.

The trader was the only important figure in Port Belon's oyster world he hadn't spoken to yet, and this was all the more urgent now, after the attack on Tordeux.

But what Dupin already suspected was this: nobody was going to tell them the story of why Mackenzie and Smith had come all this way. Either because nobody knew it or because nobody wanted to tell it.

"Any update on the blight creeping up the coast?" He couldn't stop thinking about this issue.

"They've discovered the first cases just off the Golfe du Morbihan."

Dupin considered that rather close. He didn't understand how Riwal could remain so calm about this. Apparently everyone here could.

"Our colleague Braz," Riwal said, "has contacted the authorities especially. So that they let us know immediately if there are any new developments."

"Any other updates?"

"Mackenzie didn't just confine himself to European oysters. His farm produces both kinds: *creuses* and *plates*. You wanted to know that."

Dupin nodded.

"And our colleague from Cancale who was at Cueff's house has been in touch."

Riwal summarized the relevant details. It all matched with what Cueff had told Dupin. And also with the alibi statements. Including the fact that—although Cueff had had a chance to think about it some more—nobody could attest that he had been at home yesterday before seven thirty. A neighbor, a caller, anyone.

"Our colleague knows some people in the oyster world. He is going to keep asking around about Cueff."

"Do we know where Cueff is this evening?"

"Our colleague visited him in his oyster beds and left three-quarters of an hour ago."

"Okay. What about Tordeux's *gîte*? And his story about the key and the guests?"

"I've checked," Melen said. "They're a couple. Their statements correspond exactly with those of Tordeux—he handed the key over to them."

Which didn't mean much, of course. Tordeux could have been clever in timing his journey to the *gîte*.

"Good."

In fact nothing at all was good.

Frankly, all of their findings so far were making everything seem even stranger. Every damned lousy detail of this business that they even knew was still a puzzle right now. Dupin was certain that if he had had caffeine in his bloodstream, they would have made much more progress by now.

"How long will it take Tordeux to get back from Saint-Brieuc?"

"Depending on how soon he actually leaves, roughly an hour and a half."

"Call me as soon as he gets here. I'm going to speak to Madame Premel now."

Dupin turned to leave.

"She was going to be in the oyster beds until half past six," Melen said. "I got hold of her there, then she was going to drive to a meeting of her guild. That goes on till sunset. Not—"

"Guild? A druidic meeting?" a perplexed Dupin interrupted. Surely this couldn't be.

If Melen found druidic meetings odd, she didn't let it show. "Not far from here. If you take the road from the headland to Riec. In the wood beyond the bridge, the Pont de Guilly, where the Belon is still a stream. A wild oak wood. There's an ancient spring there near a clearing. Otherwise you'll be able to find her at home later. In Riec. She lives there with her second husband and two daughters."

"Madame Premel, the oyster trader and ex-wife of Tordeux, is a druidess." Dupin said these words almost cheerfully. "Well, brilliant!"

He saw Riwal's clenched jaw.

Melen hastened to reply: "That's not at all unusual here. On the contrary. Druids—"

"What kind of association is this one that she belongs to?" asked Dupin.

"Bugel a tarzh-heol, BTH, Children of the Sunrise, not to be confused with the EBH, the Eurvezh a tarzh-heol, the Hour of Sunset, or the Bugel a derwenn, the Children of the Oak, the KAB." It was impossible to tell if Melen was aware how bizarre this sounded. "The BTH is a local druidic association, strongly committed to new humanism and tolerance. There are significant ideological differences between the groups."

"Riwal, what was the name of the association we talked about this afternoon?"

Smith's association was definitely not called that, it had nothing to do with "sunrise."

"Breudeuriezh Drouized, Barzhed hag Ovizion Breizh—the Gorsedd Breizh." Riwal had gone as white as a sheet, like he'd seen a ghost.

"The EBH is grouped under the Gorsedd Breizh, like many druidic societies," Melen carried on, "it—"

Dupin interrupted her: "Hang on, the trader is a member of the same druidic association as Smith?"

Finally a real link—albeit an odd one.

"I wouldn't say that. The Gorsedds of the various Celtic regions are umbrella organizations. Strictly speaking, she is only a druidess in a guild affiliated with the Gorsedd." Riwal was trying very hard for an unequivocal distinction that Dupin thought only partially clear.

"An association belonging to the Gorsedd," Melen countered in a friendly voice, "should actually be considered a clear declaration of beliefs. Especially since the committed patronage of the extremely liberal grand druid, Gwenc'hlan Le Scouëzec."

Dupin was feeling increasingly surprised, not just at these Breton names, but also at Melen's detailed knowledge.

"My father was a member of the Gorsedd," she proudly explained.

"This is all nonsense," Riwal said indignantly. "Smith had not been an active druid for years! So what would this be about?"

"I'll speak to Madame Premel straightaway," Dupin said with pointed cheerfulness. "We'll see if there are any specific druidic links there." He rubbed his left temple. "So what are the druids up to in the clearing this evening?"

"They are preparing for one of the eight druidic festivals of the Celtic year: Alban Eilir, which is on Saturday."

"What does that mean?" Dupin wanted to be prepared if he met a druidess.

"It means the Light of the Earth. The spring equinox. An important

Celtic date, the return of life." Melen was explaining everything with the utmost seriousness again. Even Riwal, who seemed to be recovering slowly, was clearly moved by it. But he didn't seem to want to cede this ground entirely to his young colleague:

"Easter and all Easter rituals date back to this Celtic pagan festival, including the Easter bunny and the eggs. Even the name goes back to the Goddess of Spring: Ostara. The hare is the ancient symbol of the Alban Eilir. He guards the eggs. They worshiped it way back in Egypt and Babylonia. The egg is one of the most important mysteries in Druidism in general. The egg with life inside it—that the Easter bunny brings to people."

"Really?" Dupin sighed incredulously. He felt like he'd been transplanted into a Dan Brown thriller: secret societies, lodges, associations. And behind the most important festivals and symbols of Christianity lurked occult pagan rites and ceremonies.

"It's exactly like with Halloween! The whole world celebrates our ancient Celtic festivals without realizing!"

In the end, the punchline went, the whole world was Breton. Dupin knew this all too well by now. And it impressed him too, he had to admit. The Bretons had invented, discovered, and created the most incredible things.

"Last Saturday," Dupin mused, having just recalled it, "druids held a ceremony in the Monts d'Arrée, near the bog not far from the spot where Smith was found." The commissaire began to move, walking to and fro. "And Smith"—Dupin had remembered Melen talking about an oak wood, his words taking on a touch of unintentional drama—"lay dashed to pieces on a stone next to a single oak tree. The only one far and wide." It was admittedly a bizarre, coincidental detail, but the single, striking oak was vivid in Dupin's memory.

"Druids in Brittany hold lots of ceremonies in lots of places, there's nothing unusual about that either," Melen replied. "There will have been dozens of ceremonies last Saturday, it was Digor."

Riwal added, "A druidic event celebrated by all societies alike. Digor is a public festival, all non-druids are invited too. It's mainly about the bond between the six Celtic nations. One of the rituals centers around King Arthur's sword, which was broken into six pieces, representing the six regions. And also around the vow he made before his death: to come back, forge the pieces into *one* sword again, and restore the rule of justice, fraternity, and peace."

Dupin made an effort to return to reality, where this topic was just one investigative lead of several. Even where the druids were concerned, in the end it was about real relationships between real people. That was what they needed to focus on.

As if Melen had read Dupin's thoughts, she explained, "But to be honest, I also have no idea what kind of druidic business this could be either. There must be closer links. Direct links."

Riwal looked gratefully at the young policewoman, who, with these words and her certainty, instantly swept away everything occult hanging in the air.

"So—keep me up to speed. No matter what it's about." Dupin turned around firmly and strode up the road past Tordeux's house. The wind had died down a lot in the last few minutes.

When he got to his car, Claire came to mind. She had been standing with him on the balcony so recently and revealed her unbelievable news to him. Which seemed even more surreal than this puzzling case right now. Dupin longed for the end of this day, simply to make sure that it was all real, that she was really moving to Quimper.

* * *

The commissaire was sitting in the comfortable leather seat in his Citroën.

He needed to speak to Nolwenn again in more detail. Earlier she had—very briefly—only told him about Kadeg.

"I'm back at headquarters again, Monsieur le Commissaire!"

"So how was the funeral?"

The question sounded macabre.

Not to Nolwenn.

"There was a Kig Ha Farz Léonard, you know, the famous Breton stew with a bacon base and buckwheat dumplings, it was incredibly good." Her answer, in raptures over the food, sounded more macabre than his question, to Dupin's ears at least. "It was an extremely upbeat funeral. Everyone was there. The whole family, fifty-seven people. Plus lots of Elwen's friends and acquaintances. A real celebration."

Dupin still hadn't got used to Bretons' special approach to death: Ankou, or Death, the dark figure with the scythe, was omnipresent in the Breton consciousness, but without a trace of fatality, resignation to fate, or even a death wish. Because he was not banished from life, he was simply a part of it. There were literally thousands of stories about Ankou. Dupin's favorites were the ones about how he gave Bretons a little extra time before taking them away because he was close by. Time for them to put some important affairs in order. A Breton privilege. Which made death seem slightly less terrible to them.

Nolwenn's tone changed abruptly as she said the next words:

"What's the situation with the fire?" She was of course up to speed; she always was. "A diversionary tactic? Perhaps even by Tordeux himself? Or by someone else who wants to put you on the wrong track?"

This had crossed Dupin's mind too. It was a possibility.

"I don't know yet."

"One thing's for sure: so long as we don't know who the Scotsmen were in contact with, we won't make any progress, Monsieur le Commissaire! Do you have preliminary suspicions?"

As always, she knew where the weak spot was.

"No."

"Maybe you should grill this Monsieur Cueff in person. Really put him under pressure! *That* is a concrete connection to Brittany, even if it's not to Port Belon, but it's still a link to Brittany. Who knows whether he's hiding something after all."

It did him good to feel Nolwenn's determined energy, her absolute vigor, and her attitude of not putting up with anything. Dupin had got the feeling a few times already today that he was somehow letting himself be lulled into something. He couldn't even say exactly by what or how. He had not been obsessive enough about the search for the business at the center of all this. So all he did was dash breathlessly after the events. And yes, he would definitely speak to Cueff in person.

"Thanks, Nolwenn!"

"No problem."

"I meant, I . . ." Dupin hesitated. "It's good to have you back on board!" He meant this from the bottom of his heart.

"So Kadeg will be at your service again from tomorrow morning. I'll ask Riwal to get him up to speed later."

"Good." Dupin was overcome by extremely mixed emotions. It was going to be, he could already tell, unbearable. Now that Kadeg was officially part of the "sand-theft operation."

"And Claire has told you by now." This had not been a question.

"I . . . yes."

So Claire had had Nolwenn in on it; he really should have known. "With a little bit of help," was how she had put it earlier. In the moment, he simply hadn't got round to asking what she meant by that.

"A wonderful woman! By the way, Docteur Garreg has now accepted for your party on Friday after all. He said I'm to pass on a few things to you from him as a matter of urgency."

Dupin feared the worst.

"*Naturally* he assumes that you're sticking to the strict caffeine ban even during your case, especially in stressful situations."

Dupin made to reply but Nolwenn didn't give him a chance.

"And seeing as you're now going to be spending time in Port Belon anyway, in the heart of *ostréiculture*, he firmly recommends a medicinal oyster regimen."

"An oyster regimen?"

That beat all of the recent insanity. The stupid thing was, Docteur Garreg was probably the only person who could really make Dupin feel fear. Fear, a bad conscience, guilt. He always felt like a schoolboy sitting opposite him at the doctor's office.

"He is well aware that you don't eat oysters." Not eating oysters was a flaw even for a Frenchman, but for a Breton?! "The docteur says that the little *plates* are perfectly suitable as oysters for beginners, and I fully agree with him on that. He recommends a regimen of thirty-six oysters, three sets of twelve, in the morning, afternoon, and evening. For a week." There wasn't a trace of sarcasm in Nolwenn's voice.

"Thirty-six a day?"

"Three sets of twelve!"

"And what for?"

"For your stomach."

"For my stomach?"

That was the very thing that rebelled at the thought of the oyster regimen. Dupin had heard a lot on the subject of oysters before, but this was new.

"Absolutely! For the stomach, but also to counter stress generally. To promote well-being! And yes, oysters are particularly effective in helping with acute and chronic inflammation of the stomach lining! That's due to, amongst other things, the powerful anti-inflammatory effect of the zinc. And oysters are the greatest source of zinc there is! Didn't you know that?"

"No."

"Wait." It took a moment; Dupin could hear Nolwenn typing. "Here, Docteur Garreg sent us some links, I'm quoting here: 'The essential trace element zinc plays a crucial role in a variety of metabolic reactions and processes in our bodies. For example, zinc is vital for growth, the skin, insulin storage, protein synthesis, sperm production, and particularly the immune system.' Now here's the most important bit for you: 'Zinc has a powerful antiviral effect and simultaneously improves the structure of the stomach lining, which impedes the attachment and penetration of viruses and bacteria'!"

"That sounds terrific, Nolwenn, but I've got other things to do right now." He was already near Moëlan-sur-Mer, halfway to his destination.

But Dupin's answer had, predictably, not been enough to draw a line under the subject.

"Oysters are medicinal powerhouses! Therapeutic miracles, Monsieur le Commissaire! Highly effective. The healthiest of all the foods known to science on our planet. Even in ancient times, oysters were used as medicine. A uniquely rich array of all of the most valuable nutrients and vitamins. Virtually no fat, virtually no carbohydrates, so perfect for dieting"—there had some been insinuation to her emphasis, Dupin felt—"and yet the most valuable proteins! All twenty amino acids that nature possesses."

Nolwenn broke off. And waited. Dupin would have to say something. It was the only way for him to put an end to it.

"Impressive." It sounded half-hearted.

"And we cannot forget the best bit of all: dopamine! The substance that means happiness. Oysters provide our brains with dopamine. They're intoxicating! That's what gave them the reputation as an aphrodisiac. Casanova devoured at least fifty oysters a day. The increased sperm production fits in with that."

"So they're good for the stomach then?"

Dupin absolutely did not want to have to think about Casanova's sperm production.

"Definitely!"

While they were on the topic of oysters and health, he was tempted to tell a few stories about friends who had eaten a single bad oyster and felt like they were going to die for days. In fact, he knew that many people had died from oysters. "It takes a daring man to eat an oyster," someone had said once. That was extremely apt, Dupin thought.

With the greatest sternness he could muster, he changed the subject.

"Nolwenn, have you ever heard of serious disputes between different druidic associations? Or within them?"

"Because of Smith?"

Nolwenn was instantly focused on the new subject.

"Yes. And because the oyster trader in Port Belon is also a druidess. Madame Premel. I'm just on my way to see her. Smith's and Premel's associations both belong to the Gorsedd."

"Druids are just people, and personal disputes definitely happen now and again. Do you suspect something specific?"

"Not as yet. It's still very vague. Perhaps just a coincidence."

"You definitely can't dismiss it out of hand."

Dupin thought so too.

He had reached the picturesque stone bridge that went over the Belon. On one side the river was a wildly meandering stream. On the other side, it turned into a fjord.

"I'll be there very soon, Nolwenn."

He would park his car here and look for the clearing in the wood on foot.

"Speak to you later then, Monsieur le Commissaire." Nolwenn hesitated. "I think you should take Docteur Garreg's orders very seriously. Think about it: oysters and us humans appeared on earth at the same time, more than two million years ago—*that* cannot be a coincidence!"

A moment later she had hung up.

Dupin took some deep breaths.

After the bridge, he had turned onto a path with another path branching off it. This went directly into the wood, more or less parallel to the Belon.

The sun had already drifted down a long way toward the horizon; it always went quickly at the end. The sky was split in half this evening: the translucent blue had turned into an even, warm yellow in the west, and it filled its whole domain, not the slightest trace of orange. The east, on the other hand, shimmered a granite gray. The earth and everything on it was part of the yellow world of the west. The yellow seldom revealed itself, and never in the summer. The sun itself, the burning ball, looked strangely white on these yellow evenings.

Dupin entered the wood.

It was much darker than he had expected. And much wilder. Ancient oaks overgrown with pale green-and-beige moss. Broken branches, lianas, ivy, undergrowth, lichens. Junglelike. He needed to keep an eye out for the clearing.

Dupin had worked his way deeper into the wood and turned right onto a smaller path that sloped gently upward. He usually had an excellent sense of direction. He had been in the scouts as a boy, but for some reason, he realized, he was in danger of getting lost here. Wherever you looked, things looked exactly the same and thus, in a sinister way, perpetually familiar; as if you had always been here or were walking in a circle. Seeing a patch of sky was rare.

What saved him was taking a look through the undergrowth at the stream. The oak trees seemed to be even denser now, overgrown in even more eccentric shapes; proper figures, ancient tree creatures covered in mistletoe. Dupin remembered that Docteur Garreg had prescribed him a mistletoe regimen last year, also for the stomach, a mistletoe tea regimen, one large mug three times a day. At first he hadn't been able to force the miracle regimen down, and by the end it had tasted delicious.

Suddenly it got brighter and brighter, and before he realized what was happening, the commissaire was standing in a large clearing, as abruptly as if the clearing had only just magically come into being for the first time. An idyllic meadow that stretched over a hill, the fairy-tale stream to the right with its harmonious curves. The yellow of the sky had now given way to a surreally garish orangey-pinky-red, creating an overwhelming scene.

But the real spectacle was to be seen at the other end of the meadow.

It looked like there were white robes floating there, the infinitely long shadows of the trees seeming to stretch toward them. Around a dozen phantoms were gathered in a loose circle. A little stone structure in the middle—the old enclosed spring, Dupin guessed. Large flickering candles stood on the well.

It looked archaic. From a distance it wouldn't have been distinguishable, Dupin imagined, from an ancient scene.

He approached, hesitantly at first, but then with determined strides. He was on an investigation, druidic ceremonies or not. Besides, Madame Premel herself had said he should come by, it was just "a rehearsal," after all.

A man wearing a gold headband with sprigs of mistletoe wound around it, and who was clearly in charge, was reciting something loudly, solemnly, in measured tones. Dupin didn't understand a word. Breton, no doubt. And to complete the cliché, he had a long white beard. He was holding an elegant sword in both hands. There was actually a carved egg lying on the stone in front of him. A very large egg. The sacred Celtic Easter egg.

It wasn't just the man in charge; they were all wearing the long, wide, dazzlingly white robes, and some also had fluttering head coverings made from the same material and secured with embellished headbands. A little way beyond the druid—Dupin hadn't seen them at first—a man and woman stood in normal clothes. The man had bagpipes under his arm, the woman was holding a horn that tapered at the top. Two of the druids in the circle were holding a long, twisty wooden rod. Oak, Dupin presumed, the ritual tree. Dupin's feelings vacillated between slight unease, extreme amusement, and genuine respect.

He could tell that approximately half the group was made up of women. However, he had no idea what Madame Premel looked like.

Everyone was absorbed in the ceremony; nobody seemed to have noticed Dupin. He was just wondering whether to clear his throat loudly, ask clearly for Madame Premel, or just wait a little longer, when the woman in normal clothes blew her horn briefly but all the more bloodcurdlingly for that. It sounded like a wild, furious animal, although Dupin couldn't have said which animal.

"That's it. All set for Saturday! Have a good evening, everyone!"

These words had been uttered by the white-bearded chief druid, in an altogether ordinary tone of voice, an octave higher than the one he had used before.

A few curt good-byes here and there, then the head coverings were removed and suddenly the solemn group divided into several little chattering groups.

Still nobody seemed to take any notice of Dupin.

"I've got to pick up Arthur, he's at his grandparents' house."

"Pierre and I are going for a drink, take me as far as Riec."

Two women had walked right past Dupin.

The contrast was crazy. Within the space of a few seconds, the druidic meeting had taken on the atmosphere of the end of a choir camp, when the choir leader wound up the rehearsal with some nice words and this special, cheerful, but completely mundane merriment instantly broke out.

"Madame Premel?" By this point, Dupin had decided he would ask a question very clearly.

"Ah, the commissaire. Where's your car?"

Dupin flinched; the voice had come from directly behind him.

He turned around.

A slim woman wearing jeans, a sweatshirt, and rubber boots was standing in front of him, the sweatshirt a bright red, the boots apple green, nothing matched properly, and yet the look worked. She had one of the white robes tucked under her arm, long chestnut-brown hair, piercing dark green eyes, and an energetic expression on her face, determined, but interested, kind.

"We can talk on the way to the parking lot. I've still got to pick up a few things from our Riec branch and then go back to Port Belon. Or I could take you with me in my car and drop you off in Port Belon, we'd have more time that way. But you'll need your car, I guess."

She spoke at great speed. The radiant orange of the sky had disappeared by now, as if it had been theatrical lighting for the ceremony and the chief druid had simply turned it off after rehearsal.

"I'm down there, Madame Premel, toward the bridge."

"*Salut*, Nolwenn."

Dupin looked confused. The chief druid had walked past. He had his robe under his arm too and was wearing jeans with a casual dark shirt—the beard was real, but now, when you could see the precisely cropped hairs, it looked completely different, groomed, not at all druidic.

"*Salut*, Jean. I'll be dropping in to the bank tomorrow, transfers and that . . ."

"If you've parked down there"—she was talking to Dupin again—"you've had quite a walk through our enchanted wood. There's a little bridge over the stream up there," she gestured with her head, "that'll take you straight to a parking lot, just a few minutes from here." The words came pouring out of her. "I figure you've come directly from my ex-husband's burning office—from Port Belon you've got to turn off before the bridge, not after." Dupin didn't think she was even drawing breath. "I know how we'll do it: you come with me and I'll drive you to your car. Then we won't waste any time."

She had already marched off.

Dupin followed.

"And what strikes you about the fire, Madame Premel? Where were you this evening between half past six and seven?" The commissaire had no time to lose either.

His questions didn't seem to bother her in the slightest.

"I must have just left to get to this meeting at that point. I was a little late, it actually started at seven. We live right on the river, above our business. There's always something, you know how it is. And the fire, what strikes me about it? Luckily I haven't had anything to do with that man for a long time. I don't know. There must be lots of people who can't stand him, maybe even hate him, although he always pretends to be so friendly; he has to have enemies, no doubt about it. I haven't cared about him for a long time, but sometimes we argue nonetheless. At the association's meetings, for example. Some people will tell you about that, of course, I'm not going to kid myself. I can live with that. But frankly: if you want to find out about any current conflicts, I'm not the right person."

It had sounded like one long sentence—Dupin would have managed at most a quarter of the words in the same amount of time.

"That means that at the exact time the fire was set, you were near the scene. You wouldn't have had any trouble parking a distance away from the house and getting to the annex through the little wood and the garden. The whole thing would only have taken you a few minutes."

"That's exactly right. But why would I have done that?"

"Surely it infuriated you to have lost out to your ex-husband in the bidding war for the oyster farm near Fouesnant bay."

"At that price"—her tone and speed remained the same—"he'll be up to his neck in oysters there. He probably offered a million and a half and perhaps a little something else too; it's disgraceful. I would have done the deal if it had been a deal. For him it's all about expansion. I'll leave him to it."

She seemed totally above it all now.

"You think he paid a significantly inflated price?"

"Absolutely."

"And that . . . there was bribery involved?"

"I couldn't say. But"—she paused—"I think on that occasion, he really only did it through the price. In other cases I'm not so sure."

They had reached the bridge—a wooden footbridge—and the parking lot Madame Premel had mentioned was visible from here. Several cars were just leaving. They were the last ones left.

"Do you know a Ryan Mackenzie or a Seamus Smith? Do these names mean anything to you?"

"The 'Body in the Hell-Bog' and the 'Missing Man from the Belon.' The oyster trader. There are reports about them everywhere, it was on Bleu Breizh just on my way here. But you'll want to know whether I knew them before. Whether I did business with them. No." Even her walking pace was considerably fast—Dupin was struggling to follow her. "Of course you'll say I could just be saying that now. I could be lying to you."

She seemed to be having a serious think.

"Check my business records. Although obviously they could be incomplete or doctored too."

If it went on like this, she could do the investigative interview with herself, Dupin thought.

"Do you do business with Scotland, Madame Premel?"

"No."

"What farms do you get your oysters from?"

"Mainly from the two châteaux in Port Belon. And from farmers in Riec, but only smaller quantities. Are you trying to retrace a web of relationships? That'll be a lot of work."

They had reached the parking lot. Madame Premel walked over to a white Renault van with dents and scratches on every side.

"Does anything come to mind when you think about the events—about the 'Missing Man from the Belon'?"

"There must have been some kind of fight. Someone in the oyster world knows them both, or one of them. There are endless possibilities, but it could also be purely personal. If so, it'll be extremely difficult to find it."

She had opened the car and got in as quick as a flash. She was waiting for Dupin, who had almost reached the door.

"So you don't have something specific in the . . . oyster world . . . in mind?"

"No."

Dupin got in too. The engine started at the same time.

"And in the druidic world?" Dupin left it deliberately vague.

"In the druidic world? You're interested in that?"

"The man who was the 'Body in the Hell-Bog' belonged to the Scottish Gorsedd."

"I'm glad. The Breton and Scottish associations are close. Maybe we even met at an Interceltic meeting sometime. Who knows? I don't always make it to them. The business, family . . . Maybe that was why the Scotsmen came to Brittany. We do have the traditional preparatory meeting for the big Festival Interceltique in Lorient now, in the run-up to Easter. The preparatory meeting takes place in Riec. There will be some Scottish people there. Especially since Scotland is the host nation this year."

Neither the stones flying up on all sides nor the deep potholes made Premel brake.

"Right now? Here in Riec?"

"One of these days now, yes, in Riec. Brittany's first Interceltic festival took place *here* in 1927; the festival in Lorient wasn't founded until the seventies. As early as 1927, a hundred and fifty delegates came here from the other Celtic nations, and from Scotland too. Including bagpipe bands and druids."

"And Scotland is the host nation?"

"That's been agreed for a year, everyone wrote about it!"

Although it could probably be ruled out that Mackenzie and Smith came as "delegates" to prepare the big festival, it was interesting nonetheless. In any case, this established a direct link between Scotland and the Belon. In these exact weeks. It didn't need to be about the festival itself, it could simply have been the outward reason for something else.

"So Riec is a kind of center for Intercelticism?"

"Absolutely. There are countless Celtic and Interceltic activities here. They love Intercelticism on the Belon! Even my ex-husband."

"What do you mean by that?"

"When he was younger, he belonged to a Celtic sports team. His specialty was 'Stone of Manhood' where you have to lift heavy boulders onto a pedestal. And he's one of the members of the preparatory meeting for the festival in Riec; he sponsors it too. The festival in Lorient, I mean."

"Your ex-husband is a festival sponsor?"

The festival was the biggest of its kind. Ten days, almost a million visitors from every Celtic corner of Europe. A grand festival. With live concerts. But also theater, readings, and talks.

"Yes, Matthieu likes to act generous, to the outside world. His partner, that building contractor, is involved too. They exploit the festival as an advertising space and networking forum."

"Pierre Delsard?"

His name was coming up more and more often.

"Yes."

"Did he go into business with your ex-husband? Do the two of them have a deal going?"

"I'm the last person who would know about that one too. But my ex really always wants to be the greatest all by himself."

"Does your group have direct links to Scotland? The group itself, I mean, not the umbrella organization?"

"Oh yes. A few. Links to several groups. Also to one on the west coast where the two dead Scotsmen apparently come from. The Ring of Dawn. In Tarbert. The other groups come from the north and the Highlands."

They turned onto the main road at quite a speed. The bridge was to the right, and the turnoff Dupin had taken was beyond it. They would be at his car in a minute.

"And were there or are there any tensions or disputes between your group and the one from Tarbert? Has anything happened there?"

"No. They're meetings of friendship. Of course I don't know what personal matters there might be. They are also meetings of love, of course," she said with complete sincerity. "Now you'll definitely want to know whether I am personally in touch with someone in this group? No. I wasn't on the trip over there. Or on any of the trips to Scotland. And the members of the Ring of Dawn haven't come here yet. That's as much as I have to tell you. Does that help?"

The question was meant to show in a friendly but unmistakable way that the conversation, from Madame Premel's point of view, would soon be over. Dupin was sure it had been the swiftest investigative interview of his whole career.

"How long have you been doing this?"

"How long have I been a member of this group? Five or six years. Not that long."

Smith was not an active druid by then. Madame Premel carried right on: "I presume that people aren't familiar with things like this in Paris. You probably harbor lots of prejudices."

Dupin ignored her little dig. "And the oyster farm?"

"I took over the business from my father, twenty years ago now. I've helped out ever since I was little, forever."

"Why did your marriage break down, Madame Premel?"

"I ended it." Premel didn't seem to have any issue with this question. "There came a point when I realized that Matthieu didn't want me, he wanted my father's business. It was that simple."

Dupin couldn't detect any bitterness in her voice.

They had reached his Citroën. Madame Premel drove up to it without reducing her speed, braking hard only at the last moment. They stopped right next to the car.

"What were you doing late yesterday afternoon, Madame Premel, around four thirty or five?"

"The 'Missing Man from the Belon,' I see. I was at the farm—it's high season for oysters now, in the run-up to Easter. It's a madhouse. That's why there's a night shift in the shipping department today."

"You probably weren't alone at the farm, someone saw you? Your colleagues?"

Madame Premel had started up the engine again and was stepping lightly on the gas from time to time.

"There are six of us working at the moment. In several shifts. I was also upstairs in the office part of the time. I won't have been seen there. But downstairs I was."

"What do you think about the blight, Madame Premel? Will it reach the Belon?"

"We'll see."

For the first time Madame Premel seemed impatient; all of her body language signaled: *Now get out, I need to go.*

Dupin opened the door. "Thank you so much."

"No problem."

The commissaire was just out of the car when Madame Premel drove away. He managed to slam the door shut at the last second.

A moment later there was nothing but a sluggish cloud of dust hovering above the parking lot. The sun had set, the last of the light would fade soon.

Dupin rubbed his eyes.

* * *

He had seen them all now, spoken to them all.

Everyone who was involved with oysters in Port Belon. The two farmers and the trader—Kolenc, Tordeux, and Madame Premel. The lady from the Château was the only one he hadn't seen, because she was on holiday in Morocco with her whole family. And he had also spoken to the only person in Brittany who it could be proved knew Mackenzie. And he had also made the acquaintance of the wonderfully insane Madame Bandol.

Dupin propped his hands on the hood of his car, and he stayed standing like this for a while, leaning forward, his forehead in deep furrows.

He was far from satisfied.

What continued to drive him crazy was that he didn't have direct access to the people associated with Mackenzie and Smith. His Scottish colleagues were doing flawless work, but that didn't alter the fact that Dupin was only investigating indirectly. What's more, there was no one person amongst their Scottish colleagues who was in charge, constantly poking about, even on the off chance, someone who clung to leads independently, ran around, looked around, spoke to this person and that person, to acquaintances and friends. But that's exactly what was needed.

Dupin looked at his watch. It had just crossed his mind to drop in on Madame Bandol in La Coquille after all. It would be interesting to hear what she said about the fire. Most importantly: he needed to return to the beginning of the case. To where and how everything had started. And that still meant Madame Bandol, or more specifically, her tricky, wonderful memory that might have new things in store at any moment. Then he would have the conversation with Tordeux—and finally he would drive straight to the Amiral. To Claire.

Dupin climbed into his car, started the engine, and stepped on the accelerator. No less forcefully than the druidess had done earlier.

In less than ten minutes, he was walking into La Coquille. It was full down to the last chair. It was incredibly cozy.

Madame Bandol had spotted him immediately and was waving as if she had been waiting for him, certain that he would be coming after all. Dupin greeted the lady behind the bar, who was keeping an eagle eye on the door. He slid along the counter and a moment later was standing in front of Madame Bandol. A sleepy Zizou lay at her feet.

Madame Bandol got straight to the point: "It's all extremely odd. Now this mysterious fire too!" She looked him right in the eye. "Your excellent young policewoman has brought me up to speed, by which I mean: how things stood as of six o'clock today, when she canceled our dinner on your orders. I only know about the fire from the village, I haven't heard anything from you. The smoke was drifting straight toward me." A clear rebuke— and a clear demand.

Dupin told her about the developments that evening, what they knew about the fire (nothing at all), the salvaging and the car and the conversations (most of them). Madame Bandol listened attentively, her expression becoming increasingly concerned. Even though Dupin had made an effort to summarize everything in an optimistic way.

"But none of that makes sense." Madame Bandol shook her head.

"Everything that matters is missing. *What* did the Scotsmen want to do here? Why this sudden fire? *What* is the story behind all of this? We basically don't know anything at all yet, the investigation is in a wretched state, Monsieur le Commissaire. We're running out of time." Her voice vacillated between concern, reproach, and something resembling encouragement and solidarity. "The probability that a crime will be solved decreases with every hour and every day that elapses from the time the crime is committed. Isn't that right? Hercule Poirot says that!"

Madame Bandol looked out the window at the Belon. Staring at something. On one of the fishing boats. Dupin couldn't tell what.

"Poirot, now he is a great investigator. You could learn from him!"

Dupin smiled. He wasn't offended. He himself deeply admired Poirot.

"Who might have been angry at Tordeux, Madame Bandol?"

"It doesn't have to have been overt anger. The guy isn't very popular here anyway—my friend Baptiste Kolenc is sick of that show-off. You should ask him. I don't really know Tordeux. And"—her voice turned cautionary again—"and anyway, who exactly is telling you that Tordeux is not the murderer himself and just trying to divert attention? It would be a smart move."

"Why is your friend Baptiste Kolenc 'sick' of this Tordeux?"

"He says he's violating the spirit of *ostréiculture*."

"Anything more tangible than that?"

"I don't know of anything. Ask him!"

"And Tordeux and his ex-wife?"

"Ha! She has long since forgotten him! A strong woman. She lives her life and doesn't care what people say."

Jacqueline came to the table with Madame Bandol's order, Saint-Jacques à la Bretonne. Dupin's mouth was watering. That had probably been his first ever contact with Brittany when he was a child: large pieces of fresh scallop with cream and fine bread crumbs on a large half shell. He realized he was slightly dizzy. He hadn't eaten anything since the baguette in the Monts d'Arrée. And that felt like days ago.

"I'm eating a little late this evening. This is the earliest I could manage. Have something to eat with me, don't be rude."

"I have to disappoint you, I'm afraid. I have another appointment later."

Surprisingly, Madame Bandol acted satisfied with this vague information, merely raising her eyebrows.

"If only I could remember more details about the car from the parking lot." She changed subjects as quickly as Dupin did. "That would help us so much," she said, and closed her eyes for a moment, and then shook her head theatrically. "I don't think more details are going to come to me. Too bad." She said it as if this were a scientific fact. "But since you just mentioned it, the car that you fished out of the water—I did see that."

Dupin started in astonishment.

"Sorry?"

"It came back to me as you were talking about it." She smiled. "Silver. A Citroën. Medium-sized. The car that you dragged out of the sea."

"You now recall that a silver Citroën was parked in the parking lot when you saw the dead body?" Dupin was dumbfounded. "You remember exactly? You're certain?"

"Yes! It was parked right at the end of the parking lot."

Dupin stared at Madame Bandol. A thought had crossed his mind as she was speaking, a crazy thought. But then again it was not that crazy. What if Madame Bandol could in fact remember quite a bit more than she was letting on? And was only coming out with what she knew bit by bit? What if it was a kind of game? For fun? This way she would be constantly included in the progress of the investigations.

"From the Glénan! Unbeatable!" Madame Bandol was eating a piece of scallop with relish. Then she went on. "This much is clear: Mackenzie very likely met somebody from Port Belon. Someone who is now denying it. One person or several. It seems highly unlikely that the

Scotsman suggested the meeting place if he had never been in the area before. Only the locals know that out-of-the-way parking lot. Even someone from Riec would have suggested a different place—one of the dark little woods at the end of the river, or maybe where you've just come from. No— it's someone from Port Belon."

As haphazardly as Madame Bandol's mind sometimes worked, she was going about this very methodically now. "Besides, so few cars are on the roads here outside of the season that you'd be taking a risk just by driving too far and being spotted on the way."

She let her words fade away and then added mysteriously, "Or that man from Cancale was here. As an oyster farmer, he would know Port Belon. Maybe he even has an accomplice."

She leaned back, took a sip of champagne, and her brow furrowed.

"In any case—we must get our feet on solid ground, Commissaire!"

Something else occurred to Dupin that he had wanted to ask at lunchtime.

"Why did you not take your usual route on your walk yesterday? Down by the river? Why did you leave the Belon before the cliffs and come up to the little road?"

She answered without the slightest surprise: "If it's raining as hard as it did yesterday, the path by the water gets muddy, you can easily slip. And that's when I prefer the other route. But I always walk as far as the headland, no weather stops me from doing that!"

It sounded logical.

"I need to go, Madame Bandol. Monsieur Tordeux is due to arrive any moment."

"Don't expect too much from that conversation, Commissaire."

"See you tomorrow. And you know to call me as soon as anything else occurs to you, no matter how insignificant it seems to you. No matter when."

"You can count on it."

Dupin stood up.

He was already at the bar when he turned around again and walked back to Madame Bandol.

She didn't look at all taken aback.

"Do you have," Dupin whispered conspiratorially and leaned over the table to her, "a specific hunch, Madame Bandol?" He left a brief pause. "Do you know who it was?"

For a split second there was a kind of confusion on her face, but then she burst out laughing.

"Well, you're the commissaire!"

"You don't have a particular hunch?"

"No, Monsieur le Commissaire."

"My inspectors also let me know if they have a suspicion. Everything stays within the team."

Madame Bandol gave Dupin a kind look. "I'll keep thinking. I promise."

"Great."

Dupin left the restaurant a moment later.

* * *

It was dark now. Very dark. The sky must have grown overcast, although there were no clouds visible; no crystalline glimmer from the sky anymore, no stars, no moon. Just an all-enveloping blackness.

It had become cooler too. The wind coming in off the sea had picked up again, several powerful squalls sweeping along the Belon. They blew fiercely through the village, making eerie sounds—near and far, high-pitched and low-pitched rattling, roaring, clattering, tapping, and rumbling. Neither the centuries-old oak trees nor the occasional houses could ward off the wind.

Dupin walked toward the quay and pulled his mobile out of his trouser pocket.

"Hello—hello, boss!"

Riwal came running up to him, frantic.

"Tordeux arrived five minutes ago. And we've got something!" He was standing right in front of Dupin now and left a dramatic pause. "Tordeux has a previous conviction! He was given a suspended sentence of three months. He pulled a nasty scam. He treated bigger, ordinary *creuses* from Holland with a green pigment and sold them as *fines de claire* and *spéciales de claire*."

This was a significant piece of news.

"When? Where?"

Riwal hesitated. "Nineteen years ago."

"Nineteen years ago? This happened nineteen years ago?!"

That was a hell of a long time ago.

"He still lived in Cancale at the time. He owned a little oyster farm there. With a bogus address in Marennes d'Oléron where *fines* and *spéciales* come from. He lived in Cancale, you see!"

"And?" Dupin didn't understand.

"Cueff! Nicolas Cueff. He lives in Cancale too."

"If I understand correctly, there are dozens of oyster traders in Cancale."

The oyster industry in Cancale was many times the size of the one on the Belon.

"So do we know of any link between Cueff and Tordeux?"

"Not yet, boss."

"And afterward—after these criminal activities of Tordeux's nineteen years ago—there was never another incident? Tordeux didn't do anything else wrong after that?"

"No. Not according to the police records," Riwal answered rather quietly. It was a little like with Smith's criminal past more than forty years before.

"When did Tordeux come to Port Belon?"

"Seventeen years ago. Two years after the incident."

"So he wanted to start over again here."

"Or he was planning to carry it off more skillfully this time." Riwal's words echoed darkly.

"How exactly did he go about his scam?" Dupin wanted to understand the principle behind it; maybe it could have been applied again.

"*Fines de claire* and *spéciales de claire* are excellent refined *creuses* from the Île de Oléron and the mainland across from it. They're reared in old salt ponds, they—"

"Salt ponds?"

Dupin was reminded of the case in the Guérande salt marshes the year before. He had already had his fill of criminal activities in salt ponds.

"Yes. With their special clay floors and algae, they produce the perfect nutrition for oysters. The unique thing there is an alga containing copper that has a green pigment that dyes the oysters. Which became their trademark."

"And they're particularly expensive?"

"Oh yes. The *fines* are allowed to live with a maximum of twenty other oysters per square meter during their final refinement. The *spéciales* can live with just ten—and that's for a minimum of two months! They're systematically fattened to increase the proportion of meat. Gillardeau has every single one of his oysters engraved with a laser!"

"Tordeux dyed cheap oysters green and sold them as fancy oysters?"

"Exactly."

He'd have a nice little topic of conversation if he met Tordeux soon.

"Where is he now?"

"In the little building by the oyster beds. You know the one."

Riwal and Dupin walked the remaining meters to the quay. From there they could get to the parks and Tordeux's little building.

"Did he go straight there?"

"He took a quick look at the annex. I was there. The fire has been put out, the forensic investigators have set to work very carefully."

"Has Tordeux said anything yet?"

"No."

"Good."

The news was highly significant. There was someone in Port Belon who had skeletons in his closet and had already attracted attention in the oyster world with his criminal intent. And he, of all people, he was the person who had been near the scene of the crime yesterday—even if the story about the *gîte* was true. And he was the person whose house had been on fire today. Perhaps Tordeux had really just "refined" his criminal behavior on the Belon.

But it could mean nothing. Dupin knew people who had truly changed. And others for whom that wasn't the case.

"Riwal!"

"Boss?" The inspector looked attentively at him.

"From now on, we're going to go about things differently," Dupin said emphatically. "Completely differently. We are going to grill people *in person*. It can't go on like this."

"All right, boss." Riwal was used to very determined announcements from the commissaire, but this one was extremely vague.

"You are going to take the first flight to Scotland tomorrow. And I'll drive to see Cueff, the man in Cancale, at the crack of dawn. Kadeg and Melen will hold down the fort in Port Belon. And Nolwenn will act as the central figure from the office."

"Scotland? Really? You mean I'm flying to Scotland by myself?"

"That's exactly what I mean."

"Tomorrow morning?"

"As early as possible. Call Nolwenn, she'll organize everything . . . including the formalities. And tell her that I'll be in touch tomorrow."

"Yes, okay. I'll fly to Scotland, boss. Just recently in the seminar"—there was enthusiasm in his voice now—"we talked about the famous alliance of Scottish and Breton soldiers in one of the numerous Anglo-French wars in the eighteenth century. On the battlefield, in the midst of a brutal attack by the British, Scottish soldiers recognized the Celtic language and immediately put down their weapons. Then they marched off with the Bretons. 'Les Frères d'Outre-Manche,'" Riwal said, almost affectionately.

"Riwal! This is not the time for stories. I'm going to speak to Tordeux now." Dupin turned to go. "Then I'll be in touch again."

"All right, boss."

The commissaire was pleased. This was the right decision. Long overdue. Riwal knew Dupin's way of investigating better than anyone else; he intuitively knew what would be important to Dupin. Accompanied by some precise instructions, it would almost be as if Dupin himself were in Scotland. He had considered that too: flying there himself. But who knew what else would happen here?

The door to Tordeux's house stood ajar, propped open by a wooden wedge on the ground. The fierce wind was catching on the door and making loud, strange whirring noises. The ground floor of the little building was lit by a single bare bulb, bright light falling down the steep steps from upstairs.

"Okay, then let's do it like that. Tomorrow morning, seven o'clock. *Bonne nuit.*" Tordeux's voice sounded very cheerful. But there was something domineering about it too.

Without making his presence known, Dupin walked up the stairs.

Tordeux was sitting on the sofa with his legs crossed. Dupin climbed the final steps and walked straight into the room. Tordeux had—of course—expected him.

"An appointment with my insurance rep." Not a word or gesture of greeting from Tordeux. "It was about the 'site visit.' The inspection of the fire. There has been a significant amount of damage."

Tordeux still seemed far from upset, but at least this last sentence had been fairly reasonable. He was wearing a stylish flannel suit, midnight blue with pale blue stripes, a shiny blue shirt, pants, his hair combed back with gel even more ostentatiously than this afternoon, a smug, self-assured expression on his face—as slippery as an eel.

"So—what can I do for you? What do the police want to know from me?"

Tordeux made no move to get up. Dupin picked up one of the white chairs, placing it unhurriedly in the center of the room and sitting down in a casual motion, his eyes fixed steadily on the man opposite him.

"Monsieur le Commissaire, don't tell me you're looking for a connection between the fire and the murders? What could that be?" There was a frank coquettishness on Tordeux's face.

"You could easily have set the fire yourself before your trip to Saint-Brieuc." Dupin ran a hand through his hair. "And you were in the vicinity of the scene of the crime yesterday at the time it was committed."

"Shrewd speculation, nothing more."

"People are saying that, unlike what you claimed, the building contractor Pierre Delsard did contribute to your purchase of the farm near Fouesnant. And perhaps to your investment in Cancale too?"

"Everyone is free to hallucinate as they please."

Dupin swiftly changed the subject. "From what I hear, you're an enthusiastic activist for Intercelticism? With various commitments."

"An old passion of mine. Our roots, our history, our identity." Tordeux was acting the passionate Breton now. "Is there something criminal about that? I also play the bombard now and again, by the way, less than I used to. A fantastic instrument. Very old, Celtic."

Riwal had demonstrated it once. A wind instrument, a kind of oboe. An extremely powerful sound.

"Were you also at the preparatory meeting for the festival this year?"

"Just two evenings."

"What was the focus of these two evenings?"

"Planning the schedule and logistics."

Dupin switched tack again. "What we are especially concerned with is this: What could your cunning trick here on the Belon be? Pigments aren't necessary here."

A smug smile spread across Tordeux's face. "So that's how it is. I see. Once a crook, always a crook. It's all old news, Monsieur le Commissaire, even if you're considering taking it out of the wastepaper basket." The smile remained on his lips.

Their sparring was taking place on a high level. Tordeux was quickwitted, Dupin had to give him that. And he knew that without solid circumstantial evidence, they would never be able to access his data.

"Thank you, Monsieur Tordeux. This has been an illuminating conversation."

Dupin stood up abruptly, turned around, and left. Undramatically. Without any haste. Without adding an afterthought, without some trick that Tordeux, judging by his expression, had been expecting.

"As I say, the offer stands: the best Belon oysters at special prices for your commissariat!" he called after him.

Dupin walked calmly down the steps. He covered the few meters of storeroom chaos, exited the door into the cold night air, and strode straight toward the quay. He didn't stop until he got there.

He was freezing. His jacket was in the car.

His instinct told him Tordeux had skeletons in his closet. Whatever they were and however many there might have been.

Dupin stopped again a few meters away from his car and listened carefully. Motionless. Then he stamped his feet several times, as noisily as possible. And listened again.

Nothing.

"Hello?" he called in a loud voice.

No response from anywhere.

No Toulouse goose.

Maybe Charlie had been lucky in love again.

* * *

On the tiny little streets of the peninsula, Dupin had been concentrating on not running over any of the countless rabbits—a challenge even during the day—and didn't call Riwal until he was on the main road from Riec to Pont-Aven. From there he would drive to Concarneau via Névez. Fifteen minutes at his speed.

Dupin had updated Riwal briefly. Melen had continued making inquiries. "We are too insignificant to Tordeux for him to have any conflict with us," Baptiste Kolenc had told her. There had been no talk of a suspicion that Tordeux was working in some "shady" way. Even if they all considered him ruthless where his interests and businesses were concerned. It was common knowledge that Tordeux and his ex-wife quarreled as soon as they saw each other, but nobody seemed to take it seriously. Melen had also tried to find out something about the possible joint business ventures between Tordeux and his friend the building contractor—which proved to be extremely difficult. There was a lot of speculation, but nothing solid—not even the mayor knew anything.

They still had not been able to track down the woman from the bus. Nobody seemed to have known her or recognized her.

The forensics team were continuing their work in the lab with some fabric samples from the car.

Riwal was excited, he was due to catch a plane the next morning at five forty-five. Nolwenn had organized everything. Dupin told Riwal to drive home and pack.

The phone call had lasted until shortly before he reached Concarneau.

Dupin had just driven past his usual gas station. He braked suddenly, turned around, and parked right in front of the entrance.

He was the only customer; they were about to close.

The woman at the cash register, the owner, greeted him with a sleepy nod.

"Not filling up. Just looking for something."

She looked curious now, but left him to it.

Dupin went into the "mini boutique" area and stood in front of the shelves of Breton souvenirs and specialties. The shelves were lovingly stocked: a wide selection of biscuits, other Breton baked goods, all kinds of salt mixtures from the Guérande, rillettes made from every seafood imaginable, miniature wooden boats with Breton flags, ceramic tea sets with flags on them, various clothes and textiles with Breton symbols, sweatshirts, T-shirts, aprons, and towels.

Dupin saw a dark blue T-shirt that said *À l'aise breizh*—which meant something like "In the Breton style"—one of the clothing brands that used Breton iconography. The brand had a shop next to the news-agent in Concarneau. The logo, a stylized drawing of a Breton woman in traditional costume, had become a patriotic statement. It was also used on bumper stickers that served as identifiers when traveling; in Holland, England, Spain, Germany, Italy, and France, you saw the logo on Breton cars and on cars belonging to Brittany's international friends.

Dupin chose a T-shirt in the appropriate size and went to the cash register.

"A really lovely design." The owner nodded appreciatively.

"And"—he had just seen something else next to the cash register—"and these."

Dupin had grabbed two breakfast boards in pretty wood. Presumably oak. With *Be breizh* written on them in Atlantic blue. "Be Breton." A magic spell, a sacred code. It meant everything: the unique Breton way of being—of seeing the world, things, people, life. And above all, the convic-tion that Brittany changed you, deep down inside. An elemental force. A promise. An attitude. That was exactly the right symbol for Claire's move.

The owner packed everything up into a blue paper bag and Dupin got into his car in a good mood.

He drove toward the Amiral—it was just a few minutes until he would see Claire.

* * *

Dupin parked where he always parked, directly opposite the restaurant, on the large quay in front of the local fishing harbor. The enormous fortress of the Ville Close was festively lit, the way it was every evening, the beautiful, angular church tower on the hill inside the old town walls looking particularly magnificent. Even the greenish-yellow fishing boat positioned in front of the old walls as part of the Musée de la Pêche glowed in the atmospheric lighting.

The chill and the salty wind from the west, from the open sea, had Concarneau in their grip. The fierce ringing of the little bells up on the masts of the sailing boats blended with the sound of the wind. Unlike on the secluded Belon, the little town's yellowish light illuminated the billowing, low-hanging clouds.

Dupin was glad he would soon be sitting in the Amiral—it was just as much his home as his own apartment was. He spent a significant proportion of his life there.

Claire would be sitting at his regular spot. At their soon-to-be joint regular spot.

Dupin hurried out of the parking lot between the plane trees, across the street, covered the last few meters, and threw open the door to the restaurant.

But his table was empty. No Claire. No glass, no plate, nothing. This couldn't be.

He looked at his mobile. No calls from Claire, no text messages.

"She tried to call you, Georges, but it was busy the whole time."

Paul Girard, the owner of the Amiral, was standing at the edge of the long bar. Dupin hadn't noticed him.

"It's going to be a late one tonight, I'm to tell you," he said in an offhand way, as always. "She was in the clinic and there was an emergency. Her new boss asked her to operate."

Claire had not even started working there and already she was in the thick of it.

"Thanks, Paul." Dupin sat down.

"Waiting?"

"No. No. Not waiting."

There were no two ways about it—he needed to eat something, and fast. The dizziness had got worse, although he was trying to ignore it. Besides, most likely nobody could have said, not even Claire herself, what exactly "It's going to be a late one" meant. Perhaps it would even be very late.

Paul disappeared without saying anything else. He didn't mention Claire or the obvious changes in Dupin's life. That was not his way.

Dupin leaned back.

He was confused. Exhausted. A little sad too. He had been so excited.

On the other hand, he was relieved because he had been afraid Claire would have been waiting for him for a long time. But what was even worse was this: Dupin had been worrying the whole time that Claire might have been disappointed by his behavior after her major news, although her reaction in the moment hadn't implied anything like that. "I'm leaving my life in Paris behind and I'm moving to be near you in Brittany, Georges." "Great, Claire, I've got lots to do and need to leave right now." That was genuinely more or less how it had gone. Claire had revealed perhaps the most important news of her life to him—and he'd had nothing better to do than continuing to investigate straightaway.

But then, and it didn't take long, a smile appeared on the commissaire's face. A smile that came from deep down inside and instantly banished his moodiness and gloom.

He had just realized something. And it was the crucial part: soon, this is how it would always be. Everyday life with Claire in Brittany. She would be living here with him. Which also meant doing a crazy amount of work, like in Paris, at the most ridiculous times. Just like he did himself.

Tonight, it wasn't a plan to meet like the ones they had made in the past, when Claire came to see him for a few days. The change was not still to come—it *had* already happened. There would no longer be a farewell after far too few days. They suddenly had a life together.

Dupin placed both his hands behind his head.

And for a while he just sat there.

"Voilà."

The entrecôte.

Paul had been quick. He put it down right in front of the commissaire. With the crispy homemade chips. Baguette in a little basket on the side. A bottle of wine. Two glasses.

It smelled heavenly: the aroma of seared, grilled meat, the toasted *fleur de sel* and *piment d'Espelette* on the crust; the outside crisp and dark, still *bleu* inside but in such a way that not a drop of blood flowed when you cut it. The hot mustard on the side. Nothing in the world did him as much good at the end of a grueling day of investigation as an entrecôte. Nothing else gave him so much strength. Dupin felt that nothing brought him back to earth quite like it. Along with the deep red, rich, silky Languedoc, Ivresse des Sens. Dupin loved it for the name alone: Intoxication of the Senses.

"Paul?"

"Yes?" His friend was back at the bar again.

"You and Henri, you source your oysters from the same producer, don't you?"

"Béa."

"Somewhere near Fouesnant, is that right?"

"In the large bay. Aux Viviers de Penfoulic. Oysters, *palourdes, praires,* cockles, crabs, spider crabs, sea snails." He broke off, then said calmly, "The oyster case. I see. You'll find Béa there every morning, half an hour before sunrise."

Without waiting for a response, Paul went into the kitchen.

Dupin began to eat.

He would go through his notebook later. An important ritual. How often had the solution to a case, the crucial clue, been there in his notebook for hours or days—he would reflect, summarize everything in peace, make a list for Riwal in Scotland.

That's what he would do. Until Claire came along at some point. The new head of cardiology in Quimper. It made him smile again. He was a lucky man. Commissaire Georges Dupin was a lucky man.

The Third Day

It was ten past seven and above the vast, desolate Atlantic in the west, beyond the very last jagged, storm-tossed, wave-lashed rocks of the old continent—the Pointe du Raz—the sky stretched, still as black as night. In the east it was getting very bright—the black there had given way to a shimmering, celestial, deep blue. A wafer-thin strip of lighter blue appeared above the horizon.

It was even colder and more unpleasant than last night. Now and again a shower pelted down with one of the brisk gusts of wind. The wind instantly woke you right up.

Dupin had fastened up the jacket that he really only wore in the winter months and put up the collar.

Béa was not there yet. The commissaire was walking up and down in front of the long Viviers de Penfoulic plant. Béa's mussel and oyster farm. A magical place. Not many meters from the bank of a large inlet that meandered inland. In the middle of the wide Baie de Concarneau, past La Forêt-Fouesnant. Beyond it lay the idyllic, hidden beaches of the Cap Coz in front of enormous stone pines on rich, sandy ground that reached as far as Beg Meil, the end of the expansive bay. Dazzlingly white sand, every shade of Caribbean turquoise, green, and blue: a flawless little paradise.

The Viviers de Penfoulic plant was to the front, near the inlet, only separated from the beach by a waist-high wall. There were struts at head height with green fishing nets hanging over them—no doubt to keep the seagulls away from the delicacies in the pools underneath. You could see an oblong pool, not very deep, and behind it a whitewashed shed with two blue-framed windows. At the end was a little terrace for tastings; you could enjoy everything very fresh here. The bubbling oxygen pump burbled like a romantic stream.

Claire would definitely still be asleep. In the T-shirt she had put on straightaway. Claire would be staying for the whole weekend. She had taken some of the huge amounts of leave she had amassed in recent years and didn't need to be back in Paris until Monday morning. And even better: soon she would never need to go back! She would also be there on Friday evening—at Dupin's party—which made it a good deal more bearable.

They hadn't got to Dupin's apartment until two in the morning. Claire had come into the Amiral at half past midnight. Dupin had polished off another glass or two of Intoxication of the Senses. And Paul had personally made Claire another entrecôte, as the kitchen staff had already left. After that, they had shared a little cheese plate and finally, a *baba au rhum*, a small, ring-shaped, rum-soaked yeast cake with cream.

Dupin had been able to go over his notes at his leisure. At his leisure and with extraordinary red wine in his head.

In the morning, he had snuck out of bed at five forty-five. Up till then he had been sleeping extremely restlessly, tossing and turning, and constantly waking up. And when sleep came, it had brought a peculiar dream: in it, Dupin was a tiny piece of plankton drifting in a gigantic current toward an oyster bigger than a human lying by itself on the seafloor. He would end up in its belly. He tried in vain to persuade the monster that he was not suitable as food, had the wrong flavor, certainly no green flavors!

In his right hand he was holding a (working!) mobile and was constantly trying Nolwenn's number—this too was in vain, because Nolwenn, he knew for some reason, was on the phone to Claire. Claire, who had been appointed head of a scientific subsea station. Suddenly, like a gong, there had come the sound of a metallic, booming voice. The oyster. "It's me. Me, but not me." Almost cheerful. Dupin was certain—even in the dream—that the voice reminded him of someone. Then he had woken up.

"Can I help you?"

A brisk tone that left no room for any doubt that a prompt answer was expected. A woman's voice, directly behind him.

Dupin turned with a start and said quickly: "I'm a friend of Henri and Paul. My name is Georges Dupin."

A low, husky laugh was audible. The woman's face was in shadow.

"Have I committed a crime?"

She knew who he was.

"No, Madame . . ." He realized he didn't know her last name.

"Béa to my friends. Come with me."

With these words, the oyster farmer had hurried into the plant, and a moment later the light went on, very yellowish light that turned the whole thing into a surreal theater set.

"You might be able to help me with some information," Dupin said, following her in.

"I'm intrigued."

He had walked down the concrete walkway between the pool and the shed. Several long tables with pale marine-blue work surfaces made from plastic were lined up along the wall of the shed.

"Do you like these?" Béa pulled a croissant out of the paper bag she was holding.

"Oh, I love them." Dupin hadn't had breakfast yet; he had been meaning to stop at a boulangerie later.

The croissant tasted really good, crisp and buttery. Béa had, without another word, disappeared inside the shed. He could hear metallic noises, a knocking sound, a tap. Dupin could have recognized those sounds in his sleep: an espresso machine.

He looked over the waist-high wall at the inlet that seemed so much brighter than the rest of the scenery. The receding water had exposed long stretches of sand banks that looked like whales' backs, covered in carpets of gaudy green algae in some places. It looked very nutrient-rich, the way the oysters probably loved it. A few sailing boats that appeared unnaturally white in the early morning light were in the middle of the water. There were three flatboats by the bank, clearly special boats, more like large, floating platforms that likely belonged to Béa's farm.

Béa came over with two red, chipped china mugs in hand.

"The most beautiful office in the world." She handed Dupin one of the cups and stood next to him. The coffee was perfect. Strong, but not bitter.

"Do you know Matthieu Tordeux?"

"He bought the oyster farm at the other end of the bay. I don't like him."

Béa put down her cup. Dupin had been observing her from the side. Wild, curly hair, shoulder-length, a face covered in laugh lines that spoke of life, of both pleasant and serious matters.

"Why?"

"He's a real smooth customer. But he'll cut you down without batting an eyelid if you stand in his way. With rampant egotism. He wants to play with the big boys, do business on a grand scale."

"He recently bought a farm in Cancale too."

"I know. *Think big*. Apparently a building contractor went in on it too."

"Who's saying that?"

"Jacques, the owner of the pub up on the little square in La Forêt-Fouesnant. He knows things like that."

Dupin believed this straightaway; the owners of local bars were generally well informed about these things.

"You mean Pierre Delsard from Construction Traittot?"

"Yes. Delsard is an even bigger idiot than Tordeux."

Béa had lit a cigarette. Dupin got out his notebook.

"Many years ago, Tordeux doctored cheap imported oysters in Cancale with a pigment so that he could sell them as *fines de claire*. Is there talk of him being up to any dirty tricks on the Belon?"

Béa was still looking at the water. She took a drag on her cigarette. "I haven't heard anything. Brutal business practices, yes. Snatching customers away, ousting rivals, bribes, falsely orchestrated losses for outrageous tax returns. I've heard of those."

"But no dishonest oyster deals?"

"I haven't heard anything about that yet."

"Do you know of any cases of shady refinement on the Belon in recent years?"

"No. The last verified case was many years ago. A good ten years ago. The trader was from Riec and he immediately lost his license."

"And the other farmers and traders in Port Belon—does anything spring to mind that I should know about them?"

"I know Madame Laroche from the château and Baptiste Kolenc a little, they're all right. I'm not there much, though. That trader is a phenomenon. I've forgotten her name. Hyperactive. A speed demon."

Dupin almost laughed. "Matthieu Tordeux's ex-wife?"

Apparently Béa didn't know anything about that. "Really? She was married to Tordeux? Well, everyone makes mistakes."

"What do you think—will this oyster blight make it as far as here?"

"*On verra.* It's not worth brooding over."

The same attitude as everyone else he had asked about it.

"Could an oyster farmer know sooner than other people that a blight has been detected, insider knowledge, as it were, and could you make some money from that?"

Béa understood straightaway. "It's complicated. There are several institutes and authorities testing the seawater in the oyster areas at the same time. With independent cross-checks. It would be extremely laborious."

Which also meant not impossible. Dupin would ask Melen or Kadeg to take a painstaking look at the method of examining seawater samples in Port Belon.

"Of course, the value of intact cultures of European oysters would increase manifold. Traders from the affected areas would need new breeds immediately. That's also how it was after 2008. We all needed fresh cultures. The only areas in Europe not affected were northwest Scotland and Norway."

"Perhaps there would soon be an enormous demand for European oysters from Scottish farmers. And not many farms there. They could practically ask for any price. Do some highly lucrative business. And traders in the affected areas who could have secured themselves cultures in advance, maybe even still at normal prices, would possess an immense competitive advantage," Dupin said.

"Absolutely correct. If—*if* a devastating blight were to set in."

Dupin noted a few things down in his notebook.

"Everyone has it in for *plates*, they have countless enemies." Béa's gaze came to rest almost tenderly on the pale, round baskets in the pools in front of her: dozens of European oysters. "Crabs prise their shells open, ship worms bore through them, starfish paralyze them with poisonous saliva and slurp them up, birds nosedive to peck at them, arched slipper shells compete with them for food." Béa laughed huskily. "Like everywhere else in the sea, everybody eats somebody else. But the most destructive enemy of all is the Pacific oyster."

"The *creuses*?" Dupin asked in bafflement.

"The *creuses* spread like wildfire and are displacing the European oysters everywhere. Higher reproductive rates, higher population densities, faster growth. And it's not just the European oysters they're having a terrible effect on. In the blink of an eye, they transform enormous mussel beds into oyster reefs. The *creuses* are ruthless, they destroy everything. We call them the giants."

This sounded brutal. Riwal hadn't mentioned anything about it yesterday.

"But they taste irresistible too"—Béa glanced lovingly at two baskets at the edge of the pool—"and now is the best time to eat them. They're big and fleshy but there's no fat on them. For the first eighteen months we take them to the flat regions where they often lie on dry land and get food less often, so they get tough and greedy. In the second eighteen months, we place them in the most nutrient-rich currents and they feast till they're fat—that's the old method. Do you want to take a few with you? I'll wrap them up for you."

"Thank you—no. I'm just about to drive to Cancale." Dupin didn't feel like having to explain that he didn't eat oysters.

Béa had lit a second cigarette. "The self-proclaimed oyster capital of Brittany."

"You don't happen to know a Monsieur Cueff in Cancale?"

"No. There are at least sixty farms there."

Dupin put down his little china mug. "Thanks for everything, Béa. I've got to go."

"Kind of a mess." Béa's wonderful smile was back, her eyes sparkling.

"Absolutely. See you soon."

"See you soon."

Dupin walked briskly to his car, which was parked right in front of Béa's plant, in the middle of the beach.

It would be a long journey to Cancale.

* * *

"That's enough, Kadeg! I don't want to hear any more about any of that, do you understand?" Dupin yelled. He had got the car back onto a paved road and tried to get hold of Riwal. Kadeg's call had intervened.

"Our colleagues from Lorient and I have a—"

"I said that's *enough*. Full stop. I—"

"Search warrant. We have a search warrant!"

"You have a . . ." Dupin faltered.

"Search warrant for Construction Traittot." There was unbridled, conceited triumph in Kadeg's voice. "We have sufficiently reliable evidence that a sand theft did occur in recent weeks. A whole series of them, in fact. Organized sand theft on a grand scale! We're going to conduct a raid in Lorient soon, at the building contractor's headquarters. And take a look at all of their business records. *My* photos were the deciding factor."

There he was again: the Kadeg Dupin knew. Just yesterday he was still teetering along the edge of a terrible abyss and would undoubtedly have fallen in if not for the commissaire.

"I knew it. I was right about it all."

"Pierre Delsard," Dupin murmured to himself.

It was unbelievable—there *truly* did seem to be something to this sand theft business. Which meant that there really was extensive criminal activity in the area. Carried out by a building company whose boss owned a weekend home in Port Belon and was friends with one of the local oyster farmers. Good friends.

"The prefect was extremely pleased. He—"

"Kadeg! We have our own case, an extremely complicated case—and we're right in the middle of it! Has Riwal filled you in on everything? Are you up to speed?"

It took a while for an offended Kadeg to mumble, "We talked in detail on the phone last night. I know about everything. He just called me from the airport too. He couldn't get through to you. There's some new information."

"And you're only just coming out with it now?" Dupin was about to lose his temper.

"Jane Mackenzie is Mackenzie's second wife. His first wife died twenty years ago."

"So what?"

"Riwal thought you wanted to know every little thing. Everything. He—"

"Has Mackenzie's business partner from the oyster bar in Glasgow turned up again?"

"I presume the situation is unchanged there. I didn't realize that point was so important."

"It's incredibly important. On this case, when someone wants to take a spontaneous trip, it doesn't end well. Any other information?"

"Mackenzie was involved in a bank robbery as a young man, just like Smith."

A ritual for young people in Scotland, apparently.

"Why didn't we hear anything about that yesterday?"

"They had to have a good look at old files in the Fort William police station first; this information is not on any system."

"Did Mackenzie come to police attention again after that?"

"Not at all. Riwal will be sitting in the car to Tobermory right now and he won't have reception. He—"

"What about the fire investigation? What do the specialists say?"

"That young blond woman from the station in Riec—"

"Magalie Melen, Kadeg! Her name is Magalie Melen."

"She just tried to call you too. The team leader says that they can now say with certainty that the fire broke out in the back left corner of the annex."

"Inside or outside?"

That was the crucial part.

"He tends toward outside."

"Really?"

Then it was highly likely it had been arson.

"Tordeux could of course have set the fire from outside himself—but that wouldn't make any sense. If so, he would have made it look more clearly like an attack from the beginning."

This was true.

"Any other news from Melen?"

"No. Nothing, boss. But I think you're on the wrong track with the oysters."

Dupin's blood pressure instantly shot up.

"Kadeg, I'm not on a track at all. We . . ." He composed himself and took deep breaths. It would be a waste of time to have a serious discussion about this with his inspector.

"What about that woman on the bus? Have we got her?"

"No, but the blond woman—"

"Kadeg!"

"No, but Melen is still working on it. The other one, that nice colleague from Riec, had something else interesting: Tordeux spent a week in Cancale last year. At a meeting of the umbrella organization for oyster farmers, and Cueff was registered for it too. You should definitely bring that up during your visit to Cancale."

This could be important. It would be one of the links—albeit indirect—that they were desperately searching for. From Mackenzie via Cancale to Port Belon. Clearly retraceable. Mackenzie—Cueff—Tordeux. Three people.

"I'll do that. And you speak to Tordeux again. Look into him, Kadeg."

"Whatever you say."

"And one more job: I want to know as soon as possible whether anyone from the Belon bought oysters in northern Scotland in 2008 or during another oyster crisis. As fresh cultures, to rebuild their stock. And have a careful look at the authorities that monitor oyster farming, the whole system. I want to know whether it's possible for someone to have information about the spread of a bacteria earlier than other people. Whether someone has any contacts. Keep at it!"

"And what are you aiming—"

"As soon as possible."

And with these words, Dupin hung up.

Perhaps he should have sent Kadeg to Scotland and not Riwal, he thought. Far, far away.

Dupin had reached the four-laner, which he would now stay on until Cancale. He stepped on the gas. The speedometer leapt to 170. The speed limit was 110—but he was on duty.

He tapped Nolwenn's number.

He had a few specific questions.

"*Abred ne goll gwech ebet*—You never lose when you're early, Monsieur le Commissaire. You never lose when you're early! Everyone is long since on duty."

Dupin felt instantly grounded.

"Nolwenn, this Festival Interceltique in Lorient . . ."

"'*Memoire et rêve du monde celtique*' is the motto this year. It's going to be wonderful. That's why there will be so many Scottish people who have come to Riec for the preparatory meeting. Do you think it's possible there's a link between the festival and the events in the Monts d'Arrée and Port Belon? I mean, apart from the fact that it was two Scotsmen who were killed?" Nolwenn didn't beat about the bush. "Do you think"—she sounded gentler now—"Mackenzie and Smith were using the festival as a platform for something?"

"I don't know."

With just six Celtic regions, it obviously wasn't such a great coincidence that Scotland was the host nation this time. It was just striking that the Interceltic and Scottish connections had been multiplying constantly since yesterday. Stacking up.

"You'll find plenty of connections between here and Scotland. Just think of the forthcoming Bagpipe World Championship in Glasgow in May. There are fifteen Breton pipe bands, or *bagadoù*, as we call them! They consist of bagpipes, bombards, and drums. Quimper has been producing the Breton champions for years! The regional qualifying rounds are taking place everywhere over these few weeks. And for Cornouaille, Riec was the venue this time—so there was a big Interceltic event in Riec back in February, it's not just at the moment!" Nolwenn still wasn't finished. "Or think of the abundance of Scottish-Breton friendship societies. Our parliament in Rennes has agreed to lots of cooperation agreements with all of the Scottish regions, districts, and cities."

"Tordeux, the oyster farmer, is one of the sponsors of the festival, along with the shady building contractor Pierre Delsard, who has his weekend house in Port Belon," Dupin quickly interjected as Nolwenn was drawing breath. The only thing he cared about was not talking about a forthcoming Bagpipe World Championship.

"The festival has lots of sponsors, Monsieur le Commissaire."

"I'd like Magalie Melen and a team to tackle all of the Interceltic activities between Scotland and the Belon. Especially the ones our oyster players are involved in."

"Okay. Yes, Magalie is a really excellent policewoman. We could do with reinforcement like her here in Concarneau right now." This was the tone of voice Nolwenn adopted when she was pursuing her own plans behind the scenes and Dupin was to be prepared for something in passing. The commissaire knew this tone well. "Do you actually know how similar Brittany and Scotland are? The Scottish kingdom was founded in 843, the first major Breton one in 851! The brutal annexation by England happened in 1603, the one by France in 1532! Brittany has four point five million Bretons, Scotland five point one million Scots—and most importantly: we share, as we do with all of the other Celtic nations, the harsh but wonderful fate of having been tossed far out into the raging Atlantic. Something that shapes everything!" Dupin had never heard Nolwenn speak so sympathetically about a different country. "However, we have much better weather. And of course, we have Brittany."

The commissaire didn't know how to respond.

"Celts—we are all Celts! I'll be in touch as soon as there's news, Monsieur le Commissaire. Have a good journey!"

Nolwenn hung up.

He could see the sign for the turnoff to Lorient. The venue for the festival. The headquarters of Pierre Delsard's company.

The Celts, the "bold"—the mysterious people around whom so many stories, fantasies, and legends had grown up. Every child in Brittany could rattle off the history. When the famous Celtic ruler Vercingetorix laid his weapons down in front of Caesar after the historic defeat against the Romans, the continent's last Celtic kingdom ended with the Gauls. The Celtic Britons only survived on the islands. On the biggest island, the Celtic Britons were then brutally massacred in the fifth and sixth centuries A.D. by barbaric Teutons, Saxons, and Angles. They retreated to northern Scotland and Ireland, some groups left "great Britain" entirely and came back to "little Britain," the second Celtic settlement. That was what the nation had been called ever since: Brittany. Dupin found the Celtic name much more impressive: Armorica, "land by the sea." And they had survived here to this day. And to this day the Celtic names of their last refuges on the outermost, rugged fringes of northwest Europe sounded like mythical poetry, like regions Tolkien might have invented: Éire, Ellan Vannin, Alba, Cymru, Kernow, Breizh.

In the eighteenth century, Dupin knew, people had started to remember this powerful, ancient civilization and its culture, one of the great roots of Europe, that had too often been forgotten, displaced, oppressed, or even violently fought. That's what was going on when Riwal and Nolwenn gave their impassioned lectures: it was a matter of defense, recognition, significance.

It had sounded odd to Dupin's ears initially, but that had long since stopped being the case: this was where anyone who wanted to understand Brittany and the Bretons had to start.

* * *

Dupin was approaching Rennes, the Breton capital. He was just turning onto the ring road that ran round the city to the north; from the ring road there were turnoffs for Saint-Malo and Cancale. After Lorient there had been constant heavy bursts of torrential rain, which had forced Dupin to make an infuriating reduction to his speed.

Real waterfalls, another kind of Breton rain: as if the sea were being sucked up and then poured right back down to earth from the skies.

After the phone call with Kadeg, Dupin had immediately tried to reach Riwal. Every five minutes. With no luck. He had only just got through. Riwal had arrived in Tobermory by now. The line had been terrible. Dupin had passed on his priorities briefly. First, Riwal would go to Mackenzie's wife and drive to the oyster farm.

The prefect had called soon after that, but Dupin hadn't answered. He would only get annoyed again. It was a good thing he hadn't answered, because a call from Claire had come in right after. She had been sitting in the Amiral having breakfast. There were quite a few things on her to-do list today: phone line, registering at the town hall, furniture shops, boutiques in Quimper; the move had begun. Dupin had been—without meaning to—curt with her.

The rain was pelting down so hard on the metal that he almost didn't hear the electronic beeping starting again. Magalie Melen.

Dupin had wanted to get in touch with her anyway. There must be more specific information from the forensic experts by now.

"Melen, what—"

She interrupted him frantically: "They've just showed up with an entire police van. In Port Belon! A special commission from Lorient is searching Delsard's weekend house now too. The search warrant was widened to include everything: company, personal home, weekend house."

A comprehensive measure—they really wanted to find out.

"The house next to Tordeux's house," Dupin murmured.

"Should we do something?"

Dupin would have liked to say yes. But of course it was foolish. What could they do?

"There's so much going on in this tiny village these days," he said instead.

"I don't see any kind of connection between this event, the whole sand theft issue, and our case," said Melen, again very focused. "Do you, Commissaire?"

Dupin felt the same way, and he would have expressed it with the same rigor.

"The stupid thing is just that despite all of our attempts, we do not even remotely have a story that could lend some sense to the events," he said pensively.

"By the way, every attempt to track down the woman from the bus from Plage Kerfany has come to nothing; we've spoken to all of the passengers. It's getting difficult now."

That had been an abrupt change of topic. But Melen was right, it wasn't worth continuing to spend time on the idiotic sand theft, no matter what or who the special commission was searching.

"Keep trying. Sometimes you've got to force luck, corner it. What about the fire? Are the experts able to say more?"

"They've cut the section in question out of the wooden wall and are examining it in the laboratory. They're still leaning the same way: the fire was more likely set from outside than inside, although they weren't able to detect any fire accelerants at the scene."

"So it was arson."

"It's not certain yet."

So much hinged on this answer. Completely different scenarios developed, depending on it.

"We *need* to know. Beyond doubt. Call again, apply pressure."

They simply had to make some headway.

"Will do. We have another piece of new information: your inspector just told you about a possible link between Cueff and Tordeux that we're looking into. There's a second possible connection between Cueff and someone in Port Belon: a big *écailler* meet-up took place at the beginning of March. A meet-up for oyster shuckers, and it included a competition. And do you know who was there? Madame Premel. For two days. It's probably an old hobby of hers."

Dupin remembered visiting Parisian restaurants during his childhood, hours of sitting there stiffly with his family, and there were always oysters to start (perhaps that was also why he didn't eat them?). He had hated it, the sitting around and the oysters. His mother, on the other hand, had loved oysters. He had watched them: the *écaillers*. Oyster shuckers—a highly regarded gastronomic profession, steeped in tradition. So perhaps Cueff and Madame Premel knew each other too. That was interesting.

"Madame Premel told me about the trip herself. But she said she didn't get to know a Monsieur Cueff there, as far as she could remember. Which doesn't mean a thing," Melen said.

Absolutely correct.

"Try the organizers. Perhaps you'll learn something there," Dupin said.

"We're also working on the Interceltic activities in Port Belon. And we've received a call from the authorities. The infection has reached the Étel."

The Étel was one of those incredible fjords on the south coast. It formed a small gulf with a dozen islets, similar to the Gulf of Morbihan, only smaller. It was not all that far from the Belon.

"There's still one checkpoint between the Belon and the Étel. The oyster farmers have already been informed," Melen reported matter-of-factly. "But they are still relaxed."

Dupin was again more nervous than everyone else. But, where nature, natural events, and catastrophes were concerned, Bretons were always relaxed. They knew that nature was more powerful than they were. That whatever nature wished to happen, would happen. Not that Bretons simply resigned themselves to their fates and put up with everything, that wasn't it; of course they did everything they could to protect themselves—

but they remained calm and they didn't get worked up. A big storm just elicited a shrug here.

"Speak to you soon, Commissaire," Melen said, about to hang up.

"One more thing." Dupin hesitated, but then put it firmly: "Call in to Delsard's house regularly and have a colleague tell you what's going on there, whether they find anything interesting."

"All right." Magalie Melen waited to see if there was anything else coming, then added a "See you soon," and hung up.

The gas tank light had come on a quarter of an hour ago. Dupin ignored it on principle, for as long as he possibly could. But at his speed, it wouldn't be sensible. Even though deluges of water continued to pour down and it wouldn't be pleasant to leave the car.

The gas station was before the turnoff. Dupin knew this gas station as he did every other one along the four-lane stretches in Brittany. (Which mainly meant he knew if their coffee was good. Unfortunately, it was good here.)

Dupin signaled and took the exit.

Half a minute later, the gas tank hose was in his tank. The narrow roof over the pillar was a joke. The commissaire's hair and pants were soaked through in seconds, the water was streaming down his face, through the denim, into his shoes; only his jacket was keeping the rain out. The locking device on the nozzle wasn't working—Dupin hated that—so he had to stand next to the car.

The rain was so loud that he almost didn't hear the beeping in his pocket. An unknown number. He hated that too.

He answered anyway. Anything could be important right now. He pressed the phone as close to his ear as he could.

"Hello?"

Dupin immediately recognized the self-important way of speaking: "This afternoon, I will be going in front of the press. These are really spectacular developments, mon Commissaire!"

Locmariaquer, the prefect. It was sneaky, and he had done it on several occasions recently: he sometimes just called from a different phone, without caller ID. But that didn't matter now. It was more important that—Dupin knew this from painful experience—the utmost caution was exercised when the prefect spoke of "mon Commissaire."

"Spectacular developments?"

"It's all cleared up now, of course. I'm so pleased!"

"What's cleared up, Monsieur le Préfet?"

"The case. The mysterious events of recent days."

"What?"

"Well, the two murders, all of the investigations into them have come to nothing so far. Now we've got the story at the center of it all! The people involved!"

Dupin took a few deep breaths in and out, the water running into his mouth as he did so. He was in a critical psychological state, and he was struggling to control himself.

"Hello, mon Commissaire, are you still there?"

The tank was full; Dupin had automatically hung the hose up again and was running toward the little gas station building through large oil-smeared puddles.

"Why would a Scottish oyster farmer and his seasonal worker be embroiled in a French construction company's sand theft in Brittany? And to such an extent that the first one murders the other and then he gets murdered himself? And the fire that, the forensics suggest, was probably arson? I don't see the slightest connection between these events," Dupin said.

"*That*, mon Commissaire"—the prefect had clearly decided not to lose his cool and to stay steadfastly on track—"*that is your exact task*. You'll find the connection—we've solved every case so far, haven't we? It's about the sand theft, I'm sure of it! The connection is hidden somewhere, you just need to establish it. Inspector Kadeg is absolutely certain of it anyway. We have a lot to thank him for on this case, you know that."

This was outrageous. The whole thing was.

Just yesterday the prefect had almost had Kadeg suspended, as cool as anything. Dupin had saved Kadeg's skin, and because of this, he had suggested the idea of a great coup to the prefect in the first place, in view of a sand theft that was highly improbable at the time. It was nothing but an invention born of necessity at that point in time. A lie. He was an idiot— Dupin himself had been the idiot.

"You want me to *construct* the link between the events? Invent a supposed link that connects everything to the sand theft and Pierre Delsard?"

Apparently that's exactly what the prefect was asking of him.

Dupin stayed as far away from the cash register in the shop as possible. Even though he was the only customer there. The woman at the register had already given him a skeptical glance. Dupin tried to lower his voice. He didn't really manage to.

"Even though there's no evidence of this? This is—"

"No evidence? Is Tordeux the closest friend of Delsard or not? Do the two of them do business together or not? Well, of course the fire wasn't a coincidence, an amateur can see that! Either they got into an argument or the oyster farmer wanted to destroy evidence. That's just obvious."

"It's pure speculation, and how would—"

"Mon Commissaire." The sharp tone signaled his readiness to launch fierce attacks, although the prefect was keeping any escalation in reserve for now. "If someone's head itches and lice are found, it's highly unlikely that they have fleas too. Do you know what a tiny backwater Port Belon is? A scattering of houses in a little wood! Surely you don't suppose several crimes took place there at the same time and they have nothing to do with one another?"

Again, an absurd metaphor, an absurd argument.

And the prefect still wasn't done:

"Besides, the Trenez and Kerfany-les-Pins beaches are both just a stone's throw away. Actual crime scenes! Maybe the Scotsman saw something he shouldn't have. Tragically, that kind of thing happens. Wrong place, wrong time! Wouldn't be the first time. And if I understand correctly, we're currently only talking about circumstantial evidence in that murder. Apparently we don't have a single witness. That—*that* is speculation!"

"And Smith, his laborer? He—"

"Is the investigative work my job all of a sudden? As I say, you've got specific orders, Commissaire! *This* is your investigation now. I want a connection! And I want it quickly. The press is already bombarding me. And this afternoon I'm going to report that we are on the point of dealing a decisive blow to ruthless, abhorrent criminals who are destroying our Breton coast and do not even stop at murder. And also that we will share the full story soon. I'm expecting—"

Dupin should have done it sooner: he pressed the red button.

And took deep breaths in and out. Several times.

Then he ran a hand roughly through his wet hair. They needed the real story behind all of this. As quickly as possible!

He paid and ran back to his car through the pelting rain. After getting in, he waited a little while. He needed to get his anger under control. "Never fight if you're angry." Zorro's motto sprang to mind, one of his childhood heroes. Although not fighting felt incredibly difficult to him in that moment.

Melen dropping in on her colleagues in Delsard's house was not a good idea under these circumstances. The less contact they had with all of that, the better.

As he drove away, he dialed her number.

She picked up immediately.

"Melen, leave the whole—"

"Tordeux!" Her voice cracked. "Matthieu Tordeux—he's had a serious car accident. It's unclear whether he has survived, it looks bad, they—"

"What?" Dupin was stunned.

"They're bringing him to the hospital in Lorient." The young policewoman was gradually recovering her composure. "It's touch and go. Your line was busy just now, I've—"

"What happened?"

"He crashed into a tree head-on, on the stretch of road just beyond Port Belon in the direction of Riec. Where everyone drives much too fast."

"Why? Why on earth did he crash head-on into a tree?"

"We don't know yet. The car's a write-off, an old Citroën Jumper, the pickup version that lots of people drive here."

"That cannot be a coincidence. This was definitely not an accident."

Dupin was completely fed up. What on earth was going on in this idyllic place?

"We need to find out what happened right away. A fire yesterday, a car accident today, how likely is that? This was not an accident, this—" Dupin broke off.

"Even if someone caused the accident, it may be very difficult to prove. Someone could, for example, have run Tordeux off the road with another vehicle. You wouldn't necessarily see that on his car. Someone else would have to have been watching by chance."

"Tordeux might be able to tell us himself. If he . . . is in a position to do so again."

Dupin had been back on the four-laner for some time now and had just riskily braked from 150 down to 40 kilometers an hour, taking a small turnoff at the last minute so that he could turn around.

"He's unconscious."

Dupin was silent for a while.

"Hello—Commissaire, are you still there?"

"Shit."

If it really had been an attack, then they were dealing with a third attempted murder. By an unknown number of perpetrators. The case was growing and growing; it was worsening, unchecked.

"Who found Tordeux?"

"Madame Premel."

"Premel? What on earth was she doing there?"

"According to her statement, she was on her way to Riec, as apparently

Tordeux had also been shortly before. She saw the crashed car to her right by the tree and called the police."

"Where was she before her trip to Riec?"

"We'll ask her that soon."

"And the other people from our lovely oyster world? Find out right away who was where today!"

"We'll do that."

"And make a start on searching Tordeux's house. And also the first floor of the little building on the Belon. Have some experts come for the computers, the data. I want every email, every document, and every database scrutinized, the accounts schedules, the delivery documents, whatever! All of it! Start with the last few months."

"Understood, Commissaire."

They'd have access to everything now; the suspicion of murder was enough.

"Focus on the oyster businesses and possible discrepancies." They needed to know quickly whether there was evidence of shady business—that could be where the solution to the whole case lay. "And look for Mackenzie's and Smith's names, of course. That's it for the time being, Melen. I'm on my way."

Dupin had driven over a dangerously narrow motorway bridge and was already on the slip road in the opposite direction, back to Port Belon. Cancale would have to wait.

"Nolwenn, I want Brioc L'Helgoualc'h on the scene." Dupin had just thought of this, although he had no doubt completely mispronounced the name. "The Native American from the Monts d'Arrée. He's to set out immediately. I want him to take a look at everything: the car, the surroundings. In his own way. If anyone asks, this is on my strict instructions."

"Good idea, Monsieur le Commissaire. And also because you don't have Kadeg at your disposal after all. The prefect has just assigned him exclusively to the 'great sand operation.' He called a few minutes ago, he wanted—"

"He did what?"

"He wanted us to have a prominent presence." Nolwenn's tone of voice signaled that she was just reporting what had been said—and also what she thought of the measure Locmariaquer had taken. "He has—"

"We need Kadeg."

"He's meant to look for joint business activities by Tordeux and Delsard in particular."

Deep breaths, he needed to take deep breaths—Dupin could almost hear Docteur Garreg's words. Like a set phrase from autogenic training: "Breathing is one of the best techniques for controlling anger. It instantly reduces the acidity in the stomach."

"The prefect wanted to tell you himself just now. He was extremely annoyed, he claims you just hung up. There will be serious disciplinary consequences to that one day," Nolwenn reported drily. "I'm also meant to tell you that he doesn't for one second believe it was an accident, and he sees this attack as a direct response to the search he ordered at Delsard's house. The prefect sees this incident as the ultimate confirmation that the core of this case relates to the sand theft. I'm to tell you that."

Dupin's pulse was quickening dangerously.

"These are extremely strange coincidences, of course"—Nolwenn spoke as if she were thinking out loud—"but they don't have to mean anything. The attack on Tordeux could just as easily fit with the logic of a different matter. The matter you're working on! Or it's only to do with the Delsard sand theft affair. And nothing to do with your case. There could definitely be two unrelated cases."

For a moment, Dupin wasn't sure whether Nolwenn was gently trying to get him to reflect—about whether he ought not consider the possibility of a connection after all.

As he was silent, she carried on undeterred: "Riwal just called, before the news about Tordeux. There's some new information. They've tracked down the co-owner of Oyster Heaven in Glasgow; apparently he has several homes. He doesn't have the slightest idea why Mackenzie suddenly headed off to Brittany. Mackenzie did mention several times that he knew a Breton oyster farmer, presumably Cueff, but nothing about a forthcoming trip to Brittany. Or else the owner is lying. The bar has only ever sourced its oysters from Mackenzie's farm, he says. All of the information at the Scottish police's disposal makes him look nonsuspicious at the moment."

Here, fifteen hundred kilometers away, they had no other choice, thought Dupin.

"Riwal has spoken to Mackenzie's wife." Nolwenn carried on with her report. "Everything she told Riwal matches what the Scottish policeman reported from the conversation. Apart from one thing: it does seem to her now as though her husband was behaving strangely now and again recently. He went out late at night a few times, which he had apparently never done before. He said he needed some exercise. And during work he sometimes left the oyster farm to make long phone calls. She thinks he had something on his mind."

"Since when? When did this start? Did Riwal ask her that?"

"About two weeks ago, she says."

Dupin got out his notebook with one hand and leafed through it on his right thigh, the other hand firmly on the steering wheel. He soon found what he was looking for: *Tues. 03/16, first call from S to M.* That had been two weeks ago.

It would bring back into play what had once been one of their theories: that everything had begun after a call from Smith to Mackenzie.

"Anything else?"

"No. The only other thing I was meant to tell you was that Riwal believes her. That Jane Mackenzie really doesn't know anything. That's his instinct."

That meant something: Riwal had a good sense about that kind of thing.

"He ought to be with the director of the Shelter House by now. He'll call you again soon," said Nolwenn.

"Okay."

"I've got a few reinforcements so that Magalie Melen and Erwann Braz can delegate tasks."

"Thanks." That was important, now that neither of his inspectors was available.

"And I'll inform the police in Cancale that you're not coming. How do you want to handle Cueff?"

A good question. Dupin hadn't thought about that yet. The conversation was in fact extremely urgent. And he would really have liked to do it locally. And have a bit of a look around.

"Cueff is to come to Port Belon, I'll speak to him here," he said.

Of course this was not the ideal solution, but he had a feeling it would be important to stay in the vicinity. The story was not over yet, and its center was here.

"I'll see to that, Monsieur le Commissaire. I'll call him. I've already spoken to him about your exact meeting point. I'll send him the address. I'm sure he'll want to assist the police with their investigations. And he might prefer you not to turn up at his farm anyway."

"Did you get him on a landline?"

"Yes. An hour and a half ago, he was definitely in Cancale."

"Thank you, Nolwenn."

"See you then, Monsieur le Commissaire, I'm sure we'll speak again soon."

* * *

It had been a crazy journey. Dupin's state of mind fluctuated between fury, bad temper, deep unease, and pent-up energy, and all of these feelings alike had made him floor the gas pedal. He had called Magalie Melen every five minutes during the drive to ask for news, and she had taken it surprisingly calmly.

There were no witnesses to the accident so far. What they knew was this: Tordeux had been on his way to his warehouse in Riec—the orders were prepared and dispatched here—as he did every morning. Every morning, at the same time. Half past nine. Everyone from Port Belon knew this, they were aware of his habit.

The star forensic investigator had personally arrived at the accident site a while before with his whole team, and so far they hadn't been able to find anything unusual about his car. No discernible doctoring, no "second vehicle involvement"—no missile, no stone or anything like that—so far, Reglas considered "an accident" to be "very unlikely."

Tordeux had crashed behind a blind curve. It was definitely possible to lose control of a car if it was going too fast and there was a sudden distraction or irritation; an animal, for instance. As the crow flies, the accident site was less than a kilometer from Port Belon.

The doctors in the hospital had said Tordeux's condition was still critical, extremely critical. They had not managed to stabilize him yet. He had not woken up, his hip was shattered, as was his right leg, he had many deep lacerations, but the worst of all were his severe internal injuries. They had not been able to find any signs of medical reasons for the crash—a heart attack, for example—but the doctor in charge understandably did not want to commit himself definitively at this point.

Shortly before he arrived, Magalie Melen had sent him a preliminary list of who in Port Belon had been where, and when, this morning. The most important list, Dupin felt. All interviewees had given plausible statements, but they were generally difficult to verify. Besides, if someone were to have caused the accident by doctoring the car, then it wouldn't have happened this morning anyway, it would probably have happened the night before. This had been Tordeux's first journey today, that much had been established.

Dupin had parked his Citroën a few hundred meters from the site of the accident on the narrow strip of grass next to the road, well away from the cordon.

Tordeux's car looked horrific.

It was hard to fathom that somebody had been taken out of this crushed scrap metal still alive. Dupin found the sight of accidents almost more difficult to bear than anything else. You could see the sheer physical brutality of the sudden forces at work, the speed, the masses, the crazily distorting or breaking steel—and the absolute defenselessness and fragility of the human body by contrast. If fate decreed that sheet metal or girders cracked badly, they sliced and cleaved whatever was in their way.

Dupin had stopped a few meters away from the car; that was close enough. And also because he wouldn't be able to stand a conversation with Reglas. Even now, almost two hours after the accident, there was a terrible smell. Of burnt rubber and plastic, charred paint and steel skidding across the asphalt. A sharp, aggressive stench.

Dozens of people were standing around the car. Several police cars around the sides.

Magalie Melen had noticed Dupin and was coming toward him.

"Any new findings here?" Dupin said gruffly.

"No. The press wants to speak to you, Commissaire, they turned up here early, they had had a tip-off about the search of Delsard's house and were already in Port Belon. I sent them away. The prefect has announced a press conference for noon today. He—"

"I know. Where's L'Helgoualc'h?"

Dupin wouldn't concern himself with any of that. With the press or with who would now think, say, recommend, or demand what, where, or how. He would just keep following his nose, his instinct.

"He got here half an hour ago and . . . disappeared into the wood."

"Into the wood?" Dupin looked round reflexively.

"Yes, he had a look at the car, just briefly, and then disappeared into the wood."

This part of the road ran through one of the typical little woods, the Breton thicket.

"Okay. I'll drive into the village. And talk to some people. First up, Premel."

Melen nodded.

Reglas had seen Dupin a while before, but pointedly turned away—the top pro didn't want to be disturbed. The commissaire would do him the favor.

"The forensic fire experts have been in touch. The way they were leaning has proved correct, they are now sure: it was clearly arson, from outside. Somebody set the fire. And definitely not Tordeux. On the back wall. Right down at the bottom where the wooden slats jut out slightly, they don't reach all the way to the ground. They've definitely not been able to detect any fire accelerant. But," his young colleague said in a practiced way, as if she had dealt with this dozens of times before, "with a wooden wall, it's enough to place a small piece of burning wood underneath it."

So what they had been imagining was now confirmed. It had been a deliberate attack—just like today's incident too, no doubt. Somebody had it in for Tordeux; it was good to be able to work with more than hypotheses.

"A group of our colleagues from Quimper is already examining Tordeux's residence and also the little building by the oyster beds. They're also inspecting the data."

"Good, I want to know everything."

For a while, neither of them said anything.

"Just briefly, about the Interceltic activities in this area, there are masses of them. Nolwenn has already told you, they go well beyond the annual preparatory meeting for the festival in Lorient. In Riec, we've discovered, there's even a native Scotsman, the owner of the excellent fishmonger's, and he regularly organizes a trip to Scotland. They go in a group of seven or eight, usually the same group, but never anyone from Port Belon. And no discernible connections to Mackenzie or Smith or anywhere in their area.

You know about the druidic association, that's fourteen people from Riec anyway, and Madame Premel from Port Belon. They often go to Scotland too."

"Okay." Dupin was increasingly certain that this was the wrong track, but he noted everything down to be on the safe side; you never knew in this phase of a case.

"There's something I'm meant to tell you from Kadeg. He has cleared up two more things that you wanted to know. Nobody in Port Belon bought fresh cultures of European oysters from northern Scotland after the catastrophe in 2008. Only from Norway. The second thing: he has been looking into the monitoring and information system for seawater quality. There are several institutes, it's an elaborate system. He thinks it's extremely unlikely that someone could get relevant, exclusive information first, even through bribery. All of the institutions make their respective results public immediately and independently."

That was a dead end too.

"Thanks. Speak to you soon, Melen."

Dupin turned away and was about to go to his car.

"Come—have a look at this!"

Dupin jumped.

The deep, gloomy voice had come from off to the side, from inside the wood. Dupin's muscles tensed. Magalie Melen had turned to the side in alarm too.

A moment later, a man burst out of the thicket.

Dupin recognized him straightaway: Brioc L'Helgoualc'h, with his usual surly expression.

"Follow me."

Not waiting for a response from Dupin or Melen, he went back into the wood. Melen looked inquiringly at Dupin, and on Dupin's nod, they followed L'Helgoualc'h, having to make an effort to get into the thicket at all without hurting themselves.

Silent, a *coureur des bois* in his element, L'Helgoualc'h wove his way between the trees, suddenly making a sharp left turn and stopping a few meters farther on with no warning.

At first, Dupin and Melen didn't notice anything. It was only when they followed their colleague's gaze that they saw a narrow path running through the wood at this point—not a very well-beaten path, but you could still make it out.

L'Helgoualc'h knelt down.

"Somebody ran along here after the last time it rained. These are fresh footprints, although there's no complete print anywhere."

Melen and Dupin had also crouched down. L'Helgoualc'h pointed to a particular spot with one finger. They couldn't see anything. Anything at all. Just forest floor. The tiniest twigs, dark leaves, moldy soil.

"Obvious." L'Helgoualc'h stood up and followed the path. Just a few steps and you were out of the wood. They now found themselves on the strip of grass between the road and the Breton jungle. They were right in the sharp bend, perhaps twenty meters from the accident site. Melen and Dupin had stopped right behind L'Helgoualc'h.

Without saying a word, he turned around and went back into the wood. Dupin and Melen followed close behind. L'Helgoualc'h paused. He looked and then squatted again.

"Somebody was standing here. For some time. And then left abruptly. No doubt about it," he said, sounding pleased all of a sudden.

"What does that mean?" Dupin felt an urgent sense of unease.

"Look." L'Helgoualc'h pointed out a spot with his finger again.

Melen and Dupin crouched down again.

And sure enough, it was visible now! A footprint. Two, in fact, close together, distinct, albeit perhaps only two-thirds of them. No tread marks. And along the top you could see the print indented in the soil, little sticks trodden into the ground, even more so on the right footprint than the left.

Magalie Melen spoke in a measured way, although the conclusion to be made was really quite extraordinary: "You think someone could have stood and waited here until Tordeux was close enough for them to jump out of the thicket suddenly? And confuse Tordeux?"

"All I'm saying is somebody stood here, then ran away. With some speed."

Quite a long silence followed.

Melen followed her speculative scenario to its logical conclusion. "Tordeux would have had to swerve. He pulled the steering wheel round, lost control, and sped into the tree. The simplest method of causing an accident." The young policewoman walked a few meters into the open air, looked to the left, and came back. "Beforehand, the perpetrator was able to monitor the road in peace from here."

Melen's scenario was plausible. Absolutely plausible. That's how it might have been. But of course it was still speculation, based on the interpretation of two-thirds of a shoe print. But still.

"That won't be enough for any court or public prosecutor. We need to find more," grumbled L'Helgoualc'h. "I'm going to keep looking round."

Dupin and Melen watched him go.

"Where does the path lead to?" Dupin was speaking in a low voice for some reason.

"This is one of the hunting trails, I presume, they're all over the place here. If you follow the path—it leads straight to Port Belon."

That's what Dupin had figured.

"I would li—"

The monotonous beeping of his mobile seemed eerily loud here in the wood. He reached into the back pocket of his pants.

Riwal.

"Yes?"

"You're not going to believe it, boss. This is seriously crazy, I have no idea what—"

"Riwal!"

"I drove to the Shelter House like you told me and had a look at everything here, including Smith's personal belongings. There really aren't many; in fact he owned almost nothing." Riwal's tendency to relay everything as a story increased when he was more agitated. "A handful of old photographs of people, none of whom are known to us thus far, some with captions. Everything in a little decorative wooden box, plus two fishing rods—very old models, three jumpers, two—"

"Riwal, what did you find?" It was clear that the inspector was coming to something significant.

"An old edition of Robert Louis Stevenson's *The Ebb-Tide*, two well-thumbed crime novels, and . . . an edition of *Piping Today*, published on the sixteenth of March this year."

"Riwal, get to the point!"

"Do you know *Piping Today*? It's the leading fortnightly magazine about piping and everything related to it—about the culture and history of the bagpipes, the music, the technique, the immortal heroes—"

"Riwal!"

"*Piping Today* is also the official magazine of the World Pipe Band Championships. It does in-depth reporting on all of the qualifying competitions every year. This year included. In this issue there's a comprehensive special section: a report about the regional heats." Riwal was electrified now. "And obviously about the Brittany heats too. About the two days in Riec at the end of February. With plenty of photos." He paused briefly. "To be precise, there are five photos from Riec from the twenty-seventh and twenty-eighth of February. Kolenc and Tordeux are in one of the photos in the *bagad* from Riec."

"What?"

Dupin had stopped in his tracks. This was unbelievable.

"The band itself didn't take part in the heats at all, but they helped to organize the fringe program. They played during the opening march through the village. A *bagad* from Riec and the surrounding area, and it's not bad, it—"

"The photos, Riwal! The photos!"

"Madame Bandol and Kolenc's daughter are in the background. Madame Premel is in another photo with her family at the side of the road. In the crowd. Kolenc is playing a set of bagpipes, Tordeux is playing a bombard, they're both marching in a large group. I have the photos here in front of me."

"Photos of Kolenc, Premel, and Tordeux, as well as Madame Bandol—at a music competition in Riec?" Dupin was still standing rooted to the spot. "In a bagpipe magazine that was amongst Smith's few personal belongings in northern Scotland?" This beat every previous insane thing. "A photo that Smith highly likely saw? That's crazy."

"Not really, boss. Everyone interested in piping reads the magazine—in other words, all of Scotland. This issue belongs to the residential home. They have subscriptions to several magazines and newspapers and they're available in the common room, I've just looked. Most of them are about fishing, boats, and Scottish music, which mainly means the bagpipes. You can take the magazines back to your room for a day and night."

"What does the article say? Something about one of these people, are they mentioned?"

"Nothing like that. Just a general report about the competitions, and that presumed it would be another victory for Quimper. And a few longer touristy articles. About the landscape, the people. A separate article about the oysters, the famous Belons. But that was also on the general side, no particular farm is mentioned."

This magazine, these photos that Smith had seen—it could have set everything in motion. The logical conclusion was this: Smith had seen someone he knew in the photos. One person or several. That must have triggered everything. The whole fateful incident, the chain of events.

The magazine was from March 16. The first call from Smith to Mackenzie had taken place on that exact day. Smith had seen it and then got in touch with Mackenzie. Although Dupin had no idea why. This much was certain: it was the first direct, irrefutable connection between the two Scotsmen and the people in Port Belon.

Dupin's thoughts were racing. This was exactly what they had needed. A success like this. It was clearer than ever there was a coherent story! And it had nothing to do with sand theft or with a shady building contractor.

"And there's really nothing else of relevance in this article apart from the heats and the bagpipes."

"I don't think so. I'll scan it as soon as I can and send it to you. The resolution on my mobile isn't good enough. Or this would be much easier: have someone get you a copy of *Piping Today* from Riec, you'll get the magazine quicker that way. There's a very well-stocked Maison de la Presse there, I'm sure you'll find it there."

"Okay, Riwal. Talk to the director of the Shelter House again, and to Smith's friend. I wonder if he mentioned anything that could be related to the photos. Show them the photos! And Mackenzie's wife is to see them too."

"Will do, boss."

Dupin hung up and looked around for Magalie Melen. She was standing a few meters away and seemed to have been on the phone too, because she was just taking her mobile away from her ear.

"News, Commissaire!" The young policewoman strode firmly up to Dupin. "Cueff was lying! He did leave his house the day before yesterday! He was seen in a supermarket, the big Leclerc on the first roundabout, around twelve forty-five."

"Really? Who saw him?"

This was also significant news.

"A woman who farms oysters. He was standing at the meat counter."

"And she's absolutely certain?"

"Yes."

It was unbelievable. How stupid or brazen did Cueff have to be to risk this lie? If he had been in a supermarket, he must have known about the danger of someone having seen him. Stupid, brazen—or on the defensive, in trouble.

"That means"—Melen did the calculations again—"if Cueff left Cancale around one P.M. the day before yesterday, he could have been in Port Belon at three P.M. His wife and son saw him at home at eight thirty, so he had until six thirty in our vicinity. Three and a half hours."

That would have been enough time to do everything. Yes. But Cueff was definitely not the person who attacked Tordeux. He hadn't set the fire yesterday evening or lain in wait here in the wood this morning for Tordeux. But he could nevertheless be involved.

Melen seemed to have read Dupin's thoughts. "Our colleagues in Cancale have spoken with the organizer of the *écailler* competition and emailed him a photo of Madame Premel. The organizer says that if Cueff and Premel both actively took part, it's extremely unlikely that they didn't meet, impossible really. But he cannot remember seeing them together. Cueff knows the organizer, of course. However, it's unlikely that Tordeux and Cueff saw each other at this association meeting in Cancale—there were a hundred and fifty participants. Cueff, according to his own statement, was only there for half an hour, which several people were able to confirm."

"Did Tordeux stay the night in Cancale?"

"No, he went back to Port Belon afterward. In his car. Nolwenn hasn't been able to reach Cueff yet, by the way. She has just left him a message that you can't come and that he should get in touch urgently. Our colleagues in Cancale are aware."

"Nolwenn is to try him at regular intervals."

"She is."

"I want to grill him as soon as possible. And I'll speak to Madame Premel." Dupin was not concentrating fully; his mind was still on the photos and the *Piping Today* issue.

He relayed the news to Magalie Melen in concise sentences.

"So, first and foremost we're assuming a direct connection between Smith and someone in Port Belon, whatever kind of connection that might be," Melen said.

Dupin nodded thoughtfully. "Would you do me a favor? Could you get me something from Riec . . ." The commissaire hesitated and changed his mind. "No, never mind. I'll do it myself."

It wouldn't be very far. And he wanted to see this article quickly.

Magalie Melen looked inquiringly at him.

"I'm just going to get myself the current issue of *Piping Today* quickly."

* * *

Having propped himself against an old waist-high stone wall in front of the Maison de la Presse, Dupin was engrossed in the magazine. He was right on Riec's central square, an impressive church towering up in the middle of it, and not far from the wonderful bakery. The sun was showing off its springtime strength, pretending it had been shining the whole time and was guaranteed to keep shining for days.

Dupin had already started to read the article while standing at the cash register and had stumbled out of the shop, still reading, after two minor collisions with mobile newspaper stands. The friendly owner had run after him to give him his change.

He still couldn't believe it. It was too strange. There they really were—in photos in a Scottish bagpipe magazine: the residents of Port Belon, almost the entire oyster scene. Photos that Smith had clearly stumbled across; it was at this point that speculation came in, but there was no other way to make sense of it. And then because of these photos, Smith—presumably because he recognized someone—contacted Mackenzie. Many phone calls later, the fateful Brittany trip had happened.

"Shit."

It didn't make sense.

Kolenc's bagpipes were scarlet and looked like they were made of a heavy velvet material. Tordeux's bombard looked like a long recorder but with a bulge at the bottom like on a trumpet. Both were wearing black pants, white shirts, and forest-green waistcoats.

Madame Bandol was wearing a dark red dress with a blue bolero and was standing in a small group on the edge of the crowd. A little way behind her, in conversation with a young woman whom Dupin didn't know, was Kolenc's daughter, Louann. In another one—there were five photographs of the festival in Riec in total—you could see Madame Premel at the edge with her family. She seemed to be thoroughly enjoying herself, and absolutely everyone looked cheerful. Dupin was fond of Breton festivals.

There really was nothing significant in the article—lots of touristy tips on the place and people. The only thing that caught his eye was the note at the end about the local piping club in Riec, along with an address.

Rue du Presbytère. Dupin knew it: there was always a small market there on Wednesday and Saturday mornings, where, alongside fresh seafood and other local specialties, Isabelle Barrette sold the very best cheese in France. The road branched off directly from the main square.

Dupin thought it over quickly. It was worth a try. It was almost half past twelve. Maybe he'd be in luck.

He rolled up the magazine and started to run.

It was even closer than he had expected: number 78 was practically right on the square. It was one of the pretty old stone houses, just two stories, whitewashed.

A weathered little plastic sign hung next to the doorbell. *Amis de la musique celtique/Bagad Belon.*

Dupin rang the bell. Twice in a row. Nothing happened.

He rang again.

Still nothing.

So he wasn't going to get an answer. He would ask Erwann Braz to stop by later.

"*Bonjour,* can I help you?"

Dupin spun around. A youngish man with a beard was standing behind him. He was wearing a plain jacket in difficult-to-define brown shades. Dupin knew the man. He didn't know where he knew him from, but he had seen him before. Not that long ago.

"Georges Dupin—Commissariat de Police Concarneau. Are you one of the . . . music friends here?"

"You're in luck, I've just closed the bank, lunch break." He got a key out of his bag. "Jean Danneau, head of the center here, and *Sonneur en chef* of the Bagad Belon," he said matter-of-factly but not without some pride.

Then it came back to Dupin: "You're the chief druid from the clearing!"

He must have been a very busy man. Today, in broad daylight and far away from woods and clearings, the beard, which had lost some of its magic even after the ceremony, looked completely ordinary to Dupin. It was neither long nor white. Hard to believe.

"And Nolwenn Premel collected you from the meeting yesterday. How can I help you?"

The chief druid and bank clerk, despite having the key in his hand, made no move to open the door. He looked inquisitively at the commissaire.

"Baptiste Kolenc and Matthieu Tordeux, they are both members of your group."

"Do you think there's a link between the *bagad* and Tordeux's accident?"

As always, word of the events had spread quickly. It didn't surprise Dupin. The miraculously instantaneous spread of news was an ancient and fundamental cultural technique for Bretons; they didn't need "new media" for it.

"We just want to build up a picture." Dupin couldn't have expressed this more vaguely, but that was exactly what he wanted. "Tell me about them both."

"Kolenc comes regularly, he's one of our most loyal members. Tordeux doesn't come often anymore. But when he does, he's enthusiastic. He's good on the bombard. You need strong men for it!"

"Is your group in touch with anyone in Scotland? Do you travel there now and again?"

"Oh yes. We visit a piping band in St. Andrews, in the northeast. Every two years. They come to us too. And sometimes to the festival in Lorient too. Not every year, but every two or three years."

"And Tordeux and Kolenc are always there, on the trips, I mean?"

"Kolenc is never on them. He says he can't leave his farm unattended. Tordeux, I have to think about that one." He pressed his lips together and briefly closed his eyes. "No, I can't remember him coming along in recent years. But if the Scottish band comes here, they're usually there. Those are some very fun evenings."

"Do Kolenc and Tordeux have any particular bonds with anyone in the Scottish group? Do you know of any friendships?"

"No. Monsieur Kolenc is an introvert, a quiet, important figure in Belon oysters who keeps to himself. I don't think he makes friends quickly. Tordeux acts the smart, self-confident raconteur and will chat to anyone, but I don't know of any close relationships."

"How long have the two of them been members of your group?"

"A very long time. I'm the third *Sonneur en chef* they've had. More than thirty years, I'd say."

"Do you do other things together as a group—apart from music?"

"Just music. It's about the social aspect too, of course."

"But your club doesn't do any other activities?"

"No."

"Madame Bandol, Madame Premel, and Kolenc's daughter—do they have anything to do with the *bagad*?"

"They're enthusiastic audience members. The Premel family is, anyway, in spite of the ex-husband. They're always there. The first time I saw the actress was at this event. Mademoiselle Kolenc comes every once in a while but not regularly."

"But Madame Premel was never a member or came on trips?"

"No, never."

"At the heats in Riec—did any unusual incidents take place? Did anything out of the ordinary happen?"

"What do you mean?" The chief bagpiper seemed anxious now.

"Anything odd that you can recall?"

"No. We had two distinctly pleasant days. Very quiet."

"*Piping Today* did a report on those two days here in Riec, did you see their team?"

"A journalist and a photographer, yes, they spoke to me briefly."

"Do you know anything about them? Where they came from?"

"No."

"Then thank you, Monsieur . . ." Dupin's memory for names was disastrous, time and time again.

"Danneau."

"Right."

"Is Matthieu Tordeux going to make it?" Danneau sounded genuinely concerned.

"We don't know."

"I really hope he does, we're terribly shorthanded on the bombards. It would be a heavy blow." He seemed to think it over. "But of course I especially hope so for his own sake."

He hadn't made much of an effort with this afterthought, but he clearly didn't feel bad about it.

"Well then, I hope to see you at one of our performances sometime. It will be worth your while!"

The head bagpiper turned to a postbox to the right of the front door with his key. "I just wanted to pick up the post."

"*Au revoir*, Monsieur . . . Danneau!"

Danneau smiled in a friendly way, a very friendly way.

Dupin turned away with mixed emotions. Somehow that was all very interesting, but yet again, it was extremely vague. However, the commissaire was still certain that they needed to keep at this, despite not being able to say why.

He went back to his car, tired, worn out. He yawned a few times, really yawned, which he didn't often do. Dupin had considered getting himself another coffee at the bakery earlier. In the objective interests of the case and the investigations! He would have gone ahead and done it but his stomach didn't feel at all well. A sharp, occasionally severe pain had been bothering him at regular intervals all day. Ever since that one little coffee that morning that hadn't counted.

* * *

As Dupin left the parking lot and headed on foot to Madame Premel's farm, he felt a strange mood coming over him.

The idyll of Port Belon had disappeared—the village suddenly seemed menacing. The atmosphere was eerily frantic. There was a squad car in front of each of Delsard's and Tordeux's houses, three police cars in between them, and a fire engine still in the driveway of Tordeux's house.

Two police officers were patrolling the parking lot, inspecting everyone approaching the scene. No doubt this was an order from the prefect (who had just called again, but Dupin hadn't answered).

The commissaire picked up his pace.

Down by the quay he saw a sign, a discreet one by the roadside: *Huîtres fines/Nolwenn Premel*. He turned off.

Dupin had tried to get hold of Riwal from the car. It had been busy. He tapped the number again.

"Boss?"

"Riwal, there's something else I urgently need to know."

"Yes?" Riwal knew this line from the commissaire only too well.

"Research who wrote the report and who else came to Riec at the end of February. I know of a journalist and a photographer. Maybe there were more. A group of Scottish friends of piping?" This should obviously have been researched already.

"Will do, boss. I've just spoken to the director of the home and to a few residents. Nobody knew anything about this article or about Smith having read it. The director said he often took the magazine *Piping Today* back to his room, along with an angling magazine. She doesn't know any of the people from Port Belon. He never spoke about this village or about Brittany at all. But she could vaguely recall that a long time ago, twenty or twenty-five years ago, Smith played in a piping band himself. He played the bombard—there was a small band in the Shelter House back then."

"Not anymore?"

"No."

"Tordeux plays the bombard too. Now and again."

"Speaking of a long time ago, it appears that Mackenzie and Smith were involved in the same robbery. I've found that the place and year match. So they would have had a common criminal past. That kind of thing binds people together for life, even if you're not friends and don't actually even see each other anymore."

It would explain a thing or two. Mackenzie had apparently managed to build a relatively successful, honest life, and he had obviously felt responsible for Smith.

"Does Madame Mackenzie know anything about this holdup at the bank?"

"She has never said anything about it. It was a good eleven years before she got to know him. I'd understand if he were to have kept it to himself."

While they were talking, Dupin had arrived outside a rather dilapidated stone building on the edge of a little inlet of the Belon.

"Call again, ask her."

"Will do, boss. By the way, the Scottish police have offered me the use of the helicopter service; no doubt it's nothing unusual here."

"I don't mind." Dupin was in favor of anything that made things quicker for Riwal.

"Cool."

Dupin had never heard this word out of Riwal's mouth before.

"Call—"

"Hello! Monsieur le Commissaire! Wait a moment." Magalie Melen came running up, her blond hair blowing about wildly. She stopped in front of him, out of breath.

"I just saw you walking past us. There have been two important discoveries: they've accessed the data from Tordeux's cloud. An expert from the team on Delsard's house search helped." She took another deep breath. "The volume of Tordeux's sales of the exquisite Belon oysters as a trader is significantly higher than what he can produce here as a farmer. And that's without making any additional purchases!"

"What does that mean?"

Dupin realized his inspector was still on the line.

"Riwal, let's talk again in a minute."

Dupin hung up.

Melen carried right on: "He sells more Belon oysters than he could ever produce—he's perpetrating fraud."

"Are our colleagues certain?"

"Fairly certain. It's clear something about the quantities doesn't stack up."

"How exactly is he perpetrating fraud?" Dupin hadn't grasped it yet.

"If their conclusions from the data are correct, he's buying huge quantities of finished oysters from other countries, supposedly in order to refine them, but he doesn't do that at all. Instead, he puts them up for sale as expensive Belons. That would produce a tidy profit margin, you could make a lot of money that way."

"He buys oysters from less famous regions and claims they have been in the Belon. In reality he just forges any documents, labels them as Belon oysters, and sells them on at the corresponding prices, is that how I should be looking at it?"

An extremely similar trick to his earlier idea in Cancale with the *claires* and *fines* and the green pigment. Just even more difficult to prove. Tordeux hadn't given up his fraudulent schemes at all. He had simply refined them.

"Absolutely. Another elegant way of doing it would be to use his own oysters, that would be even harder to prove. For instance, the ones from his new farm near Fouesnant."

This time, Dupin understood immediately: Tordeux would take a proportion of the yield from Fouesnant and was selling them as Belons straightaway. It was all just a question of moving things round internally.

Melen concluded: "That could be a reason for buying that farm. And why he had the money he needed to buy it."

"Brilliant." Dupin wouldn't have put it past Tordeux for one second. He was cunning and crafty, no doubt about it. "But wouldn't that have come to light a long time ago?"

"Only if someone were to take a look at all of his online accounts, otherwise no. How would it?"

"When will we know for sure?"

"The analysis of the details will take some time—but as I say: something definitely doesn't stack up, we know that already. He's selling more Belons than he gets."

That was quite something.

Tordeux would in fact have been committing crimes again, perhaps over the course of many years. And they . . . they would then have two criminals. Tordeux and, it looked like, the building contractor. Bizarre.

"The other news: the authorities have just imposed a distribution ban on the Belon until further notice. As a precaution. Simply preventatively. The blight in the Étel has got worse. It's true no infection has been detected in Port Belon yet. But still. They're going to expand the inspections here, especially out at the estuary."

"What are the farmers saying?"

"They're used to this. Purely precautionary measures. It happens from time to time. They're still calm and are carrying on with production. If the ban is lifted, they can immediately put all of the stock they've had to set aside back on the market again."

Dupin resolved to stop being surprised by the oyster community's unshakable calm.

"What kind of scale of fraud are we talking about with Tordeux?"

"The discrepancies are significant. It all mounts up. Considerable sums are involved."

"I see."

And this would in fact explain where the money for Tordeux's investments came from.

"A question that would remain completely unanswered is this," Melen said firmly. "How could Smith and Mackenzie have got involved in this fraud? Neither of their names is in Tordeux's data, and there's no reference to Mackenzie's farm. The only business relationships that can be established are those that Tordeux has already informed us about: the trader in Edinburgh and the farmer in Dundee. Of course it's possible that they received fraudulent oysters like many other people—the deliveries will have gone to all of his customers."

There was a loud noise, something metallic. Melen and Dupin jumped and looked toward the wall that ran from Premel's stone building to the road. It was too high to see anything. The sound appeared to have come from behind it.

"Thank you, Melen."

"Commissaire, just briefly on Tordeux's condition: he's out of the tricky operation now, it has gone well so far. The internal bleeding has been stopped, but he's still in critical condition. The doctors are refusing to give a prognosis."

It did sound a bit more positive, Dupin thought.

"I'll come to our tables after the conversation with Premel."

"Okay."

The young policewoman turned on her heel and strode toward the little quay.

Something else had just occurred to Dupin. It had crossed his mind earlier when Riwal had been giving his report.

He pressed Redial.

"Riwal, just a quick one. See if you can find more specific information on the bank robbery by our two Scotsmen. Any details."

"Of course, boss. What exactly?"

"Everything you can find."

"Will do."

Dupin hung up. Now he really would speak to Madame Premel.

* * *

A plain, narrow wooden door had been set into the stone wall. A small, weather-beaten sign hung over it, painted wood. Even more discreet than on the quay. *Vente et Dégustations. Huîtres plates et creuses.* The blue letters were very faded.

There was no doorbell in sight. The door was ajar so Dupin opened it.

Directly behind it was a steep staircase that led straight down to the river. The tide was in, the water was high and flowing steadily past. It almost reached the oyster plant's two long concrete pools—two meters by ten meters, Dupin reckoned—that had been built right by the bank. Inside the pools were red-and-black sacks made of woven plastic lying in piles on steel tables, three or four to each table. Large sacks full of oysters.

There were two light blue baskets in front of one of the pools, also containing piles of oysters. At the end of the plant was a square wooden terrace with a few tables and chairs. A marvelous place for a tasting. In the middle of the Belon.

Madame Premel was standing at the edge of the pool in front. She was wearing the obligatory yellow oilskin pants, long Wellington boots, a pale pink sweatshirt, and long, dark green gloves—crazy color combinations—and her hair had been tied back carelessly.

She didn't seem to have noticed the commissaire. Her exertion was visible as she fiddled with a wooden sluice gate with water flowing steadily through it. Then she turned an iron crank, cog wheels turned, and the sluice gate jolted open even further. As the cog wheels moved, there was a loud metallic noise—that's what they had just heard. The flow of water was growing by the second.

"I have some more questions for you, Madame Premel."

Dupin had come down the steep steps and was walking straight toward her. Madame Premel turned slowly. She didn't look surprised.

"No problem, so long as you have nothing against me continuing to work while you ask them. I need to be finished in half an hour. Today has been crazy."

"You mean the attempted murder of your ex-husband, I take it? The sight of the crashed car with him inside it?"

For a split second, she seemed surprised, then she answered in a measured way.

"Yes. Attempted murder. So it was that after all. Well, I'm not surprised. The fire probably wasn't an accident either, then. It's as I thought. You don't know who it was yet, I assume. And of course I look suspicious. I get it."

"How is it that you came to be driving down the road to Riec just a few minutes after your ex-husband?"

"I've wondered that myself: Why did I of all people have to be the one who happened to pass by? Well, that's what happened, it's not worth thinking about it any more. Coincidence. Or maybe not: I drive back and forth between Riec and Port Belon several times every day. Never at specific times. My ex-husband, as everyone here in Port Belon knows, drives along there every day at half past eight. How did the perpetrator actually do it, I'm interested to know—how did they cause the accident?"

She was talking much faster again. By this point she had climbed into the pool and was heaving some of the oyster bags over the little wall.

"I get the impression all of this is barely affecting you. The terrible accident, the severe injuries that your ex-husband has suffered. The fact that it was an attempted murder—"

"It's not that it doesn't affect me, don't get me wrong, but other people need to summon up sympathy for Matthieu. That's not my job anymore." She made no bones about her attitude.

"What did you do before your trip to Riec? Where were you, Madame Premel, and who can corroborate it?"

One of them had done it. One of them had tried to kill Tordeux, Dupin was convinced of it by now, someone from Port Belon. Someone who knew their way around.

"I was here at the farm, my colleagues saw me. I can't say when exactly, of course, whether they saw me at nine fifteen, or nine, or nine thirty—I left around then."

Dupin had got out his Clairefontaine and was making a point of taking a few notes. It was like with her other alibis: there was a certain vagueness to them all.

"I've heard you're a big fan of the *bagadoù* and like to go to public music performances. Especially if the Bagad Belon is involved?"

"You know about my Celtic streak. My girls love it too. We—"

"On the twenty-seventh and twenty-eighth of February, at the regional heats in Riec—did you notice anything unusual at this event?"

"We were all in great spirits, there's nothing more to tell. I—"

"Your ex-husband also marched past you with the bombard. It seems to me like you see him surprisingly often considering that you, as you say, have nothing to do with him anymore."

"Well. That's how it is in the countryside. Especially if you work in the same profession. You can't vanish into thin air. But I generally don't even notice him." She looked Dupin in the eye for the first time and started to speak marginally more slowly. "Do you know, I came to the firm decision years ago not to let anything throw me, especially not from him—"

"Commissaire!"

The voice came from above the steep stone staircase that Dupin had just come down.

Magalie Melen.

"I need to talk to you, Commissaire."

"I'm coming," called Dupin and, turning to Madame Premel, he added, "please excuse me."

"Of course." She climbed out of the pool and busied herself with the oyster sacks.

The commissaire turned round and walked over to Melen, who had started coming down the steps toward him in the meantime.

Melen spoke in a low voice: "Tordeux, he came round briefly, then went under again. He stammered out a few confused words. He was barely intelligible. The doctor tried to ask him about the details of the accident. The doctor thinks he mumbled something about a 'ghost' and a 'car.' He's still in highly critical condition."

"A ghost? What's that supposed to mean?"

Tordeux was probably delirious.

Melen was silent for a little while.

"I don't know. I was just wondering whether—supposing our theory is correct—I would have just walked into the road if I were the perpetrator? Imagine the attack had gone wrong, Tordeux had been able to get the car under control again after all, or by some miracle didn't suffer any severe injuries: he would have recognized the perpetrator and we would have arrested them already. He couldn't have taken that risk."

She seemed not to want to go on.

"And?" Dupin couldn't see what she was getting at yet.

"They could have put something on or thrown something over themselves to make sure they weren't recognizable. Anything, a rain poncho, a long coat—maybe a bedsheet? Who knows."

Now he understood. "A ghost."

"And on top of the disguise, it would have confused Tordeux even more. If a ghost walks out in front of your car—"

"Excellent, Melen."

It was just a hypothesis. But a convincing one.

"We'll see, Commissaire."

"Any news from L'Helgoualc'h?"

"Not yet. But as regards Cueff: they've tracked him down."

Dupin was relieved. Cueff's sudden untraceability had actually made Dupin more anxious than he'd realized.

"Where was he?"

"In the *Jardins de la mer,* far out. You can't get reception there."

Dupin gave her a quizzical look.

"Gardens of the Sea, that's what they call the extensive oyster beds in Cancale that stretch hundreds of meters into the sea, all the way along the coast. Nolwenn has spoken to him and he has agreed to come to Port Belon. He's just getting changed. Our colleagues from Cancale are going to drive him."

"Anything else?"

"Not at the moment."

"Have we really found out anything about the potential relationships between Smith's old group and Breton druidic groups?" He should have asked this earlier.

"Not from this side. Riwal still has to speak to the chief druid of Seashore Grove."

The chief druid was—as per Dupin's priorities—Riwal's third stop today.

"All right. See you later, Melen."

Dupin walked back to Madame Premel. Melen had already got to the wooden door at the top of the stairs.

Madame Premel was on her knees now, getting several oysters out of the bags, examining them, and placing them in the light blue baskets, all at top speed. Dupin came and stood next to her.

"I'm afraid I've got to keep working," she said, not even lifting her head.

"From what we've heard, you're pursuing another interesting hobby. The art of oyster shucking."

"An old passion of mine. I worked in the Atlantique in Concarneau as a young woman. That's where I learned it. Fascinating."

"You got to know Nicolas Cueff from Cancale at one of the competitions. Or did you know him already?"

Her eyes, an even more intensely deep green in daylight, remained totally fixed on the oysters.

"I don't know a Nicolas Cueff."

Short and to the point.

"You spent three days with him at the beginning of March. In Cancale."

"Did I? So many people took part in the competitions. I mainly used the weekend to see one of my best friends. My husband and my two girls were there too. This Cueff definitely wasn't at any of my competitions."

Several strands of chestnut-brown hair had come loose from her hairband. Madame Premel blew them away hard.

"You didn't meet him, didn't speak to him? You can rule that out for certain?" Dupin asked sharply.

This didn't make any impression on Madame Premel either.

"I don't know a Monsieur Cueff. But you can show me a photo, of course, maybe then I'll at least remember having seen him. That's possible. If he was there too."

"And no doubt you don't know a Seamus Smith either? Have another think."

This was pointless, Dupin had to admit. The person whom Smith had seen, known, or recognized in the photo had already denied knowing Smith over the last few days. And they would continue to do so; one person here was lying, and had been the entire time. One person or even several.

"No. Like I told you yesterday. And I don't know the other Scotsman either." Madame Premel did actually raise her head for a moment and look at Dupin.

"You're in a photo that we found in Seamus Smith's home."

"This man had a photo with me in it? Well, that's pretty astonishing. What kind of photo?" She had turned back to the oysters.

Dupin had initially considered keeping the photo thing—Riwal's coup—to himself. But on the other hand, the person in question should definitely know they were on their trail. That they knew about the link.

"A photo in the current edition of *Piping Today*."

"*Piping Today*? A photo of me?"

Premel clearly knew the magazine.

"Shots from the Piping World Championship heats here in Riec, with several Port Belon residents in them."

"That sounds a little crazy. But you're the commissaire . . . As I say: I don't know any Scottish people, have never previously been in contact with one, and that's that. No Smith, no Mackenzie. I quite understand that you suspect me, but I'm the wrong person. So who else was in the photos?"

"Your whole family, your ex-husband, Monsieur Kolenc, his daughter, and Madame Bandol."

Madame Premel was silent, which had not been her style up to this point at all.

"Talk to Jean Danneau, the head of the *bagad* in Riec, you know him from yesterday, he—"

"I've just spoken to him. Nothing else has occurred to him about this."

"Well. Nothing occurs to me either."

"What do you think of the sales ban?" A quick change of topic, just the way Dupin liked it. "This precautionary measure must be disastrous for you, after all."

"We'll wait and see first."

"What did you do in 2008 during the great oyster death?"

"That nearly ruined us. All of us. But my instinct tells me we'll avoid it this time."

Madame looked up, but not at Dupin. Her gaze swept over the Belon as far as the estuary. It remained fixed there. As if this was her way of warding off the evil.

"You'll be hearing from us again, Madame Premel," the commissaire said in farewell, and did nothing to lessen the threatening undertones in his words.

"I need to be on my way too." Madame Premel set about getting the bags back into the pool. The two baskets were full to the brim. "I'm out and about a lot at the moment. But you'll find me."

"That we shall."

* * *

Dupin was heading for the small quay.

Lunchtime had brought some warmth. Astonishing warmth. The sun dominated the sky, proud and unchallenged.

Dupin was sweating in his pullover. He felt that profound tiredness again, even worse than before. And at the same time an increasingly anxious discontent, an irritability. Almost a kind of anger. They needed to make the breakthrough now. They had reached the critical phase. Riwal's discovery had been so promising in this. All the more so because Dupin was certain that parts of the story they were looking for were right there, under their noses. And they just couldn't recognize them. Everything was too confused. A total mess. What he needed was a walk, half an hour to think in peace.

"Ah. Our commissaire! I missed you at lunch." Dupin had reached the quay and stopped. Madame Bandol was just coming out of La Coquille, dressed all in pale beige today, apart from her dark hiking shoes that looked like a sophisticated, stylish accent. Behind her came Baptiste Kolenc in his civvies, jeans and a red-checked flannel shirt, while his daughter was wearing a long summer dress in a pale blue that emphasized the blackness of her hair.

"Have you spotted Kiki yet?"

"Excuse me?"

"There." She pointed along the Belon toward the estuary. "Do you see?"

Around three hundred meters away was an awe-inspiringly large fin and a second, smaller one behind it. A surreal image. The dark, sinister triangle cut through the water like a knife. Dupin had seen *Jaws* and lots of other films about sharks. You could instantly believe the fish was directly related to the white monster. If the commissaire had found the name Kiki inappropriate the day before yesterday, this feeling was only stronger now.

The animal was swimming toward them at great speed. Truth be told: it was heading straight for them.

"Kiki likes the Belon. Nowhere else has such delicious plankton." Madame Bandol sounded extremely affectionate, turning her head away a moment later and giving Dupin a serious look.

"Where are we? What stage are our investigations at, Monsieur le Commissaire? And what's this about all these new developments?" It sounded like a genuine dressing-down. "You haven't kept me up to speed! We won't get anywhere like this. I've told you multiple times."

There was an amused astonishment on Kolenc's and his daughter's faces. Madame Bandol carried on unperturbed:

"I've been thinking. I actually think this is all a big trick! What does it have to do with my dead body? It's all nonsense!" Her outrage came from deep within, apparently, although it was not clear what exactly she was outraged by. "What we are concerned with is just one question: What's the real story behind what's going on here?"

"It was attempted murder, Madame Bandol." Dupin spoke loudly on purpose. "Matthieu Tordeux's accident was an attack. Someone deliberately gave him a fright behind a bend so that he lost control of his car."

Word ought to spread about what they knew, or rather, suspected. The perpetrator really ought to hear they were hot on their heels—nervous perpetrators were careless perpetrators.

"Somebody tried to murder Monsieur Tordeux?" Baptiste Kolenc had taken a step toward the commissaire, his face pale. "Are you absolutely sure?"

Without meaning to, Dupin had been keeping a furtive eye out for Kiki's fin. It was gone. Which made it even creepier. The direct relative of the great white shark was probably very close by. You just couldn't see it. Dupin forced himself to give an appropriate answer.

"We are sure, Monsieur Kolenc." It wouldn't help the impact of his strategy if he admitted that they didn't have any evidence for this assumption as yet.

"Really?" whispered an aghast Kolenc.

"So what? That just means this crime is part of Monsieur Delsard's disgraceful sand theft schemes." Madame Bandol snorted unsympathetically. "That's all. And has nothing to do with our case at all!"

"Monsieur Kolenc," Dupin said, and turned away from the water suddenly, "a vital part of our investigations is having everyone here tell us where they were this morning between nine fifteen and ten."

Madame Bandol stared at Dupin with a horrified look on her face. Kolenc forestalled her tantrum with a calm answer:

"We just told a colleague of yours: I—"

Madame Bandol interrupted him, but had obviously decided against a tantrum in the end.

"Well, this monsieur here"—she linked arms with Kolenc for a moment—"he has a watertight alibi. He and I set out at half past eight and weren't back till twelve. My walk down by the Belon! Sometimes Baptiste comes with me. Far too rarely, though."

"That's right." Kolenc smiled. "Then my daughter and I had lunch together."

"I was doing the tastings and sales in the yard. From nine o'clock onward," Louann Kolenc said in the cheerful tone of voice that Dupin had liked so much the day before. "I closed the yard at half past eleven. There were only four guests there, older couples. Port Belon is not much of a draw at the moment."

"The alibis are absolutely bulletproof. Personally, that means I'm tremendously relieved. An investigator mustn't exclude anyone from suspicion, even their best friend, until he's ruled out with absolute certainty!" Madame Bandol had spoken very firmly, but there had been an ironic smile visible at the corners of her mouth as she said these last few words.

"So what alibis do the others have? Nolwenn Premel? That building contractor? And can you definitively rule out this man from Cancale creeping around here? And," she became mysterious, "don't forget the bit players! Read about it in Poirot! Not the real bit players, but the ones in between—between the center and the outermost edge of the story. Them!"

"Who do you have in mind?"

"Well, the niece from the château, for instance. That kind of character. Or"—her eyes gleamed—"you pay attention to the people in the center. The obvious ones!"

"So do you have a hunch now, Madame Bandol?"

"For heaven's sake, no! I was just explaining. Personally I would categorically rule out the girl from the château having anything to do with it! And a lovely creature, through and through!"

"I see."

"I suppose you've heard about the current sales ban on Belon oysters," Kolenc said seriously. Dupin was glad that someone else was bringing up the topic with the appropriate level of concern.

"Yes. What do you make of it?"

"I'm not panicking. It's not worth it. *On verra.*"

"I have another question, Monsieur Kolenc."

Kolenc looked at the commissaire in surprise.

"Your hobby—the bagpipes. Have you played for a long time?"

"Thirty years. We have a brilliant *bagad* here. It's a lot of fun."

"Have the bagpipes ever taken you to Scotland? Without your *bagad*? Privately?"

"Unfortunately not. Oysters don't like to be left alone."

"And if the Scottish bands come on a visit—do you get to know them well?"

"No," Kolenc had answered harshly, quickly adding: "Although they're very nice."

"Did you notice Monsieur Tordeux becoming friendly with one of them?"

"No."

Dupin sighed inwardly. He wasn't making any headway. "Thank you, Monsieur Kolenc."

He turned to Madame Bandol: "I'm going to drop by your house later. Then we can talk."

"All right, if needs be. I'll be expecting you."

She winked at the commissaire and a radiant smile appeared on her face. The smile that Dupin liked so much.

"We—" He broke off.

Directly in front of him, less than two meters away, he saw a dark giant in the water, just beneath the surface. Up close, the twelve meters looked even bigger. Its snout open incredibly wide, Dupin could see it clearly, and even though he knew that humans were not on the menu for basking sharks, it was obvious that this snout wouldn't have had any trouble with a full-grown human being.

"Don't worry, he won't go after you, Monsieur le Commissaire."

Dupin had heard these words from owners of large dogs before and distrusted them on principle.

Kolenc's daughter smiled and took her father by the arm. "We need to go too. *Au revoir*, Monsieur le Commissaire." Madame Bandol left with them.

Dupin had given them a friendly nod and then quickly stared at the water again, as if under a spell.

The shark had disappeared without a trace.

The phone's beeping broke the spell. He glanced quickly at the screen.

Riwal.

"Yes?"

"I'm just about to meet Harold in a pub, boss. In Oban. It's extremely windy here, I hope you can hear me."

There was a terrible hissing sound on the line.

"Who are you meeting? In a pub?"

"One of the old local reporters. The police barely know anything about that bank robbery anymore. It was the pre-digital era, you've always got to bear that in mind. And more than forty years ago. An older policeman gave me the tip about the local reporter. It's a grim story. A bank clerk was shot and wounded, a third perpetrator was drowned while fleeing. There was over two hundred thousand pounds involved. Harold was the local reporter for *Fort William News* at the time. He worked on the story."

This was exactly why Dupin had sent Riwal to Scotland. To poke around. And come across this kind of information.

Hurried footsteps rang out behind him.

"Commissaire. Even more news!"

Magalie Melen and Brioc L'Helgoualc'h.

"Just a moment." Dupin put the phone to his other ear. "Anything else for the moment, Riwal?"

"Mackenzie's wife doesn't know anything about the holdup, and the photos didn't mean anything to her either. I'll be in touch again later."

The hissing on the other end was becoming increasingly unbearable.

"Straight after you speak to the reporter!"

Dupin hung up.

Melen and L'Helgoualc'h were standing in front of him. L'Helgoualc'h was holding, Dupin now saw, something that looked like fabric in his right hand. And he was wearing thin plastic gloves.

"I found this in the wood, under some bushes. On the plot of land behind Delsard's and Tordeux's houses, to one side of the path."

"And?" Dupin didn't understand.

L'Helgoualc'h unfolded what looked like a coarse tablecloth, thick linen, presumably once a dark beige, very faded and covered in dirt.

All at once, Dupin understood. Melen's ghost theory.

"Where did you say the tablecloth was?"

"Behind Delsard's and Tordeux's houses."

"To one side of the path?"

"Yes. Ten meters away from the path. I didn't find the place where the person left the path until my third attempt. The ground is covered in undergrowth and thick ivy. The person was very skillful."

"A light person?"

"Not necessarily, if they're agile."

"The size of the footprint?"

"Not particularly big, but that's hard to tell too, it's very tricky ground," L'Helgoualc'h mumbled. Dupin always got the feeling with him that he only gave information with the utmost reluctance, although he didn't mean to be at all unfriendly.

"Were you able to find any other footprints?"

"It was just one person, I think. Prints here and there, all partial, the ground is too stony. The person came from Port Belon and went back there too, via a narrow, seldom-used path, a hunting trail that starts at the parking lot and forks several times in the woods."

"Someone could have come with the tablecloth and disposed of it on the way back," Melen pondered aloud.

"How long does the path take? From the parking lot in Port Belon as far as the bend?"

"Seventeen minutes. There and back. Just walking the path itself at a brisk pace; the person didn't run. But I didn't say the person joined the path at the parking lot. They could just as easily have come from one of the back gardens and then joined the path."

"Those would be Tordeux's or Delsard's gardens," said a startled Melen, "but it would be a stone's throw for Premel and Kolenc too. There are small lanes and paths all over Port Belon."

That was true, but L'Helgoualc'h's remark was still interesting.

"Take the tablecloth to the forensic investigators." Dupin rubbed his forehead. "So the whole operation only took twenty or twenty-five minutes." That was important, particularly with inconclusive alibis. "If everything played out the way we're assuming it did."

"Maybe someone wanted to direct the suspicion toward Delsard by hiding the tablecloth in the undergrowth behind their houses. Leaving a false trail." Melen was right again.

Dupin nodded.

"Do you still need me?" L'Helgoualc'h's emphasis made it clear that he would consider it an imposition.

"Not at the moment. Thank you so much."

"Then I'll take the tablecloth away."

L'Helgoualc'h neatly folded it up and trudged off sulkily.

* * *

Magalie Melen and Dupin had walked to the command center in front of the château. Like last time, Dupin didn't sit down, pacing feverishly up and down in front of the tables instead. "We've got the alibis from Premel, Kolenc, and his daughter for this morning."

He was holding his notebook as he gave a brief report.

Magalie Melen nodded after each name.

"That tallies with all of the statements we had already taken. The young woman from the château was also doing the sales and tastings on-site from nine o'clock, over there in the château's little yard. But of course that can't be verified down to the minute. We're talking about twenty or twenty-five minutes. If not much was happening, she or Louann Kolenc could have slipped away unnoticed. And even if people had arrived in the meantime, they might have waited, left, or come back later. We won't be able to verify that."

"And Kolenc and Bandol are giving each other an alibi with their walk," said Dupin.

"All of the alibis are vague—and will probably stay that way."

There were deep furrows on Dupin's forehead. Not from worry, but from annoyance.

"Somebody needs to sound out Premel's colleagues. Very carefully."

"I'll send Braz. Just quickly, regarding Tordeux, Commissaire. The hospital has been in touch. He has fallen back into a coma again. The doctors are not venturing a prognosis. So he won't able to tell us anything for now. We—"

"Hello?"

Dupin recognized Kadeg's voice. It was cracking with excitement.

"We've got something. Something important!"

Of course.

Kadeg came running down the street. And so the dramatic scenes in front of breathtaking backdrops continued. The sun made the Belon's last stretch before the Atlantic glitter brightly. Millions of dancing diamonds.

"My data expert has accessed some of Tordeux's encrypted correspondence." Kadeg paused gratuitously and Dupin noticed the acid in his stomach rising—*his* data expert? And in any case, what did Kadeg have to do with their case again all of a sudden?

"We've found a deleted folder. And a highly significant document inside it." Kadeg had stopped in front of Dupin, a single sheet in his hand. "We have found"—another pause; this time it was meant to seem dramatic—"a blackmail letter."

"A blackmail letter?"

Kadeg held the sheet triumphantly in Dupin's face.

The commissaire took it and held it so he could read it.

I expect the money tomorrow, Thursday. In cash.

Meet me at 4 P.M.

"That's all? Just these lines? No greeting? No place?"

"Just this for the moment." Kadeg sounded offended. "We need to check whether we can de-encrypt more. It was in a folder deleted at six P.M. yesterday along with various business correspondence. We've been able to read some of it, and as far as we've been able to tell, it's not relevant."

"This isn't much, Kadeg. And it can't have been the first letter, can it? The crucial pieces of information are missing. Including the amount. Above all, the addressee."

"The experts are still looking."

"Was it possible to establish what day the data was created?" Melen asked.

"Yesterday afternoon, two o'clock."

Dupin ran a hand roughly through his hair again.

"Shit."

He had raised his voice and begun to walk in circles. Kadeg spun round with him.

How could this suddenly be about blackmail? What could be behind this? He didn't have the faintest idea. But it clearly looked as though Tordeux had tried to blackmail someone. Tordeux, again and again. He had clear and considerable criminal intent. And ambitions. Dupin had to admit that he had considered this level of criminal intent out of the question. But he had made a mistake. An enormous mistake.

His thoughts were racing. The fire had probably been a warning. That Tordeux had obviously not taken seriously.

"And this is really all you found?"

"As regards that issue, yes. But we did find out something else: when Tordeux bought the oyster farm near La Forêt-Fouesnant, Delsard did—contrary to Tordeux's statement—have a financial interest. To the tune of exactly a hundred and fifty thousand euro! We have seen the transfer on both accounts, with exact details, even the notary's case number, everything properly accounted for."

So Dupin had made a mistake on this point too. And even more importantly: Tordeux had lied again!

"And Delsard was also a co-investor in the purchase of the farm in Cancale. Two hundred thousand euro."

In both cases the amounts that Delsard had contributed were—in light of the total prices—not exorbitant sums. Nevertheless, Tordeux and Delsard were in fact doing business together, that had now been established.

"This is just unbelievable. I've had enough now."

Dupin had stopped walking, his hands balled into fists. He became lost in contemplation of the silver Atlantic beyond the Belon estuary. Half of the village must have heard him ranting.

Did everything essentially revolve around a dispute between Tordeux and Delsard? Had the pair of them quarreled? Maybe then there really would be ties to the sand theft in the end . . .

"I want to speak to Delsard."

Dupin himself would never have thought he would say these words, especially with such determination.

Kadeg couldn't hide his satisfaction. "You see, there you go. And the prefect is expecting you to call him. Immediately, I'm to tell you."

"I'm not going to do anything."

"He has postponed the press conference till four P.M. and wants to, and I quote, talk to you immediately."

"What"—this sentence wasn't easy for Dupin to utter either—"about the sand theft? Are there any updates on that?"

"It's looking more and more solid." Kadeg's self-satisfaction was insufferable. "Construction Traittot used significant quantities of sand, and its existence and purchase is not recorded anywhere. That's beyond doubt. And there's only one conclusion to be drawn from it. There are also links to a bogus shipping company in Lorient, a company with no contracts. It could have collected the sand from the beaches—I already have circumstantial evidence of that too, I had told you that. We're expecting an arrest warrant for Delsard to be issued any moment now."

"This is a disaster," Dupin blurted out. It was all playing perfectly into the prefect's hands. Including the genuine business ties that had now been proven between Delsard and Tordeux.

It was like a bad film, but he had to face up to the situation: Kadeg's ridiculous obsession with the sand theft, his unauthorized, childish surveillance farce, that had all been on the right track. Dupin had been seriously wrong. But, he thought with his gaze fixed on the river, even if all of this presumed major criminal intent made every other crime, even murder, seem possible—why the hell would someone have murdered Smith and Mackenzie in this situation?

The commissaire heaved a deep sigh.

"We're going to meet outside Delsard's house in three minutes. Three minutes!"

Dupin took his mobile out of his pocket and set off. His mood was in the doldrums.

Before he could even think about the most skillful way of beginning the phone call with the prefect, the tirade was already pouring forth.

Dupin held the receiver as far away from his ear as his arm would allow. But he still heard the words loud and clear: "disgraceful behavior," "willful boycott," "disciplinary proceedings," "suspension," there was even mention of a "transfer to the real end of the world," a phrase that Kadeg brooded over briefly: What on earth could the real end of the world be in the prefect's eyes?

Only gradually did the voice on the other end calm down.

Dupin held the phone to his ear carefully. He had taken a turnoff on his left, onto the picturesque path along the Belon.

"I've had to postpone the press conference. A second time! Which is entirely your fault. All of the evidence is there and I hear nothing! Nothing at all. Disgraceful. Only piecemeal and from this person or that person. The supposed car accident! Delsard and Tordeux's business entanglements that Kadeg had to dig up for you! The blackmail!" Dupin should have known. Kadeg had spoken to the prefect first and already informed him about everything. "That it was definitely an arson attack! You've known for hours that Delsard wanted to kill Tordeux and I—the person with sole responsibility—I don't know a thing."

Dupin thought this over quickly: with his last point, the prefect must be referring to the footprints in the wood and the tablecloth—it was evidence but purely circumstantial! And he was still not finished:

"And you—you're chasing the two Scotsmen, some ridiculous chimeras and nonsense that have nothing to do with us anyway. If you hadn't deliberately held back the evidence of Delsard's attack on Tordeux because it didn't conform to your obsessions and confused theories, then—"

"Has the forensics team found anything on the tablecloth?"

The prefect raised his voice even more. "I . . . no. But do you know where the old policeman from the Monts d'Arrée found it? Yes? In front of Delsard's house. Another piece of evidence!"

"Behind the house. Placed so conspicuously that a pro would spot it as an artificially placed clue immediately."

Locmariaquer didn't seem to have heard this.

"Incidentally, we have the extremely well paid, best forensic investigator in the world, and you have that old man from the mountains come? But we'll discuss that in detail later, along with everything else." His tone of voice was softening slightly. "So I'm not going to appear before the press until this evening now."

"And what story are you going to tell?"

There was quite a long pause. Even now, Dupin didn't think it was impossible that his question would provoke another fit.

"The story about how we're dealing with a hardened criminal in Delsard!" The wording sounded like a joke, but obviously not to the prefect. "Sand theft on a systematic scale, over the course of years, meticulously organized. An arson attack, attempted murder, potentially other murders. Dirty business dealings. And there'll be a few more things. Tordeux was his front man, Delsard did business through him, invested in various fields, definitely not just in the oyster industry, but we'll be able to prove it! Presumably he secretly used semilegal company structures to evade the tax. Exactly: tax fraud will no doubt be part of it! So Tordeux becomes aware of some things and blackmails him. He wanted a bigger slice of the pie, that's how it goes! And then there's always blackmail! So Delsard wanted to get rid of his accomplice."

It was remarkable how the prefect was twisting things.

"And the two Scotsmen, Monsieur le Préfet?"

"I've said it before and I won't say it a third time: the poor oyster farmer was in the wrong place at the wrong time—at the handover of the money. He—"

"And why would Tordeux and Delsard, who knew each other well, suddenly meet at a place like that to hand over the money like strangers? That just doesn't make any sense, they . . ."

Dupin broke off. It didn't make any sense to ask the prefect these questions. He had become fixated and there was no way to put him off course.

"Do you see?"

Dupin had no idea what that was supposed to mean.

"Your questions lead nowhere. You don't have the beginnings of an answer! We can easily leave the two Scotsmen to the Scottish police. We'll send our colleagues all of the facts. And then this matter is over and done with! Do you hear me, Commissaire? That is an official order! You are going to halt all further investigation into this issue! The two matters are unrelated, I don't need to tell you how often that happens: a coincidence, a coincidental intersection of events."

Dupin didn't speak. He knew all too well that protesting was pointless. The awful thing was that the story would, if you told the bare bones of it, sound thoroughly plausible to an outsider. The commissaire had been through this more than once: sometimes on a case, there came a point when nobody had any real interest in knowing the truth all of a sudden, in continuing to laboriously dig for it. It ebbed away, it died, it was a kind of general exhaustion. At some point—and it had nothing whatsoever to do with the actual duration of the investigation, its real length, but to do with an internal dynamic—it was enough to be able to tell a credible-sounding story that rounded everything off, just to find an ending. Regardless of whether the story still had holes or how big they were. A story that roughly linked everything together, covering the main elements. And everyone concerned was then often relieved—although their consciences prickled now and again. Dupin knew the temptation, he knew it well, but it had always been impossible for him to give in to it. It was simply impossible for him to accept something he knew was not correct.

"All right." The prefect had, of course, misinterpreted the silence. "We're in agreement then. Don't take my words too much to heart, they're meant to be more of a warning to you." The prefect took a theatrical breath in. "Ah, mon Commissaire, sometimes people get carried away, sometimes things are just complicated. So it's good to have a smart sparring partner. I have some more good news, by the way: I am personally coming to Port Belon and will carry out Delsard's arrest. And get your inspector to come back from Scotland immediately, that expensive work trip is probably already putting an undue strain on your commissariat's travel budget."

"You can . . ." Dupin paused.

"I repeat: I expect you to summon Riwal back immediately."

The commissaire sensed how serious the prefect was about this. Deadly serious.

"I've got a series of important calls to make now. I'll see you on the scene very soon!"

The prefect had hung up.

Dupin didn't know what he was feeling: disgust, bewilderment, revulsion, fury, rebellion—all at the same time.

He shook himself, once, twice, and ran a hand through the hair on the back of his head.

He had walked quite a distance without realizing. Along the Belon, around the first large inlet. There were tall stone pines amongst the oaks that went down to the bank. The water was calm here, crystal clear; some stones lay on the pale sand and little fish darted about in the shallow water.

He immediately turned on his heel and ran back, half jogging, as he held his mobile to his ear. He wanted to hear what Riwal had to report.

"Riwal, what's the—"

"Boss?"

Like last time, he could only just make out what Riwal was saying, although there were different disruptive noises in the background this time. Voices. Lively voices.

"We need—"

"I can barely hear you, boss. It's pretty busy in the pub. I ordered myself a haggis with Harold, and a pint on the side, delicious, but not for the fainthearted. People are wrong to make fun of Scottish cuisine—"

"Riwal! What did the reporter say?"

"We had a long talk. It was all very dramatic in this bank robbery. Harold really got to grips with the details back then and he thinks he still has his old notes. You'd like him, boss."

"Get to the point, Riwal!"

At least it was easy to hear him now.

"At first, the holdup was going smoothly for the three men, but then everything got out of hand. A guard drew a pistol, there was a scuffle. Mackenzie, who was clearly the leader of the gang, attacked him, seized control of the gun, and shot at the guard. He received a stomach wound and survived. But during the commotion, Mackenzie hurt himself too, which meant he couldn't escape. Smith and Ben Osborn, the third man, fled on motorbikes. Osborn had the money—it was exactly two hundred and forty-three thousand pounds! Smith was apprehended an hour later, probably extremely drunk. The third man tried to get away on a small boat but the sea was rough. A fisherman saw him putting out to sea, he didn't stand a chance." By his standards, Riwal was reporting very concisely; thoroughly but concisely. "Two days later the wrecked boat was found on a rock, along with a single shoe and the mask."

"The money?" The commissaire was walking at a brisk pace.

"The money was never found. The coast guard searched for a few more days. The assumption is that it got lost in the Atlantic. When the search was called off, the fishermen and other locals began to dive for the money. It was a sensation, of course. Such a big sum just floating around in the sea, in a plastic bag! Can you imagine? It became a kind of sport. But it never turned up again."

"And Mackenzie and Smith?"

"They confessed and were put inside for four and three years respectively. They were seriously lucky to be under twenty-one. Otherwise the sentences would have been much stiffer."

Even Dupin himself couldn't have said why this story interested him so much.

"Perhaps someone did find the money and didn't say anything," said Riwal.

"What do you mean?" Dupin had already been somewhere else in his thoughts.

"One of the fishermen could have found the money. He could have spent it bit by bit without attracting attention. Or he could have moved away."

Starting from the assumption that the money hadn't gone missing threw up endless possible stories.

There was a rather long pause.

"Or . . . or the money didn't even end up in the water because it had been dumped somewhere beforehand, or"—Dupin was running through more possibilities—"the third man never had it, Smith did. And he dumped it somewhere."

"You're right, boss, all possible. It's all based on just these two men's statements. We only know this version. It's possible they came up with a version together. Mackenzie and Smith were in the same prison. Even before the trial."

"Maybe Smith lied to Mackenzie too. Maybe *he* invented the story that the third man had the money."

"Harold said that too."

"Were there any clues indicating that?"

"No. Nothing."

"What else does this Harold say?"

Dupin was almost back at the château now. Magalie Melen was waiting for him outside Delsard's house.

"The three men had known each other since they were sixteen. They all came from the Isle of Skye, albeit from different parts, and to begin with, they learned to fish in Portree for a year. Then all three of them worked on an oyster and mussel farm. They were always hanging round together, going to the same pubs. And they got up to plenty of mischief. One time, they took their boss's boat and went on a three-day bender to the Outer Hebrides. They almost died in the process. He fired them afterward."

"Any other offenses?"

"Just harmless things, sometimes a brawl, broken furniture, a damaged car, never anything bad, no bodily harm, no grand larceny or anything like that. They wanted to take the money from the bank robbery and get out of there."

Dupin thought it would be terrible, miserable, awful: life as a young person in the seventies on a godforsaken island in a godforsaken part of the world, isolated and with no prospects. He instantly understood the wild boat trip. And, as stupid as the idea of the bank robbery had been, he understood the urge to get out of there.

"How long were they employed in oyster and mussel farming?"

"Almost two years."

"Keep poking about, Riwal. Let Harold talk."

"Another thing, boss: we've tracked down the reporter who wrote the article for *Piping Today*. He and a photographer were there for two nights. They stayed in Pont-Aven, in the Central."

Riwal waited for a response from Dupin. It didn't come. The commissaire knew the hotel well.

"They didn't notice anything unusual; they only spoke to the leader of the group, a Monsieur Danneau. The photos weren't meant to show anyone specific."

"Okay. Call Nolwenn and update her on everything. Otherwise don't tell a soul. Don't answer any calls from anyone! Apart from calls from me and Nolwenn." Dupin needed to protect Riwal. He wouldn't tell him anything about the prefect's order yet, but he wouldn't summon him back either. "Most importantly, don't answer any calls from Quimper. Or from unknown numbers. And stay in touch!"

Dupin hung up. He was standing a few meters away from Delsard's house.

Perhaps that dramatic business from years back did play a part in the present in some crazy way. The dilemma was this: How and why would this business crop up again more than forty years later, in Brittany of all places? Could the money still exist? Could it have made its way here via a circuitous route? To a person whom Mackenzie, Smith, or the third man had known back in the day? Known well? A person who had also been in the photograph in *Piping Today*?

Dupin pulled himself together.

He would get over his terrible inner exhaustion and redouble his efforts. Take another careful look, and that meant at everything!

* * *

Magalie Melen was standing in the driveway of Delsard's property, next to a dark green Porsche SUV. She had been waiting for Dupin.

You couldn't make out the house from the road—it was screened off by tall oleander, camellia, and laurel bushes, and it wasn't until you took a few steps down the driveway that you saw it: a stylishly restored old farmhouse with a barn, on the edge of a parklike garden facing east toward Riec. There was a magnificent pool in the middle of the lush garden, along with a few palm trees. Large mallow bushes here and there. Beyond the garden was the beginning of the wood and the path that cut through it, near where they had found the tablecloth.

Melen had her mobile to her ear. "All right, thanks."

She hung up and came a few steps closer to the commissaire. "He's in his study with two lawyers. He's expecting you."

It sounded like the preparation for a showdown in a Western.

"Then let's go."

Melen turned round and strode past the car; she clearly knew the way.

"Cueff will be here in half an hour," she said when Dupin caught up with her. "The bacterium still has not been detected in the Belon, but the sales ban will remain in place for now. There is further evidence of Tordeux's systematic fraud, we can now be confident there must have been a crime; nothing new on the blackmail letter, the computer experts have not been able to recover any other relevant document so far. And no trace evidence could be found on the tablecloth either."

There were so many threads.

"I had a crazy theory," said the young policewoman, hesitant now, "but it's impossible, I'm afraid. What if Mackenzie isn't dead at all? What if he only faked his death?"

"What makes you think that?"

"We don't have a body. Nothing. He could have staged it. All of it. He killed his friend on the way here from the airport, accomplished what he wanted to accomplish in Port Belon, whatever it was, and then took off, deliberately going underground."

All of a sudden, Melen's idea sounded astonishingly convincing.

"Let's just take the scene in the parking lot: Mackenzie wanted someone to see him dead, and then got rid of his car so that it fit with the murder theory and the dumped body. Someone other than Madame Bandol would have been believed straightaway! If a hiker had seen him, for instance. It would also explain why Madame Bandol maybe really did only see one car—*his*." Melen stopped walking for a moment. "Unfortunately, there would then be no explanation for other important elements." Then she calmly explained the counterargument to her own theory: "For example, why he would have gone to the trouble of staging a murder in the parking lot without creating more trace evidence. It would have been so simple for him to produce bloodstains on a piece of fabric that could have clearly identified him as the victim."

They had entered the house by now and were at the stairs to the first floor. Two policemen were supervising everything with eagle eyes. They nodded to them.

"An interesting theory."

"The only annoying thing is that it essentially leaves open the question that's been bothering us so much: What was it that Mackenzie needed to do in Port Belon?"

This was true. And yet Dupin realized there was something about it that appealed to him.

"I'll leave you to it now, Commissaire. I'm going back to the experts who are looking at Tordeux's data."

"Please do."

Dupin climbed the stairs at an athletic pace.

He found himself in an imposing room on the first floor. A long room, clearly an office, with large windows at the front facing onto the garden. Everything looked expensive—wealth on display. Objects everywhere that didn't suit the tastefully restored old house at all: a bright yellow leather sofa with a stainless steel frame, a dull stainless steel sideboard. At the end of the room was an aluminum desktop mounted lengthwise on the wall, with papers and files piled up on it and two large computer screens close together. Two men in civvies were sitting in front of the screens: the experts.

Kadeg and a tall young man Dupin didn't know were standing next to a large leather armchair that was, and this must have been inexplicably deliberate, admittedly yellow but a different shade of yellow from the sofa. In the armchair sat a slight, short man who, if this was Delsard, looked completely different from how Dupin had pictured him. A gaunt face, he was on edge, almost frightened in fact; there was something sad, something wretched, about his overall appearance. There were two stylish men in suits next to him: the lawyers, no doubt.

The tall man and Kadeg walked toward Dupin, a dynamic team.

"Jason Riefolo, head of the task force."

"One moment." Dupin turned round and got his phone out of the pocket of his jeans.

The head of the task force's face instantly turned crimson.

"You're here, you're not just going to . . ." He didn't hide his aggression.

Dupin had already stopped listening to Riefolo. He was walking back to the stairs. The phone to his ear.

"Riwal?" Dupin spoke softly.

"Boss?"

The connection was crystal clear for the first time, Dupin noticed to his relief.

"Any more news from Harold?"

"Nothing else that's relevant to us."

"Stick with it, Riwal."

Dupin hung up.

He went back and headed right past Kadeg and the head of the task force, going straight toward the slight man in the yellow leather armchair. Both of the lawyers, approximately in their late thirties, immediately moved a bit closer to the man, one on the right, the other on the left.

"Commissaire Georges Dupin, Commissariat de Police Concarneau. Monsieur Delsard, I presume? I'm investigating the murders from the last two days."

The prefect must not hear about this.

"This highly dubious search," the man to Delsard's right said, "is completely unrelated to any murders, the police's purpose is expressly different, you—"

"I don't want to search anything. I just want to speak to Monsieur Delsard. He"—Dupin had to exaggerate slightly—"bought his way into the oyster industry via his front man, Matthieu Tordeux. And both the two recent murders and the attempted murder today are presumed to be related to incidents in the oyster industry. My inquiries are about suspicion of murder, not stolen sand."

Kadeg and the leader of the task force had come over by now and had heard every word. Dupin couldn't care less at this point.

"This is ridiculous."

It was Delsard himself who had suddenly answered, his voice sounding a little shaky, but cold.

"Monsieur Delsard, you should stay silent and let us talk," his lawyer on the right-hand side urged him. The one on the left nodded in agreement.

Dupin didn't react at all; he was looking at Delsard as if he were alone with him.

"When did you get here today, Monsieur Delsard?"

"My client has been here in his house since late morning, around ten o'clock. He—"

"You weren't here when the search operation began?"

"My client was out."

"What does 'around ten o'clock' mean?"

"Around ten o'clock."

"Where were you before that, Monsieur Delsard? Between quarter past nine and ten o'clock?"

"We see no reason to respond to that."

Dupin couldn't compel them to. Delsard didn't have to say anything, and he knew it.

"You didn't arrive home here until shortly after ten, Monsieur Delsard?"

"That's what we said."

Delsard was aloof, looking out of the large windows while his lawyers spoke on his behalf.

"And did you come here alone?"

"Yes. We met our client here."

Thus one important thing was certain: Delsard had no alibi for the time of the crime.

"He came here alone?" Dupin turned to the lawyer directly for the first time.

"As I said, we met him here." It was clear that the lawyer was uneasy. He was aware that he had said something of interest to the commissaire.

Dupin turned back to Delsard. "Where were you the day before yesterday, Tuesday, between four and five P.M., and also yesterday around six thirty P.M.?"

"We will not be saying anything on that either."

The absurd game continued.

"Do you know a Ryan Mackenzie or a Seamus Smith?"

"There's no reason to ask this question of Monsieur Delsard and hence no reason to answer it."

Dupin dropped it.

He could save himself the trouble of asking more questions. Although he would have liked to have heard more, of course. About Delsard's real relationship with Matthieu Tordeux, for instance. Which Delsard would never tell him. Besides, Cueff was due to arrive soon. But, he had learned something. That Delsard had no alibi for this morning.

"All right then, Monsieur Delsard. In the matter of the attempted murder of Matthieu Tordeux, I am going to apply for a separate arrest warrant against you. That will make two of them. Let's see who gets you, monsieur. The seriousness of the crimes will be the deciding factor."

The dynamic head of the task force burst out: "That's *my* man! *We* will arrest him. On the grounds of particularly serious theft, particularly serious environmental offenses, and a whole series of other crimes. The prefect—"

"—is coming in person, I know."

Surprisingly, Kadeg had stayed out of the conversation, which was not like him at all.

"No doubt it will be a magnificent event."

Dupin turned round and went back to the stairs. He needed to get out of there.

Thirty seconds later, he had left the house.

* * *

The car bringing Cueff had been delayed by some traffic jams—heavy rain showers inland—Magalie Melen was expecting him in around twenty minutes. Dupin had decided to meet Cueff in La Coquille; it wouldn't be too busy there yet.

Two text messages had come through while he had been speaking to Delsard. Claire. *Call me.* And, a few minutes later: *Am in Lorient. Driving back at six. Dinner somewhere?* Dupin had to admit that he had virtually forgotten Claire in the whirlwind that was today. He hadn't been in touch again since their short phone call this morning. He needed to reply to her, turning her down—*Afraid I can't. Love you. G.*

Dupin had stopped to type on the road to the quay, just a few paces away from Delsard's house. To the left, along the border of the building contractor's property and before the wall to Tordeux's land, one of the paths branched off. It led into the wood and then to the hunters' trail. If you were to walk directly through the wood, you would get straight to the Belon. Dupin thought it over briefly.

Then he entered the jungle-like thicket.

It was dark here too, like at the spot where he had stood with L'Helgoualc'h and Melen.

Just two minutes later he reached the narrow hunters' trail that led to the road with the accident site. The commissaire walked straight on, slowly. He was trying to think, sort through the wealth of information. The treetops had grown close together overhead; you could smell and taste the wood on the air, the damp earth, the resin of the wood.

His conversation with Delsard had not been all that smart from a tactical point of view. His exhaustion returned, as severe as ever. No matter how hard Dupin tried, he couldn't form a single coherent thought. And yet it would be so important to sort through everything in his mind.

Suddenly there was a blue glimmer visible between the tree trunks, faint at first, then brighter and brighter.

The Belon.

Dupin's sense of direction had guided him correctly. A few more meters and he stepped out of the wood with one long stride. And stopped.

It was crazy. On the other side of Port Belon, where he had spent time over the last few days and which he knew so well from his walks, the Belon was mainly sea. Not only because you could see the estuary and the open Atlantic; no, the entire atmosphere over there was maritime. But here, on this side of the headland where the houses were, everything was different. A perfect lake scene lay before him, tranquil, quiet. From this spot, the Belon was a large blue-gray expanse, as smooth as glass, two or three kilometers long and perhaps half a kilometer wide. Utterly placid. It was still high tide, although it was gradually going out. Some of the oyster tables were visible at the edges. Including directly in front of him.

Dupin kept walking and didn't stop until he was a few centimeters from the waterline.

He had seen something gleaming. There were a few colorful, shimmering oyster shells in the shallow water—European oysters—and next to them: a "giant." An excessively large specimen. Riwal had explained it to him at the market in Concarneau once: a *pied de cheval*, a "horse's foot." One of the oysters that escapes from the parks and becomes enormous in the wild. Not as big as in his dream, but still. A forty-centimeter-large oyster was incredibly impressive. To his left, the thicket by the river thinned out and gave way to a meadow. A garden, as Dupin could tell when he looked closely. A magnificent garden. And behind three tall pine trees, in solitary splendor, stood a little castle made of pale gray granite. Enchanted, like in a fairy tale. It had to be Madame Bandol's house.

Dupin walked a little way along the stony riverside path. Hesitantly at first but then with increasing determination. He walked right across the lawn, straight toward the little castle. He had pictured it being beautiful, of course—the Bandol sisters had bought it, after all—but this beat everything he had imagined.

He approached the door, which was at the top of an imposing stone staircase.

"Hello? Madame Bandol?"

It was absurd to call out to her—the house was massive and was bound to have dozens of rooms. He would ring the bell.

"Here I am. Here!"

Dupin turned around. There was a summerhouse twenty or thirty meters away, partially covered in blossoming camellia, right on a meandering branch of the Belon, as idyllic as it gets. There was a large wooden terrace in front of the summerhouse that ran along by the water, and on it were three comfortable-looking loungers in orange, greenish yellow, and turquoise. Armandine Bandol was lying on the turquoise lounger, the backrest propped up. She made no move to get up. Zizou lay at her feet and seemed to be fast asleep.

Dupin walked over to her.

"You're very early," she said sternly. "I wasn't expecting you yet."

Only now did he realize that he had in fact promised to come by "later."

"But all right—you're here now."

She still made no move to stand up. There was a tall, narrow glass on the wooden floor next to the lounger. A champagne glass. A teapot and teacup next to it. There was a book there. A newspaper. A large, stylish red sun hat. And a little glass bell.

Dupin didn't want to admit it was a coincidence that he was dropping in, especially as he really couldn't stay long. "Everything has shifted timing-wise, Madame Bandol, the monsieur from Cancale is running late. I don't have long, but I really wanted to call in and see you."

Although there was no real logic to his words, they seemed to placate Madame Bandol.

"Come on, have a seat," she said, and pointed to the orange lounger. "Here, next to me."

Dupin hesitated, but just for a moment, then he sat down. The backrest was practically vertical.

"You ought to be silent for a moment and just let the landscape work its magic on you. I always find it tremendously helpful when I'm having a think."

She closed her eyes.

After a brief hesitation, Dupin leaned back. And looked around. He was nervous. But the world looked like a heavenly garden here. Harmony. Gentleness. Mildness. It sounded odd, but nature seemed infinitely gracious here. It was quiet; the gentle wind was the only sound to be heard.

"I see a lot more with my eyes closed. This landscape," Madame Bandol mused, "is the landscape of fairy tales, and the fairy tales take place inside us." She paused, opened her eyes, looked Dupin in the eye, and then suddenly said briskly, "Right. So! Time for work, Monsieur le Commissaire. What is the situation?"

Dupin had actually been lost in thought for a moment. Oddly enough, he had been brooding over the giant oyster. Although he didn't know why. Something had subconsciously been bothering him since then in general.

Madame Bandol's exhortation had brought him back to earth and he looked at his watch in alarm. Then at his mobile. Neither of which escaped Madame Bandol's notice.

"You can't get reception here. Ever. I'm very pleased about that."

Dupin considered what to do; he was already late. "Madame Bandol, do you think"—it was an unusual idea, but a pragmatic one at the same time—"do you think we could talk to Monsieur Cueff here at your house?"

Her expression didn't in any way betray that she found the suggestion the slightest bit odd.

"In the summerhouse maybe?"

Dupin had actually been thinking of a room inside the house, but why not. He was aware that it would make a strange impression, but still, it would be the easiest thing. Besides, they were guaranteed to be alone there. Undisturbed. And, it was never a bad thing for a suspect to be confused.

"You are doing the police a great favor, Madame Bandol."

Madame Bandol smiled, her expression revealing that she found making the summerhouse available as the scene of police work an enticing prospect.

"Of course. I mean, I am a part of the team."

She picked up the little bell next to her lounger and rang it.

"May I use your phone?" Dupin had stood up. "I need to let Magalie Melen know."

"Of course, of course."

A young woman in a black dress with a white lace apron came tripping out of the house. A far from submissive look on her face.

"Madame rang?" she asked.

"Two things, Odette: show this monsieur here our phone, he has an urgent phone call to make. Also, we will be receiving a guest in a few minutes' time, in the summerhouse. If you could prepare tea for us?"

"I think," Dupin interrupted her gently, but firmly, "a carafe of water will be enough, Madame Bandol."

"And at least a coffee for each of us!"

Dupin hesitated for a moment, then changed his mind:

"Madame Bandol, do you think Mademoiselle Odette would be so kind as to call Magalie Melen and tell her she is to come here with Monsieur Cueff, please?"

Madame Bandol turned to the girl: "We'll do as Monsieur le Commissaire says. We have the number."

"Of course, madame."

Mademoiselle Odette disappeared.

"Who maintains all of this, Madame Bandol? The garden, the . . . estate?"

"I have a small army to look after everything. A gardener, a housekeeper and cook, and then Odette too. And if needs be, those three have assistants in turn. The estate requires quite a lot of attention."

"Do you know Monsieur Delsard personally? The building contractor?"

There was confusion in her eyes.

"You're not about to entertain the idea that our case has something to do with the sand theft crimes too, are you? I'm severely disappointed, Monsieur le Commissaire. Don't lose your pride!" Whether her dismay was real or feigned, Dupin couldn't tell. "You are a true investigator. True, you're no Hercule Poirot, but you're still a fairly decent one. You're going to uncover the secret at the center of all this! And I'll assist you."

This made Dupin smile.

"And incidentally: no, I don't know him. I know who he is. No more than that. An extremely unpleasant character. He never says hello."

"Monsieur Kolenc—do you trust him completely?"

Now she looked aghast. "That's enough now. He's part of the team. One of us. Of course! He's a friend."

She considered the topic finished.

"The building contractor could be embroiled in several different matters that are completely unrelated to each other, including ours," Madame Bandol reflected. "And perhaps his friend Tordeux was not just a victim, but a perpetrator too! Maybe he even murdered the two Scotsmen. Before being attacked himself. That would be a brilliant twist: if Tordeux dies, the murderer himself would have been killed. And we would have yet another murderer!"

"That is absolutely possible. Tordeux did blackmail someone anyway. We've found a letter indicating that, but unfortunately there's no addressee. We don't know who it was meant for."

Madame Bandol's eyes opened wide. "See! He's capable of anything!"

Dupin had stood up and was pacing restlessly back and forth. He stopped at the edge of the river. His gaze swept across the tranquil Belon.

He still couldn't work out what it was that had been bothering him so much just now. But he was certain it was important.

"That's right, Monsieur le Commissaire! Meditate! That's what I meant. Then it will all become clearer!"

Dupin was only vaguely listening to Madame Bandol in the background.

He was familiar with these moments: when something within him—the term "instinct" was just a rough approximation—was working independently on something that his mind couldn't immediately grasp. Or only partially, in some vague way.

* * *

Cueff was bald, but had some closely shaven whitish-gray hair left at his temples. He wore horn-rimmed glasses that made his narrowed eyes look cunning. He had a large physique, but he was not athletic, more thick-set, in contrast to his very delicate facial features. Sometimes, Dupin thought, heads didn't match the bodies they were sitting on—or vice versa.

Magalie Melen had driven Cueff and it hadn't taken long.

Mademoiselle Odette had shown them to the summerhouse. It was painted white and adorned with opulent wood carvings. Five wooden pillars supported the dome. Underneath it stood two wooden benches at right angles, arranged so that you were looking out at the Belon, at the whole colorful panorama.

Madame Bandol had remained nonchalantly on her lounger, picking up her book and looking absorbed in her reading.

"Sit down." Dupin saw no reason to be particularly friendly. "You knowingly made a false statement, Monsieur Cueff. You did in fact leave your house the day before yesterday. We've got a witness. And you were here in Port Belon in the afternoon."

The commissaire had nothing to lose. He could try being aggressive.

After a brief moment of surprise, Cueff burst out into scornful laughter.

"I'm carted all the way across Brittany under threat of an arrest warrant just because I bought two kilos of langoustines, a salad, and toothpaste? A kilo costs seven euro at the moment—a kilo! I didn't realize you were interested in my shopping."

"I'm only interested in where you drove after going shopping."

"Straight home. Where I—"

Dupin leapt to his feet suddenly.

Cueff and Magalie Melen both looked at him, equally shocked. That was it—that had to be it: he finally knew what had been bothering him so much. He knew it. Even though it sounded bizarre. And led to a conclusion that was bold, even audacious.

The gigantic oyster in the Belon had reminded him of his strange dream from the night before. And perhaps it had not been strange at all. So much would make sense all of a sudden! So much that was absurd would be plausible all of a sudden. The photos in *Piping Today* that Smith had recognized someone in before apparently calling Mackenzie as quickly as possible . . .

Without explanation, without saying a single word at all, Dupin left the summerhouse and walked to the end of the terrace in a kind of feverish trance. Cueff had found it difficult not to lose his temper completely, but Dupin was not listening to his furious words anymore, he was so preoccupied by his own thoughts.

His brain went over the story at top speed. Motionless, he stared at the expanse of water, whose surface perfectly reflected the deep blue of the sky.

Then he turned round and went over to Madame Bandol.

There was an excited anticipation on her face that she didn't begin to try and conceal.

"A brainwave?" she asked mischievously.

"I need to make a call."

"Come on."

She got up and strode in front of Dupin, elegantly and swiftly. Cueff and Melen stared after them from the summerhouse.

Madame Bandol seemed to be positively enjoying herself. She didn't say a word. Didn't ask any questions. Which Dupin was glad about.

She showed him into a high-ceilinged, wood-paneled hallway, bigger than his entire apartment, luxuriously empty. A little table on the right, probably Empire. A velvet-covered phone with a dark red dial.

"Here you are."

Madame Bandol immediately disappeared into the garden again.

Dupin reflected briefly: Nolwenn would be the best person for this job.

That would be the most effective thing to do.

He dialed her number.

She picked up immediately.

"You need to research something for me, Nolwenn."

"Tell me what it is."

She was familiar with this kind of situation, when Dupin was extremely impatient.

"I'd like you to take a look at the lives of three people: Nicolas Cueff, Matthieu Tordeux, and Baptiste Kolenc. Research everything you can find. The biographical details. Official, public documents. Everything! And specifically the years before 1970."

"Before 1970?" Nolwenn sounded surprised.

"Birth certificate, school, education, places they've lived, that kind of thing."

"No problem."

Dupin had no idea how she would manage it. Without an arrest warrant or search warrant. But those were the words he loved to hear.

"Just for these three?"

"Just for these three."

"By the way, the prefect wants us to ask Riwal to come back immediately."

"He's staying in Scotland until we no longer need him there!"

"I've just told Locmariaquer's assistant that, on your orders, I looked for flights straightaway, but that Riwal unfortunately won't make it to Glasgow in time for the last flight today. I've booked the first flight tomorrow morning, five minutes past six. That's as much leeway as we'll get."

"That's enough, you're wonderful."

"I'll be in touch as soon as I've got something. This whole thing is to remain confidential, I take it."

Dupin had almost forgotten: he wasn't even investigating anymore. Officially, the case was closed.

"Absolutely."

She had already hung up.

He went straight back to the summerhouse.

Cueff was on his feet by now and he was furious.

Melen had stayed in her seat and she looked perfectly cheerful. Positively relaxed. Like a diva, Madame Bandol had draped herself over her lounger again in such a way that she had a view of everything.

Dupin kept it brief: "Where did you live in the years before 1970, Monsieur Cueff?"

"This is absolutely outrageous, the way you're treating me, I—"

"In the years before 1970, Monsieur Cueff."

Backed up by his massive physique—Dupin had stood right in front of Cueff—his harsh tone had an effect.

"In Cancale."

"Where were you born and raised?"

"Why?"

"Born and raised?"

"Cancale."

"Schooling, end-of-school exams, everything in Cancale?"

"Yes."

Cueff sat back down. Dupin remained standing.

If it was Cueff he was looking for, he would obviously be lying. And perhaps there was even the odd forged document. Or missing document.

"Do the police have any more amusing questions for me?" Cueff was now making an effort to seem as nonchalant as possible.

There was no point asking any more questions on his life story. Dupin would leave the research up to Nolwenn. If there was something there, she would find it.

"We're going to be taking a look at your car, Monsieur Cueff. The filter on the air-conditioning system, the floor mats, everything. They can find anything these days, you know. Microscopic traces of soil with a composition that only exists in Port Belon, for instance. At the estuary."

Dupin had phrased these sentences a little mechanically; there were still too many thoughts going through his head all at once.

Cueff burst into loud, fake laughter now. "You're a real comedian, Monsieur le Commissaire."

Dupin turned away.

A clear signal: the conversation was over.

He knew he currently had no means of putting any more pressure on Cueff, to really coax him out of his shell. He needed to wait for the results of Nolwenn's research.

Besides, it was all just a bold hypothesis. An idea.

Dupin knew that he was taking a huge risk. But he had to do it.

And it was at this point that Cueff's rage finally erupted: "You can't possibly have asked me to make a journey of several hours for those few pointless minutes. I'm calling my lawyer, he'll take over everything from here on."

Having already left the summerhouse, Dupin turned around again.

"In your shoes, I would have done that earlier. Melen, see Monsieur Cueff to the car. They're to drive him back. And keep an eye on him. If I get any fresh information, he might be back here sooner than he'd like."

* * *

Ten minutes later, Dupin was back on the quay in Port Belon. Tordeux's and Kolenc's oyster beds had become visible in the river; the receding water had left them mostly exposed. The sun no longer had the strength and radiance it had had in the afternoon, and the weather had turned much chillier.

Dupin needed to eat something. Urgently. The croissant at Béa's was ages ago. He had felt really dizzy for a moment on the way. He knew that dizzy feeling. A definite sign. He could get himself a baguette at the bakery in Riec quickly. There would still be just enough time before it closed. He could call Riwal again on the way. And Nolwenn on the way back.

Dupin walked up the little path to the parking lot. As inconspicuously as possible, which was difficult with his build. The last thing he needed now was a conversation with anyone.

"You are"—it was a terrible, bad-tempered yell and the commissaire instantly recognized it—"sus-pen-ded!" The prefect didn't seem to know how to fit all of his tantrum's furious energy into sentences. "I am hereby temporarily suspending you! Officially! You will have nothing more to do with this entire case!"

Locmariaquer had stormed up behind Dupin; he must have dashed out of the driveway of Delsard's property. The commissaire spun round. The extraordinarily egg-shaped head of the slim but very tall man with sparse hair in his—as usual—cheap-looking brownish suit was scarlet, every single cell seemed about to burst.

"The head of the task force has told me everything! Every word! You're obstructing the case. You're still investigating the issue of the two Scotsmen—and only that! That's downright sabotage! You're mocking me! And now this interrogation of Cueff too, the flimsy excuses with Riwal! I had told you that the case was essentially closed! That it was an order! Sus-pen-ded!" He lengthened the word in a preposterous way again.

"There's a new—" Dupin broke off. This was nonsense. Presenting a bold theory to the prefect in this state would not be a good idea. Besides, it would prove that he was still preoccupied by "the two Scotsmen."

"I seriously mean it. You're out!"

Oddly enough, it was these words that really got through to Dupin. Everything until this point had seemed like something from the usual tirades.

"Give me your gun. The badge! And, believe me, there are going to be serious consequences, above and beyond the temporary suspension."

Dupin was speechless.

It took everything he had to restrain himself. His hands had balled into hard fists.

The head of the special task force and Kadeg had joined them by now. There was a spectacle in the offing. A public humiliation.

Everything went very quiet.

A few seconds went by. Nobody said anything.

The prefect seemed to notice the tremendous tension in Dupin's face and body. He spoke very quietly now: "Gun, badge!"

Dupin had to restrain himself even harder.

His right hand drifted to the holster underneath his pullover. He took out his Sig Sauer. And just dropped it. On the ground next to him. He looked the prefect directly in the eye as he did so. He did the same with his badge. Only his arms moved. The badge landed right next to the gun.

Then the commissaire turned around without a word. And slowly walked away, up the road, to the parking lot.

"I expect a full report. About everything of relevance with regards to Delsard and Tordeux, especially as it relates to Delsard's missing alibi for this morning," the prefect said loudly, but with more restraint. He wasn't yelling anymore. Not a trace of triumph. In fact, he sounded a little helpless.

Dupin didn't respond.

He got into the car. Very calmly. Started the engine. And drove away in a sweeping arc.

For a few bends, he remained motionless apart from his hands mechanically steering the car.

Then he reached for the car phone.

"Claire?"

"Georges! I'm glad you called. I get that you can't—"

"We're having dinner together, Claire. Yes! That's what we're doing."

"Really? And that won't get you into trouble?"

"No, not at all. It works out very nicely."

"That's wonderful, Georges!"

"Let's meet in Rosbras. At Marie's. I'm on my way."

"And I'm just on my way to my car. I've got everything done. I'll be there in a quarter of an hour. See you soon, Georges!" He could hear how pleased she was.

"See you soon, Claire."

Dupin took deep breaths.

Then he really put his foot down.

* * *

The commissaire drove down the winding path as far as the little jetty where the bistro was. Just a few meters from the water. Not from the Belon, from the Aven. Rosbras—a handful of houses—was just a stone's throw from Port Belon.

Marie's Bistrot de Rosbras was a beautiful old building, painted a radiant white; there were pale gray windowsills with pink boxes on them containing lush blossoming flowers, wide pale gray awnings with a wooden terrace underneath, and a smattering of ceramic pots with olive trees, oleander, and small palm trees. You sat at simple wooden tables on old bistro chairs. Right by the Aven, a hybrid just like the Belon: sea and river all in one. Everything was practically perfect—but what made the place so unique was its special underlying feeling, a charm that was immediately palpable. This place had a beauty all of its own, a grace, a cheerfulness, a lightheartedness. A holiday atmosphere.

Dupin parked his car a little farther down the quay, walked to the terrace, and sat in one of the seats closest to the water. It would take Claire a little while longer.

It was very quiet, just one other table was occupied. As with everywhere else, it only started to fill up during Easter week; that's when the season gradually got going.

Dupin found himself in a strange emotional state. There was the absolute bewilderment, the reluctance to accept or even believe what had just happened. There was the unbridled fury. Dupin had tried to push it way, way down during the incident with the prefect just now, and was still doing so now. Put simply, it would have turned into a catastrophe otherwise.

Along with the bewilderment and fury, there was also the feeling of powerlessness and of utter surreality. None of it felt real. And not forgetting his total exhaustion. It was enough to make you cry and laugh, to run away and want to destroy everything. Dupin felt almost numb. Perhaps that was the right word. As if all of the powerful feelings canceled each other out.

"*Salut*, Georges, how are you? Red or white?"

Marie, the owner, had come out. Slim, with rather long, dark, tousled hair, large earrings, a red T-shirt, faded jeans, and a leather jacket. Dupin liked her, both her and her husband, who had once been a Breton football star, and also her sister, who was a superb cook. Marie and her husband had made something special out of this bar. Out of this whole place.

"Red! Gascogne, please!"

She smiled at Dupin. Warmly. Encouragingly. It did him good. And it was more powerful than any words. Then she turned round and went back into the bistro.

What should he do?

Maybe he really should keep out of everything? Let things take their course? Abandon his far-fetched theory? The fact was, he was suspended.

And he was sick and tired of it. They'd see!

Besides, Nolwenn had called on his way here to forewarn him that it wasn't easy to access the documents; she only had the first document for Kolenc—and it looked to be in order. Perhaps it would come to nothing anyway. Dupin had simply listened, he hadn't managed to say a single word about what had happened.

"The wine."

Marie was back already and placing a bottle of Domaine de Pellehaut on the table.

"Thanks, Marie."

He immediately poured himself some.

And drank the whole glassful in one go. The wine reminded him of the summer and evenings here in the setting sun.

You could really see the water flowing down the river, not gently and sluggishly—but powerfully, urgently, with speed, lots of eddies, the Atlantic reclaiming the masses of water it had lent the countryside. Like a breath in and out. The Aven was about a hundred meters wide at this point; it broadened into lakes a little bit upstream and downstream, like on the Belon at Madame Bandol's house. Dense woods turning pale green lined the banks. It was incredibly tranquil. The twittering of birds, water sounds and boats knocking together, everything muted.

Dupin poured himself another glass.

There were boats in the middle of the river on round, white buoys. Motorboats and sailing boats with their towering masts bobbing restlessly back and forth through the current. On the opposite bank, Kerdruc's handful of elegant houses towered into the air, liberally scattered and ringed by magnificently flourishing botanical gardens. There were huge stone pines there. The sun would set between them later. It wouldn't be much longer now; the sun had already moved part of the way toward them and was bathing the water and everything on the Aven in soft golden light. There still was not a cloud to be seen—the sky was a delicate pastel blue.

Dupin came here a lot, often with Claire; the Bistrot de Rosbras had become one of his favorite haunts. Mostly they just sat here next to one another, a glass of wine in hand, and stared, not talking. Watching birds, boats, eddies, the moving sun. Or not even that: simply getting lost in the atmosphere of the place and the moment.

"What's wrong, Georges? You look angry. And exhausted."

Dupin jumped.

Claire was standing directly beside him.

She must have parked the car upstream.

"I was just distracted. I'm not . . ." Dupin trailed off.

What could he say? Claire knew him.

"Have you eaten anything yet?"

"No."

"And when did you last have something to eat?"

Dupin waved her question away.

"You're crazy, Georges! But at least you've had something to drink." She looked at the glass and smiled. "Very good. As a doctor, that's my urgent order!"

Claire sat down. Every single strand of her Normandy blond hair was shimmering in the warm light.

"I'm starving too."

Dupin loved that about Claire: that she could be famished and then really ate accordingly too!

Marie must have heard Claire. She had come out to welcome her.

"We need to eat something, Marie. The Breton fish soup for me and then the *parmentier de canard*. And the *gâteau breton*. And some oysters to start—twelve. I'll have a glass of white wine with the oysters and then the red too!"

Dupin could hardly bear his hunger once Claire ordered.

"And for me too—everything. Just no oysters!"

Marie disappeared with a smile.

The *parmentier de canard* was simply divine here, creamy mashed potato with braised, deboned duck, tender and aromatic.

It would do him good. Give him strength. And much more importantly: it would be wonderful to sit here with Claire and eat. And forget everything he couldn't get his head around—for this evening, at least. Dupin got out his mobile. He pressed the Off button for three seconds. A gentle vibration confirmed it.

"I'm officially suspended from the case. The case that doesn't even exist anymore. Officially, it's considered solved. The prefect was in Port Belon in person and arrested the criminal—but this man has nothing to do with the murders."

Even these sentences had been difficult for Dupin. He had no idea how he was meant to explain the absurd affair in a few sentences, and more crucially, he didn't have the strength.

"I can't be bothered anymore, Claire. The case is over."

"We're just eating now, Georges. And drinking wine, nothing more," she said, and she meant exactly that. She poured some more wine for him, then herself.

"*Yec'hed mat*. To us!"

"*Yec'hed mat*, Claire."

Dupin drank.

He could already feel the effects of the wine on an empty stomach. In his head, in his body. And was glad. And he was also glad Claire wasn't making a fuss about his situation. She knew that this would be the most helpful thing for him.

"I decorated the whole apartment today. I'm going to take almost nothing from Paris, no furniture."

That was typical of her. Decorating an entire apartment in a single day.

"The hospital director has asked whether I can operate again tomorrow. It's an interesting case, but I said no. I'm not going to risk missing your party."

The party. That was all he needed.

Dupin had clean forgotten. It was the last thing he was in the mood for right now.

A moment later, Marie was standing in front of them with the oysters. Fresh bread on the side.

Claire expertly set about the delicacy straightaway; European oysters, the *plates*. She drizzled some lemon on top, detached the meat with the little fork, rested the oyster on her lips and slurped, then chewed, rapt. Dupin already had a piece of baguette in his mouth. And a large swig of wine.

It did him a world of good.

"I'll be able to eat them every day again. Like when I was a child. It's terrible; once you try them here, you can never eat them anywhere else."

Dupin had to smile. Although he couldn't understand this when it came to oysters, he did know exactly what Claire meant. It was true of everything here: the fish, the mussels, the crabs, the lobster, everything that the local fishermen hauled out of the waters off the coast of Brittany. It all tasted not just slightly but entirely different from the seafood in even the best Parisian restaurants. Here, a fish tasted of what it was, it had its own delicate taste, its own special flesh—with every additional hour of transport and storage, all fish started to taste identically bland.

"I saw a basking shark, Claire. Right in front of me. He only eats what oysters eat, those tiny plankton particles. Not us." Dupin was silent for a moment. "Or, if it does, it's only by mistake."

Claire gave him a quick, perplexed look.

"Kiki." He emphasized both of the *i*'s longer than he meant to. "And Charlie. A Toulouse goose."

Dupin realized his thoughts were wandering. Moving nimbly into the distance and he couldn't do a thing about it.

He stretched his legs out. Slid back slightly.

"Have one."

Claire had detached an oyster with the fork; the flesh was swimming in the little pool that had formed in the half shell.

"I'd rather not."

Claire wouldn't be put off.

"With a little vinaigrette for beginners." She drizzled vinaigrette onto the oyster and held it out to him again. Gave him an encouraging look. With sparkling eyes.

"I'd rather not. I . . . ." Dupin paused.

Maybe it wasn't such a crazy idea. He was a little nervous about seeing Docteur Garreg at the party the next day—at least if he ate this, he'd have stuck to one of the instructions. Most importantly: if they were so tremendously healthy, specifically for the stomach—real medicine, the cure par excellence—maybe it really would be worth a shot. Perhaps it would help.

Claire was about to eat the oyster herself.

"I'll eat it," Dupin said quickly.

It had sounded incredibly dramatic. He reached for the wineglass and took a large mouthful.

He was ready.

"Good for the stomach. Doctor's orders."

All of a sudden, he took the oyster from Claire, tipped his head back—this wasn't about being elegant—and slid it quickly into his mouth. Remembering Riwal's words about how to eat an oyster, he chewed quickly and swallowed. The whole thing had taken less than five seconds. He had been so on edge that he hadn't tasted much. And yet: it hadn't been bad. The little that he had tasted—mainly fresh, salty, iodine-laced water—hadn't tasted that bad at all.

Claire looked genuinely amazed. Dupin had to laugh.

He topped up his wine.

"The soup."

Marie was standing beside them, holding a tray with two deep, steaming dishes. Dupin was glad that the soup put an end to any more fuss about the oysters.

"It's very hot."

Dupin loved the thick, aromatic scent of the Breton fish soup, and also the ritual. You took the croutons, spread rouille on them, very liberally, or Dupin did anyway, placed them in the soup—they floated on it like little boats—and sprinkled it with grated Gruyère that melted on the dark, creamy soup. The flavor was unique, there was nothing like it. It was the sea, in concentrated form. A strong, well-seasoned taste, combined with the slight sharpness and freshness of the rouille.

Marie had disappeared yet again.

"Your first oyster. I'm impressed." Claire had said this sincerely, but with a little wink.

"So am I."

The soup tasted as good as it smelled.

They ate. Without saying a word.

Dupin's thoughts began to intertwine in strange ways and form large, wide curves. That's how it felt at least. The whole golden world was starting to form large, wide curves.

The commissaire reached for the wine with a smile.

* * *

A handy little police Peugeot came round the bend dangerously fast. It braked below the terrace, right in front of their table. So hard that its tires screeched.

A moment later Magalie Melen leapt out of the car and was standing in front of Dupin.

It had happened ridiculously quickly.

"Nolwenn. She's got some new information. You should call her straightaway."

Dupin didn't know how to respond. Marie, who had just brought a new bottle of wine for the duck, and Claire were watching the scene like something out of a play.

"I . . ." Dupin sat up straight, which turned out to be an awful lot of effort. "I am suspended. I mean, already suspended. I can't. How did you know I was here in the first place?" He did his best to pull himself together. Proper, coherent sentences were required.

"Nolwenn said you'd definitely be having dinner. She made a few calls; this bistro was actually her top tip but it was busy the whole time."

"And what does she have? What does Nolwenn claim . . . I mean, what news . . . new information?" Not an elegant sentence.

"I can't say. She wanted to speak to you personally."

He was no longer in a fit state. And he was fed up.

"Not this evening, no."

He had spoken clearly and firmly. The effects of the wine weren't audible.

"Tell her I'll call her tomorrow morning."

Depending on the kind of information Nolwenn had, he would then still be able to have a think. If he wanted. And he absolutely didn't think he would. With a clear head—if . . .

Claire didn't say a word.

"Are you sure?" Melen wasn't giving up yet.

"Yes."

It felt right.

Melen made a skeptical face.

"No, then. I need to get back, I left the prefect's 'big compulsory debrief' after Nolwenn got hold of me. I said I felt a bit ill. I understand, Commissaire," she sounded sad now, "I really do understand."

She turned round, got into her car, skillfully turned it around on the jetty in three moves, and soon she had disappeared.

Within seconds, the languid peace of the area was back. The scene had been like a fleeting nightmare.

Dupin was still sitting bolt upright.

He looked at Claire.

Something inside him had tensed up at Melen's final words.

He couldn't.

Not like this.

At that moment, a smile appeared on Claire's face.

"Go, Georges. You can't not." She laughed loudly. "You held out for a hell of a long time. So go! I love you."

Dupin couldn't help but laugh too. He started to feel dizzy a moment later and held on tight to the table.

He reached for his mobile, nearly sweeping his glass off the table with his elbow.

He turned his phone on. He realized that he was excited.

Nolwenn's number.

She answered straightaway. Without saying hello.

"I've got something extremely interesting, Monsieur le Commissaire.

I did manage to get access to quite a few of the three men's documents via some connections of mine."

He never asked what "some connections" meant. Nolwenn had countless contacts, including quite a number of unusual ones. Like a private detective in a classic film noir.

"And what do . . . the documents say?" The wine was still in his head, despite the excitement.

"I have all three high school diplomas. Cueff's in Cancale. Kolenc's also in Cancale. Tordeux in Brasparts in the Monts d'Arrée."

"In the Monts d'Arrée?"

"And the birth certificates, again for all three of them. But here's the thing: for two of them, I have a series of other documents from the time in between. But in just one case: nothing. Nothing at all! Not a single document. There is nothing to be found. As if the man didn't exist in the meantime."

Dupin had goosebumps. He didn't know whether it was the wine or the tension.

"I then called the local school authorities and asked about him. He doesn't appear on any school register or any list. Despite having a leaver's diploma from there. There's just this one document, he never attended the school by the looks of things. The document is a forgery, Monsieur le Commissaire! There was no—"

"Who is it, Nolwenn?"

Dupin had stood up abruptly. Hitting the table hard. The wine bottle had tipped over onto his plate.

"What is it, Georges?" Claire sounded worried, hastening to put the bottle back again.

Nolwenn uttered the name quickly and matter-of-factly.

Their perpetrator.

Dupin stood there, thunderstruck.

But it was correct.

It had to be him.

"I'll . . . be in touch, Nolwenn. I'm leaving straightaway. Straightaway . . . I think I'll arrest him."

Dupin hung up. He was trying to stand up straight.

Claire had stood up too.

"You can't drive anymore, Georges." She got out her purse and put some money on the table. Marie was nowhere to be seen.

"I'll drive!"

Dupin wanted to protest. But when a fresh wave of dizziness hit him, he decided against it.

Claire had already rushed over to her car.

Dupin ran after her, mindful of every step he took.

* * *

The sun hung low, the shadows had lengthened. It was dark in the small woods they drove through. The vast rapeseed fields in between flashed brightly in the last of the light.

One more bend and they were at the parking lot in Port Belon. Claire and Dupin had been silent for the entire journey. There was a strong, palpable tension.

Dupin had been doing his utmost to concentrate. He got the feeling the last few glasses of wine were only really having an impact now. He absolutely had to clear his head.

"A bit farther. Drive beyond the parking lot."

Claire nodded.

Dupin wanted to park directly outside the door. For various reasons. He mainly wanted to avoid having to walk all the way down the street because then he would be seen. The good thing was that nobody knew Claire's rental car. In his own car, he would have been recognized immediately.

Claire drove at a walking pace. Dupin waited until the last moment.

"Now. Here."

Claire stopped the car. Pulled the handbrake. Dupin opened the door, which elicited a loud, metallic clang. He'd hit the wall of the house.

Claire, already halfway out of the car, didn't react in any way. Dupin didn't say anything either. Instead, he climbed awkwardly over the gear stick onto Claire's seat, hitting his head twice in the process. He got out on her side.

The cool air felt good, although it made little difference to the state Dupin was in.

"Here." He made straight for the wooden gate to the inner courtyard. Opened it. It wasn't closed this time either.

"Do you have your gun, Georges?"

"No."

Without any further explanation, he stumbled across the yard with its fine gravel and stopped in front of the door.

He ran a hand through his hair, expelled all the air from his lungs, and breathed in again. Then he rang the bell. Claire said softly, "Georges, wait! I can't come in with you," but he barely noticed.

For a moment, nothing happened.

Then there were a few noises. As if furniture was being moved. Footsteps. Light footsteps.

The door opened.

In front of them stood Louann Kolenc.

Her blue eyes flashed when she saw the commissaire. She was otherwise inscrutable. She had tied her black hair back in a plait and was wearing a pale gray V-neck pullover and jeans.

"May we come in, Mademoiselle Kolenc?"

Dupin pulled himself together as best he could.

Louann Kolenc looked grave, but there was no trace of hostility or defensiveness.

"Come in. We've just sat down to dinner, my father and I." She led the way through a dark, narrow hallway. "I take it you'd like to speak to both of us."

Dupin and Claire walked into a cozy room that might once have been the manor house's kitchen. There was now—along with the aging kitchen furniture—an old wooden table in the middle of the room. A lamp with a plain, pale-colored shade hung over the table, giving off a faint, warm light. On the table: a large pot, a baguette, plates, two wineglasses, a bottle of red wine. Through a west-facing window you could see intertwined oak trees and the Belon amongst them, shimmering a golden color in the light of the setting sun.

Kolenc was sitting at the table. Composed. Calm.

He looked at Dupin and Claire without malice. But he did not greet them. His daughter sat down.

Dupin and Claire had stayed by the door.

They were silent. A long, incriminating silence.

It was some time before Dupin took half a step closer to the table. He made an effort to get his voice under control, but didn't manage it. It started to crack. Quietly.

"Ben Osborn—you are . . ." He didn't finish the sentence.

It was horrific.

But it was the truth.

There was a deathly silence in the room.

He started again: "You are not dead. And never died."

Dupin could feel the onset of goosebumps as he said these words.

Kolenc remained as calm as before.

"You didn't drown. You merely staged your own death." Suddenly the words just started to pour out of Dupin. "You had the stolen money. The entire time. You fled. Probably that very night."

Dupin's crazy idea had been correct. It had been about the bank robbery, that bank robbery more than forty years ago, yes, but in a very different way from how he had initially thought. It was not about the money that someone had somehow got their hands on—it was about the third man in the bank robbery: the supposedly drowned third man. The one presumed dead.

Baptiste Kolenc's expressionless eyes were fixed glassily on the table-top now.

Dupin stepped back a little; he could feel the wall behind him, that was good. "You left Scotland and Britain. You crossed over to Cancale. To the oyster town. Nobody bothered you, not for weeks. Thanks to the money, you had no problems getting by, and you knew all about oysters. You gradually calmed down. You began to think you would get away with it. And be able to start a new life." Perhaps the alcohol in his head was actually helping, Dupin thought—as the words flowed, the story was really starting to come together. "You learned French meticulously, as quickly as possible, you already spoke Celtic. But Cancale was not a solution. Just a stepping-stone. That's where you got everything ready. You created a new identity for yourself, got yourself new papers, a few documents as evidence of your new identity. The money—it made everything possible." Claire was still standing rooted to the spot. She was looking at Dupin, not at Kolenc and his daughter, but Dupin didn't notice. "And then you went to Port Belon. Far away from it all. With the new identity. That's how Baptiste Kolenc came into being. The wonderful Baptiste Kolenc. You bought a farm. Gradually becoming the rather private but universally respected Baptiste Kolenc. You fell in love, married a local girl. A daughter was born. You worked hard and honestly. You became an important figure in the area, an institution, above all, and this was the best protection: *an old hand*. Which you were not. For over forty years, you were something you are not."

Dupin paused. It was an absolutely insane story.

The enormous oyster in the Belon earlier had reminded him of his dream. Of the spine-chilling, sinister words that felt like something out of a fairy tale and had contained the solution to the puzzle: "It's me. Me, but not me." It was these words that had given rise to the crazy brainwave—Nolwenn and Riwal would be proud of him: a quasi-druidic lucid dream had brought the truth to light in this strange case. And oddly, there had also been echoes of a story L'Helgoualc'h had told Dupin on the peaks of the Monts d'Arrée: about the figures who turned up in the villages from time to time and were not who they claimed to be . . .

Kolenc and his daughter still made no move to speak. There was something creepy about it. Their faces expressionless, still no trace of hostility.

"At some point you stopped being afraid, but you remained careful. The probability that you would be found here in Port Belon after so many years, decades, was getting slimmer and slimmer. Everything was going well. But then," Dupin paused, "but then came a crazy twist of fate. One of those twists that happen in our lives, strange turns of events that"—the commissaire was finding it increasingly difficult to go on; it was actually a profoundly sad story—"that change everything. That seem unbelievable, but happen anyway and," Dupin was absolutely convinced of this, "our lives essentially consist of them. A reporter took photos for a Scottish magazine that Smith regularly read. And Smith recognized you in one of these photos. He called Mackenzie right away. And the catastrophe took its course."

Dupin's flow of words ebbed away. He felt sick.

Baptiste Kolenc reached for a glass as if in slow motion and drank it in small sips, extremely slowly. His daughter watched his every movement. Then she suddenly turned to Dupin, who had leaned against the wall.

"They wanted money," she said tonelessly but clearly. "Five hundred thousand euro, in cash. They threatened to go public. To destroy my father's life. But it wasn't just the money they wanted. They wanted revenge. Mackenzie wanted revenge. My father wanted to give them the money, all of it, straightaway. I was against it. They were awful people." Her voice grew hard, disdainful. "The pair of them were already fighting about the money between themselves, before they even had it. It was Mackenzie who killed Smith, on their journey here, he said that to my father outright. And he said that my father belonged to him now, that he could control him."

Baptiste Kolenc had put the wineglass down, his face stony. It was impossible to tell what was going on inside his head. His daughter went on:

"He said my father would be his personal financier now. He himself was about to get into the oyster business in Brittany. And would destroy what my father had built up over all these years."

Louann Kolenc stopped.

She fixed her gaze on Dupin. Tilted her head back for a moment. Was about to keep going, but her father beat her to it, almost inaudible: "I stabbed him to death. I didn't mean to. But I stabbed him to death."

Another rather long silence. Then Baptiste Kolenc suddenly came to life, fiercely defiant:

"I am not Ben Osborn. I am Baptiste Kolenc. Yes, I was Osborn once. But that was a long time ago. There is no Ben Osborn anymore!"

"Those two were the criminals, Monsieur le Commissaire! Mackenzie!" There was utter disgust in Louann's voice. "He—"

"Leave it, Louann. I killed him. I didn't mean to, but I don't regret it either. I would do it again."

Dupin came away from the wall and approached Baptiste Kolenc. "You suggested the parking lot as a meeting point, an isolated spot."

"I had parked my car a little way away. I had to go and get it to take Mackenzie's body away, then . . . then Armandine Bandol came and saw the body." Kolenc paused. "After that, I took the body away, sank it in the sea. I called Louann and told her everything, she came to take Mackenzie's car away." Kolenc almost seemed relieved now. "Lots of people didn't believe Armandine at first. But it was all true. Everything she said. Everything. There . . . there was a dead body."

"Matthieu saw my father—Matthieu Tordeux. The bastard. He saw him driving away from the parking lot in his car. He was coming from his *gîte*. He blackmailed my father. He wanted . . ."

"He blackmailed him?" Dupin hadn't thought of this scenario. "Matthieu Tordeux blackmailed your father? Tordeux is actually part of this business too? The fire—the car crash?"

At some point this afternoon, Dupin had—he now realized—attributed the blackmail, along with the fire and the car crash, to the whole sand theft business.

"So everything does hang together. It's all one case after all."

Nobody responded to his words.

"I couldn't allow it. It needed to stop. To be over. Once and for all." Louann Kolenc's voice had taken on a mechanical tone. "It was all meant to go back to how it always was. My father didn't know anything about what I did, I take sole responsibility for it. He would never have agreed to it! He . . . he is a wonderful person." Louann Kolenc's voice shook; she went pale and quiet and looked as if she might break down at any moment. "The grief from my mother's death was bad enough. He made a mistake as a young man. Yes. But he paid for that. A long time ago. This wasn't fair."

Kolenc had slumped in his chair, just a miserable shadow, profound sadness in his eyes.

"You should never have done it." This was a whisper. "Never. I should never have dragged you into it."

Louann Kolenc stood up. She was trembling.

She walked round the table and gave her father a kiss on the forehead. Then she sat on the chair next to him, holding his hand.

She too could barely take any more.

"I would . . ." Dupin took a step closer to them.

"Georges." Claire had turned to him, speaking softly but firmly. "Georges. It's all right. Leave it."

She was right, that was enough.

He was glad to hear Claire say these words.

Kolenc stood up.

"I'll just get a few things." He went over to a door at the back of the room. "Then we can go."

He disappeared. His daughter followed him.

Dupin knew he really ought to follow him but he didn't.

He stayed behind with Claire.

She had walked over to the window without saying a word. Dupin joined her, taking her hand and squeezing it hard. Then they looked out. The sun had disappeared behind the hills at the Belon estuary now, more or less where the parking lot was. It had set peacefully, no dramatic colors or effects, just pastel shades, pink and light orange, and a pale, translucent blue at the horizon.

"This is so tough, Georges."

"Yes."

It wasn't long before Baptiste and Louann Kolenc returned, wearing jackets. They stood in the room in silence. Looked at the commissaire.

Dupin wanted to say something, anything.

He couldn't.

There was nothing more to say.

He broke away and crossed the room, with the last of the concentration he could muster, his back straight. Claire followed.

Father and daughter seemed to hesitate for a moment, then they moved too.

Kolenc turned off the light before closing the door.

* * *

Dupin was sitting in his office in Concarneau that he disliked so much. He hadn't switched the light on, opening the windows wide instead, the yellow streetlights casting diffuse shadows into the corner room on the second floor. Bright shafts of light raced across the room now and again, a car driving down the street from the hill to the harbor.

Claire had stayed with Nolwenn in the office next door.

They had remained silent throughout the journey, cooped up in the little Citroën C2. The air-conditioning had done a bad job of the moisture exchange and Claire had had to open a few of the windows so that the windowpanes didn't mist up too much.

After arriving at the commissariat, Dupin had told Nolwenn the necessary details. Nolwenn hadn't said a word, not a single one. She had brought him a glass of water, which meant she considered Dupin's condition critical.

Two of their colleagues had led Baptiste and Louann Kolenc away.

They had left with vacant looks, Kolenc turning around once and looking at Dupin. The commissaire couldn't tell what that look had contained. A lot. But no hostility. Most importantly: Kolenc wasn't broken. On the contrary. There was a kind of pride maybe. Kolenc stood by everything he had done, even though it had turned into a tragedy. Dupin understood him deep down, if he was honest, although he wasn't supposed to.

There was one very last thing to do. Even though Dupin had no more strength left and he didn't have the nerve—least of all for this.

But he had to do it, for himself.

He heaved a deep sigh.

And dialed the number.

It was a while before the prefect answered.

"Dupin, you are—"

He cut the prefect off immediately.

"We've got the murderer of Ryan Mackenzie: Baptiste Kolenc. He has confessed. He is not Baptiste Kolenc." Dupin raised his voice. He had no idea where he summoned up the energy to do this from. "And we also have the perpetrator of the attacks on Matthieu Tordeux. Louann Kolenc. She has also confessed to everything. It's all connected. They're both at the police station in Concarneau. It has also been confirmed that Mackenzie killed Smith."

"I . . ." The prefect hesitated.

Dupin had no idea what would come next. It didn't matter anyway. He didn't intend to say any more.

"I was just saying to the young policewoman from Riec: it's a good thing I let you go so that you could keep investigating in secret! I think that was the crucial trick! Officially, the case was over and the perpetrator was lulled into a false sense of security. A brilliant strategy on my part. But I've got to say: you didn't play your part badly either, mon Commissaire. I would even say you did it very well! You'll have to tell me the whole st—"

Dupin pressed the red button. This was too dreadful. And it was worse than all of the dirty tricks he had put up with from the prefect in the last five years.

Luckily, he hadn't had even an ounce of strength left to fly into a rage. Dupin didn't care at that moment, he couldn't care less.

He stood up. Closed the windows and left the room.

Claire smiled at him as he walked into Nolwenn's office. Her inimitable, enchanting smile. It did him a world of good.

"You ought to get some sleep, Monsieur le Commissaire. Just sleep."

Like Claire, Nolwenn had got to her feet.

"I will, Nolwenn. I . . ." He couldn't go on. "Thank you."

He headed straight for the door.

Claire slipped her arm through his.

"Good night, Nolwenn," she said.

Half a minute later, they stepped out into the clear night. And shortly after that, Claire was opening the door to Dupin's apartment.

The Fourth Day

Dupin had woken around eleven o'clock. Claire had taken the precaution of turning off all the phones during the night, severing every link to the outside world. Dupin had slept like a log. And had woken up with a hangover anyway.

Claire had been up early. She had got croissants and baguettes—*sarmentines*, the tradition—in the market hall, from the bakery stall at the front. She had made just one *petit café*, which didn't count. And brought everything to him in bed. It was wonderful, apart from the headache behind his forehead. His stomach had handled the small amount of excess amazingly well; the oyster actually seemed to have done the trick.

Dupin and Claire had walked to the Sables Blancs, the legendary white beaches, at a leisurely pace, and his headache had disappeared. Then they had come back and strolled through the little streets of Concarneau. They had bought a few things for Claire's apartment, mainly dishcloths. By then it was already afternoon and they had eaten crêpes at Valérie Le Roux's—the artist who ran a crêperie with her husband on the other side of her studio. Nobody made them better. They had slept a little more at home. Later, they had bought magazines at the newsagent on the large square—no newspapers today, Dupin was not in the mood to read the headlines—and then had a drink in the Amiral.

A perfect day. So far. By the early evening he had even forgotten the "big party," or at least he almost had.

Shortly after getting up, Dupin had made just two quite short official calls. To Nolwenn, to hear the latest updates—she had been busy with the final details for this evening—and to the prefect, who had held his "big final press conference" at noon. As he had done in his phone call late the night before, he was still acting as if nothing had happened, and Dupin knew it would stay that way. That was fine by him. It was only as the prefect was saying that Dupin's gun and badge were on his desk that he had sounded hesitant for a split second, almost ashamed.

Baptiste and Louann Kolenc had made their confessions officially and thoroughly on the record last night. The sand theft had also been definitively confirmed. Kadeg had been there at the conference.

No doubt the prefect had put in a triumphant performance at the press conference with the solving of two "capital offenses," a real show.

The brilliant thing was, when the conversation ended, Dupin had instantly forgotten about it all again.

He was extremely pleased with himself.

The Kolenc thing would be a bitter blow for Madame Bandol. Dupin feared she wouldn't understand it, wouldn't forgive him for it. It was complicated. The whole business. And sad too.

It had been a tough case.

So intricate. The strangest case of his career so far. He had just, and only just, solved it. He had been closer to giving up than ever before.

* * *

The terrace of the Ar Men Du was a magical place. And not just the terrace. The wonderful restaurant with the pretty hotel on a headland was fitted with two side windows to the west and east out over the Atlantic, which meant all of the rooms had a sea view. You could see the vast horizon with the two little offshore islands. Twice a day, the Île de Raguénez exposed enough seafloor—sand, stones, shells, algae—at low tide that you could get there with your feet dry. It was a path that you shared with lively crabs of all sizes and where particularly good mussels could be found in the sandy spots and on the rocks.

It was half past seven. The sky was at its best; the Atlantic blue was immaculate and resplendent. The scraggy, storm-tossed grass that turned the island into a dark green dome shone in the wonderful evening light. Everything glowed. Including the mysteriously isolated stone house on the island, white and uninhabited, that looked as if it had only been placed there to make the already breathtaking scene even more picturesque.

Even the Atlantic, it seemed, had spruced itself up for this evening and dressed in a stylish dark blue. It lay there tranquilly, almost solemnly. Most importantly, it was infinite. You could feel it here, in all of its magnificence: the End of the World.

The Glénan loomed on the horizon. This evening, the legendary archipelago looked as if it were floating slightly above the sea. Majestic and mysterious. Dupin had had a complicated case to solve there. And he had sat in the bar of the Ar Men Du during one of his first cases, during torrential rain. Five years was a long time. And yet it had gone by in a flash.

There was a jagged rock in the sea in front of the Glénan. A gigantic Atlantic menhir, a vast monument. Jagged and above all one thing: jet black. Ar Men Du. The black rock that gave the hotel its name. It was said that anyone who caught sight of it gained their own special powers.

Alain Trifin, the marvelous owner whom Dupin thought so highly of, had arranged a long table on the terrace with white tablecloths. Nolwenn had said in advance that if it was warm enough, they would have the aperitif and the starter outside. And it was warm enough. With a pullover at least. They would go inside for dinner.

Claire and Dupin had parked down by the sea, not up at the restaurant. Everyone was already there, all of the guests, and having a great time.

There was Nolwenn; Kadeg; Riwal, back on Breton soil since 8:07 this morning; "his commissariat," "his troops"; the gangly Goulch, a police-man from the coast guard who had helped Dupin enormously during the case on the Glénan; Marc Leussot, the marine biologist and amazingly ruthless ecologist who had become the new director of the renowned Institute for Marine Biology after his predecessor had been arrested as a side effect of Dupin's investigation; his friend Henri and Henri's wife Héloise; Paul Girard from the Amiral, of course, and Paul's wife Corinne, Dupin had seen them just earlier; Fragan Delon, the old friend of the murdered hotelier in Pont-Aven whom the commissaire went to see occasionally; Docteur Garreg, who eyed Dupin skeptically—which was no doubt to do with the coffee ban and oyster regime he had prescribed. Dupin felt he had stuck to both orders, more or less. Commissaire Rose was not there yet, but he did spot someone who was clearly a spontaneous invitation on Nolwenn's part: Magalie Melen. He had to admit he had grown somehow fond of her over these last few difficult days. He was seeing her in her civvies for the first time: a floral skirt, white blouse, and dark blue pullover.

Alain Trifin was celebrating with them, of course. (To make sure that the prefect was *not* celebrating with them, Nolwenn had researched a date very early on when he had an important evening meeting in Rennes.)

"Monsieur le Commissaire, glad to see you found your way too!" Nolwenn had spoken in a stern voice, but then a warm smile spread across her face. She had been waiting for him and Claire near the steps to the terrace. She greeted Claire with two kisses, then Claire and Dupin made their rounds.

Nolwenn had supplied them with glasses filled with Dupin's favorite red wine at Alain's, the one for festive occasions: Confidentiel, a Gigondas.

Dupin had sworn to watch his alcohol intake this evening but was, by the time they had finished their rounds of greeting everyone, already on his third glass.

"Let's have one official toast. Even if you don't like it." Nolwenn had positioned herself at the head of the table, everyone else was around it, and had raised her glass: "To the commissaire! To you! To these five years! You've done a reasonably good job." High praise indeed from Nolwenn. "With good teachers"—her gaze roamed around kindly—"you have completed the first steps on your way to becoming a '*vrai* Breton.' Bravo!" There was laughter. "And the best teachers are vital, especially for a Parisian. *N'hall ket an den ober ul lamm hir gant ur vazh verr!* You can't jump far with a short pole. So, to us all! *Yec'hed mat!*" The loud, festive clinking of glasses rang out.

The incredible amuse-bouches were already on the table: *langoustines rôties, tartare de mangue et ananas, gelée de langoustines.*

"And," Nolwenn raised her glass again, "to Claire! The Norman who is becoming a Breton! A positive step!"

Claire smiled; it was clear she was moved.

They clinked glasses again.

Then Riwal took over.

"Boss, we've got something for you. Two things, actually. One of them is here." He bent down and picked something up off the floor. A fishing rod. A magnificent fishing rod. With a reel and fishing line.

He carried on: "There are some things you're not at all bad at, boss; there's just one thing you're terrible at. But we think you ought to learn it: relaxing. Docteur Garreg"—he looked over at Dupin's GP, who nodded in agreement—"strongly recommended it to us. These are doctor's orders: two or three hours of fishing at least once a week. And," Riwal became solemn, "fishing will undoubtedly make you even more Breton!"

He handed the fishing rod over to Dupin with a ceremonial gesture and hugged him in a rather clumsily tight embrace. Everyone around them applauded.

Dupin didn't know what to say. Anything to do with intentional relaxation just made him more anxious. He needed tips (or hours that happened to turn out as happily as today). But perhaps fishing would do the trick.

All eyes were turned eagerly to the commissaire.

"Excellent! I'll go fishing then!"

Fragan Delon muttered in his bass voice: "I'll take you sometime too."

"I will too, if absolutely necessary." Leussot grinned at him.

Henri looked conspiratorial.

Dupin knew how much this meant. For Breton men, fishing spots were sacred.

Suddenly, and this didn't seem planned, Kadeg walked toward the commissaire, a bright red bucket in his hand.

"You'll need this for fishing! I've just remembered."

He put the bucket right at Dupin's feet and looked rather embarrassed. Then he held out a hand to Dupin.

"I . . . thanks—I just wanted to say that," he stammered. Dupin knew that Kadeg didn't mean the situation and the bucket.

He gripped Kadeg's hand hard.

The loud bang of a car door being slammed with some force put paid to any more emotiveness. Every head turned toward the parking lot.

Rose—Commissaire Sylvaine Rose from the Gwenn Rann.

With supreme calm, she got a small package out of the dark Renault that Dupin remembered so well—he had even spent a night in that car. She walked toward the terrace at her own pace.

"Now for the sentimental gift." Nolwenn took over again, solemnly presenting Dupin with a picture frame.

"An advance printing. An article that will appear in the *Ouest-France* tomorrow on the occasion of your work anniversary. Researched and written by Michel Guéguen, a distinguished Concarneau historian."

Dupin didn't understand a thing.

"Don't worry, it's not really about you, it's about your heritage, your name." Nolwenn took a deep breath. "In 1832, a particular Breton was born: Guillaume Dupin! In the Guérande. At first, he becomes a fisherman like his father, then at twenty-six he meets an extremely beautiful Concarneau woman, Mauricette Rocherdreux, who works at one of the sardine factories. He moves to Concarneau to be with her and the couple settle down in the Ville Close. He takes a job as a guard at the Institute for Marine Biology. And becomes a legend amongst the fishermen. He guards the famous barometer in the garden of the institute that gives the fishermen the crucial information they need every morning: set sail! Or: you'd better not. He could read it like nobody else! A question of life and death. He died in 1898. And left behind two sons, who both turned their backs on Brittany and in fact . . . guess where they went!"

Dupin still didn't know what Nolwenn was trying to get at.

"Far to the east. Past Paris even."

"To the east?"

"To the Jura!"

So this was the point. His father's family came from the Jura.

"That could have been your great-great-grandfather, Monsieur le Commissaire! Guillaume Dupin. A Concarneau man."

The essence of this was clear: the Dupins—they were in fact Breton, or, to put it another way: Brittany had made them!

"Remarkable." It really was a crazy story. A truly lovely story. He would ask his mother about it when he got a chance. The Dupins weren't a long-established family in the Jura, he knew that much. "Thank you so much!"

The lively conversations started up again straightaway, a festive wall of sound.

"Monsieur le Commissaire!" Rose was standing right in front of him now. "Wind and sun did permit me to make it." She was wearing faded jeans, a tight black roll-neck pullover, and a longish black jacket, looking casually elegant as always.

She set down a little package for Dupin.

"That's just for refills. The present is here."

She pulled a tiny wooden box out of her pocket. No more than three centimeters long.

"You carry it on you all the time."

She opened it up and Dupin immediately saw what was inside: *fleur de sel*! The little box was full to the brim.

"So that you never have to sprinkle any other salt on your entrecôte!" She eyed him briefly, then laughed. "You've earned it."

Rose handed him the little box like a medal. It was very beautiful.

"Thank you!"

Alain Trifin had personally planned the celebratory menu for this evening: for the starter, *terrine de foie gras maison* with pineapple-and-apple chutney. The best foie gras in the world, legendary. The brilliant, crazy chef at the Ar Men Du, Patrick Le Guen, used a secret blend of spices for it that he only produced late at night and in small quantities, once everyone had left, so nobody could find out the recipe.

"The main dish today will be *turbot rôti* with *galettes de pommes de terre*." Nobody could present the food like Alain Trifin, with no fuss, but with a huge impact. "Caught four hours ago, on a line, one by one, not in those nets that damage the flesh. They were caught by Philippe Briant, one of the local fishermen. The turbot was immediately gutted on the boat and wrapped in damp linen cloths. The flesh stays succulent that way."

Dupin had seen the solemn ceremony before, when the fisherman—who kept his boat at the Pointe de Trévignon and sold fish there every day—arrived in his truck an hour before the restaurant opened. The chefs formed a proper guard of honor; everything else could wait.

"For dessert, a great classic: *millefeuille à la vanille de Tahiti*."

Dupin's mouth was watering.

Nolwenn leaned over to him. "I had taken the liberty of inviting Madame Bandol too. She called and says to tell you she's 'indisposed.' And that she's angry at you; apparently Kolenc is not the real culprit. But that she can imagine her anger will abate again. And that you might eat together at La Coquille when you get a chance."

This made Dupin smile. That sounded just like Madame Bandol, and it also meant they were still friends. However, he could understand why she was not in the mood for celebrating. Dupin had already decided this afternoon that he would visit her soon.

"She impressed you, didn't she, Monsieur le Commissaire?"

"Yes, she is one of a kind."

Nolwenn looked out over the Atlantic. "One of the real greats! A strong woman. Just at the end of last year she lost her twin sister, that—"

"What?" Dupin couldn't believe his ears. "She died?"

"A fashion designer who lived a very reclusive life in Paris. Sophie Bandol was really close to her twin sister. Last November. There were just a few small notices in some fashion magazines."

Dupin almost jumped out of his skin.

"Really? That way round?"

Nolwenn looked at him, her eyes wide. And didn't make any move to answer this obviously confused question.

That would mean Madame Bandol really was Sophie Bandol, the actress. And . . . Dupin pulled himself together; it didn't make any sense to brood over it. Suddenly he had to laugh. And laugh loudly, which didn't seem out of place in this cheerful atmosphere. It was crazy. And wonderful.

"Boss." Riwal took the floor again. "Boss, there's one thing we'd like from you this evening. You've finally got to tell us the real story of why you were given a disciplinary transfer to the End of the World. Why you were really fired in Paris."

Dupin knew that new legends had been growing up around this for years. He had run over the toy poodle belonging to the chief of police's wife. He had had a brawl with the mayor of Paris, knocking out one of his teeth. Or he'd picked a fight with the mafia and was in a witness protection program. In any case, it was rumored, he must have seriously upset somebody.

"I . . . let's see how the evening goes," laughed Dupin. "Who knows what it still has in store."

It would be a long night.

A magnificent Breton night.

Read on for a look at Jean Luc-Bannalec's
next baffling Brittany Mystery,
The Killing Tide — Available February 2020

Day One

"What a load of shit," Commissaire Georges Dupin muttered.

The stench was appalling. He felt sick to his gut. He had been overtaken by a fit of nausea almost to the point of fainting. He had had to lean back against the wall to support himself; he wasn't going to last much longer if he stayed here. He felt cold sweat running down his forehead. It was 5:32 A.M., but no longer night and noticeably cool. Dawn was creeping slowly across the sky. Dupin had been dragged from his bed by a phone call at 4:49 A.M., when it was still the middle of the night. He and Claire had only just left the Amiral shortly after 2:00 A.M.; they had been at one hell of a party to mark the beginning of the longest day of the year: the summer solstice. In Celtic they called it Alban Hevin. Brittany was naturally blessed with enthralling light, but at this time of year it became magical. The sun didn't set until 10:30 in the evening, and yet long afterward a brilliant light lingered in the atmosphere; the horizon was clearly visible across the Atlantic, yet at the same time the brightest stars could already be seen. This "astronomical twilight," as they called it, lasted almost until midnight before total darkness united sea and sky. There was so much light it almost made you drunk. Dupin loved these days. Really loved them.

The room, with its yellowish tiles reaching up to the ceiling, was cramped and cold in the harsh neon lights, with its tiny windows tilted open but not letting in anything like enough fresh air. Half a dozen dark gray containers as high as a man stood on rollers in two rows of three.

The young woman—in her midthirties, Dupin guessed—had lain in the container to the front on the left; a cleaner had found her. Two policemen had turned up here at the fish auction hall in Douarnenez harbor right away. Together with the crime scene team from Quimper, who had taken the body out of the container and laid it on the tiled floor before Dupin arrived.

It was a revolting spectacle even for the hardened observer. Dupin had never come across anything like it in his whole career. The body was covered in rotting fish, guts, stomachs, intestines, a mixture of all the more or less liquid waste that had been in the container. Even whole pieces of fish, tails, and bones stuck to the woman, to her hair, her hands, and—though there were only a few places where their original color could be made out—her light blue sweater, bright yellow oilskin pants, and black rubber boots. Her short, dark brown hair was tangled with sardine heads. Her face was a mess too. Fish scales glittered in the light, particularly macabre where one extremely large fish scale covered her left eye while her right eye was wide open. The slimy mess on her upper body had intermingled with the woman's blood. A lot of blood. There was a four-to-five-centimeter cut across her lower throat.

"Dead as a dormouse," said the wiry pathologist with red cheeks, shrugging. He didn't look in the slightest like a comedian and didn't seem in the slightest bothered by the stench. "What is there to say? The cause of death is no more a puzzle than the woman's state of health. Somebody cut her throat, probably yesterday between eight P.M. and midnight, though I'll spare you the reasoning behind that." He glanced at Dupin and the two crime scene specialists. "If you have no objections we'll take the young lady to the lab. And the barrel too. Maybe we'll find something interesting." There was a jovial tone to his voice. Dupin was overcome with another wave of nausea.

"Not a problem for us. We're done. There's nothing more to be added to the crime scene investigation for now."

The chief forensic officer from Quimper, Dupin had been pleased to note, was away on holiday, and his job was being done by two assistants, both of whom had the same unbounded self-confidence as their lord and master. The shorter of the two took over: "We were able to take a number of fingerprints from the top of the container, where it opens—twenty or so different prints altogether I'd say, although most of them weren't complete or were one on top of the other. Hard to say much more at present. Even though we will," he hesitated a moment, "need to look more closely at the interior."

Kadeg, one of Dupin's two inspectors, who seemed fully awake and composed and stood too close to the corpse, cleared his throat. "We could do with a little bit more information. On the knife for example." He had turned toward the pathologist and mimed for the experts: "I believe the blade must have been very sharp; the wound looks almost surgical."

The pathologist wasn't going to be impressed. "We'll examine the wound carefully in due course. The state of the wound depends not only on the blade but also on the skill of the perpetrator, as well as the speed with which he made the cut. Someone who knows his knives can make almost any cut with any knife, even in a fight. Mind you, I would probably rule out a machete"—he clearly thought this really funny—"but any of the hundred, maybe two hundred knives carried by the fishermen who use this hall could have done it."

"Just who might be carrying a knife with him," the smaller forensics man said ironically, "isn't a question you're going to get very far with here. Everybody who lives by the sea, whether they fish, hunt, collect mussels, own a boat, or are looking for work—in other words virtually everyone who lives here—owns at least one good knife and knows how to use it."

Kadeg looked as if he was about to make another objection, then dropped it and quickly changed the subject. "How often and when are the barrels emptied? Have you been able to find that out? There must be a regular schedule."

He aimed the question at the rookie policeman from Douarnenez, who, along with his colleagues, had been the first to turn up and seemed a down-to-earth local.

"Twice a day, we already know that. The men who gut the fish sometimes work late into the night and so the barrels are emptied very early in the morning before the first fishing boats come in. And once again around three P.M. The cleaners who empty them were totally distraught and called in one of the warehouse staff, who reported the incident to us at the police station. Then he closed off the hall."

"Without even glancing into the barrel himself to see if he might know the person?"

"There was only a leg visible."

"What about a phone?" Kadeg asked. "Did you find a cell phone on the body?"

"No."

"Okay," the pathologist said, obviously in a hurry. "Then let's pack up the corpse and—"

"Boss," Riwal, Dupin's other inspector, interrupted. He was standing in the doorway of the little room, which was already too full. There was a woman behind him who looked remarkably similar to the dead woman, except that she was probably about fifty years old.

"Gaétane Gochat, the chief of the harbor and the auction hall here, she's just turned up and—"

"Céline Kerkrom, that's Céline Kerkrom." The harbor chief had stopped in her tracks, staring at the body. It took a few moments before she got her voice back.

"She's one of our coastal fisherwomen. She lives on the Île de Sein and usually brings her catch here to sell."

Gaétane Gochat sounded completely unmoved, no trace of shock, horror, or sympathy, which, Dupin had learned, meant nothing whatsoever. Each person reacted totally differently when it came to sudden brutal or tragic events.

On his last case, in the Belon area, they had moved heaven and earth to find out who the murder victim was; here the identification of the deceased seemed remarkably simple.

"I need a *café*," Dupin muttered. It was only the second sentence he had spoken since he arrived. "We have a few things to talk about. Come along with us, Madame Gochat. You too, Riwal!" He was in no state to hide the grumpy tone in his voice.

He suddenly tore himself away from the wall, walked past all of them without waiting for their reaction or noticing the puzzled, surprised expressions on their faces, and was out of the door. He needed coffee. And now. He needed to shake off the stupor, the infernal stench, and the exhaustion that meant he was seeing everything as if through a hazy veil. To put it in a nutshell: he needed to come to himself, to plunge back into reality, and quickly. Get his mind wide awake, clear, and sharp.

The commissaire made his way through the big halls to where he had on his way in spotted a stand with a little bar, and a large coffee machine and a couple of scuffed bar tables. Riwal and Gaétane Gochat had trouble keeping up with him.

Everyday professional life in the plain tiled fish market had resumed, paying little heed to the dramatic news which had obviously already done the rounds; things were busy. Fishermen and fish sellers, restaurant owners and other customers were going about their business. Hundreds of flat plastic boxes were spread around the big hall on the damp concrete floor, in garish colors: fire red, neon green, signal blue, bright orange, just a few in black or white. Dupin recognized the boxes from Concarneau; they were a standard item in all the fish warehouses and the chief utensil in all the auction houses. They contained heaps of ice, on top of which lay everything the fishermen had caught in their nets: vast quantities of fish and sea creatures in every shape, form, color, and size; every sort of exotic sea creature you could imagine in your wildest fantasy. Huge, prehistoric-looking monkfish with their jaws ripped open wide, shining mackerel, fierce-looking lobsters, grayish black squid squeezed together, masses of langoustines, different types of sole, top-quality examples of sea bass (a fish Dupin loved, primarily served as carpaccio or tartare), delicious red mullet everywhere, gigantic spider crabs. There were also fish and shellfish Dupin didn't know the names of, as well as some he had never seen before, at least not knowingly, maybe already prepared on his plate, but not like this. He had to admit that as a good Frenchman his culinary interest went far beyond the zoological. In one box he came across a sadly confused-looking shark, in another next to it, a meter-long, almost completely round-bodied yet at the same time somewhat flat fish with a disproportionately large back fin. A sunfish, if Dupin's memory served him well. It was only recently that Riwal had shown him one in the Concarneau fish hall. Brittany was a paradise in many ways, particularly for lovers of fish and seafood; nowhere were they better or fresher. That was why the adjective "*breton*" stood alongside the name of almost every fish dish in almost every starred French restaurant: *Langoustines bretonnes, Saint-Pierre Breton*—there was no higher praise.

The busiest part of the hall was the rear, where the auctions took place. Along the sides were half-open rooms where some of the fish were already being prepared. Men in white protective suits, with hairnets, white rubber boots, and blue gloves worked with large, long knives at stainless steel workbenches.

"Two *petits cafés*." Dupin had reached the stand quickly, despite having to zigzag between the boxes. The old lady behind the counter gave him a suspicious look but placed two cardboard cups beneath the machine.

Dupin turned to the harbor chief, who was standing next to Riwal.

"Are you related to the deceased, madame?" The thought had occurred to Dupin because they looked so alike.

"Not at all," said Gaétane Gochat dismissively. It seemed she had been asked the question more than once.

"Have you any idea what happened here?"

"Not in the slightest. Was she killed here in the auction hall? At what time was the murder?"

"Apparently between eight P.M. and midnight yesterday evening. Whether or not she was killed here is something we don't know yet. How late were you here yesterday?"

"Me?"

"Yes, you, madame."

"I think up until about nine thirty. I was in my office."

"Whereabouts is your office, if you don't mind me asking?"

She replied with an impassive face. "Directly next to the auction hall. That's the administration center for the harbor."

Madame Gochat was the prosaic type, one who concentrated on doing the things that needed to be done, speedily and rationally. She was a stocky person with presence, short brown hair, brown eyes, little worry lines around her eyes and lips; businesslike rather than stubborn. Dupin thought she could be feisty if it came to it. She wore jeans, a fluffy gray fleece, and the obligatory rubber boots.

"What sort of fishermen come here? Those from the big boats too?"

"The deep-sea trawlers come in around five in the morning, the ones that have been at sea for a couple of weeks; the local boats that have been out for a couple of days come in around midday; and then at about five in the afternoon we get the coastal fishermen who've set out at around four or five in the morning, while the sardine fishers have gone out the evening before. The auctions begin as soon as the boats have come in. We were very busy yesterday. It was the beginning of the holiday season; a few of the coastal fishermen were still here by the time I left."

"Did you see Madame Kerkrom?"

"Céline? No."

The elderly lady behind the counter had set the two *cafés* down in front of Dupin. The expression on her face as she did so was hard to decipher.

"What about earlier?"

"About seven P.M., I think, I saw her briefly then. She was carrying a box into the hall."

"Did you speak to her?"

"No."

"What were you yourself doing in the hall at that time?"

There was just a hint of testiness in Madame Gochat's look.

"Every now and then I look and see if there's my sort of guy."

Dupin drank down his first *café* in one gulp. A proper *café de bonne soeur*, a "nun's coffee," as the Bretons called weak coffee. *Torre*, bull coffee, was what they called a strong one. For really bad coffee, undrinkable and disgusting, there were a multitude of names, serious Breton names: "Bardot piss," which supposedly meant something like "mule piss," or *café sac'h*, water squeezed through an old pair of stockings.

"You said Céline Kerkrom *usually* brought her catch here. What do you mean by that? How regular was she?"

"Almost every day, just as the auctions were starting. She specialized in *lieu jaune*—pollock—bass, and bream. Most of the time she fished with a line. She rarely used a net, as far as I know."

"So yesterday she brought her catch here?"

"Yes."

"But not every day."

"Maybe she missed out five or six days in the month. Every now and then she would sell direct to a couple of restaurants." To judge from her tone of voice, Madame Gochat wasn't happy with that.

"The killer could more or less reckon on her being here?"

Madame Gochat looked irritated for a brief moment, before continuing. "Absolutely."

"Did she have a crew? Fellow workers?"

"No. She always went out on her boat alone. Lots of the coastal fisherfolk are one-man or one-woman operations. It's a hard way to earn a crust."

"We need to know when she came in yesterday, who last saw her, and where and when. Everything."

"Obviously," Riwal replied.

"If I understand properly"—Dupin had turned back to face the harbormistress, pulled his red Clairefontaine notebook out of his pants pocket, and his Bic ballpoint from his jacket—"I imagine none of the fishermen who were here this morning were here last night."

"Certainly not."

"Who, apart from the fisherfolk, is here during the auctions?"

"At least one of my colleagues, the customers—fish merchants, restaurant owners—the workers who're already working on some of the fish. And two people to deal with the ice."

Madame Gochat noticed Dupin's curious look. "Everyone needs vast amounts of ice. There's a huge ice silo directly next to the auction hall. It's a service we provide."

"We need as soon as possible a complete list of everybody who was in the hall last night between six P.M. and midnight and/or who had been at the quayside beforehand."

"My colleagues will work on that," Gochat said. She seemed used to giving instructions. "We'll get together the people who were in the hall, but it will be harder to find out who was on the quayside. That part of the harbor is freely accessible. Anglers really like the quayside and there are always biggish groups of them there. Tourists like to pass by too; there's always something to see. Apart from that, three Spanish deep-sea trawlers have been moored there since mid-day yesterday, each of them with at least eight crew members."

The entrance was open, at least ten meters wide, and once in the hall it wasn't far to the little side room where the body had been found.

"I want to know about everybody who was here." Dupin repeated his instruction, stressing the "I." "What each and every person who was here was doing, from when and until when. And then we can tackle each and every one of them."

"It'll be done, boss," Riwal replied. "Our colleagues from Douarnenez have in any case already spoken with the member of Madame Gochat's staff who was here last night and closed up the hall. Jean Serres. At 11:20 P.M. The last fisherfolk had left shortly before. He had seen Céline Kerkrom a few times in the course of the evening."

Like Kadeg, Riwal gave the impression of being lively and relaxed, but then that had been the case ever since the birth of his son, Maclou-Brioc, four weeks earlier; despite the lack of sleep, his paternal pride had left him looking invincible. "He didn't notice anything unusual or suspicious. So far nobody's said they noticed anything."

It would have been too easy.

"At what time did this Jean Serres see the fisherwoman last?"

"None of our men said."

Dupin drank his second *café*. Yet again down in one gulp. It didn't taste any better than the first one. Never mind.

"One more, please," he said. Right now it wasn't about taste, it was the effect that mattered. The woman at the stand fulfilled the order with the slightest of glances.

"Madame Gochat"—Dupin turned to face the harbormistress—"I would like to call your colleague and ask him when he last saw Céline Kerkrom last night."

"You mean you want me to call him *now*?"

"Now."

"As you wish."

Madame Gochat took her cell phone out of her pants pocket and stepped aside.

"Jean Serres," Riwal continued, "said that at about nine P.M. there were some ten to fifteen fisherfolk in the hall. Of those, five were preparing the fish, and there were maybe five buyers, and a couple of men dealing with the ice. At about nine P.M. the first coastal sardine fishermen had come in from the nearby harbor basin. It was busy on the quayside. The afternoon rain had suddenly stopped about six P.M. and the sun had broken through, which had brought the anglers and promenaders out."

In Concarneau, Dupin himself was one of the promenaders who always strolled by the fish auction hall. He liked the lively, colorful goings-on around the harbor, the way it was reliably repeated every day, perfectly choreographed. There was always something going on.

The elderly woman on the stand had set a third paper cup on the counter in front of Dupin, and was now dealing with four older fishermen who had just turned up.

"I want all the workers in the hall put stringently under the microscope, Riwal," Dupin said loudly.

"Leave it to me, boss."

Dupin threw back the third *petit café*.

The harbormistress came back over to them, her phone still in her hand. Serres said he had last seen Céline Kerkrom about 9:30 P.M. In the hall. He reckoned she had come in around 6:00.

"Did he notice anything in particular?"

"No. She'd been absolutely normal. But then he had no reason to pay her any particular attention. They didn't speak."

"I want to speak with the man myself—Riwal, tell him to come here now."

"Consider it done." Riwal left the counter and headed toward the exit from the hall, where a small group of police was standing.

"How long do the coastal fish auctions last usually, Madame Gochat?"

"It's very variable, it depends on the season and the weather. December, coming up to the holidays, is the busiest time. Even busier than in June, July, and August. At that time of year we work until after midnight. Now it's up to about eleven P.M. or eleven thirty."

"What do the fisherfolk do after the end of the auction?"

Madame Gochat shrugged. "They go back to their boats, take them to their moorings. Sometimes they hang around for a while, tinkering with their buoys, chatting on the quayside. Or maybe they go for a drink."

"Here?"

"Down at the Vieux Quai, Port de Rosmeur, right next door."

For the first time that morning Dupin's features lit up. The *quai* and the area behind it were fabulous; he could spend hours on the old pier side with its fishermen's houses painted in shades of blue, pink, or yellow, sitting in one of the cafés or bistros watching the world go by. His favorite was the Café de la Rade, painted in bright Atlantic blue and white, a former fish canning factory. Everything there was unstaged, nothing put on for show. There was a view of the harbor and the bay of Douarnenez, breathtakingly beautiful. Dupin liked Douarnenez, in particular its wonderful old market halls—the coffee there was great—and the Port de Rosmeur, the charmingly aged harbor quarter, built in the nineteenth century, the golden age of the sardine. If you needed to name a center of operations in Douarnenez, then the Café de la Rade was the perfect place. The commissaire, who had a tendency toward ritual, in every one of his cases designated either a bar, a bistro, or sometimes even a location out in the open air as "center of operations." It would be the scene for interviews and, if necessary, for official interrogations too. Dupin was famous for his dislike of offices of every kind, in particular his own. He escaped from them as often as possible. He solved his cases from the scene of the crime, not from a desk. Even when the police prefecture was close by, Dupin needed to be outside, in the open air, amongst other people. He had to see things for himself, speak to people himself, live in their world.

"Did you know any more about the deceased, Madame Gochat?"

"No. Like I said, she was a coastal fisher from Île de Sein. She'd been married. As far as I know her ex-husband was one of the technicians in the island lighthouse." The harbormistress, even now, talking about the dead woman, showed no sign of emotion.

"When did they get divorced?"

"Oh, that was years ago, ten at least. They get married young on the islands. And if it goes wrong, they're on their own again young."

"What else? What else can you say about her?"

"I don't know, she was thirty-six, one of the few women in this business. She spoke her mind and had a few hefty disagreements with some people."

"She was a rebel, a fighter," said the elderly woman at the coffee stand, who was busy with a few glasses at a little washbasin. She seemed angry.

Displeasure was written all over Madame Gochat's face. Dupin was quick to follow up. He was curious.

"What do you mean, Madame . . . ?"

"Yvette Batout, Monsieur le Commissaire." She had now positioned herself directly opposite Dupin on the other side of the counter. "Céline was the only one who stood up to the self-appointed 'king of the fishermen,' Charles Morin, a criminal with a big fleet, half a dozen deep-sea trawlers and more coastal boats. *Bolincheurs* primarily, but a couple of *chalutiers*. He has more than a few skeletons in his closet, and not just in the fishing business."

"That'll do, Yvette." The harbormistress's tone was cutting.

"Let Madame Batout say what she wants to say."

Madame Batout batted her eyelashes briefly at Dupin. "Morin is unscrupulous, even when he plays the *grand seigneur*. He uses giant dragnets and drift nets, even along the sea bottom, causes piles of unnecessary catch, ignores the quotas—Céline even caught him out a couple of times inside the Parc Iroise, right in the middle of the conservation area, even though he denies it all and threatens his critics. Céline reported him to the authorities several times, including those at the *parc*. She had the balls to do it. Just last week six dolphins who'd been crushed in one of the nets were found dead on a beach at Ouessant."

"Did he threaten Céline Kerkrom directly?"

Dupin was making thorough notes, in a rapid scribble that looked like a secret code.

"'You need to take care, you'll see,' he told her here in the hall, back in February, in front of witnesses."

"He was threatening to take her to court for slander, not to kill her, there's a bit of a difference, Yvette." Gaétane Gochat's memory was curiously mechanical; there was no way of knowing what she actually thought.

"What exactly happened back in February?"

"The two of them," the harbormistress said before Madame Batout could answer, "bumped into one another by chance here, and they quarreled. Nothing more."

"It was more than a quarrel, Gaétane, and you know it." Madame Batout's eyes were blazing.

"How old is Monsieur Morin?"

"Late fifties."

"What did you mean about 'skeletons in the closet, and not just in the fishing business,' Madame Batout?"

"He had a finger in the pie in a whole raft of criminal affairs, including smuggling cigarettes across the channel. But for some reason or other nobody ever caught him. Three years ago a customs boat was close on his tail and nearly caught him, until he sank the boat. The only piece of evidence! And there was nothing else to hold against him."

"Be careful what you say, Yvette!"

"Has Charles Morin ever been the subject of a police investigation?"

"Never," the harbormistress said firmly. "Everything against him, I'll say it outright, amounts to nothing more than extremely vague accusations. Rumors. I think that given the number of illegal actions he's accused of, the police would have been on his tail at some stage."

Dupin unfortunately knew all too many cases where that hadn't been what happened.

"Great," he mumbled.

His first conversation and already he had not only one hot topic but two: illegal fishing and cigarette smuggling.

Fishing was a huge affair in Brittany. Anyone who regularly read

Ouest-France and *Le Télégramme*—and Dupin did so with particularly strict regularity—came across news from the fishing industry every day. Almost on a par with agriculture and tourism, it was one of the most important branches of the economy, a proud Breton symbol: nearly half of France's fishing catch came from Brittany. A venerable branch of the economy that was deep in crisis. There were several factors at work causing trouble for the Breton fleet: overfishing; the destruction of the seas by industrial large-scale fishing; the rising temperature and pollution of the oceans causing serious damage to fish stocks; climate change and the associated quirks in the weather which led to ever-diminishing catch sizes; the brutal, almost lawless international competition; fishing policies that had long been failing, on regional, national, and international levels; and fierce arguments, bitter quarrels, and conflicts.

And the prefecture had—to the commissaire's chagrin—been on them for years about the tobacco smuggling. No matter how bizarre it might seem in modern times in the middle of Europe, tobacco smuggling really was a serious problem. A quarter of all the cigarettes smoked in France entered the country illegally; the loss to the public purse was a multibillion sum. And since sales over the Internet had been banned, the situation had got even worse.

Don't Miss the Bestselling
Commissaire Dupin Series

"*A charming mystery.*"
—*New York Times Book Review*

AVAILABLE WHEREVER BOOKS ARE SOLD